"Something wrong?" Judd asked.

Kat strode to her pallet. "I'm beginning to think the mind plays peculiar tricks on a person in the wilderness. For a moment there I—"

"You what?"

Kat dropped down on her knees in front of him. She was magnetically drawn to Judd, lured by some power beyond her control. It was as if she had been led to this particular place in time, as if all the stars and moon had become aligned for some monumental occurrence.

"Diamond?" Judd's voice came out of the darkness. "You better go back to your pallet."

"I haven't thanked you properly for saving my life," Kat murmured.

"You're welcome. Go to bed."

Kat reached up to skim her forefinger over his lips and stared into eyes that blazed like golden flames.

His hand clamped over her wrist. "You're playing with fire, Diamond."

"I know," she whispered as she reached up with her free hand to trace his lips again. "How hot will it burn, Panther?"

"You don't want to know," he said roughly.

"Oh, but I do," she assured him. "No strings attached. Just for tonight . . . please, Lassiter?"

"It's a little late for formality," he whispered as his lips feathered over her neck. He combed his fingers through her frothy golden curls, letting the strands glide over his hand.

"Teach me to please you," she whispered, as he eased her down beside him on the pallet. . . .

BOOKS BY CAROL FINCH

RAPTURE'S DREAM
ENDLESS PASSION
DAWN'S DESIRE
PASSION'S VIXEN
MIDNIGHT FIRES
ECSTASY'S EMBRACE
WILDFIRE
SATIN SURRENDER
CAPTIVE BRIDE
TEXAS ANGEL
BELOVED BETRAYAL
LONE STAR SURRENDER
STORMFIRE
THUNDER'S TENDER TOUCH
LOVE'S HIDDEN TREASURE
MONTANA MOONFIRE
WILD MOUNTAIN HONEY
MOONLIGHT ENCHANTRESS
PROMISE ME MOONLIGHT
APACHE WIND
APACHE KNIGHT
ONCE UPON A MIDNIGHT MOON
COMANCHE PROMISE
MINE FOREVER
CANYON MOON
RIVER MOON
CRIMSON MOON
A BID FOR LOVE

Published by Zebra Books

CHEYENNE MOON

Carol Finch

Zebra Books
Kensington Publishing Corp.

http://www.zebrabooks.com

ZEBRA BOOKS are published by

Kensington Publishing Corp.
850 Third Avenue
New York, NY 10022

First Printing: November, 1999
10 9 8 7 6 5 4 3 2 1

Printed in the United States of America

*This book is dedicated to my husband Ed,
and our children Kurt, Jill, Christie, Jon and Jeff
and our grandchildren Brooklynn, Kennedy and Blake, with
much love.*

CHAPTER ONE

Texas—1878

Judd Lassiter was so exhausted, so anxious to sprawl out in a real bed, that even the hell-town known as The Flats looked good to him. As rowdy Texas towns went, The Flats was one of the worst. The community had sprung up on the banks of the Clear Fork of the Brazos River, at the foot of the hill where the military post of Fort Griffin sat. The place was jumping alive with outlaws, prostitutes and gamblers who preyed on buffalo hunters who came to sell their hides and the travelers passing through town.

Wearily, Judd dismounted, then patted his horse—his closest friend and constant companion. The buckskin known only as Horse blew out his breath, then slurped a drink from the trough beneath the hitching post.

"Give me an hour and you can have all the hay and grain you can eat," Judd murmured, giving Horse another fond pat.

Squinting into the late afternoon sunlight, Judd listened to reveille being played atop the hill at Fort Griffin. A grim smile pursed his lips as he untied his saddlebags. He found it ironic that a fort, which adhered so strictly to regiment, tolerated a hellhole like The Flats.

The town was a necessary evil, Judd supposed as he headed for Breezy's Bathhouse. Soldiers looking for excitement descended "Government Hill" to entertain themselves at the dance halls, saloons and gaming houses that lined the streets of The Flats. During previous visits to town, Judd had broken up several fights between professional gamblers and drunken soldiers, before innocent victims caught a stray bullet.

Sometimes he arrived too late to do more than contact the mortician, who was doing a thriving business.

The only advantage that Judd found from making an occasional overnight stop in a town that had been nicknamed Hell's Fringe was that most folks here didn't treat him like an outcast—because most folks here were outcasts themselves. The more civilized communities in Texas were as welcoming as a tomb. Citizens were all-fired anxious to see him leave. The legends surrounding the man known as Panther didn't invite many close friends.

Not that Judd gave a damn about what folks thought of him and his mixed heritage. He had learned not to care years ago. He had learned that most folks labeled half-breeds as third-class citizens—misfits who didn't fit in anywhere.

Hell, Judd could have been the kindest, most generous humanitarian on the face of the planet, but the eerie lore that followed him gave "decent" folks pause. More often than not, people prejudged him because his mother was Cheyenne and his father a French trapper. Judd had learned to shrug off those wary glances and condemning stares. He figured the Great Spirit would give those bastards their rightful due on Judgment Day.

Fortunately, Breezy Malone, owner of the barbershop, bathhouse, dance hall and a local hotel, didn't care who a man was, as long as he could pay cash for a shave, haircut, bath and rented room. In addition, Breezy had taken a special liking to Judd, who had once saved him from a stabbing during a barroom brawl.

"Panther, what brings you out this way?" Puffing on a cigar

as thick as his beefy finger, Breezy bounded from his barber chair. His bald head shined like a coin in the shafts of sunlight that slanted through the window. Dust particles danced like miniature gold nuggets, giving the shop a surreal appearance. "From the looks of your shaggy hair I'd say you've been roughing it for a while, my friend."

Judd, who had never been long on words, nodded and said, "Been a while."

Breezy motioned for Judd to take a seat. After snuffing out his stogie, he scooped up a pair of scissors. "You've got enough of that black mop on your head to braid," he said teasingly. "Thinking of reverting to your old ways, are you?"

The reference to Judd's upbringing in the Cheyenne village wasn't meant unkindly, and Judd took no offense. Breezy was the closest thing to a friend—aside from Marshal Winslow— that Judd had in The Flats. After the lifesaving incident, Breezy always gave Judd preferential treatment when he arrived in town.

"Got the best room open at my hotel if you want to stay the night," Breezy said as he combed Judd's thick mane of shoulder-length hair.

"Thanks. I've spent the last three weeks dreaming of a feather bed."

Breezy chuckled. It was a deep, throaty sound. "And you'll be wanting a sudsy bath, too, I expect. You're one of the cleanest sons of bitches I've ever met. Most of the riffraff around here think a weekly bath is pushing it some. I'd be a rich man if other folks felt inclined to bathe as often as you do. If cleanliness is next to godliness"—whack, snip—"then you'd be in line for sainthood, Panther."

Judd didn't bother to tell Breezy that bathing was a purification ritual inspired by his Indian heritage—a ritual Judd felt compelled to observe after so many confrontations with the filth and evil in the world. He simply sprawled leisurely in the chair while Breezy snipped and tugged at the long, thick strands of raven hair. Breezy kept rambling—the man talked more than anybody Judd had ever met—but Judd didn't mind all that much because he spent so much time alone that he grew tired of the sound of his own voice.

"Marshal Winslow is going to be mighty glad you're in town. He was in here jawing this morning, wishing you'd show up. Guess he got his wish," Breezy went on while he clipped hair around Judd's left ear. "The marshal received some Wanted posters on a gang of rustlers and stagecoach robbers who have been raising hell and creating havoc for ranchers in the area. A real vicious bunch, according to Winslow. They went on a murdering spree down San Antone way, then robbed our westbound stage last week. There's good bounty money on that wild bunch. You interested, Panther?"

Judd didn't nod, for fear Breezy would clip off a piece of his ear. "Maybe."

"The good folks who live near Buzzard Peak and Possum Creek sure would like to have some peace of mind. Between those damn Indian raids—no offense—and those ruthless rustlers, settlers are losing horses and cattle left and right. And I don't have to tell you how ineffective those soldiers up on the hill usually are at quelling disturbances 'round here. Government never has functioned as efficiently or effectively as private business. Wonder if it ever will."

"Doubt it," Judd put in.

"Damned ticklish situation we got here." Snip, whack. "The soldiers are supposed to round up Comanche raiders and escort them north to Indian Territory, but the Texas Rangers have a policy of exterminating any Indian who poses a threat. That puts the soldiers in conflict with the Rangers, and settlers and townsfolk are caught in the middle."

Judd was well versed on the trouble that plagued Texans. He was of the opinion that Texas settlers brought most of their troubles on themselves. They had invaded the fertile valleys and rolling hills that were set aside for Indian hunting grounds in the Medicine Lodge Treaty of 1867. Although settlers had trespassed on Indian land, the soldiers tended to look the other way. The settlers demanded protection from Comanche raiders who fought for the return of their land, and Texas Rangers chased after them with gun barrels blazing.

Deep down inside, beneath Judd's exterior of seeming indifference, he sympathized with the Indian tribes that had been rounded up like cattle and herded into Indian Territory. They had been stripped of their vast land holdings when the white settlers cast greedy eyes on the property. The Comanches and Kiowas were trying to protect what trespassing settlers had unlawfully acquired, but invading whites didn't really give a damn what the Indians wanted.

Judd often wondered if those holier-than-thou settlers ever stopped to realize what hypocrites they were. They were outraged that the original owners of the property were trying to take back the land. Didn't those settlers get it? Couldn't they figure out that Indians were every bit as outraged by the injustice as the whites?

"You wouldn't believe what came rolling in on the stage this afternoon," Breezy yammered, hopping from one topic of conversation to the next, "Prettiest creature I ever saw." He sighed whimsically.

"She is traveling with an older gent who wears the fashionable trappings of gentry. There are two bodyguards following after them who look a mite rough around the edges. Don't know the scoop on the lot of them. Don't know if the pretty little lady is the gent's daughter, his young wife or his kept woman. But I can tell you for sure, Panther: When word got around town that an extraordinary bit of fluff arrived, the news cleared out the saloons and gaming halls in nothing flat. Men lined the boardwalks to catch a glimpse of her. Even followed her around town until she disappeared into the hotel. Too bad she didn't rent a room at my hotel. I would've found some excuse to pass the time of day with her myself."

Judd made a neutral sound while Breezy snipped at the hair that brushed his shoulders. Judd had seen too much destruction centered around attractive women to pay much mind to Breezy's gossip. It galled Judd that so many females seemed to enjoy having men fight and fuss over them. He sure as hell wasn't stupid enough to get involved with the female of the species.

When he felt the urge to ease his male needs, he paid for the service and then went his way. He certainly knew better than to cast his eyes in the direction of a respectable woman—not with his mixed heritage, his profession and his reputation. There were unspoken laws prohibiting *his kind* from associating with women of so-called *quality*.

"You're damn lucky you decided to show up this week instead of next," Breezy said as he set aside the scissors and then snatched up the razor. "Buffalo hunters are due in soon. This town will be stinking to high heaven when those hides are stacked in the streets to await transport from the teamsters."

That was another sore spot with Judd. Buffalo herds that provided food, clothing and shelter for Indian tribes were being slaughtered at alarming rates. Too often, the animals were killed for sport, their carcasses left to rot on the prairies. The killings were condoned by the government in an effort to force Indian tribes to remain on reservations and depend on the rations and supplies provided by military posts. The reservations were nothing but glorified prison camps, and it got Judd's dander up just thinking how unfairly Indians were treated.

Judd tamped down his angry frustration. He'd faced the fact that he couldn't single-handedly wipe out every injustice in this world. He had learned to live one day at a time, to survive the best he knew how and not to make anybody else's troubles his own—unless he was paid handsomely for it.

Although he still adhered to the beliefs of his mother's people, he wasn't an idealistic fool. He simply did what he was good at and got paid for it. He avoided the entanglements of civilization as often as possible. As long as there were still wide open spaces on the continent, he would continue his lone-wolf existence and rid the world of criminals who preyed on innocent victims.

If Judd was forced to change his ways . . . Well, he would deal with the situation when he encountered it, and not a minute before. In his dangerous profession, a man was a fool to look too far into the future.

"Tip back your head, Panther. I'm going to shave under your chin."

Breezy Malone was the only man Judd allowed near his

throat with a sharp blade. Anyone else was considered a mortal threat.

"Cattle will be coming up the trail soon," Breezy reported conversationally. "You ever been in town when those cowboys come riding in here, shooting up the place, chugging whiskey and fighting over the calico queens?"

"Yeah," Judd said carefully—he didn't want Breezy to take a chunk out of his jugular.

"Word came in yesterday that the trail drive from San Antone should be here tonight. My business will be booming again, I reckon. Had to replace a tub in the bathhouse last fall when two drunken cowboys got into a fracas over who was the first in line for a bath. One of them shot a hole in my tub by accident. He was aiming at the other cowpoke, but the man was so drunk and blurry-eyed that he missed by a mile."

Judd was thankful he didn't have to fight over a quiet, relaxing bath. He wanted the bathhouse all to himself, wanted to soak until his tight, aching muscles were the consistency of hasty pudding.

"There you go, Panther," Breezy said as he stepped away to admire his handiwork. "I can see why the fallen angels over at Sadie's brothel think you're a handsome devil. Always wondered if I could have found myself a wife if I hadn't turned bald at thirty and wound up with this paunch and this mug that only my mother could love."

Judd shrugged at the compliment. He had been told he was handsome—"in a rugged, earthy sort of way"—whatever the hell that meant, but he didn't let compliments go to his head, because he wasn't responsible for how he looked. That was the Great Spirit's doing, or God's maybe.

Having been raised in two contrasting civilizations, Judd wasn't sure who was in charge of that place called heaven but he knew, firsthand, what hell was like. He had waded through it a score of times while he tracked bloodthirsty criminals who had no respect or consideration for anyone's life except their own. He had stared death in the face more times than he could count, and he had survived because he had overcome the fear of dying years ago. The way Judd figured it, a man had to make peace with death before he could deal with the hazards of living.

Nothing touched Judd emotionally these days. Thirty-three years of hard living had taught him to keep his feelings to himself, to control the emotions. He was not easily impressed or surprised. He simply went his own way and expected everybody else to do the same.

"I've got water boiling for your bath," Breezy announced. "I reckon you'll want a private bath, same as usual."

Judd nodded. Breezy knew the drill. When Judd Lassiter— more often known as Panther—hit town, he wanted a hot, solitary bath, a pint of whiskey to wash away trail dust, and an hour of well-soaked privacy. Judd paid Breezy exceptionally well for the privilege of having the bathhouse to himself.

"You're my best customer, Panther," Breezy said when Judd paid for services rendered. His stubby arm swept up in an expansive gesture. "The bathhouse is all yours. Enjoy, my friend."

Judd took the whiskey offered to him and ambled into the back of the shop. He sighed appreciatively at the three brass tubs sitting on stone pedestals in the cedar-paneled room. The moment Breezy poured boiling water into the middle tub and closed the door on his way out, Judd peeled off his grimy clothes.

Out of habit, Judd laid his pistol, knife and bullwhip on the floor—within arm's reach. Smiling in pleasurable anticipation, Judd lowered himself into the water. If he ever decided to settle down, the first thing he was going to purchase was the largest bathtub money could buy. Money wouldn't be a problem, Judd reminded himself. Hell, he could be living like a king, if he wanted, but this streak of restlessness in him simply wouldn't allow it.

Judd clamped the cork from the whiskey bottle between his teeth. The cork gave way with a muffled pop. The liquor burned its way down his throat and took the edge off his nerves. Three swigs later, Judd was lounging merrily in his bath without a care in the world. He'd just dozed off, only to be awakened by a booming voice coming from the front of the shop.

"I need to see this man called Panther immediately!" the authoritative male voice demanded.

"Well, you'll have to wait," Breezy Malone rapped out, loud and clear. "Panther doesn't like to be bothered when he's bathing."

The voices quieted momentarily, then the door burst open. Judd reached for his pistol and took the measure of a tall, lean dandy dressed in an expensive three-piece suit. A salt-and-pepper goatee covered the man's square chin. Slate-gray eyes widened in alarm when he faced the spitting end of Judd's pistol.

"Put that thing down, Mr. Lassiter, or Panther—whatever it is that you prefer to be called. I mean no harm. I have urgent business to discuss with you." The man drew himself up to dignified stature and said, "My name is John P. Trumball. It is a pleasure to make your acquaintance."

Judd didn't give a damn if the President of these United States was standing in the doorway. "Get the hell out, Trumball," he snarled.

"But I have a proposition for you. I've been told that you are a gun for hire, among your other legendary talents."

"I make it a policy never to be propositioned in the bathtub. Get out!" Judd growled, then acquainted the intruder with The Look. Sure enough, it worked. Trumball swallowed visibly and stepped back a pace.

Breezy poked his bald head around the door. "Sorry, Panther. He barreled in before I could stop him."

Trumball wheeled around to glare at the proprietor. "Close the door. This will only take a minute."

Breezy glanced apprehensively at Judd, who looked no less intimidating and dangerous while sitting naked in a tub than he did when fully clothed and packing an assortment of hardware.

Muttering, Judd motioned for Breezy to close the door. The door shut with a decisive snap, indicating Breezy was no more pleased about the intrusion than Judd was.

"Make it damn fast, Trumball," Judd muttered, but didn't lower the gun barrel.

J.P. Trumball shifted uneasily, then raised his chin. "I under-

stand you are a legend in these parts. I wish to acquire your
services to accompany my stepdaughter to Santa Fe.''

"No."

J.P. blinked. "But I have yet to explain the situation."

"Doesn't matter. Not interested," Judd bit off. He didn't
like the looks of this dandified rooster with a Louisiana accent.

"You will be well paid for being an escort for no more than
a quarter of the one-way trip," J.P. put in quickly.

Judd frowned curiously. "What the hell does that imply?"

J.P. strutted forward, then pulled up short when he heard
Judd cock the trigger. "It means it won't take you long to
accomplish your duties. My stepdaughter has foolishly taken
it into her head to travel west. I have objected but she is
adamant. I want you to frighten her into returning to The Flats
so she can catch the first stage back to Louisiana where she
belongs."

Judd had been offered hundreds of jobs as a bounty hunter,
cattle detective, bodyguard and scout for supply and wagon
trains, but never had he been asked to scare some wool-brained
female home after acquainting her with the dangers lurking in
the wilderness. He had to admit the proposition held amusing
possibilities, but Judd Lassiter wasn't a baby-sitter, especially
for some citified female who probably didn't know one end of
a horse from the other and was completely out of her element
in the badlands of Texas.

"We can discuss the details over supper," J.P. insisted. "All
you need to do is leave my stepdaughter alone for a few hours
at night and let fear of the unknown in the darkness get the
best of her. I'm sure she will be more than ready to abort this
ridiculous trip to New Mexico. Easy money for two or three
days' work—I promise you that."

Judd thought it over for a half second and said, "No."

J.P. scowled. "Damn it, man. I need your help. This is
important—!"

J.P. squawked in surprise when the lash of the bullwhip—
that seemed to leap into the gunslinger's hand—bit at the hem
of his breeches. The whip hissed, then curled around his ankles
like a snake. Before J.P. could brace himself, his legs flew out

from under him and he sprawled in an undignified heap on the floor.

"The answer is no. Now get the hell out," Judd snapped. He flicked his wrist and the whip slithered across the floor toward him.

Muttering, J.P. clambered to his feet, rearranged his twisted jacket, then stalked away. "Damned, irascible half-breed," he grumbled.

J.P. tramped from the shop, then glanced left and right. Surely there was someone else in town who could be coerced into accepting this task. There had to be someone who could follow specific instructions for the turn of a coin.

Checking his gold-plated timepiece, J.P. scurried toward the gaming hall. He had heard it said that men in this hell-town could be bought easily—except for the man called Panther, obviously. J.P. decided he would invite himself into a poker game and pose a few nonchalant questions.

No matter what, though, his infuriating stepdaughter was not going to escape his control, not until he got his hands on the fortune she was trying to run off with. Damn it, he had to have money—and quickly. Otherwise everything he had schemed and plotted to acquire would be stripped away and he would be left penniless.

That was not going to happen, J.P. promised himself. Katherine Diamond was *not* going to arrive in Santa Fe. She was going to suffer an untimely accident. But damn it, first J.P. had to find an escort who didn't realize he had been hired as a pawn in a cleverly arranged murder.

In swift, determined strides, J.P. entered the nearest gaming hall and sat himself down to appraise his poker hand.

CHAPTER TWO

Kat Diamond scrunched down behind the wooden barrels and crates that lined the darkened alley, impatiently waiting for the legendary Panther to exit from the livery stable. The bounty hunter had spent an unbelievable amount of time brushing down his horse and making sure the animal was well fed and properly stabled. Kat had never encountered a man so devoted to a horse!

When Kat heard footsteps in the alley, she shrank into the shadows. She was working on a very short clock. Her stepfather would be coming around to check on her, and it would not bode well if J.P. discovered she had sneaked down the back steps of the hotel and eluded the two henchmen who had been standing guard outside her door.

During the trek from Louisiana to Texas, Kat had come up with a plan. She was a woman who needed a plan, needed to know where she was going and how she was going to get there. Especially now when it could mean the difference between life and death—hers!

According to the gossip she had gleaned around The Flats, there was only one man who possessed the skills and experience to escort her safely to Santa Fe, only one man who could counter J.P. Trumball's scheme of murder. That man was the legendary bounty hunter called Panther—or so the maid at the hotel claimed.

The maid had conveyed fantastic stories about Panther's unerring ability to track criminals through the wilderness. His success rate was phenomenal and he was hired to track down the worst of the worst. Panther, or Judd Lassiter, whichever name he preferred to answer to, was Kat's salvation—if only she could persuade him to guide her across Texas to New Mexico. Without his help she would never have the precious freedom she had waited years to enjoy.

If J.P. had his way, Kat would not survive the week.

Although Kat had feigned ignorance, she knew exactly what J.P. was up to. She knew perfectly well that the two so-called escorts who accompanied her and her stepfather from Baton Rouge to The Flats had been hired to dispose of her. She couldn't say she was shocked by the dastardly assassination plot. She had lived under the same roof with J.P. for almost half her life, after all.

Kat's wandering thoughts scattered like buckshot when she heard the sound of crates being overturned in the alley. Muffled voices sent a flare of panic through her. Oh God! J.P. and his henchmen were scouring the alley in search of her!

Clutching the leather poke tightly in her fist, Kat bounded to her feet and sprinted away. She had nothing but her wits, and her departed mother's pearl-handled derringer, to protect her. The one-shot handgun wouldn't stand up against the loaded six-shooters those burly henchmen packed on their hips.

Sending a hasty prayer heavenward, Kat raced toward the street, hoping her disguise would protect her from the hoodlums who were hot on her heels!

Judd ambled from the livery stable, assured that Horse was well tended. The bath he had taken an hour earlier had been reviving and relaxing—except for Trumball's unwanted intrusion. Thankfully, the pompous dandy hadn't dogged Judd's steps. Though it wouldn't have mattered much, Judd mused.

No way in hell would he agree to play nursemaid to some incompetent, bullheaded twit who had decided to strike off on her own. Judd reckoned he would have enjoyed scaring the petticoats off the foolish lady, but—

Pelting footsteps put Judd on immediate alert. He reached for his pistol with the speed of a hiccup as he rounded the corner to Main Street.

"What the hell—?" Judd staggered clumsily when an unidentified body slammed into him broadside. The momentum of the grimy-faced lad who had burst from the alley like a cannonball knocked Judd off balance and they both went rolling in the dirt. Judd instinctively clamped hold on the kid.

To Judd's everlasting shock, he realized the urchin was not a boy at all! There were definitely breasts beneath that dingy shirt—and Judd's hand was clamped over them.

"Argh!" Judd grunted when a knee connected with his groin. He felt a frantic hand grab at the pocket of his breeches, felt the whoosh of his breath as the disguised female surged off his belly and raced across the street.

From his downed position, Judd swiveled his head to see the woman in men's clothes disappear into the dark alley on the far side of the street.

Judd didn't bother to check his pocket to see what the mysterious female had stashed on him. The raucous streets of The Flats were no place to flaunt a coin purse—not unless a man wanted to find himself quickly separated from his money and his life.

Judd came to his feet, then stared pensively in the direction the woman had gone. He had taken only two steps toward the Malone Hotel when scuffling footsteps resounded in the alleyway where the woman had first appeared. Judd stopped short when two men, packing drawn pistols, burst into view and raced across the street and into the adjacent alley the woman had entered.

Casually, Judd brushed his hand over the poke in his pocket, then continued on his way.

"Ah, Panther, I heard you were in town." Sadie Norris lounged in the doorway of her brothel, wearing a revealing red and gold kimono that advertised her ample wares. Tossing her head, letting the cascade of jet-black curls tumble over the swells of her breasts, she flashed Judd a come-hither smile, then struck her most seductive pose. "Come on in, sugar. I'll make sure you feel welcome in town."

Ordinarily Judd would have veered in Sadie's direction, but not tonight. He had recently been plowed over by a female locomotive who had two gunmen trailing her caboose, he had a pouch stashed in his pocket, and his hand still tingled from accidentally groping a well-endowed chest concealed by baggy men's clothes. He had the unmistakable feeling that the mysterious female would be looking him up to retrieve her stash—if she survived being chased by those two gun-toting ruffians.

A stab of guilt made Judd wince as he strode up to Sadie. A tiny voice kept nagging at him to check out the situation with the mysterious woman, but he had found himself in one too many showdowns lately. Why should he care why the unidentified woman was trying to outrun her two ominous shadows? He was just curious, was all. It was none of his business.

"Well, sugar?" Sadie purred provocatively.

"Sorry, Sadie, not tonight," Judd declined. "I need a hearty meal and a decent night's sleep. Tomorrow, maybe."

She pouted, then sent him a wink. "I haven't had a good ride since last time you passed through. Tomorrow it is then."

Judd strode away, too cynical to think he was God's gift to womankind, as Sadie implied. Most likely Sadie fed the same line to all her clients.

Following the insistence of his growling belly, Judd entered the restaurant to wrap his lips around a juicy steak and the best fried potatoes in all of Texas.

Kat's heart pounded like a hammer as she shinnied up the supporting beam at the back of the bakery shop. She slung her leg onto the roof and slithered up and out of sight. If she hadn't been agile as a cat—and afraid for her life—she would have been overtaken by the two henchmen giving chase. Kat was

beginning to think J.P. had changed his plans about the time
and place of her murder. According to the conversation she'd
overheard a week earlier, she was supposed to meet her Water-
loo in some desolate stretch of countryside on the Texas frontier,
not in the middle of town! There were folks here—like the
marshal—who might pose questions about her unexpected
death.

"Damn it, we can't have lost that gal," Chester Westfall
muttered as he stared in every direction.

"Looks to me like we just did," Hugh Riggs grumbled.
"J.P. ain't gonna be none too happy about this."

"Well, J.P. never seems too happy about anything. This ain't
our fault," Chester insisted. "J.P. should have told us the gal
was clever. Now we know why she gave that little urchin at
the stage station at Fort Worth the time of day. She must've
bought those grimy clothes from the kid so she could skedaddle
without calling attention to herself. She must have known we
were up to something. Wonder what tipped her off."

"If we lose the chit, J.P. will have our hides," Hugh mused
aloud. "This was supposed to be a quick, easy job, but it ain't
turning out that way."

Kat held her breath while the hooligans milled around
beneath her hiding place. Enviously, she stared across the street
to see Judd Lassiter sauntering into the restaurant. He would
be feeding his face while she clung to the roof by her fingernails.
She had been living on nervous tension for a week and hadn't
had a decent meal in days. She couldn't even chew on her
fingernails to stave off hunger, because they were presently
clenched in the shingles.

Kat decided, there and then, that Judd Lassiter may possess
legendary skills as a gunman and scout but he had no conscience
and no heart. The insensitive scoundrel hadn't bothered to come
to her rescue when Hugh and Chester barreled after her. Oh
no, not the almighty Panther! He had sauntered off to appease
his hunger pangs.

Kat wondered if the notorious gunslinger had pulled the poke
from his pocket to inspect the contents. If he had, she needed

to contact him immediately—before he absconded with her inheritance.

Damn, maybe she had given the legendary bounty hunter more credit than he deserved. Of course she had! All she had was the testimony of a starry-eyed hotel maid who behaved as if Panther hung the moon.

Well, it didn't matter, Kat told herself. She'd had no choice but to stash the pouch in Lassiter's pocket for safekeeping, for there was no guarantee that Hugh and Chester wouldn't capture her. She simply could not have the pouch in her possession if the worst happened!

"Well, what are we gonna do now, Chester?" Hugh asked.

"Not much we can do except to report to J.P. after he finishes his poker game. He can stand watch at the hotel while we comb the streets for the gal. For sure, she has to return to her room to gather her luggage."

That's what those two baboons thought. Kat wasn't going anywhere near her room again. Recovering her luggage wasn't worth the risk of confronting J.P. and his hired guns. These men had seen the last of her—she hoped.

"Don't know why the stupid bastard is gambling in the gaming hall at a time like this," Hugh said, scowled, then strode off. "Don't know why we took this job in the first place."

Kat knew why J.P. had detoured into the gaming hall. He was an incurable gambler. His addiction had brought the wolves to the door of a once-prosperous plantation and brought J.P. mounting debts. It was the reason Kat had been forced to sacrifice the home that had been in her mother's family for generations. It was the reason she had decided to head to Santa Fe, hoping to shed the albatross of a stepfather.

J.P. Trumball had become the curse of Kat's life, and she knew she wouldn't survive his dastardly scheme if she didn't escape here and now.

She had escaped, but she was stuck between the devil and the deep, forced to place her trust in a man she didn't know and doubted she could trust. But for sure and certain she knew she couldn't trust J.P. Trumball, because he wanted her dead!

Resolutely, Kat pulled herself onto all fours and crept across the rooftop. She saw Judd Lassiter exit the restaurant and mosey toward the establishment called the Malone Dance Hall and Hotel. Kat focused on the weathervane perched atop the hotel and crawled south, refusing to look down. It seemed ironic to Kat that she had been forced to overcome her fear of heights in order to save herself from the first attempt on her life. Odd how the fierce instinct for survival had cured her lifelong fear in the time it took to blink.

Judd kicked off his boots and stretched out on the bed. What the room lacked in tasteful wallpaper it compensated for in space. True, there was little luxury in the room, but Judd didn't mind. He had bedded down in places that made this place look like a castle. Hell, he had stayed in rooms so small that he barely had room to change his mind, much less his clothes.

In the dance hall below, Judd could hear the sound of a tinny piano and the whine of a fiddle. Breezy Malone, entrepreneur of The Flats, had built his hotel above his popular dance hall. In short, Breezy's investments were making him a wealthy man. As money went, Breezy was second only to Johan Vukovich, the big, red-haired Swede who owned two saloons, a supply store and the bakery.

The sound of laughter seeped through the cracks in the floorboards as Judd removed his hardware and set it on the nearby nightstand. He jerked instinctively when the sound of a gunshot drifted through the open window on the spring breeze. From all indication, some poor bastard had met his bad end in this hell-town where gunfights were all too common an occurrence.

Judd eased back on the bed, resting his head on linked fingers. He hoped the woman he had run into—literally—hadn't become the victim of gunfire. Much as Judd hated to admit it, he still felt guilty about leaving her in the lurch. But how was he to know if she was a victim or a predator? She could have been getting exactly what she had coming, for all he knew.

The Flats boasted far more outlaws, schemers and miscreants than decent folk. Breezy Malone and the big Swede were two of only a few good men in town. The woman he accidentally bumped into could have been a prostitute who had made off with her unsuspecting client's purse, Judd mused. It was probably best that he hadn't gotten involved.

The thought provoked Judd to fish out the leather poke. He might as well find out what she had stashed on him.

Judd opened the leather pouch and poured the contents into his hand—and nearly choked on his breath. A priceless collection of diamonds, rubies, pearls, peridots, moonstones, opals, emeralds and sapphires winked in the lantern light.

He stared at the gems with his mouth gaping. "I'll be damned," Judd gasped. Who the hell *was* that woman who collided with him? And where the Sam Hill had she gotten jewels that looked to be worth a king's ransom?

One by one, Judd held up the stones to the light, then dropped them back into the poke.

"Oh yeah," he said to himself, "the mysterious female will most definitely be looking me up to collect her treasure."

Judd grabbed his pistol and dagger, then tucked them under his pillow. Knowing he was holding a treasure valuable enough to get a man killed—especially in this dangerous neck of the woods—Judd decided to sleep with one eye open. He was damn well going to be ready and waiting when the mysterious female came calling. He was not going to be the *deceased* eyewitness who could identify the woman who had been temporarily separated from her fortune in gems.

The faint creak of the roof brought Judd straight up in bed. Instinctively, he reached for his pistol. A muffled noise near his second-story window had him twisting sideways. His keen sense of smell identified the intruder seconds before he saw the shadowy form crouch on the windowsill, then ease into the darkened room.

Despite the grimy clothes the woman wore, Judd had picked up the aroma of roses while he clutched her to him in the street. That same scent drifted toward him on the breeze now.

A half smile pursed his lips as he watched the moon-drenched silhouette tiptoe across his room.

"Looking for something, little lady?"

Kat halted in her tracks at the sound of the low, baritone voice, accompanied by the click of a trigger. She wondered if protocol dictated that she raise her arms over her head like an apprehended criminal. But since she didn't consider herself a criminal, she refused to use a gesture that implied guilt or wrongdoing. Instead, she drew herself up to full stature and stared steadily at the shadowed form of the gunslinger known as Panther who held her at gunpoint.

"You're probably wondering what is going on," Kat said for starters.

Now, there was an understatement if ever he heard one!

Judd heard himself chuckle. That was an unusual occurrence, because in his serious line of work he encountered very little amusement. His own laughter sounded foreign to him, but this female provided an instant, unexpected source of mystery and amusement.

Judd levered up on his elbow and kept his loaded gun trained on her chest. "Now why would I wonder what the hell's going on?" he drawled. "I found myself run down on the street by what I presumed to be an urchin. Quite by accident I discovered you are a woman. I can't help but wonder if you were planning to tell me that, had I not discovered the truth for myself."

He noticed that his guest shifted uneasily from one cloddish boot to the other. If he were guessing, he'd say her footwear was several sizes too big. She had apparently confiscated her wardrobe from a boy who had yet to grow into his big feet.

The woman's awkward shift of weight made Judd wonder if she was embarrassed that he had touched her so familiarly and if she was remembering the sensuous contact of his hand on her breast. Or was she simply nervous because he held her at gunpoint? He wasn't going to toss aside his weapon to find out. No telling what this unconventional female had up those baggy sleeves of hers.

"And why," he continued belatedly, "should I be surprised

to see you skulking in through my window to retrieve the leather pouch you stashed on me?''

''If you'll kindly put down your weapon, I will be more than happy to explain all that,'' Kat said in a rush.

''Why would I be foolish enough to disarm myself?'' Judd flung back. ''I have no reason to trust you. Our chance meeting—''

''Believe me, sir,'' Kat interrupted. ''There is nothing chance about it. I was waiting for you to stroll from the livery stable. Obviously you care a great deal about your horse, because you spent an extraordinary length of time fussing over the animal. If I hadn't had to wait so long for you, I might not have found myself running for my life.''

Judd was stunned to learn that this woman had been stalking him, and that she was highly intelligent and perceptive. She had noted his lengthy attention to Horse. No, Judd realized, he definitely wasn't dealing with the village idiot. Her poise and manner of speech indicated she had been formally educated. Judd, on the other hand, had graduated from the school of hard knocks and untold experience.

''Had I known you would be so long detained, I would have hidden elsewhere so my two would-be assassins couldn't track me down,'' she went on to say. ''And thank you so *very* much for coming to my rescue when you realized I was in dire straits!''

Judd squirmed in response to her accusatory tone. He had indeed felt a twinge of guilt—something he rarely dealt with—because he hadn't investigated the situation. ''How was I to know the pouch you stuck in my pocket wasn't stolen? Who was to say that you weren't getting what you deserved?'' he countered.

Kat contemplated that and realized he had a logical point. He didn't know her from Adam, so why would she expect him to volunteer his assistance and jeopardize his own life? She knew for a fact that he was highly *paid* to stick his nose in dangerous places.

Out of habit, Kat began to pace, mulling over her situation, her immediate plan of action, and the man who held her at gunpoint. "What time is it?" she asked out of the blue.

Judd frowned as he watched the woman wear a path on the braided rug. Being a man who made a habit of knowing his enemies and figuring out what made them tick, he noted that time was important to this woman. He never paid much attention to time, because every hour of every day was pretty much the same as the next in his world. Also, he realized this little lady did her best thinking while she paced. He, however, preferred to contemplate while staring off into space. Another obvious difference between them, he pointed out to himself.

"I'd say it's close to ten o'clock," Judd replied as he monitored her restless pacing with the barrel of his pistol.

Kat's stomach growled loudly. "I realize this is an outrageous imposition, but I haven't eaten since breakfast, haven't eaten much of anything for a week—"

"And you expect me to trot over to the restaurant to pick up supper?"

Her shoulders slumped and she dropped her gaze to her oversize boots. "Forget I asked. That was presumptuous of me." Kat drew a deep breath when a gnawing ache and feeling of light-headedness stole over her. "I—"

Hunger and anxiety combined to send the darkened room into a spinning blur. Kat reached out to steady herself against the commode and inhaled another deep breath—but it didn't help. She had been operating on sheer nerves for a week, and the lack of nourishment quickly took its toll. Her legs buckled beneath her and she wilted on the braided rug.

The instant before she lost consciousness she reminded herself that she had never passed out in her life—until now . . .

CHAPTER THREE

Judd watched the woman's legs fold up like a tent. She hit the floor with a quiet thud. He stayed where he was, wondering if she was playing possum to gain his sympathy or if she had actually fainted.

Cautiously, taking her measure down the sight of his pistol, Judd eased off the bed. He hunkered down beside Kat's crumpled form to run his free hand over her arms, checking for a concealed weapon. He told himself it was only precaution that prompted him to brush his hand over her breasts to make sure she hadn't stashed a weapon . . .

"Should've known," Judd muttered when he felt cold steel nestled between her breasts.

He flicked open the buttons of her dingy shirt to retrieve the pearl-handled derringer that was tucked in her chemise. Further inspection turned up an envelope tucked inside her sock. The envelope held a small amount of cash.

Cynical and mistrusting though Judd was, he had to admit that frisking his mysterious visitor had its appeal. Despite the shapeless garments, there was a well-endowed feminine body concealed beneath. He had made a quick, thorough study of her alluring assets—and relished every moment of it.

Well, hell, thought he, now what was he supposed to do with this tempting, unconscious female? Should he turn her over to Marshal Winslow for questioning? Probably. But something stopped Judd from following that impulse.

Instead of hoisting up the woman, tossing her over his shoulder like a feedsack and toting her to the jail where a dozen drunken soldiers, ruffians and cowhands usually spent their Saturday nights, Judd scooped her up and placed her on his bed.

After he lit the lantern, he reached out to tug the grimy cap from her head. Mesmerized, he watched a glorious mane of red-gold hair spill over his pillow. Judd used his kerchief to wipe soot from her face and found himself staring at a peaches-and-cream complexion and delicate features of extraordinary beauty.

"Holy—" Judd's breath hitched when he noticed the unsightly bruise on her cheek. Anyone who dared to mar such perfection deserved to be whipped and shot. Who had left that mark on her, and why?

For a moment Judd simply stood there absorbing the woman's beauty, realizing that even the most self-disciplined of men could be taken in by her. Just because of the way she looked it would be easy to *want* to believe anything she said, *want* to help her. However, Judd was a man who constantly dealt with black-souled outlaws. He had learned to trust nothing and no one. Desperate people employed desperate means to survive, he reminded himself.

He suddenly recalled what she had said about waiting for him outside the livery stable. She had sought him out for a purpose, and he had yet to learn what that purpose was.

Judd ambled over to get the tasseled cords from the faded drapes, then secured the woman's hands and feet to the bedposts. It wasn't that he didn't trust her to be here when he returned with food and drink—it was that he made it a hard and fast rule never to put blind faith in anyone.

Judd made his way through the dance hall on the first floor, declining offers from calico queens to buy them a drink, swirl them around the dance floor, then take his lusty pleasure. He was on an urgent mission to provide nourishment for his mysterious visitor—and then get some straight answers.

The moment he stepped onto the street, two proper ladies and their escorts gasped in alarm, then scattered like a flock of quaking ducks. He usually had that effect on genteel folks who had learned to recognize him on sight.

Having no idea what kind of food the woman preferred, Judd placed a quick order for bread, cheese, Borden's Eagle Brand milk, and canned cherries. Carting the tray heaped with food, Judd retraced his steps across the street, scattering a few more decent folk, then reentered the dance hall and climbed the steps to his room.

Kat moaned groggily, then tried to roll onto her side. When she realized she had been physically restrained, she blinked, trying to orient herself. Her conversation with Judd Lassiter came back in a flaming rush.

Kat couldn't say she was surprised to find herself staked out on Judd's bed when she regained consciousness. As of yet, she had given him no reason to trust her. She hadn't had a chance to explain the reasons for her odd behavior.

Apprehensively, Kat glanced at the door, wondering where Judd had gone. Her first guess was that he'd trotted over to the marshal's office to report that she had broken into his room to retrieve the hefty pouch of jewels.

Kat sighed, exasperated. It was going to be difficult enough to explain her situation to Judd Lassiter, but it would be impossible for her to feel comfortable about broaching the subject with the marshal. The lawman would be obliged to question J.P. Trumball, who would give a contrasting version of the story, just to save his miserable, conniving hide. It would be her word against that of J.P. and his two henchmen. J.P. certainly wasn't going to admit that he had set her up for a convenient murder.

No, Kat repeated to herself, involving the marshal would invite serious trouble!

Damnation, if only she hadn't fainted she might have had time to persuade Lassiter to guide her west, to protect her from anticipated danger. How was she going to convince Lassiter this was a matter of life and death?

The moment the door swung open, Kat sagged in relief. Lassiter carried a tray of food and he was alone—thank goodness! She was prepared to launch into an explanation, but staring up at the imposing figure of the man she was seeing in full light for the first time left her lying there like a tongue-tied idiot.

Judd Lassiter moved with feline grace, though he stood six feet four inches in his boots. His dark shirt and breeches accentuated the powerful muscles of his arms, chest and thighs. Wild nobility was stamped on his angular features, giving him a rugged, eye-catching appearance. His sheer male presence dominated the room and held Kat spellbound.

His shiny black hair and intense greenish-gold eyes contributed greatly to his physical appeal. His eyes, she decided, must have helped earn his nickname of Panther, for those fascinating pools—large and almond-shaped, with dark brown pupils—were so like those of the great cats she had seen and read about.

Kat had never seen such an astonishing example of vibrant masculinity in all her twenty-three years. This, she realized, was a man to be reckoned with, who deserved every ounce of credit bestowed on him by the legends surrounding the man called Panther. He possessed a predatory aura, a cunning awareness of all that transpired around him. It was in his intense, sweeping glance, his constant alertness. She couldn't help but wonder what kind of background had molded Judd Lassiter into the remarkable man he was.

"You're awake." Judd scoffed at himself for stating the obvious, but he was caught off guard by the woman's all-encompassing stare.

Judd felt as if she were dissecting him part by part, then putting him back together to appraise him as a whole. Her vivid green-eyed gaze kept sweeping from the top of his head to the toes of his worn boots, as if she couldn't quite believe what she was seeing. He didn't know whether to be flattered or insulted by that intense attention. He decided to be indifferent, because indifferent was what he did best.

"I brought you something to eat," he said as he sank down on the edge of the bed. "A little bit of everything, in fact." He reached over to untie her right hand so she could pick up the slice of bread. He opened the can of milk and handed it to her.

"This is very kind of you," Kat murmured, forcing herself to stare anywhere except at him.

She felt like an imbecile for gaping, as if she had never seen a man in her life, but this man was nothing like men she had known in Louisiana. He was . . . well . . . Kat couldn't find the appropriate words to describe the startling effect he had on her feminine senses. He just affected her on some primal, instinctive level that made her feel awkward, uncertain and awestruck.

Kat ate and drank hurriedly, determined to begin her explanation. "I know you are puzzled by my appearance and intrusion into your privacy, but I face a situation of grave consequence and I have come to strike a bargain with you."

Judd raised a thick eyebrow, but remained silent. His gaze wandered over her, wondering what sort of bargain she had in mind. No doubt it would be as unusual as the woman herself.

"I have been sentenced to death," she blurted out.

That certainly got Judd's attention. His eyebrows shot up like exclamation marks. "Why?"

"My stepfather, J.P. Trumball, sees me as an inconvenience and he wants me out from underfoot, permanently."

Judd went very still. He wondered if the explanation J.P. had given earlier that afternoon was going to be in direct contrast to what this little lady was about to tell him. Undoubtedly.

Kat muttered in frustration. Despite all her mental rehearsing, she had begun badly. Judd's eyebrows were shooting up and down like fireworks and he was staring dubiously at her.

"My name is Katherine . . . Kat . . . Diamond," she introduced herself. "After I announced to my stepfather that I intended to leave my home in Baton Rouge to travel to Santa Fe so I could visit my aunt, I overheard J.P. making arrangements with the two men he hired to serve as our so-called escorts—"

"These two men wouldn't happen to be the ones who were

chasing you when you bumped into me, would they?'' Judd
interrupted.

"The very same," Kat confirmed. "J.P. left this afternoon
and he ordered the guards to stand watch outside my hotel
room. Knowing I would probably have to make an indiscreet
exit, I purchased the clothes I'm wearing from a young boy
who worked at the stage station on the route. I gave the lad
what money I could spare for these garments.''

"Whatever you paid was far too much," Judd inserted, grinning wryly as he appraised the grubby, ill-fitting clothes and
boots the size of shoe boxes.

Kat nodded in agreement and took no offense, because he
spoke the truth. But necessity had demanded that she make
prior arrangements if she was to escape J.P.'s clutches.

Kat was relieved when Judd settled back to listen to her
story. He was an intent listener, she noted. She suspected that
he was intense in everything he did.

"My stepfather is a compulsive gambler and somewhat of
a con artist," she continued. "He courted my mother, as if he
were a proper, respectable gentleman, after my father was killed
during the war. J.P. catered to my mother, who had been in ill
health for many years. She saw J.P. as a possible protector and
provider, but he turned out to be neither. He squandered money
from the plantation with his excessive gambling debts.

"When my mother finally realized that he was bleeding our
finances dry, she took the precaution of hiding the heirloom
jewels so I wouldn't be left penniless. When my mother died
last year, J.P. began searching for the gems. He knows I would
never have left the plantation without the jewels, and he desperately needs them to pay off his debts. I decided to leave Baton
Rouge before he absconded with the jewels and left me with
no means of support.''

At this point Judd wasn't sure who to believe. Both J.P.
Trumball and Kat Diamond told a convincing tale. But one
thing was certain: Judd Lassiter was no one's foolish pawn.
He would reserve judgment until he'd heard both sides of this
story—in detail.

"J.P.'s first tactic to recover his failing finances was an

attempt to marry me off to a wealthy gentleman, but I refused to be sold into matrimony,'' Kat elaborated. ''J.P. tried to compromise me twice, but my dearest friend vouched for my integrity.''

Judd suspected that men would line up on Kat's doorstep to claim her. She was stunning, eye-catching. She was also incredibly soft, shapely and tempting beneath a man's questing hands . . .

Judd gave himself a mental kick for allowing his thoughts to veer down that lusty avenue. He still wasn't certain what kind of woman he was dealing with. It was important to keep his unruly urges under wraps and pay close attention to what the little lady said—and didn't say.

''As anxious as I am to escape J.P.'s manipulative control, I have no intention of finding myself married off to a man who bears J.P.'s stamp of approval. I want the freedom to make my own choices, to lead my life as I see fit. I will no longer tolerate a man with J.P.'s unscrupulous morals and flawed character to dictate my future!''

Her voice rose to an indignant pitch, and Judd was pretty sure the little lady had a strong independent streak, just as J.P. claimed. Also, as J.P. claimed, this young woman was accustomed to wealth and pampering. She would be out of her element if she tried to cross the Texas frontier. She didn't have a clue what hardships she would encounter en route to her chosen destination.

Kat popped a chunk of cheese in her mouth and chewed vigorously, then continued. ''I was waiting to approach you this evening because I want to hire you as a guide and protector for my journey to Santa Fe. J.P.'s scheme involves hiring his henchmen to dispose of me in the wilderness, never to be seen or heard from again. He, of course, plans to return to Baton Rouge to convey the shocking tale of my unfortunate death. He wants all the jewels for himself.''

Judd wasn't sure if Kat possessed a lively imagination or if she was giving him the truth. Her story definitely did not coincide with J.P.'s. Although Judd had no reason to doubt her, neither did he have reason to believe her. It was entirely possible that she had stolen the jewels from J.P., who had sent his guards to chase her down. The jewels could have belonged to J.P. and Kat had swiped them out of spite and desperation.

Who the hell knew for sure?

Well, there was only one way to find out, Judd decided. First thing tomorrow morning he would confront J.P. Trumball and hear his detailed version of the story.

Kat stared Judd squarely in the eye. "I am willing to share the jewels, which . . . uh . . . comprise my inheritance, if you will agree to see me safely to Santa Fe."

Judd was quick to note her hesitation in midsentence and he wondered if it was significant. He didn't have a chance to ask, because Kat kept talking without taking time to catch her breath.

"I realize your life might also be in jeopardy if those pistol-packing guards are able to track me down, but I promise you will be well paid for your trouble. Only a man with your renowned reputation with weapons can discourage Chester Westfall and Hugh Riggs from carrying out J.P.'s scheme."

Kat frowned when she suddenly realized the handgun she kept for protection was not lying against her skin. Her free hand flew to her chest. Her gaze widened when it dawned on her that Judd had touched her familiarly in order to confiscate the weapon.

"You searched my person?" she croaked, her vivid green eyes shooting daggers at him. "How dare you!"

He watched embarrassment enflame her cheeks, saw her hand glide down to check for the stash of money in her sock. Those piercing, pine-tree-green eyes zeroed in on him again.

Before she got all huffy, Judd blurted out, "What the hell did you expect, lady? Precaution is the trademark of my profession. Of course, I relieved you of your derringer and checked the contents of your envelope. I have no reason to trust you."

Her chin went airborne. "I demand that you return my money, jewels and handgun immediately. All of them belonged to my mother, and now to me."

Judd handed over the money and the handgun—minus the bullet. The jewels he refused to return because he still wasn't certain who actually owned them—Kat or J.P. As for the hooligans Kat claimed were hired to kill her, well ... Judd didn't know about that, either. The men could have been ordered to return Kat to her hotel room simply because she was at risk on the perilous streets of The Flats.

Judd was certain of one thing. This *had* to be the woman Breezy Malone claimed had caused such a sensation when she stepped off the stage. And no, Kat Diamond definitely would not be safe on the streets after dark. There were too many men hereabout who, with or without the influence of whiskey, might pounce on her. This woman definitely needed a bodyguard's constant protection.

Judd just wasn't sure he wanted to get mixed up with this female. She was the worst kind of distraction for a man.

"I would appreciate it if you would untie me," Kat requested, squirming uncomfortably. "I don't know how you could possibly consider me a threat to you. After all, you're the one with the impressive reputation as a bounty hunter, detective and scout. Surely you don't think I plan to harm you. Surely you don't think I'm *capable* of harming you. That is utterly preposterous."

Judd didn't know what she was capable of—that was the problem. Furthermore, Kat Diamond was a threat to his sense of well-being and self-discipline. The damnable truth was that she intrigued him, piqued his curiosity and stirred yearnings he had ignored during his exhausting foray to track down two brothers who had murdered, plundered and raped their way from San Antonio to Fort Worth. Judd was tired, ready for some R-and-R and ill prepared to deal with this mysterious, alluring female who told tales of deception and attempted assassination and carried a pouch of priceless jewels.

"I know I'm asking a lot," Kat said, squirming restlessly. "But I have one more imposition."

Judd braced himself, wondering what she wanted from him now.

She smiled hopefully at him. "Would you mind terribly if I camped out on your rug? I cannot possibly return to my hotel room."

She wanted to sleep with him? Judd felt as if she had plowed her fist into his midsection, sending air gushing from his lungs. *Sleep with him?*

Well, that wasn't precisely what she'd said, he reminded his rioting male body. She had asked to bed down on his floor. There was a distinct difference between the two, he quickly reminded himself.

Judd eyed her for a long, ponderous moment. A feeling of mischief flared inside him as he stared at his bewitching intruder. He was going to find out exactly how serious and determined Kat Diamond was about this journey across Texas. He was going to rattle her cage a bit.

"What would you say if I did agree to this bargain—for a reasonable cut of the rocks in the pouch, of course?" he asked.

"Then I would be forever beholden to you," Kat said, smiling in relief.

"But what if I tacked on a stipulation that, beginning tonight and throughout our trek to New Mexico, I wanted you in my bed, not camped out on the floor or in a separate bedroll on the prairie? What would you have to say about *that,* Kat Diamond? Hummm?"

CHAPTER FOUR

Kat choked on her breath. She was sorry to say she'd had so many other pressing details on her mind that she hadn't considered what she might have to lose in order to acquire her freedom from J.P. Trumball.

Good gad, was Lassiter serious? The payment of jewels would make him a wealthy man. Why was he insisting on turning her into his convenient harlot, too? Did this man have no more scruples than J.P.?

Her mind raced in circles. Were there even more sacrifices to be made for the chance to enjoy her freedom and independence? Already she had turned her back on the family plantation, her childhood friends, her way of life. Was she to sacrifice her innocence, too? And to whom? To a man who saw her as a convenient conquest, a man who wanted to retain the upper hand in this bargain?

She should have known better than to expect this gunslinger to be an honorable gentleman. As soon as that hotel maid started yammering about the fantastical and phenomenal feats Panther accomplished, Kat should have realized the starry-eyed maid had embellished the truth for no other reason than to repeat a fairy tale. Judd Lassiter's reputation was nothing but a crock of superstitious gossip, and he probably didn't have an admirable, respectable bone in his body.

For the second time that day Judd felt a chuckle bubbling in his chest. He could tell by the emotions chasing each other across Kat's face that she hadn't anticipated his shocking stipulation to her proposition. He wondered if she had shared her tantalizing charms with other men when she was determined to make them do her bidding. Probably. Who knew for certain if Kat had been a willing participant or actually compromised by the two eager suitors she had mentioned? Her "dear friend" could have lied for her. And who was to say that "dear friend" wasn't a man who had been sexually compensated for corroborating her story?

That was neither here nor there, Judd tried to tell himself. His only purpose for blurting out the stipulation was to rattle her, startle her—or so he told himself. Never mind the licentious thoughts that had been buzzing around his head since he'd frisked her and savored the silky texture of her curvaceous body beneath his hand.

While she lay there, staring at him in profound concentration, he reached down to untie one ankle, then the other. "Well, Diamond? Are you still all-fired anxious to take a jaunt through the *Comancheria,* across *Llano Estacado* where a sip of water is as precious as your pouch of jewels? Do you have the slightest inkling what you're getting yourself into?"

When he freed her hand and feet, she sat up cross-legged, never taking her eyes off him for a second. Kat was still pondering his counterproposal of intimacy. She was certain that he was more man than any of those dandies J.P. had paraded past her, hoping for a marriage contract that would bring him needed money. She had capably thwarted unwanted advances, dodged slobbery kisses. If nothing else, she was experienced at eluding men's amorous attentions.

Yet there was something dangerously appealing about Judd Lassiter. She wasn't opposed to testing her reaction to him— physically speaking—to a small degree. But she was opposed to being *forced* into it because of a bargain. Strong-arming was a tactic J.P. used on her repeatedly, and she rebelled against it. Was she going to allow Lassiter to twist her arm a half dozen different ways, too?

Before Kat realized it, she was up and pacing the floorboards. She had to think this through, to weigh the advantages and disadvantages she might face. Lassiter wanted to know exactly how much her freedom was worth to her, didn't he? He was upping the ante to see how serious she was about this journey to New Mexico. Didn't he understand she had already risked her life for her independence? Didn't he believe her situation was as precarious as she claimed?

Judd suppressed a grin as he watched Kat circumnavigate the room, her head bowed over her cloddish boots, her hands clamped tightly behind her back. What was she thinking? Was she plotting to manipulate him?

After a good five minutes of pacing, Kat halted directly in front of him, drew herself up proudly, and met his inquisitive gaze.

"I would like for you to return my stones to me, please," she requested politely.

"Why? Are you going somewhere?"

"No, but they are mine, after all."

Or so the little lady claimed, thought Judd.

"I have no guarantee that you won't sneak off while I'm asleep and leave me with what little money I have left," she added.

"What guarantee do I have that you won't club me over the head while *I'm* sleeping and relieve me of the money in *my* pocket?"

"We definitely have a conundrum," she agreed.

Judd frowned, bemused. "A what?"

"An intricate and difficult problem, a dilemma," she explained to him. "There is no trust between us, no *cause* for trust between us. I don't know you and you don't know me. All you have is my version of the story and all I have is the sensationalized rumor of your reputation, a view—I might add—offered to me by a dreamy-eyed hotel maid who appears to be one of your female admirers. In my book, that doesn't count for much."

"Just what does count for something in this book of yours?" Judd asked, biting back an amused grin. "I think I'd like to read it before we enter into any sort of agreement."

Kat slanted Judd an annoyed glance when he poked fun at her. But her irritation evaporated when another thought replaced it. She had finally figured out the crux of the problem. What she always wanted most, what she respected most in this world, was *trust.*

Since J.P. had come into her life, she had learned not to believe anything he said. She had learned not to rely on effusive flattery bestowed on her by would-be lovers who saw her as a conquest. She had never believed in love, because her parents had been united for convenience, for financial security and the propagation of well-respected Southern families.

Monica Diamond had not married J.P. for love. That had never entered into the equation, Kat knew. Monica believed she needed a husband because that was expected in society. Monica's frailty and prolonged illness prevented her from enjoying independence, but at least she had been wise enough to foresee the problems that lay ahead for her only child, after Monica made the unwise decision of marrying that silver-tongued charlatan, J.P. Trumball . . .

"Well?" Judd's impatient prompt jostled Kat from her pensive musings. "What do you think we should do about this conundrum, Diamond?"

Kat mentally scrambled to discard thoughts of the past and focus on the present problem of offering a guarantee that wasn't built on trust or friendship.

She eyed him consideringly. "You are half Indian, I am told."

He nodded confirmation, then appraised her warily, wondering what that had to do with whatever thought was swirling around in that sharp mind of hers.

"The Indian agent in Louisiana is a personal friend of my family. He once told me that, in the Indian culture, regardless of the clan or tribe, a man's word is his honor, his dignity, his pride. If you offer your promise that you won't relieve me of my jewels, then I will believe you are an honest man. It would be refreshing to know that in at least one culture a man and his word of honor cannot be separated."

"Then I give it, as a warrior of the Cheyenne nation," he assured her.

An indescribable sensation unfurled inside Judd. For the first time in his adult life someone from white society looked upon his deep-seated Indian beliefs with something akin to respect. This enchanting female was offering a symbolic hand of good faith. She neither scoffed nor scorned Indian custom. She didn't look down on him, as if he weren't her equal, just because Indian blood pulsed through his veins.

Should he think less of her because he had yet to ascertain the hidden agenda behind her insistence on traveling to Santa Fe? The simple fact was that Kat Diamond was offering him a job as her bodyguard. Her past and future weren't part of this bargain, only the immediate present. All Judd had to decide was if he wanted to take the job for a cut of the expensive jewels.

"Well, Panther?" she prompted. "I have agreed to turn my back on you, without fearing betrayal. Are you willing to offer that same faith if I give you my word of honor that I won't betray you, beginning tonight?"

Judd rose from the edge of the bed. Though his attention dropped to the lush curve of her mouth, and he wondered if she would taste as good as she looked, he extended his hand. "You can have my bed for the night, Diamond. I'll bunk on the floor."

She shook her head, causing the riot of curly hair to catch and burn like a flame in the lamplight. "No, Panther. You paid for the use of this bed. *I* am the intruder and *I* will sleep on the floor."

Her sense of reason and fairness were points in her favor. Judd liked that about her—even if he still wasn't sure her noble offer wasn't another manipulative act aimed at gaining his cooperation. If she *was* on the level, his respect for her would elevate several notches, come morning.

Kat turned away to roll up one end of the braided rug to serve as her pillow. To her surprise, Judd dropped the quilt at her side. The pouch of jewels plunked softly atop the quilt. She peered up at him, noting a hint of a smile playing on the corners of his chiseled mouth.

"They're yours. You keep them," he said.

Kat scooped up the poke and tossed it back to him, noting the lightning-quick reflexes of his hand. "No, you keep them, Panther. If something beyond your control, and mine, prevents me from reaching Santa Fe, the entire pouch will be yours. That is *my* stipulation to our bargain."

He cocked his head, studying her astutely. Kat knew he didn't trust her completely, but she didn't understand why. Learned cynicism perhaps? Lack of faith in all women maybe? Whatever the reason, Judd seemed to be pondering her reasons for putting him in charge of her valuable inheritance.

"About *your* stipulation . . ." she added hesitantly.

"Yes?" Judd found himself holding his breath.

She stared at him steadily from her position at his feet, but there was nothing subservient about her manner, Judd observed.

"I'm going to be perfectly honest with you," she said. "I have known no other man. I have been taught that the gift a woman can give only once in life should be given to a man she trusts and respects above all others."

Judd was quick to note that Kat had not included love along with respect and trust. Evidently she wasn't some starry-eyed romantic who believed in something Judd couldn't confirm existed. Love for parents and friends, he understood, but a strong bond between a man and woman? Judd had seen very little evidence of that. His father had taken a Cheyenne wife in order to gain a foothold in the village, in order to receive hunting and trapping privileges, in order to appease his needs when the mood struck. The marriage had nothing to do with love.

Judd had to admire Kat for rejecting his counterproposal, though the man in him was all too eager and willing. Although she claimed to be in dire straits, she refused to sacrifice her integrity and self-respect.

If she was to be believed, he reminded himself cautiously.

"I freely admit that I don't know how to cook, build a campfire in the wilderness or hunt, but I want to learn to be self-reliant. I want to learn to ride—"

"You don't ride?" Judd choked. Just how incompetent *was* this woman?

"No, but I will be your willing student," she assured him quickly. "And what I'm not experienced enough to offer you in . . . um . . . intimate satisfaction I will compensate for by providing personal comfort on the trail."

Judd stared down at her, feeling the coil of lusty desire tighten like a clock spring. The man in him wanted to declare that he would teach her to provide sexual satisfaction and he'd take care of the cooking.

Damn, this journey was going to be more difficult than he thought. He was going to be transporting a tenderfoot across rugged country, teaching her survival skills, safeguarding a sack of rocks and a damn virgin! What was he going to get out of this besides a lot of hard work, frustration and a few shiny rocks?

Judd snuffed out the lantern, lay down on his bed and asked himself at what point he had lost control of his own destiny. He decided it must have been the moment Kat Diamond came barreling from the alley. Experience and self-preservation warned him not to trust her completely. Already, he was driving himself crazy trying to second-guess her hidden motives, frustrating himself by picking apart her comments in hopes of separating lies from the truth.

Although Kat Diamond sounded sincere, it could be that she was trying to deceive him into thinking she spoke the truth because she needed his cooperation to get herself, and those sparkling jewels, across no-man's-land.

In the darkness a soft, sultry voice floated toward Judd, putting his male body on full, tormenting alert.

"Thank you, Panther. I was hoping I could count on you."

"Don't thank me yet, Diamond. We are one helluva long way from Santa Fe," he muttered as he tucked his pistol within easy reach beneath his pillow.

* * *

As tired as Judd was, he was getting no sleep whatsoever. It was unnatural to trust anyone implicitly, so he lay there waiting to see if Kat tried to put him to sleep—permanently.

Because Judd couldn't relax, it didn't take long for him to react to the thud against the door. His pistol was in his hand in a heartbeat. He was on his feet, jerking Kat up off the floor and sending her cartwheeling across his bed to land in an unceremonious heap against the wall. He didn't have time to apologize for his less than gentle abruptness. The door banged against the wall and two staggering drunks stood with their pistols drawn.

"Get out, pal," one intruder slurred. "Me and Clem decided to use this room for the night."

"Not this room," Judd said with quiet menace. "It's taken."

"Two six-shooters to one says this room suits us just fine," Clem said, and smirked. "The marshal already dragged off one dead body tonight. Doubt that he'll get all sentimental about hauling off another one—yours. Especially after we testify you tried to steal our room."

From the corner Kat watched Panther face down the drunken cowboys. She marveled at his calm demeanor. Clearly he had encountered lopsided odds before without backing down. It made her wonder what odds Panther considered risky. Certainly not two-to-one odds.

As of yet, the foul-smelling cowboys hadn't realized there was another occupant in the room. Although Kat had the element of surprise on her side, she wasn't sure what to do with it. Her handgun was unloaded, and all she could do would be to throw it at the intruders. That, she decided, wasn't good enough.

While Panther and the cowboys held each other in stalemate, Kat glanced at the rickety bedside table to see the bullwhip curled on top of it. She inched her hand forward to grab the stock. Without the slightest idea how to use the weapon, Kat lashed out with a snap of her wrist.

Leather popped, striking her cheek as it hissed across the

room. She bit back a cry of pain and ducked beside the bed when the intruders whirled toward her. To Kat's relief, Panther pounced on them. The two men were propelled back into the hall and hit the opposite wall with *thunks* and squawks.

Kat bounded across the bed to make sure the men didn't have Panther at another disadvantage. It was a waste of effort on her part. Panther had clubbed them over the head with the butt of his pistol. He jerked the red bandannas off their necks and used them as improvised handcuffs. In a matter of minutes the two unconscious troublemakers were bound together to sleep off their bout with too much whiskey.

"Do you know these men?" Judd whispered.

Kat shook her head. "They aren't the henchmen my stepfather hired, if that's what you're asking."

Judd closed the door and jammed a chair beneath the latch. "Glad to see that ingenuity compensates for what you lack in strength and skill, Diamond," he murmured. "Hope I didn't hurt you when I tossed you aside. I didn't want you to catch a stray bullet and there wasn't time for explanation."

Kat smiled up at him. "I assume you're the type who shoots first and asks questions later."

"No," he contradicted in a cold, emotionless tone, "I'm the type who shoots first and asks *no* questions later."

Judd paused in front of Kat to inspect her for bruises. When he saw blood glistening in the scant moonlight that came through the window, he cursed under his breath. "Sorry. I guess I was a little rougher on you than I thought."

"That wasn't your doing," Kat assured him. "I never used a bullwhip before—"

Kat's breath evaporated when the pad of his thumb swept tenderly across her cheek. She hadn't expected his touch to set off such a strange reaction. Unsure how to deal with the arousing sensation, Kat retreated into her own space.

"Using a bullwhip is the first thing you're going to learn after you mount a horse," he insisted. "Can you use a pistol—and I'm not talking about that piddly derringer you carry—without shooting yourself in the foot?"

"I don't know."

"What does that mean?"

"It means I never shot off the kind of pistol you pack, so I don't know if hitting myself in the foot will be a problem."

Judd sighed loudly, making his frustration known. "My fee as guide and bodyguard is going to keep going up. It's gonna cost you if I have to teach you every little thing you need to know, Diamond."

"As I recall, we never got around to agreeing on a price," she pointed out.

"I want a diamond and a ruby," he negotiated.

Kat wasn't sure which diamond he was referring to—her or one of the sparkling stones in the pouch. She thought she had made it clear that her ability to please a man was as untried as her ability to handle weapons.

"Which diamond?" she asked him flat-out.

Even in the dim light she saw a devilish grin purse his lips. "The one of greatest value."

Well, that pretty much put her in her place, didn't it? He considered her worthless at protecting herself, worthless as a potential lover. "Fine, it's yours, Lassiter."

"Is it?"

"I said so, didn't I?"

Kat plunked down on the rug like a dog, her confidence waning. Spending too much time with a man like Lassiter was hard on a woman's pride. The man eclipsed her in more ways than physical size and stature. He was so . . . adept, skillful, omnipotent in the face of danger. She was so . . . helpless, inept, damn it!

But not for long, Kat promised herself faithfully. She would learn everything Judd Lassiter could teach her. She would make him, and herself, proud. She was going to become more than a defenseless lady of quality who had been raised in the lap of luxury. She was going to be independent, reliable and resourceful.

He'd see, she vowed fiercely. If nothing else, she was going to earn Judd Lassiter's grudging respect and trust.

Judd kept silent while Kat flounced on the floor. Maybe he should apologize for those wisecracks, but he wasn't feeling charitable. He was exhausted, and that little fracas with the drunks had soured his disposition. He kept telling himself this bargain was a mistake. Why had he let Kat talk him into this?

Okay, so he did know why, Judd admitted. Kat Diamond fascinated him, intrigued him. The slightest touch of his hand against her cheek stirred him. Knowing what generous curves and swells lay beneath those tawdry garments tormented him. He wanted her, and he wasn't accustomed to denying himself when it came to appeasing his need for a woman. But Kat Diamond wasn't anything like the other women he knew.

That was another major problem.

The fact that Kat had pitched in to distract the drunken cowboys had impressed him. Most women would have skulked in the corner and waited out the showdown. Not Kat. She had drawn attention to herself, put herself at risk, to even the odds.

Judd could only hope this intriguing fascination he had quickly developed for Kat didn't turn out to be the fatal variety.

CHAPTER FIVE

Judd jerked awake, reflexively groping for his weapon. He blinked, shook his head, then stared down at the makeshift pallet on the floor. He saw Kat curled up under the quilt, her knees tucked against her chest, her arms wrapped around herself like a lost child. Judd knew that self-encompassing position well. He'd spent a considerable amount of time huddled up like that after his mother was killed and his father took him to live in white society. He had taught himself not to be insecure, not to let inner feelings or fear get the best of him.

Uprighting himself, Judd stared at Kat for a long, thoughtful moment. Impulsively, he reached out, wanting to brush his fingertips across the purplish bruise and the self-inflicted wound on her cheek—a wound she had sustained in an effort to protect him from harm. The thought had him shaking his head in amazement. No one had ever stepped forward to protect him before.

Before Judd touched her, he retracted his hand. The sensations that touching her last night had aroused in him deprived him of much-needed sleep. He had to keep his distance from her—physically and emotionally. He would simply admire her from afar. That was for the best.

Judd Lassiter was not in the habit of carrying emotional baggage or secret yearnings when he struck off into the lawless wilderness of west Texas. He sure as hell wasn't going to start now. He had accepted this assignment, unusual though it was, and he was going to be paid for his trouble. He would do his job and go his own way, just as he always did.

Rising, Judd grabbed the shirt he had draped over the iron headboard, then donned his boots. His stomach was growling something fierce—a hazard of being a big eater, he supposed. He needed a strong cup of coffee and a hearty breakfast. Kat would probably appreciate nourishment, too, he mused. He had brought her finger food the previous night . . .

His hand stalled over the chair he had jammed against the latch; then he found himself glancing back at Kat. Until this morning, he had never had anyone to look after, except himself. But suddenly he was taking Kat's needs into consideration. He hoped to hell he didn't get too attentive and considerate. It would ruin his reputation as a hard-nosed bounty hunter, not to mention costing him his edge when he focused absolute concentration on the vicious outlaws he was hired to track down.

Frustrated by the direction of his thoughts and the forbidden yearnings gnawing at him, Judd let himself out the door. The two drunks he had trussed up in the hall were draped against each other, snoring in chorus. Judd grabbed the men by their heels and dragged them toward the staircase.

Might as well keep his bad-ass reputation intact, he decided as he sent the drunkards somersaulting down the steps.

Groaning, the stubble-faced men pried open their puffy eyes. Judd loomed over them, acquainting them with The Look. It was a cold, deadly, uncompromising expression that drained the nerve out of most folks.

"The name is Judd Lassiter, sometimes known as Panther," he snarled at the men.

Name recognition was a grand thing, Judd noted. The cowboys shrank back in fear, as if expecting to be gobbled up in one bite.

"That's right, boys. You messed with the wrong man last

night. Do it again and you won't need a room to bed down in. You'll be fitted for coffins, buried six feet deep on Boot Hill."

Judd swooped down to confiscate their pistols, then tethered the men to the banister. "Since you boys have no manners, I'll help myself to the big irons on your hips to compensate for the inconvenience you caused me last night."

"But we need those pistols," Clem wheezed. "We're riding with the cattle drive headed to Dodge City."

"Your problem," Judd snapped unsympathetically, then stepped over the sprawled men. "Just consider yourselves lucky that I didn't decide to let you wake up dead this morning."

With that, Judd ambled through the vacant dance hall and stepped into the street to inhale a breath of spring air.

Several passersby ducked their heads and scurried off, as if expecting him to wave his arms and turn them into toads.

Absently, he glanced up the slope of "Government Hill" to see the log huts of Fort Griffin sparkling with dewdrops that reminded him of diamonds.

Judd muttered under his breath. He did not need reminders of diamonds, not when he didn't know what to do with the one camped out in his room.

"Panther, you're just the man I've been looking for."

Judd stared across the street to see Marshal Winslow lumbering from the crude wooden building that served as law enforcement office and calaboose. Winslow was a middle-aged man with a middle-aged spread above his belt buckle. He had shoulders like a buffalo, legs like tree stumps and a sandy-brown mustache that reminded Judd of a caterpillar wiggling on his upper lip.

"Got a telegram last night from the sheriff in Haskell County," Winslow called as he galumphed across the street.

"And?" Judd pivoted toward the only restaurant in The Flats that served breakfast. His belly was growling to beat the band.

"And I've got Wanted posters for three men who made a second strike against the stage line. The bastards dressed up like Comanches to rob the coach and made off with several thousand dollars. The stagecoach guard shot and killed the fourth outlaw. That's how he knew they were white. The outlaws killed a male passenger and took his wife captive.''

Winslow scowled, then stared into the distance. ''The renegades left her on the side of the road after they finished taking their turns with her.''

''Did she survive?'' Judd asked quietly.

''No,'' Winslow muttered angrily. ''This account is just the latest in a series of atrocities these bastards committed. The Texas Rangers have been looking for them, but all this time we thought it was renegade Indians. The bounty on the three men is sky high. You want the job?''

Judd decided he might as well take the assignment since he was headed west. But at no time was he going to put Kat's life in danger in order to collect. ''All right. I need descriptions of these desperadoes.''

''Don't have much to go on,'' Winslow said. ''The sheriff thinks he knows who is behind this Indian disguise business, but it's just his educated guess.''

Winslow fell into step beside Judd, then muffled a chuckle when several elegantly dressed ladies and their children darted from Panther's path. The marshal pulled the telegram from the pocket of his leather vest and waved it in Judd's face. ''The names and descriptions I have are for Rowdy Jack, Arkansas Riley and Crazy Ben Corothers. The dead man was known to ride with this bunch. They've left a trail of death, cattle rustling and robbery from here to the western border of Texas. Bunch of cutthroats,'' he grumbled.

When Judd entered the restaurant, several patrons cast him wary glances, gobbled their food and skedaddled. Winslow remained on his heels and invited himself to the table.

The marshal grinned in amusement when Panther cleared the restaurant with nothing more than his intimidating presence. ''We really need to do something about the effect your reputation has on people. One look at you and they run scared.''

Judd shrugged as he took his seat. ''I'm used to it.''

Winslow sprawled in his chair and sighed. ''Last night was a rough one in town. I had more drunken cowboys than I knew what to do with. They got into a fight with some of the soldiers, and it took several clubs to knock some sense into them.''

''I know,'' Judd replied. ''I met up with two cowboys who had a mind to rout me from my hotel room.''

''Aw, damn.'' Winslow muttered. ''Don't tell me I've got two more dead weights to drag to the mortician's office.''

''No, they're alive, tethered to the banister at Breezy's dance hall.''

Winslow slumped in relief. ''Good. I already have one death to investigate. Found that fancy-dressed gentleman, who arrived on yesterday's stage, with a bullet in his back, sprawled face-down in an alley with his pockets cleaned out.''

A cold knot settled in Judd's gut. ''J.P. Trumball?''

Winslow perked up immediately. ''You know him? He drew all sorts of attention when he arrived because he was traveling with a dazzling female. Men lined up on the street to feast their eyes on her.''

''So I heard,'' Judd murmured. ''Breezy told me.''

''The girl disappeared without a trace,'' Winslow went on to say. ''Her luggage is still in her room. The two bodyguards who were traveling with the pair claim the girl and her stepfather got into an argument last night. They think she shot him and then hightailed it out of town.''

Winslow reached into his pants pocket. ''I drew up this notice and took it to the newspaper office to have copies made. I want to question the lady if I can find her.''

Damn it! Judd raged silently. Had Kat neglected to tell him that the reason the henchmen where hot on her heels was because they had seen her kill Trumball? Had she stolen the jewels from her stepfather and then come to Judd with her prefabricated tale?

Judd was just beginning to trust Kat and then, *wham!* Now he didn't know what to believe. She claimed she couldn't handle a weapon . . . Judd frowned, remembering her exact words. Kat claimed she couldn't use a heavy six-shooter, but she had been carrying a derringer that could inflict fatal wounds at close range.

''I've traced Trumball to a poker game at one of the saloons,''

Winslow continued. "He was on a winning streak, but his luck apparently turned sour after he left the saloon."

"Could be that an unhappy poker player decided to reclaim the winnings," Judd murmured.

"Could be, but the two bodyguards don't think so. They swear they saw the girl dressed in men's clothes scurrying through the alley." Winslow shook his head morosely. "Reckon you can never be sure about a woman in these parts, even if she's the most gorgeous thing you ever laid eyes on. Only goes to prove that looks can be deceiving. The biggest mistake a man can make, I reckon, is misjudging the fairer sex."

Words to live by, thought Judd. *Lies from a stranger, no matter how alluring she is, should never be accepted as truth.*

Winslow handed over the notice that bore a crude sketch of Katherine Diamond and a request for information as to her whereabouts. "If you happen across the woman, I'd appreciate it if you would send me a telegram. The bodyguards I questioned claim the woman is clever and cunning. Apparently she made off with the money the guards were expecting to be paid for their services."

"And you believe them?" Judd asked.

"Don't know what I believe. Won't know until I get some answers from the woman."

According to Kat, she had very little in the way of ready cash. Judd had turned up no more than a few coins and banknotes from the envelope tucked in her sock. Maybe he hadn't made a thorough search. He hadn't checked the lining of her dingy cap. He hadn't looked inside the soles of her clunky boots, either.

Judd sat there listening to Winslow ramble about the trouble he anticipated with the cowboys who would be milling around town for the next few days while they restocked supplies, then headed through Indian Territory to reach Dodge City. Judd's attention drifted to the explanation Kat had given him. He wondered if her version of the story was anywhere close to the truth. Problem was, Judd didn't know her well enough to form an opinion of what she was capable of doing.

J.P. Trumball hadn't told the same tale when he intruded on Judd's bath. The town marshal's information also conflicted with Kat's statements. Who the hell was Judd supposed to believe? That cat-eyed beauty, the marshal or J.P. Trumball's bodyguards?

True, Judd's first impression of Trumball wasn't good, but in all fairness, Judd didn't like citified dandies in general. They reminded him of those years when his father attempted to indoctrinate him into white society and Judd had been snubbed and ostracized because of his mixed breeding.

Well, hell, Judd didn't know what to think, who to believe. For all he knew, the bodyguards could have told Marshal Winslow the truth. Or they could have lied through their teeth and stolen Trumball's poker winnings. Or the bodyguards might have even been in cahoots with Kat and decided to dispose of Trumball. Or Kat may have been in cahoots with Chester Westfall and Hugh Riggs and they decided to double-cross her.

Or worse, Judd thought with a grimace, Kat could have acquired his services to lead her westward, while her two bodyguards followed at a discreet distance, waiting to dispose of *him* when he was no longer needed. There was no telling what kind of betrayal he would face in the wilderness when he had Kat Diamond in tow.

The assassination attempts Kat mentioned could have been the one that left Trumball dead, and the one she slated for Judd when he was of no more use to her. She may have no intention of splitting the jewels with him.

Grimly, Judd tucked the notice with Kat's sketch in his pocket, then took out enough money to pay for the meal he'd ordered.

"Holy hell, Panther!" Winslow grunted as he stared at the huge feast the cook delivered. "You gonna put away two cups of coffee and all that food?"

"I'm a big eater," Judd reminded him. "Always have been."

Judd stood up, then grabbed the tray. "No insult intended, Marshal, but I plan to eat in my room, then catch a few more hours of rest before I start tracking Rowdy Jack's bunch."

Winslow flicked his wrist to shoo him on his way. "Sure,

sure, I know you like your privacy. When you meet up with those vicious cutthroats, send me a telegram with the details. You can collect your bounty at any law enforcement office in Texas.'' His gaze narrowed meaningfully. ''Dead or alive, Panther. Makes no difference to me. Just watch your back. Those outlaws don't play by gentleman's rules.''

''Neither do I,'' Judd mumbled before he turned and walked away.

Kat stirred beneath the quilt. Sleeping on the floor left her feeling stiff and achy. But, she reminded herself optimistically, it was a small price to pay for her first step toward independence. This was the first day of the rest of her life. J.P. no longer had control over her or her finances. She would be on her way to Santa Fe, and the past would become only a fading memory.

Levering up on her elbow, Kat raked the tangle of hair from her face. She noticed that Judd had crept from the room without her knowing it. For a moment she feared he had absconded with the jewels, but his whip and dagger lay in plain sight. He wouldn't leave without his arsenal of weapons, she assured herself.

The cut on Kat's cheek and the bruise on her chin—compliments of J.P.—were taut. Kat moaned softly as she worked out the stiffness in her muscles. She rose to wash her face with the pitcher and basin on the commode, then blinked in shock when she saw her reflection in the mirror. None of her former acquaintances from Baton Rouge would recognize her, except for the mop of curly hair that defied a brush. She looked like a heathen from the streets, not the genteel lady her father would have expected her to be.

Using a corner of the towel, Kat rinsed her face and wished for a bath to ease her aches and pains. She suspected a proper bath was a luxury she wouldn't enjoy until she reached Santa Fe. But ah, to soak in a tub for a leisurely hour!

When Kat heard approaching footsteps, she dashed over to snatch up the knife lying on the bed. When the door whined open, Kat was poised and ready to confront an unwanted intruder.

She broke into a smile when Judd shouldered through the door, carrying a tray heaped with food. "Morning," she murmured in greeting.

"Yeah, it is," Judd mumbled as he kicked the door shut with his boot heel.

Kat frowned curiously. *My, the man obviously woke up on the wrong side of his feather bed.* "Something wrong, Lassiter?"

He jerked up his head and glanced in her general direction. "What makes you ask that?"

Kat's frown deepened when he practically bit her head off with his question. "You aren't your charming self this morning," she observed.

"Where the hell did you get the impression I'm teeming with charm? Nothing could be further from the truth. Headhunters aren't paid to be sociable and charming."

Kat swore, there and then, not to let his surly mood spoil the first day of her promising future. She smiled brightly. "I hope one of those cups of coffee is for me. And part of the food?" she asked expectantly.

Judd stared at the air over her left shoulder. "Take what you want." His hand shot out, palm upward. "Give me the dagger, Diamond. I don't want it buried to the hilt in my spine when I turn my back."

Judd's conversation with Marshal Winslow caused demons of suspicion to swirl in his mind. He wanted to believe Kat was a Southern damsel in distress—really he did. But he had a survivor's mind and a survivor's instincts. He would not let his guard down until he was absolutely, positively certain he could trust her. Right now he was certain of only one thing: He was unwillingly attracted to a woman whose name might eventually be listed as his cause of death.

Judd had survived treachery for a dozen years because he refused to trust what people told him. He assumed nothing, took the necessary precautions, left nothing to chance or wishful thinking.

At that very moment, while he watched Kat clasp the coffee

cup in her hands, take a sip and smile in appreciation—as if he had brought her a touch of heaven—he hated her, hated this feeling of satisfaction that came from knowing his act of kindness and consideration pleased her immensely.

Kat sighed approvingly, closed her eyes and let the second sip of coffee stream down her throat. "Ah, Lassiter, for this cup of coffee I'll love you forever."

"Will you?" He studied her suspiciously.

She glanced at him from beneath a fan of long, thick lashes. "You really aren't a morning person, are you? I hope your mood improves as the day progresses."

"Don't hold your breath waiting for that to happen," he said, and snorted. "Now turn your back. I'd like to change into traveling clothes."

Kat did as ordered, focusing her attention on the juicy steak, eggs and biscuits. "What time is it?"

"Do I look like your timepiece?" he snapped as he shucked his shirt and reached for a clean one.

Kat ignored his irascible tone. "Close to seven, I suppose. When will we be leaving town?"

Judd watched her devour the food on the plate. "As soon as I gather supplies, find you a change of clothes and buy a horse. You can't leave town with only one set of clothes."

"Why not?" Kat glanced back at him, then whipped her head around. But it was too late; the sight of washboarded muscles revealed by his gaping shirt was emblazoned on her mind. "Sorry."

"What if someone saw you in the same getup?" he asked as he fastened the buckskin shirt.

"I'm not planning on being seen," Kat said between bites of fluffy biscuit. "I plan to leave the hotel the same way I came in. I don't have sufficient funds for clothes or a horse. I was hoping maybe we could ride double."

"Horse is not carrying extra weight," Judd let her know right quick. "Where we're going, riding double is an invitation to let trouble catch up with you."

Despite his order to keep her back to him, Kat swiveled on

the edge of the bed. Judd jerked his breeches up quickly, noting the heightened color in her cheeks.

"Sorry," she bleated. "But did you say Horse? You named your horse Horse?"

"It's my horse, isn't it? I can call him what I want, can't I?" he said defensively.

Kat whirled back around to stare at the food on her plate, but the sight of Judd's horseman's thighs protruding from the long hem of his shirt was right there alongside the mental photograph of his sinewy shoulders and muscled chest. Sweet merciful heavens! She had caught two accidental glimpses of his masculine body and now she was speculating about anatomical parts she had yet to see. No matter what, she was not—repeat *not*—going to turn around again.

"Are you sure you can't afford another set of clothes?" he asked very deliberately.

"You know I can't," she replied. "I'm sure you checked the envelope to see exactly how much money was in it before you returned it to me."

Judd glanced toward the dingy brown cap that lay on the floor, wishing he could check it for a stash of money. Same went for the oversize boots.

Later, he promised himself. If she had lied to him about having J.P.'s poker winnings in her possession, she would discover hell had no fury like an enraged man—or however that saying went. Judd couldn't recollect. He hadn't spent enough time in white society during his formative years to pick up on all those clichés.

"Fine, then, I'll add the necessary costs to my expense account and you can pay me at the end of the trail."

"Thank you." Kat sipped her coffee. "When I . . . am reunited with my . . . aunt in Santa Fe, you will be paid in full."

Judd's brows flattened suspiciously. He noted that Kat had hesitated in midsentence. He had the unshakable feeling there was something she wasn't telling him. Recently, he had been having that feeling with alarming regularity.

Hurriedly, Judd stuffed his feet in his moccasins. While he

trekked through the wilderness he preferred to look exactly what he was—half white and half Cheyenne. It gave most folks pause, wondering which half of society he preferred, wondering how to deal with him.

That was the way Judd liked it.

"You can turn around now. I'm decent," he announced.

Kat glanced over her shoulder, and her mouth scraped her chest. "My goodness," she chirped.

Her astounded gaze traveled over his brawny physique, marveling at the tawny-colored garments that altered his appearance from semicivilized to downright dangerous. The black Stetson shaded his face and concealed his gaze. The double holsters sported two lethal-looking pistols. The strap around his thigh sheathed the dagger that Kat knew for a fact was razor sharp. The ammunition belt lay diagonally across his broad chest. A necklace of panther claws encircled his throat.

This, she realized, was the man called Panther—the powerful creature who had revealed himself last night when drunken cowboys crowded his space. Judd did indeed look the part of a skilled, ominous gunslinger. His sheer size, combined with his rugged garments, gave him an intimidating, imposing appearance.

"Why are you looking at me like that?" Judd demanded as he reached for a biscuit. His arm accidentally brushed hers and he quickly eased away.

Kat wasn't sure how to respond to his terse question. She was looking at him like *that* because it was impossible not to stare in feminine appreciation and awed fascination. He reminded her of a powerful warrior of the plains who borrowed just enough from white society to put the final touches on a package of powerful strength and blatant masculinity. He was . . . magnificent.

Kat shook herself loose from her awed thought. "You look very nice," she said lamely.

"Nice? *Nice!*" He snorted. "I hope to hell you don't think that is supposed to be a compliment!"

"You look nice in an interesting sort of way," she said, confused by his offended tone. "Is that what you want to hear?"

To her surprise, he curled his fingers tightly around her forearm and jerked her to her feet. He stuck his face in hers and said, ''All I ever want to hear from you is the truth and nothing but. You got that, Kat Diamond?''

His harsh tone and manhandling were provoked by emotions Kat couldn't begin to comprehend. She had the uneasy feeling they were discussing more than her comment about his appearance. But for the life of her she didn't know what he expected of her. What she did know, with sudden clarity, was that standing this close to the man she was instinctively attracted to, looking into the slits of his eyes that glowed with pinpoints of amber, was causing the most phenomenal sensation.

Her gaze settled helplessly on the compressed line of his lips, wondering, speculating, tempted to test the texture of his mouth. Would his kiss be as harsh and overpowering as his mood? Or would his kiss be soft and gentle, giving pleasure as well as accepting it?

Judd didn't like what he saw in those entrancing green eyes. He didn't like the way she was staring at his mouth. He had given her The Look that made most men wilt like a sun-baked rose, but she didn't seem to notice.

He shifted uncomfortably, certain she was speculating about what it would be like to kiss him . . . because he wanted the same damn thing so badly he swore he could taste her from here! But one kiss from those lying lips and he might be poisoned against the truth of who and what Kat Diamond really was—a scheming, cunning siren who fed him lines to gain his cooperation, until the time when she had no more use for him and she'd leave him as a meal for circling buzzards.

To break the spell he felt settling over him, Judd gave her a firm shake. ''Got that, Diamond?'' he repeated. ''Nothing but the truth. If I find out that you've lied to me about anything, you have no idea how sorry you're going to be.''

Scowling, Judd released her to devour his meal. Kat stood beside the bed where he sat. He could feel her gaze on him but he didn't glance in her direction. He knew he baffled her, left her thunderstruck. But damn it, he felt the need to lash out at her, because he didn't know how in the hell to deal with the onslaught of conflicting feelings she stirred up in him. She made him feel vulnerable, angry. She made him ache with longing and burn with an anticipatory sense of betrayal.

She could smile and leave him thinking the sun rose in this very room. She could stare at him with sensual curiosity and turn his knees to mush. She made him ache with the want of her. And all the while, Judd kept telling himself she might be using him for an ulterior purpose.

"Lassiter?" she said softly.

"What?" he snarled in question.

"I haven't lied to you, if that's what you're thinking."

Empty words and deeds, he thought to himself. Time would tell the tale.

CHAPTER SIX

Kat voiced not one word of complaint when Judd returned an hour later with a sack of supplies, a new set of men's clothes and a large-brimmed hat. He ordered her to make a quick change, then shinny down the support beam on the rear balcony where he would be waiting with the horses. Considering Judd's black mood, Kat feared getting her head bit off if she didn't make a snappy descent to the ground.

The man had her totally confused, Kat mused as she changed into the crisp, clean shirt and breeches. Sometimes he behaved as if he liked her—a little. Then at other times she swore he despised her. Like a clock pendulum, his disposition tick-tocked from gruff to gentle. He kept her mentally off balance, intensely aware of him and unsure how to react.

While Kat inched along the balcony, telling herself not to look down for fear her dislike of heights would swamp her, she vowed to simply be herself, despite which way Chief Thundercloud's turbulent moods blew. As long as Judd upheld his end of the bargain, she had no right to ask more of him.

Problem was, if his price went up each time there was something new to teach her on the trail, she might arrive in Santa Fe with an empty pouch . . .

Kat gulped when she made the mistake of looking down as she swung her leg over the balcony railing. It was a good twelve feet to the ground. Her fingers dug into the wood like cat claws and she couldn't force herself to let loose of her handhold to shinny down the rough-hewn beam. Climbing up had been infinitely easier, especially when motivated by an intense fear of imminent death.

"Hurry up," Judd snapped while she hung there like laundry on a clothesline. "We don't have all day, Diamond."

"I'm . . ." Kat groped for solid footing and found none. "Scared," she admitted on a shaky breath.

"Height didn't bother you last night."

"Last night it was dark and I couldn't see how far off the ground I was. I was also more afraid of being shot to death than falling off a roof."

Muttering, Judd stood up on the saddle and grabbed her dangling leg. When Kat kicked instinctively, she nearly sent Judd windmilling off Horse.

"I'm trying to help, damn it. Let go of the railing and wrap your leg around the beam."

"Easy for you to say," she bleated.

Impatiently, Judd hooked his arm around her hips and yanked her loose. Like a cat, she twisted in midair, then wrapped herself around him. Her broken nails dug into his back, her legs circled his hips, as she buried her head against his chest and squeezed the stuffing out of him with her arms. Judd could feel her heart pounding like a tom-tom, feel his betraying male body reacting to close contact.

"You can let go now," he muttered at her.

"Okay," she said unevenly, but she didn't let go.

Judd sank down on the saddle with Kat curled around him like a boa constrictor. He grabbed the mare's reins and guided the mount beside Horse. Then he pried Kat loose and planted her in the saddle, which was surrounded with supplies and bedding.

Judd glared into her peaked face. "You're afraid of heights, you can't ride, and you claim you can't handle a pistol. Is there anything else you can't do that I need to know about before we haul ass across Texas?''

Claim you can't handle a pistol? Kat frowned at the way he phrased the terse comment. ''From the sound of it, you don't believe me. Why not?''

He shrugged an impossibly broad shoulder.

Kat took up the reins, just as she'd watched Judd do with such experienced ease, then crammed her oversize boots in the stirrups. ''Well, it doesn't matter what you believe, because very soon I am going to be as proficient with a weapon as you are.'' Head held high, she nudged the horse forward.

''Wrong direction, Diamond,'' he said behind her.

Kat tugged on the reins to turn the bay mare so she could follow the man dressed in buckskin who was riding the buckskin gelding. She concentrated on emulating his casual ease in the saddle.

Judd led the way down the alley and veered toward a grove of pecan and elm trees that skirted the riverbank. He charted his course northwestward and they rode in silence for several miles.

Kat marveled at the changes in the panoramic valley that spread out before her. The lazy-flowing river was flanked with mesquite-and-oak-clad hillsides. Judd continued to remain within the shelter of the trees that formed a continuous line along the river. Kat presumed he didn't want to call attention to himself while they trekked cross-county.

She smiled in satisfaction as she glided in rhythm with the mare. For the first time in her life, she was living an adventure she had only dreamed about. Inhaling a deep breath of fresh air, Kat thanked the Lord above for seeing her through the harrowing night and giving her this new lease on life.

''Why did you decide to become a bounty hunter?'' Kat asked four miles later.

''Revenge,'' he said shortly.

''Revenge? Against whom?''

''No one you know.''

Obviously, Lassiter did not wish to discuss that topic. Kat moved onto another one less sensitive.

"How did you become such an accomplished rider?" she asked.

"Years of practice."

Well, wasn't this going to be fun? thought Kat. Lassiter had become as closemouthed as a clam—worse than usual, she realized. "Would you mind elaborating on that?" she coaxed him.

"Why? Are you planning on writing my biography?"

Kat gnashed her teeth, reminding herself that she was not going to let Judd's unsociable attitude dampen her spirits. "I'm not asking you to reveal your deepest, darkest secrets," she assured him. "I only wondered if you were taught to ride during your Indian upbringing or if you were raised in white society."

Judd wondered if Kat was trying to lure him into conversation for devious reasons. Was she attempting to distract him while her two cohorts picked up the trail? It would take a while, because Judd had made an inconspicuous departure.

Did she have any idea that her double-crossing cohorts had told Marshal Winslow that she had disposed of her stepfather?

"I was raised as a Cheyenne warrior in the Colorado mountains until I was sixteen," Judd replied finally. "Both boys and girls from our clan were taught to ride at the same time we learned to walk. Pastime games were designed to practice horseback skills and train mounts properly."

"I wanted to learn to ride proficiently," Kat recalled. "But my father came from the old Southern school of tradition which dictated ladies were born to carriages. They were to be seen, not heard. They were to obey father and husband without question. The fact is that my father was sorely disappointed that I wasn't the son that every blue-blooded Southerner was expected to have. He held it against me, and I never realized why he withheld his affection until I was old enough to understand those resentful comments he hurled at me."

Kat smiled ruefully in reflection. "When I was a child, I defied Papa's hard-and-fast rule and raced off on bareback while he was away from the plantation. The horse jumped a creek and I landed in the middle of it. I nearly drowned. If not for one of the field hands who heard my screams and saw the riderless horse charging across the pasture, I probably wouldn't have made it out of the creek alive.''

Judd swiveled around on the saddle to frown at her. "Don't tell me—let me guess. You don't know how to swim, either.''

Kat dropped her head when he stared at her in annoyance. "No, I don't. After the incident, which my father referred to as the beginning of my 'rebel phase,' I was ordered never to mount a horse. He confined me to the attic for two weeks as punishment. He was determined to break my willful streak so I would become proper marriage material for a proper Southern gentleman.''

Despite his mistrust, Judd found himself feeling sorry for the young girl who grew up entrenched in tradition. He could understand why Kat craved freedom so much, after being deprived of it all her life.

The whole outdoors had been Judd's playground. He had come and gone at will, discovering the wonders of nature, learning the habits of animals that his people incorporated into a way of life. Kat had been confined and restricted, denied the simple pleasures Judd had taken for granted.

"So what did you do with yourself for those two weeks in the attic?'' he had to know.

She stared into the distance, and Judd noted the hint of sadness that dulled the usual sparkle in her eyes. "I read about all the fascinating places in the world that I doubted I would ever see. At least I did until my father showed up unexpectedly, carted away the books and ordered me to copy the sentence he spouted at me.''

"Which was?'' Judd prompted.

" 'I will not defy my father's orders again so long as I live under his roof,' '' she repeated. "He made me write it exactly five thousand times. I cannot recall how many times my hand cramped and a child's angry tears spilled on the parchment, forcing it to be torn up and rewritten. Smears and smudges, according to my father, were unacceptable.''

For years Judd had buried his resentment about the cruel twist of fate that had taken his mother's life and sent him away from the mountain village in Colorado to his father's office on the bustling streets of St. Louis. But never had anyone lorded over him the way Kat's father had—if her story was to be believed . . .

The suspicious thought left Judd wondering if Kat was embellishing the story to gain his compassion. For all he knew, this could be a carefully plotted fabrication to gain his trust.

"How did you adapt when you left the Cheyenne village at sixteen?" Kat asked.

"Not well," Judd admitted. "My father and I lived in a home near the river while he ran his fur-trading company. I felt smothered by the hordes of humanity and I struggled in the school where he sent me to be educated. I agreed to the schooling, only if he allowed me to spend my summers with my mother's clan. I knew I would never be at home in white civilization.

"After a few days in the same place, restlessness catches up with me. Now that the Cheyenne have been confined to a reservation, I'm no longer at home in that world, either."

"The proverbial misfit," Kat murmured. "I can easily identify with that. I was named after my great-great-grandmother who lived an adventurous life during the Revolution. According to the story, Kat fell in love with the dashing Captain Diamond who, with the help of his younger brother, organized a spy ring against the British, using a lighthouse to send messages to the rebels.

"It was a grand story," Kat said. "I even tried sending messages, in hopes of being rescued, while I was locked in the attic for punishment. My father discovered what I was doing, and I had to write a few thousand sentences for being 'deceptive,' as he referred to it. He told me on numerous occasions, and my mother echoed the sentiment, that I was born at the wrong time and place, with an uncontrollable wild streak." She glanced briefly at Judd. "It seems you and I have more in common than I thought."

"We have nothing in common, other than the fact that we're riding in the same direction. And speaking of riding, there are skills you need to learn before we encounter trouble. We *will* meet with trouble," he guaranteed. "This is lawless territory inhabited by lawless men who will separate you from your scalp, your horse and your money if you give them half a chance.''

''Are you trying to frighten me? If so, I am fully aware of the dangers.''

''I'm offering you lessons in reality,'' Judd insisted as he halted at the edge of a grassy valley flanked by picturesque hills.

Kat smiled appreciatively as she stared across the meadow where white daisies and yellow buttercups lifted their colorful petals to the sun and rippled like a banner in the wind. The sight of running streams glistening like silver ribbons, rolling grass and tree-covered hills filled her senses.

Perhaps there were wastelands to the west, but the scenery Kat viewed begged to be captured on canvas. ''This is beautiful country,'' she murmured.

''Then you can understand why the Comanche got all bent out of shape when white settlers laid claim to the land, same as they laid claim to the panoramic mountains and valleys in Colorado where the Cheyenne roamed since the beginning of time.''

Kat noted the bitterness in his voice and felt a twinge of guilt, for her family plantation had once belonged to tribes that were shuffled out of the way in the name of progress.

''Now pay attention,'' Judd said, jostling her from her thoughts. ''Rule Number One: Never ride into a clearing without checking for signs of unwanted guests.''

He gestured toward the trees on the north slope of the hillside. ''The sudden flight of birds indicates predators are nearby, whether they be the two-legged or four-legged variety.''

Kat nodded and tucked away the information for future use.

''Rule Number Two: Know your own limitations and those of your mount.''

Kat glanced down at the bay mare that appeared to have a docile disposition. The horse wasn't as spirited as Judd's buckskin gelding. Horse threw his head and pricked his ears constantly. The animal was as alert to its surroundings as Judd was.

"I'm not well enough acquainted with this animal to know her strengths and weaknesses," Kat said.

"You will be soon," Judd promised. "You're taking your first crash course in riding as soon as I scout the hills to make sure no danger awaits us."

"What am I supposed to do while you're scouting?"

"Practice with the bullwhip," Judd ordered sharply.

He unhooked the bullwhip attached to his saddle, then dismounted. When Kat tried to slide off the right side of the mare, he jerked her upright. "Wrong side," he told her. "Always dismount on the left. Only Horse and Indian ponies are trained to expect a rider to be all over them."

He placed her hand on the lead-weighted stock of the whip, then guided her arm up and away from her hip. Judd told himself to concentrate solely on needed instruction, not the spontaneous surge of desire that crashed through him when he caught Kat's feminine scent and made familiar contact with her. He didn't flaunt his own skills with a whip that he had learned to make an unerring extension of his own arm and fist; he simply put Kat through the fundamental motions.

While Judd guided her arm through a series of precise, economical movements, Kat watched the popper attached to the braided leather lash out like a striking snake. A tree branch fell a dozen feet away when Judd gave an abrupt tug.

"You can make the whip crack like a pistol shot with a mere flick of your wrist and the downward momentum of your arm," he informed her. He took her arm through the rapid motion, and bark flew off a nearby tree as the whip hissed and cracked like thunder. "You can take the head off a rattlesnake with this weapon, or peel hide off lobos before they attack. Remember that, Diamond. Practice intently while I'm gone."

His fingers grazed the mending wound on her cheek, and Kat gulped air. Already she was intensely aware of the man who had hovered behind her, filling her senses with his musky aroma and masculine strength. Now she gazed up into those amber-green eyes, fanned by feathery black lashes, then stared at the sensuous curve of his mouth. That same alluring curiosity that had claimed her the previous night came back full force, leaving her to wonder how it would feel to have those male lips moving upon hers, to have those sinewy arms meshing her to the powerful contours of his body.

Judd noted the look of speculation on Kat's face and cleared his throat to alleviate the sudden constriction of his voice. "Don't shred your cheek again, Diamond," he rasped. "I like it just the way it is . . ."

Abruptly, Judd wheeled toward Horse, wishing he had kept his hand to himself and his trap shut. There was a lesson for *him* to learn, he realized as hungry awareness thrummed through him. He was going to have to figure out a way to give Kat instruction from long distance. Standing close enough to absorb her scent and feel her curvaceous body brushing erotically against his was the kind of tormented distraction Judd didn't need.

He jerked upright when he heard the hiss of the whip. Out of pure reflex, Judd whirled around and aimed to fire his pistol.

The teasing smile slid off Kat's lips when she found herself staring down the lethal end of the Colt. Again, she was reminded that Judd's deadly, unerring reflexes were the stuff legends were made of. He reacted out of habit and—as he had bluntly informed her—asked no questions later.

"Mischief will get your head blown off," he snapped as he holstered his pistol. "Practice until I return. If you can't handle the bullwhip to my satisfaction then, we aren't leaving the confines of these trees until you can. Got that, Diamond?"

Something flashed in her eyes, and Judd knew immediately what prompted the reaction. He knew what she intended to say before the words were out of her mouth.

"You are not my father, Panther. I will eagerly practice what you teach me so I can learn to guard your back as well as you guard mine. But do not even think to treat me the way my father and my step—" Kat clamped her mouth shut and glanced away.

"Stepfather," he finished for her. "Would he be the one who put that bruise on your chin?"

"For the very last time," she said solemnly.

Judd rode away, wondering if that hurtful blow had prompted

Kat to leave J.P. Trumball sprawled in a dark alley. He couldn't say he blamed Kat if she had retaliated against the abuse, but he couldn't tolerate it if she had lied to him about it.

When he and Kat were miles away from The Flats he would confront her with what Marshal Winslow told him, Judd promised himself. He believed a man should own up to his actions, and the same applied to the stunning female who was dredging up a riptide of emotion with each passing hour.

Judd still wasn't sure how far he could trust Kat . . . And when it came to this fierce awareness of her, he wondered how far he could trust *himself.*

Kat practiced with the whip until her arm gave out. Tree branches lay around her like casualties on a battlefield. Shaking the ache from her arm, she began again, emulating every motion Judd had taught her, vowing to impress him with what she had learned.

If a man of his vast, perfected skills could ever be impressed, she tacked on.

A warm tingle skittered down her spine as she cracked the whip and watched a leafy branch plunge to the grass. She could feel Judd's lingering presence, his tantalizing scent. She wondered if their close contact affected him as drastically as it affected her. Probably not. She suspected he had been with dozens of women. The brush of a hand or hip would have little effect on him.

Kat was not a woman prone to romantic fascination. Or at least she hadn't been. But she did admit that Judd Lassiter intrigued her on the most elemental level, left her thoughts parading down sensuous avenues.

Great. Just what she needed—to find herself infatuated with the legendary Panther who was everything she wasn't—but hoped to be eventually. Independent? Most certainly Judd Lassiter was that. Skilled in survival? Obviously. His self-defensive instincts never failed to astound her.

Although she could tell Judd didn't quite trust her—refused to let himself—Kat desperately wanted to earn the respect of the only man whose opinion of her mattered. Odd, she mused. Never in her life had she given a fig what folks thought of her, though her father had tried to pound it into her head that impressing one's peers was paramount. Kat had always been confident enough not to be ruled or influenced by others' opinions. So why was she suddenly striving to please a man who didn't seem to like her all that much?

While Kat was trimming trees near the river, Judd was keeping lookout from the oak-clad hills. He noted the silhouettes of two riders through his spyglass. He suspected they were the guards J.P. Trumball had hired, since they were coming from the direction of The Flats. The men, novice frontiersmen at best, neglected to conceal themselves by following the tree-lined river. From the rise of ground, Judd estimated the men were a few hours behind them—and he intended to keep it that way.

Pensively, Judd turned his attention to the grove of pecans where he had left Kat wielding the bullwhip. She was just beginning the first of many instructions she needed to survive in the wilderness, but he made a pact with himself to fix it so she felt the need to depend on him, rely on him. He wanted to convince her that he was indispensable, hoping she wouldn't turn on him—in case she wasn't exactly what she pretended to be.

Judd sighed heavily, wavering between believing Kat was just what she seemed—a woman who had been restricted and confined so long that her free spirit demanded release—and not what he suspected. He didn't want to be suspicious of everything she said or did, because the fact was he enjoyed her company.

She was a novelty to him. While other folks trod lightly around him, avoiding him whenever possible, Kat appeared to have no fear of him. He'd convinced himself that he liked his wanderlust way of life. But having Kat underfoot had already begun to grow on him, though he did his damnedest not to let her know it.

Over the years, Judd had been tested by savvy, wily outlaws. He had heard all the desperate excuses before, all the cries of

pretended innocence. He had gained a formidable reputation
that swirled with legends of his fantastic feats. He sure as hell
didn't want to be brought down by a mere slip of a woman.

His maternal grandfather had taught him to view situations
from every angle, to be prepared for anything, to assume nothing. Judd had applied that theory to Kat Diamond, trying to
figure out her angle, her underlying motives. Thus far, all he'd
done was wear himself out trying to determine what she was
up to and trying *not* to think about how much she appealed to
him as a man.

He felt as if he were walking on quicksand, never knowing
which step would be his last.

For a moment, Judd let his first and only conversation with
J.P. Trumball slide through his thoughts. It was J.P.'s scheme
to frighten Kat back to Baton Rouge—or so he said. J.P. had
wanted Judd to leave Kat alone in the darkness long enough
to let the unidentified sounds and sights work on her nerves
and imagination.

Judd had every intention of reshaping Trumball's scheme to
suit his own needs. He would make sure that Kat Diamond
turned to him for protection and compassion. If she developed
a fond attraction for him, then all the better. It might discourage
her from following through with a dastardly plan to dispose of
him before he took a cut of the jewels.

This was a matter of survival, Judd reminded himself for the
umpteenth time. Unconsciously, he brushed his hand over the
pouch of gems that he had tucked in his pocket. On impulse,
he drew them out and poured the glittering stones into his palm.

A faint smile tripped across his lips as he watched the stones
glisten in sunlight. Whether or not the jewels were truly Kat's
inheritance, or stolen from J.P., they reminded Judd of her. The
emeralds were the color of her eyes in artificial light. The rubies
reminded him of her lush lips, the pearls the color of her skin,
and the diamonds winking up at him symbolized the brilliance
of her infectious smiles.

Judd brushed the pad of his thumb over a pair of peridots—
amber-green–colored stones that were the same shade of his
eyes while he scrutinized her, wanting to believe the best and

constantly on guard against the worst. Vigilant eyes that sought the truth—whether it brought relief or disappointment. He would leave these gems with her as a reminder of him when they parted company. He would keep one diamond and a ruby to remember this forbidden fantasy that followed him like his own shadow.

"Damn, Panther, when did you get so philosophical and sentimental?" he asked himself. "You've let that woman creep too far beneath your skin."

Judd kept telling himself the reason Kat affected him so strongly was because he had never spent so many consecutive hours in the presence of any woman—certainly not enough hours to gain insight and form the semblance of friendship.

It didn't help matters that he had been so long between women, either, he reminded himself sourly.

Judd glanced in the direction of the riders, then frowned. Tonight he would have to take a closer look at his two shadows and set about to waylay them. He didn't need those two men breathing down his neck. He needed time to convince Kat that she needed him until she reached the outskirts of Santa Fe.

Time for a riding lesson, Judd decided as he picked his way down the mesquite-and-oak-covered slope. And then he was going to give Horse his head and set a swift pace that would leave his trailing shadows in his dust.

CHAPTER SEVEN

Long before Judd reached the edge of the clearing he heard the hiss and pop of his bullwhip. He swallowed a chuckle when he saw the broken branches strewn in the grass. Kat's face was flushed from exertion, but she had followed his instructions to the letter. It wouldn't be lack of practice that prevented her from developing competence with the whip.

"Thinking of pruning trees for a living?" Judd asked as he ambled up behind her.

Kat squawked in surprise when the voice came from so close behind her. "Lord," she bleated, clutching her palpitating chest. "You scared me half to death. How did you get here without my hearing you?"

His lips twitched as she pivoted to stare owl-eyed at him. "The stalking panther is the totem of my mother's clan. Warriors are instructed to study and emulate the movements of the great cats. When in the wilds, you do as the cat does in order to survive."

She cocked her head to study him from a different angle in the shadows of the trees. His eyes had taken on an amber glow, and there was something about him that sent an eerie tingle sliding down her spine.

Your imagination is working overtime, Kat told herself. But she couldn't help but remember that strange legend the maid from the hotel conveyed. At the time, Kat had shrugged it off as superstitious nonsense, but the more time she spent with this man called Panther, the more she began to wonder if the phenomenal myths carried a few shreds of truth.

The maid had mentioned something about Panther being an Indian shaman who took on animal form when good clashed with evil. And something about a Phantom Panther of the Plains, as she recalled. All myths, she suspected, but still . . .

"Yes?" Judd prompted when he noted lively curiosity flickering in her eyes.

Kat blinked, stunned. Either this man could read her mind or her thoughts were transparent in her expression. *Must be the latter,* she convinced herself. "You don't happen to hold some sort of official title with your Cheyenne clan, do you?" she came right out and asked him.

"Why do you ask that?" he questioned her question.

"Because of something I heard while I was pounding the streets of The Flats, pumping everyone for information about a reliable guide and bodyguard. The hotel maid—"

"The one you think is my secret admirer?" he cut in, grinning wryly.

Kat nodded. "She spoke of you as if you were God's brother—a miracle worker and a wizard, all rolled into one. It must be flattering to have so much respect and admiration bestowed on you—"

"You were saying?" Judd interrupted.

Kat smiled at his subtle tactic of referring her to her previous topic of conversation. "I was saying that fantastic legends follow you."

"The Phantom Panther of the Plains?" he supplied. "The guardian spirit of *Llano Estacado?* Are you referring to the myth about how I, in the heat of the deadliest battles, transform into my namesake and wield phenomenal powers?"

He said it so casually, as he tossed her a sly smile, that Kat felt foolish about broaching the subject. But there was no mistaking that unexplainable aura of feline grace and controlled power that she sensed swirling around him. It had become even more evident after they'd left civilization behind, as if Panther had returned to his natural element.

"Nights of a thousand watchful eyes that carry a curse to the damned?" he added, his smile broadening as he watched her study him intently. "Yeah, I've heard the tales bandied about when no one thinks I could overhear. Makes a fantastic ghost story to pass around a campfire, doesn't it?

"Or maybe you have me confused with the legend about the Comanche half-breed who is said to call in the wolves when he clashes with the worst hombres in the West."

"Calls in the wolves?" Kat repeated curiously.

"So the legend goes," Judd said. "Then, of course, there is the myth of the Lone Horseman, also a Cheyenne shaman, who commands the ghost horses that rumble across the High Plains to wreak havoc on evil white men who have trespassed on Indian hunting ground."

That said, Judd pivoted to retrieve Horse from his tether in the trees.

"Are all three legends a product of someone's overactive imagination?" she called after him.

"Lesson Number Two," Judd announced as he swung effortlessly into the saddle, purposely ignoring her question. "Mount up, Diamond. You are going to learn to stay on the back of a horse at full gallop. There may come a time when we have to beat a hasty retreat while crossing the *Comancheria.* I don't want to look over my shoulder and see you spread-eagled on the ground. The Kiowas and Comanches have a fetish for a thick head of hair. Either they raise a scalp or they abduct female captives to sire their children. After the whites poisoned Indians with strychnine to exterminate them, the Comanches propagate their tribe by using white and Mexican slaves.

"You don't want to know what happens to white squaws with stubborn streaks like yours," he added quietly.

When Kat gulped hard, Judd was assured that she had forgotten about the myths surrounding the Phantom Panther, the Wolf Prophet and Lone Horseman. He had her speculating on the disasters that might befall her if she didn't learn all the necessary survival skills he could teach her.

"Use your knees and feet to steady yourself on the horse," Judd instructed. "Move with the horse's gliding motion, not against it. Curl your upper body over the pommel." He gestured to the three scraggly hackberry trees that were spaced apart in the meadow. "When you round each tree in a figure-eight pattern, lean opposite the horse for balance. Watch and learn."

Judd touched his heels to Horse's flanks. The animal gathered itself and plunged off, ears laid back, tail in the air. Kat studied the poetic motion of man and horse moving as one graceful creature that executed sharp turns with amazing precision.

Kat squirmed uncomfortably in the saddle. She hadn't let on, for fear of Judd's ridicule, but her inner thighs and backside were already sore and tender from hours in the saddle. She wasn't sure she had the stamina or endurance to complete the obstacle course Judd charted. But she would be damned if she fell on her face when a raiding party of Comanches swooped down on her. She had no intention of letting anyone separate her from her scalp while she still had need of it, and she balked at being toted off for breeding purposes.

Determined to pass the second test Judd tossed at her, Kat grabbed the reins, dug in her heels and held on with her knees when the mare took the bit in her teeth and thundered forward. Stark fear coiled in Kat's belly as she covered ground at alarming speed. She leaned away from the mare as they executed the first turn, then scrunched down for the straightaway.

The second tree came at her with such startling speed that Kat wasn't able to shift her weight quickly enough. She and the mare parted company in midturn, and the reins ripped across Kat's hand like the lash of the bullwhip. She tried to drop and roll, but she cartwheeled into the tree, bounced sideways and found the waving grass coming at her before she could thrust out her arms to brace herself.

"Damn," Judd muttered as he gouged Horse. He'd intended to push Kat to determine her limits, but he'd obviously expected too much from her first riding exercise. The moment he reached her, he bounded from the saddle to hunker beside her.

"You okay, Diamond?" he asked.

"C-can't . . . br—ea—the—" she wheezed.

Judd slid his arm beneath her, rolled her over, then propped her into sitting position against him. When her eyes rolled back in her head and her face turned white as salt, he shoved her head between her bent knees. Her hat tumbled from her head, sending a waterfall of curls over her ashen face. Judd whacked her none too gently between the shoulder blades—once, twice, three times. Finally, she sputtered, gasped and coughed.

"Scalped," Judd said grimly. "Sometimes hapless victims don't die for hours. Lobos and panthers usually arrive first. The buzzards swoop down to take what's left."

He knew he was scaring the living daylights out of Kat. That was the whole point. The tactic appeared to be working, because she twisted around and flung herself into his arms, same as she had when the fear of heights had overtaken her. She clung to him like a barnacle on a ship, and Judd let her hold onto him for a full minute. He noticed the raw flesh on her hands where the reins had been ripped from her grasp, knew her fingers were stinging like hell on fire. He figured Kat had earned this moment of compassion after her spectacular fall and his grim depictions.

When she tipped her peaked face up to stare somberly at him, Judd had to battle the insane urge to kiss the breath back into her. This survival lesson was about to backfire in his face—on his lips, to be precise. His arms enfolded her involuntarily, securing her quaking body to his.

He was oh so close to losing himself in those hypnotic green eyes and petal-soft lips—until she said, "Promise me that if I fall when we're pursued by Comanche warriors you'll shoot me and end my misery before the torture can begin."

"I—" Judd couldn't speak for the intensity he saw on her face.

"Promise me, Panther," she demanded shakily.

Judd didn't even want to consider that grim scenario, but Kat forced him into it. Still, he wasn't making any such promise. Honest to goodness, he didn't think he could pull the trigger, even though he had never been squeamish about drawing and firing when the situation demanded.

"Just make double damn certain that you don't leave me with that option," he growled as he hauled her to her feet. "Now run the obstacle course again, with no mistakes. Do it *now,* Diamond."

He expected her to burst into tears and refuse to mount up immediately after she'd taken a spill. He felt an unprecedented sense of pride sweep over himself when Kat squared her shoulders, stepped back on wobbly legs and tilted her bruised chin. This little lady might give out occasionally, Judd realized, but her strong will and determination refused to let her give up.

When Judd whistled softly, Horse jerked up his head from the patch of grass where he grazed. The second whistle brought Horse trotting obediently toward him. "Take my horse," he insisted.

"Why? Does he come with a written guarantee of a softer landing?"

Judd grinned as he gave Kat a boost onto the saddle. "No, but he knows this drill better than your mare. This time I won't come running if you fall off, so don't fall off."

When he turned and walked off to retrieve the mare, Kat inhaled a cathartic breath, focused absolute concentration on the distant tree—and prayed. She was not going to fall off, even if she had to wrap herself around Horse like a vine.

The light touch of her heels sent Horse into a lunging gallop. Although Kat was a novice rider, it only took an instant to realize this powerful animal had a much smoother gait and could run circles around the plodding mare.

Kat concentrated on moving with the graceful motion of the gelding. She shifted her weight as Horse dug in his hooves, then circled the tree, exploding onto the straightaway like a discharging cannon. The second tree posed no problem because Kat was getting the feel of the maneuver and anticipated when to shift sideways, then upright herself.

Two down and one to go, she told herself, teeth gritted, eyes straight ahead. *No mistakes, no miscalculations, Diamond. Get it right.*

A warm sense of accomplishment channeled through Kat as she completed the circuit, then pushed her weary body beyond its previous limits. She ran the course again, and again, gaining confidence with each change of direction, each shift of the reins in her tender hands.

Kat couldn't contain her beaming smile as she trotted Horse back to where Judd waited. She was expecting a heartwarming comment such as: *Job well done, Diamond.*

She didn't get it. Judd merely tipped his head to the sun and stared into the distance.

"We'll stop for supper just past dark," he said before he galloped off on her mare, headed toward the concealment of a distant grove of trees.

Kat's aching muscles were screaming so loudly she swore Panther could hear them, but she said not a word. She had learned Lesson Number Three: No one receives awards for survival, only the personal satisfaction of knowing she has met the challenge and lives to tackle the next one.

"You're leaving?" Astounded, Kat watched Judd swing effortlessly onto Horse's back.

They had taken their meal of hoecakes and the wild turkey he'd dropped with a crack of the whip. Kat had cleaned and stored the utensils, then plunked down to give her screaming muscles a rest. Suddenly Judd was on his feet, prepared to ride off without a word of explanation.

"You have the bullwhip," he threw over his shoulder. "If a predator ventures close, apply what you've learned."

"Where are you going? When will you be back?" she questioned uneasily.

"I'm going to scout the trail, and you can look for me when you see me coming."

Kat muttered at his indefinite answer, then glanced apprehensively at the swaying shadows. Judd had informed her that this area was a known habitat for wolves, coyotes and panthers. The thought of defending herself against such deadly predators put her nerves on tense alert. She hadn't had time to acclimate herself to her surroundings. Every unidentified noise made her flinch.

"I can't believe you're leaving me alone in the dark," she said, and scowled. "I hired you to protect and guide me."

"This is part of what I was hired to do," he reminded her briskly. "To *scout*. You have to learn how to adjust to the darkness and its nocturnal prowlers. It doesn't do a damn bit of good to practice skills if you are never allowed to test them. This is the reality of your training, Diamond. You learn to take care of yourself when no one is around to do it for you. The code book of the wilderness states that nine times out of ten, no one is around to save you when you need saving most. No one but *yourself*."

"And that's the book *I* would have liked to read before we set off," she shot back.

Judd grinned inwardly when she threw his words back at him—words he had flung sarcastically at her the previous night. But he didn't let her know that she had amused him. He simply nudged Horse and vanished into the shadows.

Kat's shoulders drooped as she stared at the spot where she had last seen Panther. The inky black shadows of the trees seemed to swallow him up, as if he had vanished into thin air, as if beyond those shadows was a vacuum that swallowed all sound. She wondered if his vanishing act was one of the reasons myths and legends swirled around him. Probably.

Uneasily she glanced around, telling herself she had nothing to fear but fear itself—and not quite swallowing that malarkey. The fact was that fear of the unknown was eating away at her nerves. Judd had told her that in addition to the wildcats that prowled the hills and valleys, rattlesnakes, scorpions and tarantulas were known to hide in the grass and under rocks and fallen limbs. Kat scooted closer to the small campfire Judd had built to ward off the evening chill, then wrapped her hand around the stock of the bullwhip.

While she sat there, staring in every direction at once, she remembered the legend of the Phantom Panther—especially that eerie part about nights with a thousand watchful eyes staring from the darkness. That was when Kat's imagination hit full stride. She experienced the unnerving feeling that she was being watched, stalked. Every sound that erupted in the night was amplified by the contrasting silence.

Tension whipped through her, causing the hair on the back of her neck to stand on end. When a distant coyote howled, Kat nearly came out of her skin, then huddled as close to the campfire as she could get without setting herself on fire.

"Damn you, Judd Lassiter," she muttered as she bounded up to pace in circles around the campfire.

Kat decided to walk down to the creek to cleanse herself as best she could from the bank. Maybe a makeshift bath would calm her jittery nerves.

Glancing every which way, she scurried through the brush to bathe, but it didn't help much. Shivering from the chill of the water, Kat returned to camp, then pulled the bedroll around her like a cloak. She double-checked the inky shadows for unwanted intruders.

Judd had to know she was frightened—terrified was nearer the mark. Never once in her life had she found herself in unfamiliar territory without a reliable escort. Judd knew she was completely out of her element, with only rudimentary survival skills for protection. Yet he had left her alone on the very first night on the trail, damn him! When he said he was giving her a crash course on survival, he hadn't been kidding.

Cautiously Kat patted the bedroll from top to bottom. Judd had warned her that snakes often slithered into bedrolls for warmth. She wasn't stupid enough to snuggle into the pallet without giving it a good shaking first, but . . .

But what, Diamond? she asked herself. *You know you're exhausted. Why don't you just lie down and catch up on your sleep? Afraid?*

Kat muttered at the taunting voice, then decided to shake out the pallet once more for good measure, then get some shuteye—

When the underbrush rustled, Kat twisted around, the bullwhip upraised—just in case. Her heart hammered against her rib cage and her hands shook. She waited, anticipating the worst.

No attack came, thank God!

"Probably just a rabbit. Raccoon or possum maybe," she told herself.

Was it best to sing and talk? she wondered. Would the sound frighten away predators? Or was noise an invitation for human predators to strike?

Judd had told her that Comancheros who traded illegal goods and rifles to Indians were known to steal white women and children for the Comanches in exchange for horses and safe passage through hunting grounds. Were Comancheros lurking out there? Or outlaws perhaps?

After two hours of apprehensive solitude, Kat could endure no more of the unidentified sounds that came at her from a dozen different directions. She belted out a few gospel hymns, then shifted her position in the camp to huddle in silence, listening intently for the approach of predators.

This was turning out to be the longest night of her life, and Kat couldn't get one wink of sleep, for fear someone—or something—would sneak up while she was unaware. She had to stay awake, to keep the vigil. And while she did, she cursed Judd Lassiter for every unnerving minute of torment she endured.

"You sure we oughta be out here?" Hugh Riggs questioned as he passed the pint of whiskey to Chester Westfall. "We don't know where the hell we are or who we might meet up with."

Chester took a swig of liquor, then resettled himself against the saddle that served as his pillow. He glanced at the glowing coals of what had been the campfire, then at the swaying shadows cast by overhanging tree limbs. "You wanna give up on them jewels that Trumball claimed the gal has on her? There's a fortune inside that pouch, friend. We can be sittin' pretty for the rest of our lives if we can get our hands on them."

"Yeah," Hugh agreed halfheartedly. "But I don't like the company the lady is keepin'. I heard those incredible tales that folks in The Flats were spoutin' when Panther arrived in town. The man worries me.''

Chester scoffed. ''You believe that rubbish? It's nothin' but wild imagination and superstition.''

''Maybe, maybe not. But how do you account for the fact that this particular bounty hunter has a perfect record for tracking down the worst outlaws Texas can throw at him? Answer me that, will ya, Ches? You explain to me how a man can trail desperadoes through woodlands, prairies or deserts and survive without some kind of supernatural powers.''

''Well, hell, Hugh, the man's part Injun, ain't he? Those savages grow up learnin' to live and hunt like animals. It gives 'em an edge. I wouldn't be surprised if that headhunter didn't start all those wild rumors himself, just to scare the bejeezus outa anybody who decides to go up against him.

''If I started the tale that you transformed into a bat and flew off in the night before I could capture you, the story would be all over Texas. Nobody could prove me wrong, and the myth would just keep growin' and growin'.''

Although Hugh wasn't long on brains, he decided that made a certain amount of sense. But still . . .

''What was that!'' Hugh bolted upright and floundered for his pistol. He aimed toward the rustling underbrush, then fired when he heard an eerie growl.

''Gimme that damn gun, you idiot!'' Chester snapped as he dived across his partner's barrel-shaped belly to confiscate the weapon. ''Hellfire, Hugh. Save them bullets for what you can see, not what you can't—''

Loud caterwauling rose from the darkness, drifting in from a new direction every few seconds. Then it was as if a chorus of wailing snarls struck up in the night. The two men hunkered by the dwindling campfire, squinting in one direction, then another.

''Look there!'' Hugh croaked, pointing a shaky finger toward the glowing pinpoints of what he swore were nocturnal eyes reflecting the dim light. ''And there! Holy hell, what are those things?''

Chester gulped, forcing his catapulting heart down his throat to his chest where it belonged. "Fireflies most likely," he wheezed.

Another strange growl erupted from the overhanging trees. Both men dived for their pistols.

"Geezus!" Hugh whimpered, terrified. "He's here. He's watching us! I can feel it! Can you feel it, too?"

"Ain't nobody here but us," Chester hissed with more bravado than he felt. "This is how them legends are born. You get a little nervous, and poof. You start thinkin' you're seein' things that ain't there, hearin' things that have logical explanations if you just think about it."

Hugh Riggs was not totally convinced. The hair on the back of his neck was standing at attention. He felt as if someone— or something—was breathing down his neck. He couldn't see who or what, but he could feel it.

"Ain't no pouch of jewels worth dyin' over," Hugh murmured.

"Nobody's dyin' here," Chester insisted, his gaze circling the inky-black shadows. "We'll just let that Panther character lead us across the territory until we find the perfect spot to ambush him. We'll have the jewels and we can light out for California." He took another sip of courage from the whiskey bottle. "You keep the first watch tonight and I'll get some sleep."

Chester scrunched down on his pallet, took another sip of liquor to fortify his nerves, then squeezed his eyes shut.

Hugh breathed a huge sigh of relief when the winking pinpoints in the darkness evaporated into nothingness, and only the sound of toads and cicadas called to him. The occasional call of a hoot owl reached his ears. He sat there for two hours, trying to tell himself that he'd let his imagination run away with itself. Then his eyelids grew heavy and he slumped on his pallet.

He wasn't sure how long he'd slept, but he awoke with a start and jerked his pistol into firing position. "Lord have mercy!" he screeched.

Chester bolted up, fists raised to fend off the expected attack.

"What the hell's wrong?" he scowled when he saw nothing but darkness surrounding him.

Hugh pointed the trembling pistol barrel toward the mellow dirt that encircled the glowing coals of the campfire. "Cat paws," he said hoarsely. "Big ones. Look at the size of those tracks!"

Chester crawled onto all fours to brush his hands over the prints—as if destroying the evidence would break the curse of the darkness.

"Why'd you do that?" Hugh questioned, bewildered.

Chester sank back on his haunches. "Dunno. Met up with a voodoo woman down in New Orleans once. She said if you remove the pin from a voodoo doll you remove the curse of inflicted pain. Figured maybe the same held true for this kind of black magic."

"So you think there is something to those legends?" Hugh murmured, eyes rounded. "You think the mark of death has been put on us? That's what you're thinkin', ain't it, Ches? You've been scoffin' about the folklore all the livelong night, but you're as worried as I am. I say let's forget about that gal and her jewels."

Chester forced himself to calm down, to think things through. He'd been destitute all his life, without a pa to raise him and his sister. They'd never had enough food to fill their growling bellies, nor enough clothes to keep them warm. Chester wanted to know how it felt to have money to spend on whims. If a man wanted more than he had, then he had to take some risks. He'd taken his fair share of risks, broken most of the Ten Commandments at least once, without his conscience bothering him about it. He wasn't going to let some stupid superstition ruin his chances of getting his hands on that poke of gems. No, sir, he'd come this far and he wasn't turning back.

"I ain't givin' up," Chester vowed fiercely. "And I sure as hell ain't traipsin' through country I don't know without following that bounty hunter's tracks. If we don't follow him, then we'll definitely be lost."

"We could turn back," Hugh suggested.

"Back to what?" Chester snorted. "Back to sweepin' up in

taverns for the price of a meal? Back to sleepin' in storerooms with nothin' to show for ourselves but the clothes on our backs? Back to disposing of rich men's enemies so they won't have to get blood on their elegant hands?''

After a few moments, Hugh nodded his bushy head. ''Okay, so we ain't left much behind, except warrants for our arrests. I ain't arguin' about that. But I don't see *dead* as much of a future, either.''

''Nobody's gonna scare me off with hocus-pocus,'' Chester said defiantly. ''I say we keep followin' that headhunter. I'm the boss, so that's what we're gonna do.''

Hugh slumped back on his bedroll and stared into the night. He had a real bad feeling in his bones, but he tried to ignore it as best he could. Hugh had done plenty of things guaranteed to put a noose around his neck, but he had dodged a couple of near hangings and moved on to places where nobody knew who he was or what he'd done. Then he met up with Chester and they had committed a few more crimes that made them candidates for hell.

Hugh supposed that was why he wasn't in a hurry to die, especially out here in the wilds of Texas, where he was so far from the familiar settings of towns and dark alleys that he could duck into and lose himself in.

No, he wasn't in a great hurry to push up daisies, because he knew the devil was itching to get his hands on him. Far as Hugh was concerned, the devil could wait.

CHAPTER EIGHT

Eyes closed, Judd inhaled deeply, steadily, then let his breath out slowly. Although Horse was shifting uneasily beneath him, Judd opened his eyes and focused absolute concentration on the woman who sat by the campfire in the distance, her glowing mass of hair shining like flames. She was learning to keep the vigil, assuming nothing, waiting in a state of readiness.

Again, Judd closed his eyes and drew himself up to another plateau, separating himself from the dark depths of concentration where absolute control of spiritual power originated.

Since he had accepted the forces at his command, he had developed the ability to transport himself from one level to another, but it always took time to readjust when he turned all conscious thought inward. It drained his strength and forced him to regenerate energy.

His skin still tingled, his ears rang. After several moments Judd stared into the distance again, seeing only as a man should see, not as a stalking predator. The three black pumas beside Horse prowled, awaiting Judd's command. He gave a slight nod and the great cats slinked soundlessly into the trees to become lost in the inky shadows.

As Judd neared camp, he smiled devilishly. He struck out

with a moccasined foot to rattle the underbrush beside Horse. He bit back a snicker when Kat whipped around to seek the source of the abrupt sound. In the dwindling firelight he could see the whites of her eyes, the taut lines bracketing her mouth. She clutched the bullwhip so tightly in her fist that her knuckles turned white.

The color matched her complexion, he observed.

He hoped the past several hours of solitude had convinced Kat that she preferred his presence to solitude. Judd had lived alone for years, but Kat hadn't. Obviously, she hadn't learned to function in complete privacy. It was something the Cheyenne learned at an early age. They were taught to commune with nature, to seek their guardian spirits, to confront their fears. They knew of the special, unseen powers bestowed by the spirit world, accepted them as part of their existence . . .

And few warriors were chosen to wield those special powers.

Kat knew nothing of those Indian customs, had practiced none of the rigorous physical and mental training. She wasn't coping well. Judd could see fear written on her exquisite face in bold letters.

Dismounting, Judd crouched in the underbrush behind Kat. He uncurled his hand, allowing the quail he'd caught to fly free. He swallowed a bubble of laughter when Kat squawked like a plucked chicken and scrambled away from the unexpected sound. While she composed herself, mumbling something about a ''damn bird,'' Judd circled around to make his entrance from the opposite side of camp.

When he stepped into view, Kat vaulted to her feet. Propelled by hours of barely controlled panic, she sprinted toward him. ''Thank God you're back!''

Judd braced himself when she launched herself into his arms like a homing pigeon returning to roost. It was damn nice to be welcomed and wanted, he realized as she squeezed him in two. Although he had designed a series of evening events to keep Kat off balance so she would come to depend on him, he couldn't account for the warm coil of sensations that unfurled inside him when she hugged him as if he were the other half of her missing soul.

He looped his arms around her hips, his body stirring instantaneously when her breasts brushed against his chest. She tucked her chin beneath his shoulder like a trusting child, still holding on to him for dear life. He should have been exceptionally pleased to know his devious scheme had produced the wanted results, but masculine need kept overriding his original intentions. He kept wondering why it felt so good, so right, to nestle Kat in his arms.

He should know better, he told himself. He was not and never would be the kind of man any woman needed, especially a gently bred lady like Kat.

Mostly, folks took a wide berth around him, never ran *to* him the way Kat just had. He was a trained predator. Yet it was oddly satisfying to be Kat's haven for comfort rather than an object of fear and wariness.

Enjoy the moment, but don't get too accustomed to this, Panther. You know your limitations, your destiny, came the quiet voice of reason.

"How long does it take?" Kat murmured against his buckskin shirt.

Judd felt her words vibrating across his flesh like a caress and he had to refrain from pulling her closer than she already was—which was too damned close for his comfort. Needy sensations were bombarding him like a barrage of gunfire.

"How long does it take for what?" He had no idea what she meant, and his mind was focused on the ache pulsing in his lower regions.

She tilted her head back to peer at him through that fan of thick lashes. "How long to get used to being alone at night in the wilderness?"

For the life of him he couldn't take his eyes off her quivering lips. It was like staring at a feast while on the verge of starvation. His floundering brain had difficulty processing the question, because his attention was focused on her sensuous mouth.

"Days? Weeks, years, forever?" she prompted when he simply stood there staring down at her.

Judd gave himself a mental shake and willed his voice to be

steady. "Depends on what you're used to," he said as his betraying gaze slid back to her lush lips.

He was going to have to kiss her, Judd decided suddenly. Despite his vow to keep his distance and remain emotionally uninvolved, he needed to test this attraction that was beginning to monopolize his thoughts and leave his male body on a slow, steady burn.

Just one kiss, he told himself. It wouldn't alter the course of their separate lives or crumble the mistrust that he wore like a suit of armor. He'd kissed dozens of women and his world hadn't come crashing down. He just needed to appease urges that had been deprived for more than two months, was all.

He didn't want to frighten her, because he'd done plenty of that with his scare tactics. Although gentleness wasn't his forte, Judd forced himself to proceed with tender patience.

Ever so slowly, subtly alerting her of his intent, Judd lowered his head. He watched her lashes flutter shut when his lips brushed lightly over hers. He felt the tension drain out of her— and pour into him like chain lightning. Desire exploded through him when Kat reached up on tiptoe to wrap her arms around his neck. Her uninhibited response nearly drove him to his knees. With a groan, he clutched her to him until her feet were dangling in the air. He deepened the kiss, exploring the sweet recesses, tracing the edge of her teeth, fencing with her tongue.

He heard another moan—was it his or hers? He wasn't sure, didn't have enough mind left to figure it out. He was burning up inside, bombarded by hot, achy sensations that left the hard evidence of his arousal pressing blatantly against her thigh.

His acute senses turned against him. So attuned to her was he that he couldn't draw breath without breathing her, couldn't touch her without absorbing the feel of her. Her shapely body was pressed against his muscled contours, but he couldn't get close enough to satisfy himself. The layers of buckskin and cotton that separated them frustrated him. And yet he thanked the powers that be that there was something stopping him from melting into her.

Sweet mercy! It was as if she were made to fit him perfectly, he thought as he drank the honeyed nectar of her kiss, savoring every last drop of unexpected pleasure. It was as if she were born to match this deep well of passion that bubbled up in unlimited supply!

Never had Judd experienced such uncontrollable reactions to a woman. He couldn't get enough of Kat. Damn, this wasn't supposed to be happening to a man who had spent his entire life practicing self-discipline!

Kat felt her senses reeling—not unlike on the previous night when the hotel room had spun in a dizzying blur, not unlike the frantic sensations she'd experienced when she had taken a fall during her riding lesson. Now, as then, she lost the ability to breathe normally, couldn't formulate thought. Her body was bursting with life and whirring with amazement. She had never felt more secure in a man's arms—or so completely undone.

Judd's woodsy scent became hers, and they clung so tightly together that she couldn't distinguish where his flesh ended and hers began. It was as if they were sharing the same breath, the same skin, the same thundering heartbeat.

Was this desire? This wild, desperate, hungry feeling that overrode every other emotion, even fear? When Judd kissed her, the fear that haunted her for hours on end vanished into nothingness. She held on to him, learning by example, returning the pleasure that sizzled through her, feeling the most incredible sensations scald her inside and out.

When Judd shifted her in his arms to brush his hand over the swell of her breast, Kat instinctively arched to meet his caress, stunned by her own eagerness. With this man—only this man—she felt wild and wanton and unfulfilled.

When his roaming hand slid between the buttons on her shirt to swirl around her nipple, Kat went up in flames. The woman she had once been was no more. This man's bold caresses gave her life, put her in touch with her own feminine needs. And what she needed was more of him, all of him, whatever it took, however long it took to ease these burning sensations that multiplied, intensified, with each ragged breath.

Kat tunneled her hand beneath his buckskin shirt to explore the rippling muscles on his chest and belly. She felt him flinch, then tremble. She was pleased to realize that her touch affected him as fiercely as his affected her. Touching him was like skimming her hands over a living statue of masculine perfection, and having him react to her caresses did wonders for her feminine pride.

WHAT IN THE HELL DO YOU THINK YOU'RE DOING! The indignant voice roared in Judd's ears, startling him to his senses. It took every smidgen of willpower he could muster to release his possessive hold on Kat, to set her back to her feet, denying himself the pleasure of her wandering caresses. When he did, she stared at him with a startled sense of wonder. Judd was pretty sure he was seeing the reflection of his own dazed expression.

Her mouth was swollen from the intensity of their kiss, her boyish shirt gaped open to reveal the satiny skin he had dared to touch. Desire glistened in her eyes, and there was no question that she had been as totally immersed in that amorous embrace as he had.

Damn, nothing had ever hit him that hard—that fast—before. He'd lost control in the blink of an eyelash. Just like that—*wham!* He and Kat were like fire and gunpowder—a dangerous, explosive combination.

Judd dragged in a shuddering breath. He should say something. Unfortunately, his tongue felt as if it had melted on the roof of his mouth. He didn't have enough air in his lungs to speak, even if his vocal cords were functioning properly—which they sure as hell weren't. And his unruly body? Now, there was the greatest problem of all. He was so hard it hurt, and the bulge in his trim-fitting breeches was a testimonial to the arousing effect Kat had on him.

Big mistake, Lassiter. Huge! You just found out something you were better off not knowing—and on your first day on the trail to boot. You are dangerously vulnerable to this woman. You aren't even sure you can trust her. You aren't sure she isn't plotting to use you, then deceive you, to cheat you. And here you've got the worst case of lust ever recorded in the annals of history. Don't let her know how strongly she affects you—in case she hasn't figured it out already.

"We better go to bed—" Judd swallowed a groan. "What

I mean is that we need to get to sleep. We . . . um . . . have a strenuous ride"— *Damn it, don't even think about strenuous rides, you idiot!*—"ahead of us tomorrow."

Kat angled her head and studied him astutely. "I could swear you're blushing. How sweet."

Sweet? Judd jerked upright. He had to get this situation under control immediately. He had to remain in charge. He had to stop blurting out the first thing that came into his head. "I've been called many things, Diamond, but sweet never made the list. And if I was blushing I was doing it for *you.* What the hell are you doing? You shouldn't have let me kiss you like that, touch you like—" So much for not blurting out the first thing that came into his head. "I thought you said you'd never . . . well, you know. So why did you? Why with *me?*"

Kat's gaze narrowed. She didn't like the sound of his accusing voice, didn't like the implication that she should have been the one to break the kiss, as if *he* were simply an innocent bystander. "Are you saying that you think I lied to you about not being intimate with men because I kissed you back?"

"Yes," he rapped out.

Her chin shot up. Despite all the wonderful things she had been thinking about this big brawny hulk of man the previous moment, she wasn't thinking nice things about him now. He was questioning her integrity and honesty, just because she had gotten carried away kissing him. She had done nothing to warrant his cynical suspicions.

Well, okay, she had withheld a teensy-weensy tidbit of information from him, but that had absolutely no bearing on what had just happened between them. He was behaving as if the incident was *her* fault, damn him!

Anger burgeoned inside Kat and she matched him glare for glare. The Look he flashed her didn't faze her one iota. And damn him for taking something wondrous and spontaneous and turning it into his personal version of the Spanish Inquisition. She would have accused him of just that, but she figured she'd have to explain what the Inquisition was. Annoyed as she was with him, she imagined she would have sounded condescending when he asked her to explain what she meant.

He had hurt her—deeply—insulted her and, despite her attempt to hold her tongue, she lashed out to wound him as she had been wounded. "Judd Lassiter, you are a wool-brained idiot!" she all but yelled at him.

"No argument there, Diamond."

"And let me tell you something else," she snarled as she stalked up to stab him in the chest with her index finger. "Just because you kissed me and I liked it, you don't hear me whining because you have been with other women. I'm not standing here passing judgment because you kiss like every woman's dream come true. I haven't cursed you because of your experience!"

Judd couldn't begin to follow whatever twisted female logic she had applied to the kissing incident. "What the hell does that mean?"

"You don't get it?" she asked sarcastically. "Fine, then I'll translate into *Idiot* for you. It means"— she stabbed his chest again for good measure—"that for that one marvelous moment when the world stood still, it didn't matter what had come before, not for you, not for me, because we were just *us.*"

"We were just *us?*" he repeated, dumbfounded.

Kat retreated a step. It dawned on her suddenly that to him there must not have been a *them* in what she considered a magical moment. She felt like a naive fool, and she realized she was way out of her league with Judd Lassiter.

He had undoubtedly kissed dozens of somebody elses. He didn't feel stars collide in cosmic explosions, because this was nothing new or special to him. *She* was the only comet around here that had gone up in flames.

"Just forget I said anything. Obviously I don't know what I'm talking about." Hurt, humiliated, embarrassed, Kat stamped over to snatch up the bedroll she had discarded in her haste to fly into Judd's sheltering arms . . .

Kat squeezed her eyes shut and called herself ten dozen kinds of fool. She, in her state of panic, had thrown herself at him, invited him to kiss her. What was the man supposed to think when she reacted the way she had? No wonder he didn't believe she had little sexual experience. She had behaved like a depraved harlot the moment he returned to camp.

"Hey, Diamond."

Kat gnashed her teeth so hard she practically ground them smooth. He always called her by her last name when he wanted to keep things impersonal—which was most of the time. "What, Lassiter?"

He wanted to say he had felt the *us* she referred to, but he couldn't bring himself to arm her with that dangerous knowledge, not when he was waffling between suspicion and trust. When she was in his arms, he felt so vulnerable as to forgive her anything. But there were some things a man couldn't forgive, not if he wanted to survive.

Judd stared at her rigid back, because she wouldn't do him the courtesy of turning to face him. "You probably should know that your stepfather is dead—if you don't know it already."

Hell! Why had he added that? He was handing her yet another weapon to use against him. Again, he had alerted her that he didn't believe what she'd told him. If she knew he was suspicious, she would make a greater effort to gain his trust.

Judd waited, hoping she would turn around so he could gauge her reaction to his remark. But she didn't face him, just stood there, stiff as a flagpole. Then she began pacing back and forth between a distant tree and the campfire, her hands clasped behind her, her head bowed over her cloddish boots. She didn't ask how Trumball had died, didn't ask when, just wore a path in the carpet of grass.

Her lack of questions sent his suspicions into full-scale riot again. Scowling at the disaster he had made of the evening, Judd stalked over to his pallet and plopped down.

"Aren't you going to stand watch?" she asked, looking up suddenly.

"No," he bit off.

"What if someone, or something, sneaks up on us? You said we had to maintain constant vigil. You said—"

"Forget what I said. Nothing will bother us tonight."

She stared at him as if he had lost his mind. "How can you possibly know that?"

"I just know, damn it!"

Kat assessed him wonderingly. How could he know such things when she had heard all sorts of unidentified noises in the darkness? They could become wolf bait before dawn. And what about those rattlers he'd mentioned? Did he honestly expect her to sleep after enduring apprehensive solitude, after what had passed between them, after he blurted out that J.P. Trumball was dead? Why hadn't he elaborated? Had J.P. died mysteriously and Judd had no details to offer?

Kat sincerely doubted that J.P. had died mysteriously. Either that compulsive gambler had fallen prey to ruthless cardsharps or his two henchmen had turned on him.

Just where were Chester and Hugh? she wondered. Were they out there in the darkness, waiting for their chance to separate Kat from the inheritance her mother had hidden away for her?

Had *Lassiter* disposed of J.P., so he could get his hands on the jewels? Maybe this wily bounty hunter had it in mind to haul her miles away from civilization, then leave her while he galloped off with all the priceless gems. Perhaps Kat had been too eager to trust him, too eager for a confidant and friend. Maybe she had played right into Lassiter's hands.

A dozen different thoughts—and an equal number of suspicions—swirled through her mind as she paced, then paced some more. She needed to devise an alternate plan—in case she found herself betrayed and abandoned in the wilderness.

She had to think things through, she told herself urgently.

Fact Number One: She knew nothing about Judd Lassiter that really counted. Why, he wouldn't even confide how much of the myths surrounding him were truth. He had answered her questions with questions—which meant he hadn't been completely honest with her. What was he hiding?

Fact Number Two: Judd had given his word as a Cheyenne warrior that he wouldn't betray her. But he was a half-breed. Did that mean that he agreed to keep *half* the bargain and *all* the jewels?

Fact Number Three: Given Fact Number Two, it stood to

reason that if Lassiter gave *half* his word, then he would lead her *half*way to Santa Fe and ride off into the sunset.

There then, she mused, were the cold, hard facts. To trust Lassiter completely would be an invitation for deception. Kat needed to pick Lassiter's brain to become an honor student in survival skills. When she learned everything he knew, she could strike off on her own before he had the chance to betray her. If she didn't become like him, armed with skills and knowledge of the wilds, then she might perish.

If Judd ever left her alone again at night, she could not, would not allow fear to dictate her actions. She would not leap into his arms like a helpless fool. Never again would she allow herself to seek comfort in his strength. She would strive to control her fears and conquer them. She would practice with weapons until she could defend herself, and she would learn to imitate The Look he wore so well when he encountered trouble. She would learn to intimidate, and Judd Lassiter would indeed see the spitting image of himself when he looked at the woman she was going to become!

Once Kat had all her thoughts in order, her ducks in a row, her plan mapped out, she plunked down on her bedroll. The bullwhip was within reach. She mentally prepared herself for whatever trouble lurked in the darkness.

In the course of one night Kat taught herself to sleep lightly, to distinguish between sounds of potential danger and harmless noise.

She, who dreamed of independence and freedom, was asserting herself to achieve a decade of hopes and dreams. She was not going to let herself depend solely on Judd Lassiter, she vowed as she huddled in the bedroll, keeping an ear tuned to the sound of danger. She was going to learn to rely on no one but herself!

CHAPTER NINE

Judd couldn't decide if he was relieved or disappointed that Kat had been giving him the cold-shoulder routine since the "kissing incident." She was still operating under the theory that he was not a morning person and she didn't try to have a conversation with him until they halted at midday to eat and rest the horses.

At one o'clock—give or take a few minutes—she asked for his best guess of the time. He taught her how to gauge time by the position of the sun; then she began firing a barrage of questions at him. Kat wanted to know how many days it would take to cross the *Comancheria*. She wanted to know how to become inconspicuous when the terrain changed from tree-clad hills to waving grama grasses, prickly weeds and flat prairie.

Judd showed her how to lie down carefully in the thick grass, inching arms and legs between the stems to conceal herself. Then he taught her how to search for water by studying animal tracks and following the flight of birds.

When the terrain changed again, and they rode toward the rock-ribbed canyons with their sheer cliffs, deep, winding arroyos and gray-hued buttes that stood in lonely isolation, Kat claimed the landscape reminded her of the medieval castles she had read about in the books she pored through during her childhood confinement in the attic. She compared the dark, serrated ridges of rock formations to dragons' spines and found imaginative beauty in everything she encountered on the trek west.

She voiced no complaints when her clothes snagged in the armor of thorns from cactus and briers that lined the bone-dry creeks, or when she stared at distant water holes that turned out to be too stagnant for human consumption.

Judd taught her to slice cactus open to sip its milky fluid to stave off thirst. Then he ordered her to use the tracks left by animals and the flight of birds so that *she* could lead them to clear, clean water holes hidden in the fingerlike trenches that cut jagged gashes through the High Plains.

To his surprise, Kat led them unerringly to a clear pool shaded by the towering walls of an eroded cliff. He realized that she hadn't just been listening to what he said—she had *absorbed* his teachings. She was making every effort to perfect her survival skills.

Although he knew she was stiff and sore from endless hours in the saddle, she never once pleaded with him to stop to rest. She waited until he called a halt, as if she were trying to prove that she could match his endurance.

Judd suspected that Kat had spotted the two riders who followed their trail across hills and ravines but she made no mention of it. That made Judd twitchy. It was as if she expected to be tracked across this unforgiving terrain.

If there had ever been a *them*—even for that magical moment out of time—it no longer existed, Judd mused. Kat Diamond had become an entity unto herself. She was his impersonal companion whose only interest lay in what he could teach her.

Kat insisted on lessons in handling his dagger when they stopped for the night, and she practiced faithfully while Judd tended the horses and hunted game. Of course, Judd kept a cautious eye on her during the practice sessions with weapons. He never turned his back on her—just in case she decided to make his spine her target.

Judd put his foot down when Kat asked for instructions in

using his pistol. Sound carried too far in this barren land and echoed through the labyrinth of canyons. He did, however, allow her to learn to load his Colt, to familiarize herself with handling the weapon, to draw and aim. Firing, he told her, would have to wait until they reached the natural fortress of Palo Duro Canyon to the north.

During their two weeks of traveling, Kat also learned how to build an inconspicuous campfire and cook the game Judd killed and cleaned. She worked tirelessly beside him, never standing close enough to touch or be touched, never turning to him for safety or protection when an unidentified noise startled her.

When Judd left her to her own devices in the dark of night to scout and keep a distant watch on her, she greeted him with little more than a glance when he returned to camp.

Well, so much for frightening her into dependence, he thought sourly. Even when she encountered a rattlesnake during his absence, she killed the varmint with the whip, skinned it and served it up for a bedtime snack.

This was not the same woman Judd had met in The Flats, he realized. True, she was still extremely appealing to him and he was vividly aware of her, but she was now hell-bent on proving her competence—to him and to herself—in the wilderness. Judd admired her determination, her transformation—in an exasperated sort of way. Judd hated like hell to admit it, but he had enjoyed having her turn to him for protection and compassion. He missed those sensations that had stolen over him that night she'd thrown herself into his arms, that unforgettable night when he had savored the enticing feel, the scent and the taste of her . . .

"What is that?" Kat questioned, jostling Judd from his all-too-arousing thoughts.

He glanced toward a butte whose base was covered with a whitish hue. "What you're seeing is dried bones scattered across the ground. It's the site of MacKenzie's Massacre," he explained in a bitter tone. "General MacKenzie and his soldiers rounded up fifteen hundred Indian ponies and slaughtered them."

"Why?" she asked, aghast.

"Horses are the Comanche, Cheyenne and Kiowa's pride and joy, an integral part of their livelihood. In the past, horses were raised and trained for battle and used to trade for supplies, blankets, cooking utensils, guns and ammunition. It was a common practice to will a string of prize horses to a warrior's best friend at death, and to give a horse as a treasured gift, or in exchange for a generous favor or good deed," Judd explained. "When MacKenzie destroyed the tribes' horse herds, he essentially destroyed a way of life and broke the warriors' spirits. The general also laid the Cheyenne, Comanche and Kiowa encampment in Palo Duro Canyon to ruin so the Indians would not only be left afoot but forced into confinement in Indian Territory.

"According to the legend, when the moon is full, you can see ghost horses racing across the High Plains. They symbolize a way of life that has come and gone for the Indians. Also according to the legend, the Lone Horseman leads the ghost horses on their silent trek across the prairie, trampling the evil brought by the hated white-eyes."

Kat grimaced at the thought of destroying yet another facet of the Indians' livelihood in an effort to steal land the white settlers had cast their greedy eyes upon. The buffalo herds were dwindling in alarming numbers, land was taken away, and horses were slaughtered. Kat sympathized with the plight of the Indians, because she understood that fierce craving for freedom, the distaste for monitored confinement.

In silence Kat rode several miles, studying the caprock escarpments that cut through the plains. She imagined what it would be like to call this rugged land home and have soldiers order her to move to a locale of *their* choosing. Kat could well imagine the anger and frustration the Indians were forced to bear. She could understand why the tribes fought desperately to preserve their culture and traditions.

"Oh my!" Kat breathed in awe when she topped a hill to stare down at a yawning canyon.

Judd shook himself from his own musings to see what had demanded Kat's attention. In the distance, from the canyon rim where they halted, she surveyed one of the few true oases in this rough country. Cedar and cottonwood trees formed a semicircle around a sparkling pool fed by an underground stream that rose from the limestone canyon floor, then meandered lazily to the southeast.

"What spectacular scenery," she murmured, smiling for the first time in days.

Judd was oddly disappointed that he wasn't the one who incited her pleasure.

Thoughts like that will get you in trouble, Judd lectured himself, battening down the tingles of unruly desire.

"A bath, Panther?" she asked hopefully. "I have asked for nothing in days, but this . . ." Her voice trailed off as she stared longingly at the pool that glittered like the diamonds stashed in Judd's pocket. "Could we stop for just an hour?"

When she turned that radiant smile on him, Judd was nodding agreeably before he realized it. "We'll make camp for the night. Just don't drown in the pool, landlubber," he mumbled.

"I won't, because you are going to teach me to swim," she said as she sent the mare sidestepping down the rock-strewn slope.

"I am?"

Kat nodded assertively. She was determined not to neglect even one facet of her survival education. She was learning to control her fear of heights by riding close to the canyon rims, forcing herself to look down and appreciate the rugged beauty of the countryside. Her sense of panic had waned after several trips up and down steep slopes of canyons and gullies.

By evening, she hoped to have her fear of water under control as well. The memory of the day she foundered in the creek near her family plantation would be just that—a distant memory—she vowed.

She stared at the inviting pool, marveling at how the mere sight of it lifted her sagging spirits. For a short time, she was going to relax, bathe and learn to paddle across the natural pool.

"I can understand why the Kiowa, Cheyenne and Comanche refused to give up this area," Kat said.

"Then you won't hold a grudge if a war party suddenly swoops down from the canyon rim to oust you from this site. Whispering Springs is one of several landmarks considered to be sacred ground by the tribes," Judd informed her.

"The pool is filled with holy water?" Kat asked interestedly.

"In a manner of speaking, but it's more of a spirit spring, a place where guardian spirits are summoned, where spirits whisper their commandments in the wind. Some white men contend that this site is haunted."

"Ah, the stuff that legends are made of," she said with an understanding nod.

Judd let Horse pick his own way down the eroded inclines. "This is the sight where warriors once came for vision quests. It offers a secluded, solitary haven so a warrior won't be disturbed while he seeks insightful knowledge from his totem."

Fascinated, Kat glanced over her shoulder at Judd. When he spoke of Indian spiritual magic, she had the unmistakable feeling that he was speaking from personal experience. Kat craved insight into this intriguing man whom she had tried exceptionally hard to ignore—and failed miserably—for the past two weeks.

"Tribal custom teaches that unsought powers are bestowed on warriors who have proved themselves as wise leaders among their peers. The power-giving spirits offer their greatest blessings to those who stand up to them bravely and courageously. The guardian spirits give blessings by placing the magical powers in a warrior's mind and body."

"You are referring to the Comanche Wolf Prophet and the Lone Horseman," she presumed.

"Exactly."

"And the great Phantom Panther of the Plains?" she added, watching him intently.

He shrugged noncommittally. "Perhaps."

Kat frowned at his evasive answer. *Well, fine,* she thought. He was letting her form her own opinion, and her opinion was that there was something to the legend and that it applied to him. How? Kat had no idea. She wondered if she would ever find herself in a situation that would grant insight into Panther's mysterious depths.

"Perhaps I will seek my own vision quest here," she announced. "I have nothing against a visitation from guardian spirits. I have always believed there is more to life than what we see, hear and learn. There is more power in what we sense and feel in our hearts and souls, if we can learn to harness it."

Judd smiled cryptically. "Is that so, Diamond?"

Kat met his gaze directly. "It is so. I learned to do my first soul searching while locked in the attic, and I have practiced meditation on many occasions since then. I have read about metaphysical experimentation and strange occurrences that defy scientific explanation."

"So you have no fear of what legends call magical and supernatural?"

"I am learning that fear is the obstacle that separates people from their greatest potential," she said philosophically.

Judd chuckled as he eased Horse up beside the mare. "Very profound, Diamond. But talk is cheap. It takes courage to confront the omnipotent spirits of Indian culture, to accept the responsibility of wielding such devastating powers. Some see imposed power as a blessing as well as a curse that dictates destiny."

I have the unshakable feeling you would know all about that, Panther, she replied silently. "I trust you can occupy yourself while I bathe and meditate."

Judd glanced southwestward, then called her attention to the ominous clouds gathering on the horizon. "It will be dark soon, and it looks as if we'll be in for a rough night. Enjoy your oasis while you can." He smiled wryly at her. "And give my regards to any guardian totems you scare up during your vision quest."

Kat was too busy staring at the inviting spring-fed pool to pay much heed to his taunt. She had waited forever for a good, leisurely soaking, rather than those birdbaths beside the creeks and rivers. After dismounting, she peeled off her clothes, washed both sets of garments, then hung them over tree limbs to dry.

The limestone slab that formed the spring bank provided perfect footing for wading into the clear water. Watching where she stepped, Kat ventured into the pool until she was standing shoulder deep.

Ah, if only she could spread her arms, lean forward and glide across the water like a graceful swan!

She practiced the technique in the shallows, hoping there would be time enough before the storm descended for Judd to teach her a few simple swimming strokes—from a distance, of course. She couldn't risk humiliating herself as she had the night she melted into his kiss and practically begged for his touch.

As the sun sank into the looming clouds and darkness descended on the canyon, Kat lounged in the shallows, absorbing the stillness before the approaching storm, letting her mind wander where it would, wishing that she, like Panther, had been schooled in the natural wonders of nature. But she had been restrained and confined, and she yearned to become attuned to every facet of her surroundings, to become an integral part of it.

Her parents were right, she realized. She had been born in the wrong time and place. She envied the childhood freedom and the valuable lessons of life that Judd had learned while living with the Cheyenne.

Kat closed her eyes, breathed deeply. She sought a state of total relaxation, letting her mind become a blank slate, letting her senses overflow with the beauty and peacefulness of her hidden oasis . . .

Out of nowhere, she heard an eerie, otherworldly wail that chased itself around the rocky precipices above her. Kat opened her eyes to the darkness. Her breath lodged in her throat when the startling image of a white, incandescent mountain cat condensed from a hazy fog that hovered on an outcropping of rock above her.

When the oversize creature turned its head toward her, chills chased each other up and down her spine. Eyes like glowing coals burned down on her with such alarming intensity that her first reaction was to shriek in fear and shrink away. Yet she swallowed her cry and stayed where she was. The creature growled and snarled threateningly; then, with lithe, powerful grace, it pounced to the ledge below, landing with the soundlessness of a skipping shadow.

Kat was too mesmerized by the vision to be afraid of it. Fascinated, she watched the evanescent specter leap from one outcropping of rock to another until it stood on the opposite bank of the pool. The vaporous predator snarled at her. The intimidating sound rolled across the water's surface, followed by three accompanying yowls from the rock cliffs. Kat glanced up to see three coal-black shadows perched on the ledges behind the phantom cat.

Kat rose to her feet and moved deeper into the pool. She wasn't sure why she chose to advance rather than retreat. She supposed it was because Judd had informed her that the guardian spirits of Indian culture admired courage and bravery. Or perhaps it was because those flaming eyes were calling to her on some subconscious, elemental level.

She recalled that most cats didn't naturally gravitate to water, unless to quench their thirst or hunt game. The great white panther only prowled the limestone bank, watching her intently. Fool though she would probably turn out to be, she practically dared the phenomenal specter to defy its aversion to water and come get her.

Caterwauling, the great cat stalked the bank, then paused to lash out with its paws, as if it wanted to strike her and couldn't quite make brutal contact.

Arms outstretched, Kat leaned forward and paddled vigorously with her feet. For a split second, when she realized she had floated past the underwater shelf and was in over her head, fear paralyzed her. Then she reminded herself that she was no longer a child foundering in the creek near her home. She was a woman who had made a pact with herself to break free of her limitations and live up to her full potential. Kat relaxed and moved with the instinctive skill of treading water.

Again, the great white cat pounced at the lapping waves and swiped at the air. The ghostly creature practically purred a taunt to venture closer—if she dared.

Kat paddled with arms and legs, aware that she had reached the deepest, most dangerous part of the pool, aware that she was most vulnerable, but her fascinated attention was on the prowling specter with glowing eyes and daunting snarls.

When the creature sprang into the shallows, sending up a spray that sparkled like diamonds in the moonlight, Kat smiled at the intimidating display. She wasn't certain what possessed her, but she stared at the evanescent creature in defiant challenge.

"Meet me halfway, phantom cat. Come out here where we both are at risk . . . if you dare . . ."

The graceful creature blustered and sent up a shrill, ear-splitting wail while Kat paddled in circles, laughing with the pleasure of realizing she had taught herself to swim and had conquered yet another inhibiting fear. She was actually swimming, and loving every glorious moment of it!

When she paddled back in the direction she'd come from, her amusement vanished, because the snarling specter bounded around the pool to wait for her on the other side.

Here, Kat realized, was the ultimate test of her endurance— the moral to the myth, as it were. The ghost cat was cunning and patient, letting her taunt and tease him and expend a great deal of energy treading water, while he waited on solid footing for his overconfident prey. She realized that she had been cleverly outsmarted by all that snarling bluster.

"Another lesson to live by," Kat mused aloud. "Is that it? Cunning, patience and foresight are worth their weight in gold? You played the waiting game far better than I, but in the end, phantom cat, *you* lose, because I have learned from your knowledge and wisdom. You no longer hold the advantage over me, because *I* know what *you* know."

The revelation prompted Kat to draw closer to the shelf of limestone where she could find solid footing. She was still too far away for the intimidating specter to attack without swimming into depths over its head.

Kat waited, wondering if she was about to be tested again. The graceful creature circled the pool once, twice, then lunged onto the ledge of rocks where the three black cats waited like sentinels in the night. A parting wail reverberated around the canyon walls and the phosphorescent creature, accompanied by three black guard dragons, vanished from sight—as if they had never been there at all . . .

Kat blinked and stared at the dark stairsteps of rock that ascended to the towering precipices. For a moment she wondered if that strange creature bounding from the ledge to toy with her had been a chimera, an illusion of her overactive imagination. Was this what a vision quest entailed? she wondered. Had she fallen asleep and dreamed that encounter with the Phantom Panther?

Kat had no time to ponder what she swore had just occurred, because the rolling clouds swallowed the moon and a cold downdraft of air, clogged with choking dust, plunged down the cliff.

The stillness of the night was shattered by the rumble of thunder and whistling wind. Kat waded ashore hurriedly. She watched the suffocating cloud of dust descend, and she barely had time to grab her clothes before they could be whisked off in the fierce gale. She donned her garments quickly, staggering for balance each time a strong gust buffeted her.

Kat had never weathered a dust storm before, but she predicted she was in for a long, harrowing night. Disoriented, she clutched the spare garments to her chest and scampered toward the shelter of trees that rimmed one side of the pool.

A strong, steady hand folded over her forearm, and Kat knew instinctively that Judd had come in search of her. She accepted his support, but she refused to snuggle up against his muscled warmth as she had done that first night on the trail.

"There's a cave about fifty feet up the face of the cliff," Judd yelled to be heard over the howling wind.

Kat jogged to keep up with his swift pace and struggled to draw breath in air saturated with dust and moisture. Lightning flared like bony fingers above the canyon ridge, and Kat gasped when she saw the ominous cloud looming above them. She had never seen anything so imposing as the swirling, churning clouds that obviously carried the topsoil from New Mexico and west Texas in its violent updrafts.

When thunder exploded, ricocheting off the stone cliffs, echoing around the chasm, Kat instinctively ducked. Mother Nature's special effects were intimidating, reminding her that in the rugged beauty of this land there was always danger. Kat expected to see multiple tails of twisters drop from the storm clouds any second.

She grabbed Judd around the waist when a wind gust threatened to pitch her over the narrow ledge of rock on the face of the cliff. Kat refused to look down, refused to let terror consume her.

"It won't be much farther," Judd assured her.

Huge raindrops pelted them as they sidestepped to higher elevations, using handholds of rock to steady themselves against the churning wind. Kat couldn't imagine how Judd could see to lead the way, but then she reminded herself that she was traveling with the man known as Panther and that he was in his natural element. Each time she floundered, he offered support. Each time fear threatened to weaken her determination, he seemed to sense it and reached out to tug her along with him to the next stairstep of rock.

Although Kat had vowed to become self-reliant, she found herself relying on Judd, trusting him to guide her and protect her from harm. It had become as natural as breathing, though she had taken great pains not to rely on him too often.

Rely on him for just a few minutes, she allowed herself. *When we reach safety, put that physical and emotional wall between you and him and everything will be fine.*

Kat clung to that thought, and to Judd's hand, as they braved the perils of wind and storm to find safety.

Unfortunately, disaster struck in the time it took to blink. Kat lost her footing when a fierce gust of wind whipped around the face of the cliff, and her rain-slick hand slipped from his grasp. She screamed when she found herself clawing air. Frantically, she reached out to anchor herself to a scraggly cedar tree that grew between the cracks of stone. Panting for breath, Kat wrapped herself around the spindly tree—the only thing standing between her and a forty-foot plunge to the canyon floor.

"Kat!" Judd bellowed over the roaring gale. "Are you all right? Hold on!"

"Hold on?" Kat laughed hysterically. Did he think she could let go when there was nothing beneath her but a bed of solid rock?

A lifetime later, when Kat's trembling arms were close to giving out, she saw the popper of the bullwhip flapping in the wind.

"Grab hold," Judd hollered at her. "I'll pull you up."

Kat stared at the braided leather that swung above her head. "Let go?" she chirped in question.

"Do it now," Judd demanded tersely.

Kat swallowed with a gulp. She wasn't sure that one aching arm would support her weight while she stretched upward to grab the braided leather that was slithering like a snake against the rock.

"Now, damn it!" Judd roared.

Kat's hands were slick with rain, and fear clawed at her. Letting go was the most difficult thing she had ever done. Bracing her oversize boots against the stone cliff, she unclenched her left hand and reached up, cursing when the whip slipped from her grasp.

"I can't hold on," she wailed in frustration.

"Hold out your arm," Judd instructed.

Summoning her composure, Kat steadied her sliding feet against the rock and thrust up her left arm. To her relief, the whip snapped and curled around her elbow. Scrabbling against the stone face of the cliff, she moved upward, towed toward the narrow ledge.

When Judd's arm hooked around her waist, Kat came down on all fours to make sure the whipping wind didn't catapult her off the ledge again.

She looked up into Judd's eyes, and caught her breath when she noted the strange glow, felt the strength of his grasp on her waist. She shivered uncontrollably as a cold chill rippled down her backbone.

Was that the aftereffect of fear? she wondered shakily. *Must be,* she decided as she drew a steadying breath.

"Come on, Diamond," Judd said as he hoisted her to her feet.

Kat frowned at the hollow quality of his voice, then decided it was the wind that distorted the sound—that and the kind of fear that left her ears ringing and her heart thumping. It was only her imagination that Lassiter's voice sounded as if it were echoing through a stone tunnel.

CHAPTER TEN

Thunder cracked overhead as Judd ducked into the dark niche that offered shelter from the raging storm. He groped along the rock wall for the lantern that hung on the railroad spike that had been driven into the stone. Gold flames flickered to life, illuminating the two bedrolls that had been laid out on the rock floor.

Kat blinked, then stared at the thick timbers that supported the walls and ceiling of the cavern. It didn't take a genius to realize this was an ancient mine shaft. "This is where you had planned to spend the night, even before the storm struck?"

He nodded. "The cave provides a bird's-eye view of the canyon. If unwelcome visitors arrive, I can see them at a glance."

Kat studied the lantern and driven spike. "Obviously you have taken refuge here before."

"I always stop here when traveling through this area, though there is another legend about Whispering Springs that says—"

"Why am I not surprised to discover this place is teeming with legends and myths, and that you are unaffected, or should I say *immune* to them?" she interrupted, frowning speculatively at him.

"The legend says," Judd went on, ignoring her comment, "that several prospectors and treasure hunters ignored the fact that this is a sacred Indian haunt. They holed up here, searching for the lost mine where dozens of gold bars, nuggets and valuable relics from a Spanish mission, and its small settlement, were hidden. According to the tale, a ruthless band of Comancheros plundered the mission for valuables and killed the inhabitants when the fabled gold relics could not be found."

"Have you searched for the lost fortune?" she asked curiously.

"No. The Indian legend also states that evil spirits placed a curse on the treasure. Anyone who seeks the hidden treasure finds death as a reward. The prospectors never emerged from the mine shaft alive."

Kat glanced around uneasily, deciding she wasn't going to venture into the dark shaft in front of her. She had gone as far into the jaws of this mountain as she intended to go.

"Supper will be a simple affair." Judd glanced at her quickly, then his gaze flitted away. "We'll have to take a rain check on your swimming lesson, Diamond."

She plunked down cross-legged on her pallet. "I already learned the rudimentary skills of swimming on my own," she informed him. "Challenge and necessity are very good instructors."

He smiled wryly as he handed her a stick of beef jerky and a canteen. "And what of your vision quest? Did the storm interrupt your spiritual meditation?"

Kat had the sneaking suspicion that Judd Lassiter knew the answer to the question before he asked it. She used the tactic he had employed when he refused to answer her pointed questions—she quickly changed topics. "Mmm, even this jerky tastes good tonight. I'm famished after the long day's ride and the strenuous swim."

Judd was famished, too, but the food didn't appease the hunger prowling through him. Keeping watch over Kat at the pool, while she was unaware, had proved to be sweet torture for him. He had seen his own spectacular vision in the twilight—one that was emblazoned on his mind like a brand.

Kat Diamond, he had discovered, was feminine perfection, every shapely, curvaceous inch of her. Most likely, he would be spending the evening in a state of arousal, remembering the beauty he had beheld, restraining himself from venturing close enough to map her luscious contours with his hands and lips.

"Panther?"

Judd jerked up his head to find Kat staring quizzically at him. "Yeah?" His voice cracked like porcelain.

"I asked you if this ferocious dust storm is a common occurrence in west Texas. I've never experienced anything like it."

He nodded his tousled head as he munched on his meager meal. "Dust storms are a hazard of the spring and fall seasons. There isn't much a traveler can do except hole up and wait it out. The storms last a few hours at the least, two days at the most."

"What about our horses?" she questioned in concern. "Will they be all right?"

"They are tethered against a windbreak at the base of the canyon," he reported. "I used the empty feed sacks for masks so Horse and the mare don't have to breathe dust."

Kat jerked upright when a lightning bolt speared in front of the cave entrance. Thunder crashed and rolled. "Are you sure we haven't offended the Great Spirit by seeking sanctuary on this sacred ground?"

Judd chuckled and grinned at her. "When a sudden storm rains its towering fury, it does make one wonder, doesn't it?"

Kat rose to her feet and ambled to the mouth of the cave. She watched crackling flames and smoke swirl up in the wind, saw the lightning-struck tree near the pool—the same tree where she had draped her clothes to dry.

An odd sensation snaked down her spine as she watched the stricken tree glow like a coal. Then an indefinable feeling of power overcame her as she stared down on the canyon. She felt as if she were part of the storm that pummeled the valley, a part of the wilderness. She had never experienced such sensations while living in the noisy throngs of civilization, but out here she felt as if she were coming to life, coming into her own.

She frowned, wondering if the lifelike incident she'd experienced beside the pool had been a hallucination brought on by weariness, solitude and hunger. She was ready to swear she'd seen the phantom cat that bounded down the face of the cliff, accompanied by three devil pumas. The incident had seemed so real at the time, and yet unreal. She wanted to discuss the incident with Judd, but the incident defied words.

It was too personal and private to share with anyone. No, Kat mused as she watched the storm rage. The vision was *her* secret, *her* private lesson learned.

"You may as well come to bed, Diamond," Judd said, interrupting her thoughts. "It's a long ride to the northern caprock of Palo Duro Canyon, and there is nothing between here and there except rugged, unforgiving terrain that will test your stamina."

Kat turned her back to the storm, then faltered when the lanternlight reflected off Judd's amber-green eyes. For a split second, she swore she had seen that same glow in the eyes of the evanescent specter that had prowled around the pool, taunting her, challenging her, snarling at her, testing her will to survive. She swore she had seen it again when Lassiter pulled her to safety on the stone ledge.

No, it couldn't be, she tried to assure herself. But deep inside her, in the darkest reaches of her soul, she had a strange feeling—an indefinable sense of knowing—that the incident by the pool was an enlightening vision. She was just having trouble sorting out all the possibilities of what she was thinking.

Kat remembered all the legends Judd had described to her the past two weeks. She wondered if he was subtly trying to tell her something—something as personal and private as the feelings and visions she'd experienced while swimming at the oasis pool.

Again she stared at Judd in the flickering lanternlight. She was confused by the limitations of what she *assumed* to be real and true, baffled by the conflicting implications of what a silent voice whispered for her to believe.

"Something wrong?" Judd asked with a husky purr in his voice.

Kat shrugged off the strange sensation and strode to her pallet. "I'm beginning to think the mind plays peculiar tricks on a person in the wilderness. For a moment there I—" She clamped her mouth shut and stared at him.

He cocked his head, watching her intently. "You what?"

"Impossible," she murmured. What she was thinking was impossible . . . Wasn't it? And yet . . .

"Diamond?" he prompted, going very still, studying her astutely.

Impulsively, Kat dropped down on her knees in front of him. She stared into his fascinating eyes for a long, speculative moment. An unexplainable sensation trickled through her, making her forget her vow to keep her distance from this man she found so wildly attractive, so utterly intriguing. Though she'd been hurt once, and didn't want to endure that feeling again, she was magnetically drawn to Judd, lured by some nameless power beyond her control.

For more than two weeks her life had teemed with unpredictable experiences and unprecedented challenges. She had lived adventures she had read about in books. And true, she thought to herself, what she was thinking was foolhardy, but she wanted to recapture that moment when Judd had kissed her and unveiled a world of splendorous sensations. She had no idea why it should be here—in this place, with this man—but everything seemed so right . . . almost predestined.

Kat was sure she was harboring some silly notion that she had been led to this particular place in time, as if all the stars and the moon had become aligned for some monumental occurrence. Obviously, she had spent too much time in the company of her own forbidden thoughts, for she was compelled to act upon this need to discover what transpired between a man and woman.

"Diamond?" Judd's voice wobbled as he watched her watch him with such unblinking intensity. "You better go back to your pallet."

"I haven't thanked you properly for saving my life," she murmured.

"You're welcome. Go to bed."

He was warning her away, but Kat had learned to face danger at every front. Tonight had been a night of astonishing discoveries and startling revelations, Kat realized. She wanted more, especially from this remarkable man who wasn't just the *subject* of legends but a *true* legend.

Losing her innocence to this man, in this place, didn't frighten her. Indeed, the prospect intrigued her. She wasn't asking for a lasting commitment from this human tumbleweed, not when she had come to crave her freedom as he craved his. But for tonight, for only this one night, she wanted to discover where those wild sensations he once incited in her could lead, to *know* him as she had known no other man.

Kat reached up to skim her forefinger over his lips and stared into eyes that blazed like golden flames.

His hand clamped over her wrist. "You're playing with fire, Diamond," he rasped.

"I know," she whispered as she reached up with her free hand to trace his lips again. "How hot will it burn, Panther?"

"You don't want to know," he said roughly.

"Oh, but I do," she assured him as she trailed her fingertip over the high ridge of cheekbones that denoted his Indian heritage. "No strings attached. No regrets for either of us. Just for tonight . . ."

When her lips fluttered over his, Judd groaned in unholy torment. He could feel his deprived body straining toward hers, feel his arms encircling her, crushing her to him. *This shouldn't be happening,* he told himself. He shouldn't want her like hell blazing—but he did. To see her gliding across the pool was to want her in his arms as she had been at the oasis—naked silk, softer than anything he'd ever beheld or touched. He wanted nothing between them but this ravenous need to touch and be touched, to possess and be possessed.

He told himself that she had come to him tonight knowing her own mind, offering herself up to the ungovernable attraction between them. And very soon he would know if Kat had told him the truth about her lack of intimate involvement with men.

But at this moment the feelings leapfrogging through him had nothing whatsoever to do with answering suspicious questions and testing her honesty. It had everything to do with satisfying an ache that had become his constant companion since Kat had crept into his hotel room in The Flats. No matter what she was really up to, he was going to be compensated for this uncertain bargain between them.

"Lassiter?" she murmured as he deftly unbuttoned her shirt.

"It's a little late for formality," he whispered as his lips feathered over the rapid pulsations on her neck. He savored her feminine scent, the satiny texture of her flesh beneath his hungry lips. He combed his fingers through the frothy gold curls, letting the wet strands glide over his hand.

"Teach me to please you," she murmured as he eased her down beside him on the pallet.

Why? he wondered. So she could acquire power over him? Was that why she wanted to know how and where he liked to be touched?

"Patience," he insisted when she reached up to help him doff his shirt.

She smiled up at him, her green eyes twinkling like emeralds. "Odd that you should say that." Her nimble fingers glided beneath the hem of his doeskin shirt to make stimulating contact with the muscled ridges of his belly. She raised an eyebrow when he flinched in response. *"Need seems to be as much the instructor as necessity."*

The knowledge that her slightest touch pleased him enormously bothered him, incited a breathless kind of *im*patience. Judd had it in mind to caress her thoroughly, to leave her teetering at the peak of sensual abandon, to prove that the greater power lay with him, to prove that he was less vulnerable than she. Yet, when her palms splayed over his belly and skimmed the waistband of his breeches, he trembled like the trees beneath the raging storm outside the cave. His flesh burned at each place she touched, and his intention of remaining emotionally detached sailed off like a leaf in the wind. Judd realized that making love to Kat would demand the kind of involvement he had never permitted himself with a woman. She had the power to touch his heart and soul, as well as his body.

He wanted to savor her, to greet every inch of satiny skin he exposed to erotic caresses, but the feel of her hands pressed against his hips, the feel of her supple body meshed to his aroused flesh, undid him.

Groaning in defeat, Judd shifted to pull off her baggy breeches and free himself from the confinement of buckskin. He didn't take time to remove his shirt, for fear she would see the scars that marred his back, afraid she would become distracted and repulsed.

And damn, for a man whose skills in patience were legendary, he was acting carelessly, frantically. He swept his hands down her bare legs, then up again, hearing her gasp, feeling her tremble beneath his touch. Gently, he tested the dewy heat of her feminine core with his fingertip, then drove himself into her. He felt the undeniable barrier give way, heard her hiss in pain and felt her tense beneath him.

Judd cursed himself soundly, went completely still, then braced his weight above Kat. He hadn't believed that she was totally innocent of men, and he had made her first intimate encounter a moment to remember—but not pleasurably. He was stunned to realize that he felt guilty about disappointing her. He had sought his own pleasure without attuning himself to her needs. He had shattered whatever romantic fantasy had brought Kat into his arms after two weeks of avoiding all physical contact with him.

Judd cursed himself again when he met Kat's wide-eyed gaze, saw the look of tension and confusion on her exquisite face. "Not what you expected?" he said, smiling apologetically.

She shifted gingerly, forcing herself to relax against his masculine invasion, reminding herself that she had asked for what was turning out to be a major disappointment. "No, it wasn't," she admitted. "Now that we're finished, would you mind getting up? I think I'll take your good advice and retire to my own pallet."

She thought they were finished? Thought the deed was done? Judd nearly laughed at her naiveté. If he was going to make a mistake with her, then, by damned, it was going to be the best one he ever made. Although his deprived male body cried out to ride to completion, Judd refused to appease himself at Kat's expense. He simply couldn't do that to her.

"Are you going to get up?" she asked when he didn't move.

"I don't think so." He smiled down at her.

"We aren't going to stay . . . um . . . together like this for the rest of the night, are we? Is that common practice?"

Judd couldn't bite back his amused chuckle before it flew free. He had never expected the initiation rites of an innocent to set off such a myriad of emotions inside him. He had experienced hungry need, suspicion, impatience, guilt and amusement—and they were just getting started, though she hadn't figured that out yet.

"You're laughing at me!" Kat braced her hands against his chest, trying to push him away, trying to blink back her tears of shame and embarrassment. "Damn you, Panther. I don't need help making a fool of myself. Just let me—"

His lips slanted over hers, silencing her, cherishing her with newfound patience and tenderness. He brushed the pad of his thumb over her nipple, then withdrew from between her thighs. He shifted beside her, drawing the rosy crest of her breast into his mouth to suckle gently. He heard her breath break on a sigh, felt her arch up to him in instinctive invitation. He treated the other budded peak to the flick of his tongue, the whisper of his lips, and felt her shiver beside him.

"There is far more to learn than what you think, Kat," he murmured against her soft skin. "I began badly and I'm sorry. We're starting over. And Kat?"

"Yes?"

"We've only just begun . . ."

Judd dedicated himself to erasing the pain he'd caused her, to replacing her unpleasant initiation with erotic sensations. He vowed that, when his own release came, she would be with him all the way to oblivion. He owed her for the disappointment, for his suspicion, for his lack of gentle consideration. She wasn't a harlot who offered herself for a quick tumble in exchange for coins. To treat Kat in such an impersonal manner was unforgivable, and it played hell with Judd's conscience.

Even if she never came to him again, even if this was their first and last tryst, he would do all within his power to see that she had been loved, and loved well.

Like a summer breeze whispering in the night, Judd kissed her, caressed her. His hands and lips glided over her flesh, peeling away all the garments that shielded her perfection from him. He spread a row of moist kisses over her flat belly, brushed his lips over the silky curve of her inner thigh. He cupped her softest flesh in his hand, then glided his finger into the honeyed fire that he called from her.

"Panther?" she whispered brokenly. "What are you—?"

"Teaching you what lovemaking is all about," he interrupted as he stroked her with his fingertip, arousing her until she offered him the most secret, satisfying kind of caress.

"Oh, God!" Kat gasped as a wild wave of pleasure swamped her from out of nowhere, leaving her aching to the very core of her body, to the depth of her soul. What was happening to her? Where had this helpless feeling of ineffable pleasure come from, and when would it stop?

Over and over again, he built the climactic pleasure and held her in his hand while she shimmered with the hottest, sweetest fire she'd ever known. She cried out his name in a breathless plea to end the fervent torment, and he came to her as gently as he should have come to her before. She clutched at him with such frantic desperation that Judd couldn't refrain from smiling in satisfaction. But this time Kat didn't take offense at the purr of laughter that bubbled from his lips as he drove hard and deep, filling the ache of need he had summoned from her.

Although her eyes were drugged with desire, her lips swollen from his passionate kisses, she met and matched his knowing smile. "You should have told me," she murmured as she curled her legs around his hips.

"And miss showing you that you were mistaken?" He chuckled softly. "Not a chance, Kat. When we're through, then you can tell me if you prefer to sleep alone on your bedroll."

He eased away slightly, then glided rhythmically toward her, arousing her and himself, watching her watch him lose control, letting her view the intense need that claimed his facial features, his body and emotions—as he had viewed her in the throes of ecstasy moments before.

The intimacy of this moment, the profoundness of need they called from each other, stunned him. This wasn't simply about appeasing basic urges, Judd realized as they moved together in perfect rhythm, racing across the night sky like a flaming meteor. Every part of who and what he was was intently involved in this passionate union. This was nothing like anything he had known in the past. It was all-consuming, magical.

When desire seared every part of his being, Judd understood what Kat had meant when she said she had felt the "us" at first kiss. Their identities were being fused with the kind of indefinable intimacy that shook the very foundations of his soul. And for that incredible moment when pleasure pulsated through his body, he lost the ability to think, only to feel. It didn't matter that there were things about him that he couldn't confide to Kat, things that would frighten her, confuse her. All that mattered was the shared pleasure that held them aloft like an eagle gliding on an updraft of wind.

Kat let out her breath on a ragged sigh, marveling at the multitude of sensations that assailed her at once. If she had known *then* what she knew now, she would never have made that silly remark about preferring to sleep alone. Judd was right, the *showing* was much more enlightening than the telling. The thought made her giggle.

"Should I be offended by your laughter?" he teased. "As I recall, you cursed me for doing that earlier."

In the most forgiving of moods, Kat looped her arms around his broad shoulders and smiled at him.

"Promise me something, Panther."

Judd tensed. The last time she'd asked it was for his promise to ensure that she didn't suffer if she fell from her mount and found herself at the mercy of a war party. He didn't even want to think about that again.

"Promise you what?" he asked cautiously.

Her smile faded as she met his gaze directly. "From now on, until we reach Santa Fe, I want to . . . sleep in your arms."

Now, what man in his right mind wouldn't agree to a bargain like that? The prospect left his body stirring with a need Judd swore had been thoroughly sated. But once hadn't been enough for him, he realized. The answering passion they had discovered in each other demanded to be fed, again and again.

When he took so long in replying, Kat wondered if he thought she was asking for a commitment he wasn't prepared to give. "No strings," she assured him quickly. "That was the bargain, then as now . . . oh, my!"

Her eyes widened as he surged powerfully against her, assuring her that he was willing to accommodate whatever needs she wanted satisfied in the dark of night.

"Little lady, you've got yourself a deal," Judd rasped. "But I may be more demanding than you anticipated."

"I don't think I'm going to mind all that much." She moved sensuously beneath him, reveling in the sensations they aroused in each other so quickly, so easily, so naturally.

To Judd's delighted astonishment, Kat urged him to his side, then to his back. She pulled away the shirt he hadn't bothered to remove and she caressed him with her hands, lips and body. She trailed whispering kisses over his chest, his belly, his thighs, then enfolded him in her hand and left him groaning in aching torment.

She teased him, pleased him as no other lover had. Heat curled and expanded when she invented ways to make him beg for mercy—and made him enjoy every moment of utter defeat. When she took him into her mouth and caressed his aroused length with the delicate touch of tongue and teeth, he groaned aloud. She measured his sensitive masculine flesh with fingertips and lips and left him gasping for breath. The sound of his breathless need echoed around the cavern, and he wondered suddenly if this was what it felt like to die—not caring if he lived from one second to the next, because profound sensations had already swallowed up his very existence.

When Kat sank down upon him, guiding him into the hot, silky center of her body, he was hopelessly lost. Again, they watched each other became lost in the whirlwind of mindless passion. The intense intimacy they shared burned away the image of every woman he'd ever known—save this one woman. Judd was certain he was going to see that enchanting face, embedded with luminous green eyes, surrounded with a mane of flaming red-gold curls, from now until long past eternity. She had touched him way down deep in his soul, in that dark, secret place he reached into to wield the powers of his guardian spirit. But now, the thought of Kat would be there each time he summoned the supernatural strength within him.

If the day came when she betrayed him for the pouch of heirloom jewels and the freedom she craved, he wondered if he would also hate her until long past eternity.

"Panther?"

Judd pried open his eyes—and discovered it took all the energy he had left. "Mmm," was all he could get out.

"I—" Kat sighed, shook her head, then cuddled up against him. She decided it would be best not to confide the tender emotions she felt for him. Those were not the sort of words Judd wanted to hear, or words she expected to hear herself voice.

These wondrous feelings were just the aftereffects of a magical, unprecedented moment, she convinced herself. An illusion that would fade when reality returned.

What had she intended to say, then didn't? Judd wondered. Was she about to offer a confession of honesty after their intimate tryst? Was her conscience starting to bother her?

Hell and damnation, he wished he could trust her implicitly, wished he knew for certain if she had conspired with the two men who followed their trail. It would be easy to trust this woman who gave him the gift of her innocence so generously, so intensely. And because it could be too easy, Judd rebuilt the crumbling wall of his defenses and tucked away vulnerable emotion. He was cautious—had to be. That was what kept him alive when dealing with the ruthless elements on the frontier.

In his profession, *blind trust* was that last step a man took before he ended up *dead wrong*.

Even as Judd reminded himself of that grim fact, he felt his hand gliding over Kat's hip, and he buried his face in the curve of her neck. Weariness overtook him and he slept peacefully for the first time since he could remember.

CHAPTER ELEVEN

Chester Westfall and Hugh Riggs cursed mightily as the dust clouds engulfed them. Like ships blown around by a tropical storm, they veered off course, unable to follow Panther's tracks. Dust granules pelted their eyes and left them choking for breath. They blindly searched for a haven from the storm. They made their way north, following the caprock that provided a windbreak from the threatening clouds, pushed by the winds at their backs. Long past midnight, they found a deep, V-shaped arroyo to tuck themselves into.

Since the storm had overtaken them before they could prepare their evening meal, and with the last of their pemmican gone, there was nothing to eat but flying dust.

Windblown, hungry and miserable, Chester and Hugh huddled against the walls of the ravine, then cursed when the sky opened to rain mud. Water streamed over the ledges of rock, and the water rose higher and faster in the narrow gully. Before they could be washed away in flash-flood water, the hapless men mounted their horses.

"If we get out of this alive, I'm in favor of givin' up this hunt," Hugh bellowed to be heard over the raging wind and rain.

"After what we've been through? Hell!" Chester growled. "We deserve to have them jewels, and by damn we'll have them!"

At the moment, Hugh didn't think that even a king's ransom was worth the trouble they had encountered, but he wasn't about to strike off on his own now. He had no choice but to stick to Chester like glue and hope they survived the night.

Kat awoke, serenaded by the warble of birds, greeted by rays of sunshine slanting into the cavern. It only took a moment to realize she woke up alone. The whip, pistol, dagger and pouch of jewels were gone. Frantic, she grabbed her clothes and dressed. Surely Judd hadn't decided to abandon her in the middle of nowhere . . . had he? Now that his male urges had been appeased, he hadn't ridden off without looking back . . . had he?

Kat stepped onto the narrow ledge, then plastered herself against the face of the cliff. She had no idea they had climbed so far up the canyon wall last night! Sweet mercy, the glittering pool below her looked a third its natural size!

Get hold of yourself, Kat, she chided. *You have spent the past two weeks developing a resistance to that cold, prickling fear that consumes you when you stare down from dizzying heights. Remember?*

Kat inhaled a deep, cathartic breath, then wobbled back inside to roll up the pallet—Judd had taken everything else when he left unexpectedly. Returning outside, Kat surveyed the perilous stairsteps of rock that descended to the canyon floor. Going up was easier than climbing down, she decided. Besides, what was the point of climbing down? She saw nothing of Judd or the horses.

Feeling angry, betrayed and abandoned—and not for the first time, she recalled—she stuffed the bedroll in the back of her baggy shirt and stared determinedly at the narrow footholds of rock that led up the chasm wall. Kat grabbed hold of the stump of a scraggly juniper and pulled herself up, refusing to look down and scare herself witless.

She would pull herself onto the canyon rim and follow the caprock that cut through the High Plains, then she would veer northwest. That was the direction Judd said they would go to reach the old Indian camp at the head of Palo Duro Canyon.

"Devious traitor," Kat scowled as she dug her fingernails into the outcropping of stone and scrabbled to a higher elevation. "If you had taught me to use a pistol, I would unload it on your sneaky hide! I should have known better than to trust you, to trust anyone but myself. If I live through this, I will never make the mistake of trusting anyone again!"

Fueled by anger, Kat scaled the rock ridge to see that the terrain to the west flattened out into unwelcoming miles of barren land that led to the buttes to the northwest. She pulled her hat down around her ears and stalked off, looking like a one-humped camel wandering in the desert.

Judd Lassiter had better hope she never caught up with him, she thought resentfully. She'd shoot, stab and poison him, then she'd stake him out on a red ant hill and leave him for the buzzards!

God, she had been such a naive fool! She had allowed her attraction for him to get the better of her—and he had certainly got the better of her because of it! Kat was ashamed of herself for thinking there was more to Judd Lassiter than what reality had cruelly taught her. He had turned out to be a bandit who stole her innocence and her jewels. And worse, she had asked him to!

Kat cursed Judd Lassiter every other step, alternately praying that she wouldn't encounter an Indian raiding party or swarm of outlaws.

So much for empty promises, thought Kat. Judd Lassiter wasn't a man of his word, after all. He was just like the rest of his gender—unreliable, self-centered and greedy. Well, this was the very last time she depended on another living soul, Kat told herself as she hiked off across the cactus-ridden plains.

"Diamond?" Judd frowned when he was met with silence as he stepped into the cavern. A vile curse exploded from his

lips when he realized Kat had left. While he'd been readying
the horses, packing supplies, and scouting for the men who
were following in their tracks, she had taken the jewels he'd
tucked in her bedroll and disappeared!

"Damn her," Judd snarled as he whirled around and stalked
to the edge of the rock shelf. He was certain now that Kat had
faked her fear of heights, because she had obviously scaled the
canyon wall. If she had descended to the canyon floor, he would
have seen her. Apparently, she hadn't wanted that to happen.

"Scheming witch," he muttered as he picked his way down
the rock footholds to reach the horses.

Did she think he had let his guard down after they had been
all over each other like a rash the previous night? Did she think
she had learned enough survival skills to strike off on her own?
Had she lost her mind! She didn't even have a horse or supplies.
What did she plan to live on? Her deceit?

It never occurred to Judd that Kat believed *he* was the one
who had abandoned *her*. He was too wary of her hidden motives
to even consider that possibility. He was the one who had been
betrayed and deceived. When he caught up with Kat Diamond,
she would pay dearly for this!

Chester Westfall stirred like an overturned beetle and tried
to get his bearings in the bright sunlight. He didn't have the
foggiest notion where the hell he and Hugh were—except
huddled against the stone face of caprock that lay like a stone
spine on the High Plains. No doubt the dust storm had caused
them to drift so far off course they would never find Panther's
tracks again, especially after the storm destroyed the trail.

Coughing and sputtering, Chester pounded the sand and dust
from his clothes, then reached over to whack Hugh on the
shoulder. "Wake up. We've gotta figure out where we are and
how to get back to where we were. That gal and her guide are
gonna get too far ahead of us."

Moaning groggily, Hugh levered onto his elbow to survey
the surroundings. All he saw was a lonely stretch of plains

dotted with gullies that stood in water, and a stone cliff towering over his head.

"I'm famished," Hugh croaked, then sputtered on dust.

"So am I, but we ain't got nothin' but our fingernails to chew on for nourishment." Chester came to his knees, then to his feet to work the kinks from his spine. "Way I figure it, we gotta backtrack south."

Hugh squinted into the sunlight. "Which way is south?"

Chester made a stabbing gesture with his arm. "That way, you moron. You've got the worst sense of direction I ever saw. Now get off your sorry ass and let's get movin'."

Reluctantly, Hugh clambered to his feet to dust off his clothes. "At least I'm gonna take time to fill my empty canteen. Maybe we ain't got food, but I'll damn sure take my fill of water."

Hugh and Chester slurped water until their bellies sloshed like whiskey kegs. Once mounted on their horses, they climbed the slope of the canyon to reach higher ground that would grant them a broad view of the plains.

Hugh blinked in surprise when he spotted a figure walking toward them. He directed Chester's attention to the unidentified silhouette. "Is that a mirage?"

"Hope not. Maybe that lone traveler's got some food to tide us over," Chester said as he drew his pistol and nudged his steed forward. "If the sonuvabitch don't wanna share, then he can kiss this world good-bye."

Hugh licked his lips in hungry anticipation, drew his pistol and followed the swift pace Chester set.

Kat's eyes widened in alarm when she saw two riders sweeping down the caprock, heading straight toward her. She cursed herself a thousand times for not paying attention. She had been too preoccupied in cursing Judd Lassiter and formulating a plan to reach Santa Fe to notice she was on a collision course with disaster.

When she scurried toward the shelter of a scraggly cedar

that clung precariously to the stone wall of the gully, gunshots whined and zinged off the rock beside her leg.

"Damn it," she hissed as she stared at the slope above her. She was trapped—and without a weapon of defense.

"Well, I'll be damned," Hugh erupted as he drew down on the woman dressed in men's clothes. "Look who we have here, Chester. The gal played right into our hands."

Kat stared up at the whisker-faced, scraggly-haired riders who held her at gunpoint. "Double damn," she muttered under her breath.

"Let's make this easy on all of us, little gal," Chester said as he walked his horse closer to the stunted cedar tree that Kat was trying to hide under. "Hand over them jewels and we'll leave ya be. The jewels for your life. Seems like a reasonable trade."

Kat rose to her feet and stepped into view. "Is that the deal you made with J.P.?"

When Chester and Hugh glanced at each other, then bore down on her with the spitting end of the Colts, Kat nodded sagely. "You killed him, didn't you? It wasn't some spiteful gambler who was trying to reclaim his losses. Not that there was any love lost between me and my stepfather, you understand. I'm only curious to know what really happened to him."

"He got—"

"Shut up, Hugh!" Chester growled. "We don't have to tell her nothin'."

"You just did," Kat insisted. "I presume you cleaned out J.P.'s pockets to pay all your expenses."

"Well, he had it comin'," Hugh burst out indignantly. "When you sneaked off that night in The Flats, J.P. started shootin' off his mouth about how we was gonna have to take a smaller cut of them jewels, because we couldn't keep track of you for one evenin'. He swore he wasn't gonna pay us one red cent, so we bustled him into the alley to shut him up. Then we figured you must've hired Panther to guide you. We decided to take over J.P.'s plans for ourselves—"

When Hugh slammed his mouth shut and Chester swore ripely, Kat felt an uneasy tremor trickle down her spine.

Although she was aware of J.P.'s assassination plot, it was difficult not to become apprehensive when that moment of reckoning came. These two scoundrels had no intention of trading the jewels for her life. They planned to leave her in the same condition they'd left J.P.

"Hand over them jewels," Chester snarled as he trained his pistol on her chest. "We don't have the inclination to stand out here jawin'."

"I don't have the jewels," Kat informed the men, glancing discreetly around, trying to figure out how to give herself a sporting chance to survive this encounter. "You arrived too late, I'm afraid. I was double-crossed early this morning. Panther rode off with the jewels, and my horse is trailing behind him."

Chester eyed the hump on her back. "Whatcha got there?"

Kat pulled the bedroll from beneath the hem of her shirt and tossed it on the ground. "Sleeping gear. That's all Panther left me. No food, no water, not even a map for direction. You want it? It's yours. It's one less thing for me to carry. I may as well be down to nothing."

The fact that Kat showed no interest in the rolled-up pallet assured Chester that it contained nothing of value. He spouted several obscenities as he stared northwest.

"Now what are we gonna do, Ches?" Hugh asked as he followed his partner's gaze. "You reckon that gunslinger is headed to that place called Tascosa, or maybe Sweetwater?"

"Reckon so. Them soldiers at Fort Griffin said there ain't but two towns out here, and a few stage stations. Then again, he might have decided to switch directions and head back to The Flats."

His gaze circled back to Kat, and she knew the instant that Chester decided she had become a disposable commodity. All she was doing was taking up these two killers' breathing space. Kat knew, there and then, that she was staring death in the face.

"Well, little gal, it's been nice knowin' ya," Chester muttered as he cocked the trigger. "Thanks for nothin'."

Kat dived sideways when the pistol discharged—missing her hip by scant inches.

A war whoop resounded like the howl of doom. Kat found her worst nightmare materializing on the ridge above her. Comanche raiders! Dear God! Chester wouldn't have time to kill her and put her out of her misery before she was scalped or dragged into captivity!

Frantic, Kat wheeled around and dashed through the narrow canyon. She stumbled, fell, then clawed her way to her feet, ignoring the biting pain in her hands and knees. Behind her she heard Chester and Hugh discharging their pistols in rapid-fire succession.

Arrows hissed through the air, followed by a rifle blast that sent Kat sprawling in the grass. She remembered what Judd had told her about the Comancheros trading rifles and ammunition to the Comanches for horses and safe passage across Indian hunting ground. The war party that had managed to escape from the reservations to the north had come well armed. Kat knew she didn't have a chance of survival, but stark fear put wings on her feet and left her praying for a miracle.

Her frantic thoughts scattered when she heard a piercing howl of pain. She glanced over her shoulder to see Hugh Riggs staring at the arrow that protruded from his barrel-shaped chest. Chester was already slumped over his saddle. Two arrows were imbedded in his back.

Blood-pounding terror racked Kat's body as she raced downhill. She cursed Judd Lassiter repeatedly as she darted to and fro, dodging the hiss of arrows. If not for Judd's heartless abandonment and betrayal, she wouldn't be running for her life.

And double damn him for not being here to keep the promise she'd asked of him. She had begged him to prevent her from being tortured—in the event that they were chased by a raiding party. Now she was at the mercy of five warriors who plunged down the cliff to lift her scalp.

Kat's heart was pounding so furiously that she swore it would break a rib—not that it would matter. She was as good as dead . . .

She suddenly recalled what Judd had told her about Indians admiring bravery and courage. The thought prompted her to spin around to meet her enemies. She swept the hat from her head, letting the waterfall of red-gold curls tumble free. She swallowed her fear, shot the approaching riders The Look that Judd Lassiter leveled on his foes, then tilted her chin in defiance.

She would fight the way Judd told her Indian warriors were taught to fight—to the death. According to Judd, a warrior was at his most dangerous when cornered, because he was determined to take as many enemies as possible with him during his last earthly battle.

Kat intended that the Comanche kill her quickly, because she planned to attack, not defend. Mimicking the war whoop she had heard echoing around the ravine, she raised both arms, clenched her fists and stormed directly toward the riders. The first bronze-skinned brave stared bewilderedly at her—until she whacked his horse, causing the steed to bolt sideways.

Letting loose with another shrill shriek, Kat barreled toward the warrior carrying the rifle. She had decided she preferred a bullet to arrows as a means of death. The warrior snapped the weapon into firing position as she ran headlong at him, screaming at him to end it now, because she planned to pull him from his horse and claw him to shreds if he didn't.

Kat heard one of the braves speaking in a foreign tongue as she leaped off the ground to grab the warrior by the lacings on his shirt. She expected him to end her misery at close range, but he whirled the rifle in his hand to konk her over the head. Kat was still clawing at him when the second blow caused her head to explode with intolerable pain.

"End it now!" she shrieked as she tumbled off the side of the warrior's pony.

By the time Kat hit the ground, she didn't feel a blessed thing . . .

Judd exhausted his vocabulary of curse words while he watched the confrontation through his spyglass. He had seen it all, from Kat's rendezvous with the two men who had trailed them since their departure from The Flats. No doubt the three conspirators had been working out the details of their arrangements when the Comanche raiding party overtook them. Although Judd's view had been obstructed by the scraggly tree Kat clung to, he could see the threesome huddled together. Hugh and Chester had their backs to his spyglass, blocking Kat from view.

Judd knew he should have disposed of Chester and Hugh that first night on the trail, but he had wanted to give Kat the benefit of the doubt about her connection with Hugh and Chester. He kept hoping she had been truthful with him when she claimed the two henchmen were as much her enemies as J.P. Trumball.

Obviously Judd had been living on false hope. The rendezvous was like a signed confession of guilt and conspiracy. Kat had been tried and sentenced in that crucial moment.

As disappointed as Judd was to see his worst suspicions confirmed, he couldn't help but admire Kat's gumption as she faced the Comanche warriors. Kat displayed amazing courage in the face of mortal disaster. Her defense had been a fierce offensive attack that obviously impressed the warriors. Otherwise, the raiding party would have ridden off with her lovely head of hair as their coup.

Hounded by conflicting emotions, Judd watched Kat's unconscious body being tossed over the horse Chester Westfall had been riding—and no longer needed. He also noticed that the two scoundrels had been relieved of their scalps—a practice, Judd reminded himself, that had actually been started by white men. Too bad the newspapers didn't remind the public of that fact. Publicity was anti-Indian, because greedy white settlers wanted land, and the government saw that they had it.

Judd pocketed his spyglass as the raiders rode north. He kept telling himself that traitorous female was getting exactly what she deserved. Yet, deep down inside, Judd couldn't quite forget that Kat Diamond had touched emotions in him that no other woman had ever stirred. The frustrating fact was that if Kat Diamond was to get her due, Judd wanted to be her judge and jury, because her betrayal demanded his personal retribution.

When the braves and their captive disappeared into the canyons to the north, Judd rode to the site of the ambush to retrieve the bedroll. To his amazement, the pouch of jewels was still tucked in the bottom of the pallet. Obviously Kat and her conspirators hadn't had time to divvy up the jewels before disaster struck.

"Damn lot of good those priceless gems will do you now," Judd muttered to Kat's floating image.

Judd rode past the two dead henchmen without a sideways glance. He speculated the braves were returning to their secluded camp. He suspected the raiding party was also on a mission to bring down a few buffalo before returning to the reservation.

Judd figured that if the raiding party was nearby, then so were the buffalo hunters. More than likely, Judd would be picking up the scent of rotting carcasses very soon.

Sure enough, Judd stared down the slopes to see massacred buffalo stripped of their hides and left to rot on the plains. Because of his heritage, he was overcome by the same sense of outrage as the Comanches when he witnessed the results of senseless slaughter.

Indians made use of every buffalo they brought down. The carcass meant beef for the winter, bedding and clothing. To the whites, the hides were taken—sometimes for sport and sometimes for profit, because each hide sold for three dollars and seventy-five cents. The vultures got what was left.

Although Judd realized that times were changing, that the frontier was shrinking rapidly, and the white plague would never go away, he knew he was never going to adapt completely to this so-called progress of society. Wide-open spaces were a part of his soul, his spirit. He may have been born half white, but his heart was pure Cheyenne. He wouldn't fit into white culture any better now than he had as a teenager. Despite the government's relentless attempt to indoctrinate Indians to the white man's way of life, he could not forget the traditions and philosophies that were the root of his very existence.

This wasn't the first time Judd wished the Great Spirit had seen fit to reverse the roles of Indians and whites, letting the invading hordes know how it felt to give up everything they believed in when they were herded onto reservations and told what to do and how to behave.

Judd shrugged off his bitter thoughts and focused his concentration on rescuing Kat—whether she deserved it or not. He didn't have much time if he wanted to save her from whatever plans the Comanche had for her.

CHAPTER TWELVE

Kat was sorely disappointed to realize that she had awakened and that life as she knew it still existed. She had hoped to be removed to a higher sphere.

Damn the luck.

Hands bound at the wrists, Kat had been staked to the ground like a sacrificial lamb. The Comanche warriors looked to be having some sort of powwow. Probably discussing her future—or lack thereof—she presumed. Several pair of dark eyes darted to her at irregular intervals.

What were those warriors planning? she wondered. Were they drawing straws to see who violated her first? Or was she doomed to become somebody's wife?

"Damn you to hell, Lassiter," Kat scowled resentfully. "The one time I really need you, you aren't here."

Kat decided she may as well hold true to the bold image she'd projected during her confrontation with the braves. She was not going to lie here meekly, while a bunch of men decided her fate. She had spent her life being ordered around by the male of the species, and she had declared her freedom. She would force the Comanches to shut her up—permanently—or they could listen to her rail at them until they went deaf or she lost her voice, whichever came first.

"Untie me this instant!" Kat yelled, despite the headache that pounded against her skull.

That got everybody's attention.

"Yeah, you!" she shouted, then shot the braves The Look. "I'm talking to all of you. I have no intention of being anybody's good time, so you can forget that idea. And furthermore, I will not be anyone's dutiful wife! All you'll get from me is defiance, a barrel full of it. I promise you that. Do you hear me? I will not cooperate!"

The brave who had clubbed her over the head with a rifle butt rose from a crouch and stalked toward her. He spoke sharply, upraised his rifle, then glowered at her.

Not to be outdone, Kat called him a choice name and glared right back.

He struck out with a moccasined foot and kicked her in the thigh.

She retaliated by raising the heel of her clunky boot and jabbing him in the shin. The onlookers barked laughs when the brave yelped and leaped back, as if he had been attacked by a rabid dog. Then the brave who appeared to be in charge of this powwow summoned his cohort back to the circle.

Kat presumed the warrior with the white feather braided into his hair was in charge of the war party. Obviously, he was well respected in the tribe, and the other men looked to him for guidance and leadership.

Kat began singing at the top of her lungs, then recited the Preamble to the Constitution. She refused to shut up, even when the self-appointed leader marched over to drench her with water. Kat blinked to clear her vision, then gaped at the brawny warrior who towered over her. Although his hair was dark and his skin was bronzed by the sun, his light-colored eyes hinted that he was white—all white from the look of his facial features. Had he been taken captive as a child? she wondered. Could he speak English? Would she be able to reason with him?

Although the leader spoke curtly to her in Comanche, Kat kept right on singing, reciting and tossing snide remarks. Dry-

throated and hungry though she was, Kat kept putting up a
racket until she was hoarse. Then she wheezed a few more
songs and recitations.

Kat had the feeling her captors would arrive at some sort of
decision by nightfall, because the raiders huddled together for
another powwow. The men sank down cross-legged for their
in-depth discussion. Kat moistened her lips as best she could
and serenaded them.

Damn it, what did it take to make these warriors killingly
furious? Why wouldn't they shoot her and get it over with?

Suddenly the whole passel of brawny warriors bounded to
their feet and stared northward. Kat tried to see what they were
staring at, but the outcropping of rock above her blocked her
view. Whatever was going on above her was lost to her. But
whatever—or whoever—had arrived now demanded the Comanches' rapt attention.

Kat decided she might as well give her vocal cords a rest,
because no one was paying the slightest attention to her.

Wild Hawk's attention was no longer focused on the man-
woman whom he and his raiders had captured earlier in the
afternoon. Although the yammering creature was the subject
of controversial discussion, Wild Hawk was too distracted to
decide what was to be done with her. While two members of
his clan were certain the man-woman was touched in the head
and was a very bad omen that should be avoided, Wild Hawk
disagreed.

Some of the warriors suggested torture as retaliation for
the awful noises the man-woman had been making since her
captivity. Blue Eagle offered to claim and tame the creature as
his slave. But Wild Hawk admired the female's courage and
spirit. He favored taking her as a wife to bear his children. But
the decision was put on hold when the hazy specter condensed
from the shadows that clung to the canyon wall.

Wild Hawk stared at the translucent apparition in rapt fascination. The specter had taken on the kind of eerie quality that
commanded reverence among the Comanche clan. Tales of

similar sightings in this area were numerous. Other raiding parties had returned to the reservation, speaking of the Phantom Panther that prowled the plains and canyons of the *Comancheria*.

Wild Hawk knew Three Wolves, the half-breed Comanche shaman who wielded the powers of his guardian spirit. Wild Hawk had traveled with Three Wolves in the old days—before the whites came with their empty promises and stole land that had belonged to the People since time began. He had also heard of the Cheyenne warrior known as the Lone Horseman who led the ghost horses across the canyon rims and through the mountain passes in Colorado.

Here again was one of the chosen few who commanded and wielded omnipotent powers of the spirit world, Wild Hawk realized as the vaporous image took shape on the outcropping of rock of the chasm. He was honored that the Cheyenne prophet known as Panther, and his three intimidating ghost cats, had appeared to him.

As darkness swallowed up the twilight, Wild Hawk watched the four intriguing shadows take animal form, saw the glowing, green-gold eyes fix on him. Although most white men feared what they could not explain, Wild Hawk and his people marveled and understood, for they were scholars of nature who gathered knowledge from the cunning creatures that lived alongside them.

Wild Hawk had seen his own vision, heard the mystical voices calling to him in the wind, but he had not been granted the powers that Panther, Three Wolves and the Lone Horseman had attained.

A silent voice called to Wild Hawk, ordering him to walk among the shadows of the great cats that prowled the rocky ledges of the canyon. A shrill, unearthly scream rolled through the ravine, a warning and summons in one. The wild scream rose higher, amplifying, calling down the night.

To his stunned amazement, Wild Hawk realized the other warriors had not heard the summons. They were staring at the intimidating images above them, yet those shrill, unearthly cries had reached only Wild Hawk. When he strode to the footpath that led up the slope, his companions called him back, unsure that he should confront the powerful spirit creature alone.

Wild Hawk didn't heed the warnings. He ascended the winding path, guided by the light of the moon and the glowing pinpoints of eyes that called to him on the deepest level of his soul. He sensed the dangerous presence that lurked on the outcroppings of stone, knew he was being stalked and watched, yet he moved steadily toward the misty images, hearing that silent scream that was his name.

The great shaman who walked among white man and Indian alike summoned, and Wild Hawk was humbled to be called to stand in the powerful presence of a Chosen One. Even when Wild Hawk heard a vicious snarl close behind him on the narrow path, he did not turn, did not flinch in fear. He continued to climb toward the evanescent plume of fog that hovered above him.

"My brother Three Wolves has spoken of you," Wild Hawk called out. "He is one of us, yet he is like you. He can call in the wolves, while you command the great cats that stalk the wilds. What is it that you wish of me, Panther?"

"Leave the woman behind and go in peace. She must not be taken into captivity on the reservation. The great chief in Washington scorns that practice. Your people will be punished if you try to continue the old custom in a changing world."

The purring voice was quiet, as deep as the night, as soft as the whisper of the wind, but an icy chill surrounded the place where the ominous presence hovered.

"The man-woman displays tremendous courage, invincible spirit," Wild Hawk said as he stepped closer to the hovering specter whose eyes flared like gold-green flames. "We will give her to you as an offering of peace and kinship, if that is your wish."

"It is my wish," came the hollow, echoing purr. *"In exchange, I will grant you safe passage north through the canyons. You will not feel the slash of claws that show no mercy, the bite of fangs that draw lifeblood.*

"Soldiers from Fort Elliot search for you, Wild Hawk. They are camped a half day's ride to the east. You must ride north

through the ravines if you are to avoid them. They are many and you are few.''

"So it is, always, with the whites," Wild Hawk muttered bitterly. "They will not be satisfied until all that we have is theirs, until our spirit is broken and our way of life has vanished like the buffalo."

"White men can never destroy what is more precious than hunting grounds and warm buffalo robes, my brother. The whites cannot take what is in our hearts and souls. It will be our quiet victory, because our greatest source of power and strength comes from within. They have not learned to channel that special source of strength and wisdom. They do not hear and respond to the inner voices. But they are still a threat to your people if you continue to defy the orders not to raid and retaliate.''

"We have not come from the reservation to make war on the settlers," Wild Hawk explained. "We sneaked away to hunt for our starving people and to track down the white outlaws who have deceitfully dressed as Comanche and left a trail of terror and death behind them."

He paused to stare down to the place where his warriors waited, where the woman was staked. "We thought we had overtaken the three outlaws who have given my people a bad name. Instead, we found the woman dressed as a man and her two companions. The men turned their weapons on us, and we gave them the battle they initiated. We were trying to decide what to do with the man-woman when you appeared."

Panther breathed deeply, steadily, calling himself back from the depths of the omnipotent powers bestowed on him. In his lifetime he had revealed himself to two men only. One was the powerful Cheyenne shaman called Lone Horseman; the other was to the Comanche prophet known as Three Wolves. But Panther made another exception in Wild Hawk's presence, because he knew of this warrior's prestige among his people. Panther could sense the spirits swirling around this courageous warrior, who resented his white heritage and had committed his heart and soul to the Comanche who raised him. Wild Hawk would soon find his true calling, and he would be challenged to follow the destiny the Great Spirit presented to him.

Wild Hawk wobbled unsteadily, gasping in disbelief as the hovering image altered right before his eyes. The thick, crystal-like fog changed shape, then took on a muscular human form. The man called Panther stepped from the translucent haze, wearing a breechcloth, leather leggings and moccasins. Sharp, polished claws and colorful beads encircled his neck on a thin leather strap. He towered in height, and bronze muscles rippled as he inhaled a deep, controlled breath, as if he had emerged from a mystical trance. Indeed he had, because Wild Hawk had watched the transformation take place!

Wild Hawk fell to his knees, awed by what he had been allowed to see. "Chosen One, I am humbled in your presence. I have seen such feats only once before. When Three Wolves returned from that place where spirits dwell, I saw him rise from a curl of dark smoke, in much the same way you condense from the shimmering fog."

He stared questioningly at the omnipotent Cheyenne shaman. "You have appeared to me in both spirit and human form, because of the daring man-woman? What other powers does she possess besides unfaltering courage and bold defiance in the face of possible death? Those powers I have seen for myself and greatly admired."

Panther laid his hand on Wild Hawk's broad shoulder. "Take your braves and ride through the night. You are meant for greater things than to die at dawn at the soldiers' hands."

Curiously, Wild Hawk peered into the chiseled face, commanding features and mesmerizing amber-green eyes. "You can foresee what awaits me?"

Panther nodded gravely. "The gift is both blessing and curse, my brother. Three Wolves knows of this burden of guardian spirit power, as does the warrior called Lone Horseman. When *you* are summoned by your totem, use the gift wisely, cautiously."

Wild Hawk swayed on his knees, startled by the oppressive strength he felt bearing down on his shoulder, stunned by what he had seen and heard in the shadows on the cliff. Still the pinpoints of glowing eyes burned down on him like starlight. Still the prowling restlessness in the powerful presence radiated around him, assuring him that he knelt among the omnipotent spirits Panther commanded.

"I am not worthy of such powers," Wild Hawk murmured. "I carry the curse of being born white. My people have honored me by making me a chief among them, but I am my own enemy!"

His tormented cry reverberated around the canyon, returning to him time and time again, like the torturous thought that was his constant companion.

"It is that which you perceive as your greatest curse that is your greatest strength, Wild Hawk," Panther murmured. "You have been called upon to translate for your people so they can communicate with the whites. You have walked in both worlds and you will again, when destiny calls you. Until you come to terms with your white heritage, you cannot help the Comanche you love as if they were your own blood kin.

"Think on this, my brother. You must learn to see the world around you from the broad viewpoint of the hawk that soars over land and sea. The guardian spirits are waiting for *you* to accept who you are, so they can empower you for the good of your chosen people."

"But I gave my word that I will not leave Texas until the evil whites who strike terror on their own kind, and blame their cruel deeds on the Comanche, are dead," Wild Hawk insisted.

"Then go with caution, Wild Hawk, but do not forget what I have told you. You are to become one of the chosen. The time is coming when you must face your waiting destiny and answer your calling . . ."

And then, as if awakening from an indescribable dream, Wild Hawk felt the oppressive weight lift from his shoulder and pull him to his feet. He found himself alone, staring at the empty space where Panther had risen from the silvery pocket of fog, then vanished like the night fading into daylight.

Wild Hawk retraced his footsteps along the narrow path and descended to the canyon floor. His warriors waited anxiously for him to explain, but he spoke only the command to mount up and ride toward the canyons to the north.

When the warriors broke camp and thundered off into the night, Wild Hawk stood over his captive. She began singing in her native tongue, her voice recoiling off the stone walls and ricocheting in the darkness. He studied her astutely, wondering why Panther ordered this woman to be spared, wondering how she fit into the Cheyenne shaman's destiny.

Wild Hawk smiled wryly as he stared at the woman with luminous green eyes and spun-gold hair. She would make a good mate for the Panther, if the shaman could find a way to tame her without destroying her fiery spirit.

Kat braced herself for what she expected to be the battle of her life. She didn't know what had happened on the rocky ledges above her, but she had heard a voice cry out in the night. She wondered if this warrior, who looked to be white rather than Indian, had drawn the longest straw and had come to claim his prize. She expected that he had in mind to force himself on her before he lifted her scalp and rode off to join his raiding party.

"You will have a fight on your hands—I promise you that," Kat hissed at Wild Hawk, then struck out with her foot in warning not to venture one step nearer. But Wild Hawk simply stood there, staring down at her with those silver-blue eyes, sporting a smile she couldn't interpret. It seemed she had somehow amused him when it had been her intent to provoke him into ending her captivity quickly, mercifully.

Kat had accepted the inevitability of her death hours ago. She was prepared to meet her Maker, but the suspense of not knowing when the moment would come frustrated her no end. She struck out at Wild Hawk again, though her blow connected only with air.

"End it, damn you!" she railed at him.

To her astonishment he spoke to her in stilted English. "I am known as Wild Hawk. I will not take your life, for I was commanded to spare you. My warriors and I mistook you for the treacherous white men who hide behind Indian buckskin and war paint to accomplish their selfish deeds. Your companions gave us no choice but to defend ourselves. Only you will be left alive.''

Kat stared after Wild Hawk as he turned on his heels and strode toward his horse. She watched him disappear into the darkness, heard the clatter of the horse's hooves die into silence. Kat still couldn't believe she had been left in one piece to die of starvation or thirst—whichever came first.

Where the hell had those Indians gone? And what had Wild Hawk meant about searching for white men who dressed as Indians? Kat figured she wouldn't have the chance to find out, because she would be stuck here until the day she died.

"I wouldn't be staked out here at all if not for you, Judd Lassiter," Kat muttered. "If not for your betrayal I wouldn't be here in purgatory!"

Hot tears scalded Kat's cheeks as she slumped on the hard ground, wondering if she would become the evening meal for unseen predators stalking the canyon. Ah, so much for the freedom she craved, she thought, disheartened. She would never know what it was like to become her own woman, the mistress of her own destiny!

Kat decided, there and then, that if she met up with Lassiter in the hereafter she was going to have several choice words to hurl at him. She could forgive him for not caring about her and abandoning her in the middle of nowhere, but what she could never, ever forgive was his betrayal of her trust. Neither could she forgive *herself* for seeing more in that man than was actually there.

He was not a man to be admired and respected, after all. He was a man to be despised. And Kat did despise him, because he had made her care about him in ways she had cared about no other man. She had been nothing to him but a convenient amusement.

As it turned out, she had bargained with the devil—and lost!

CHAPTER THIRTEEN

Tormented by conflicting emotions, Judd approached the place where Kat had been staked. He wished like hell that he could feel nothing but indifference—but he couldn't. He didn't want to be hurt and disappointed by Kat's betrayal, and he shouldn't have spared her life. She was nothing to him but one of the many assignments he had taken over the years. When she reached her destination, they would go their separate ways. So why should he care what happened to her when she didn't give a damn about him?

If by chance—Judd told himself—he encountered the deadly trio of outlaws who were wanted for robbery, murder and impersonating Comanche raiding parties, then he would deal with them. If not, he would track them down *after* he delivered Kat to Santa Fe. But for sure and certain Judd was not going to let this scheming, crafty female have any more influence over his emotions. She'd made him too vulnerable already, and *that* he refused to tolerate!

Without a word, Judd reined in Horse and the trailing mare to a halt, then dismounted. He noted that Kat didn't bother to greet him, either. Her silence implied that she felt awkward

with the knowledge that he was wise to her scheme of taking
the jewels and tramping off to rejoin her cohorts.

When Judd leaned down to cut the leather straps that bound
Kat's wrists, she glared at him. "Why did you bother coming
to look for me? Don't tell me your conscience bothered you,
because I don't believe it. You have everything you wanted
from me."

The resentful comments surprised him. How the hell could
she pretend to be the injured party when *she* had taken the
jewels and left without a word of explanation? What game was
she trying to play with him now?

"You're welcome for saving your hide," he said, and
snorted. "Would you prefer to remain staked out until you
become a predator's bedtime snack?"

She glared mutinously at him. "I've been devoured by one
predator already, then captured by a few others. What difference
could it possibly make now?"

Without one word of thanks Kat bounded to her feet and
stalked toward her horse. Judd stared at her in stunned disbelief.
True, he didn't understand women, hadn't spent enough time
with them to analyze how their minds worked, but he sure as
hell couldn't imagine where Kat got off snubbing *him*. Damn
it, he had saved her life. She should be a tad beholden!

Muttering at his inability to remain indifferent around this
infuriating female, Judd swung into the saddle. "The price for
getting you to Santa Fe just went up again. I want four gems
instead of two."

Kat gaped at his broad back as she followed him through
the canyon. "You already have all the jewels," she reminded
him harshly. Suppressed frustration bubbled up like a volcanic
eruption. "You left me alone in the cave, took everything
except my bedroll and vanished from sight! You knew damn
well that I have an aversion to heights and you *left* me there.
Probably laughed yourself silly over it, too! And after the
day I've had—*because of you,* I might add—you have the
unmitigated gall to expect me to thank you for showing up?
You have the nerve to demand more in payment? Have you
lost your mind!" she shouted.

Judd swiveled in the saddle to glower pitchforks at her.
"Who the hell do you think you're dealing with here? The
village idiot? There is no way you can twist what happened to
make me the guilty party! You think I don't know you made
off with the jewels and then met up with your cohorts?"

Kat's mouth dropped open and she gaped at him.

"Well, you're wrong, Diamond. I saw you rendezvous with
Westfall and Riggs. The only hitch in your devious plan was
the arrival of Comanche raiders. For a woman who has had to
change her deceitful plans and is now left to rely entirely on
me, you damned well better change your tack!" he yelled at
her.

Kat's expression was still frozen in a look of total disbelief.

"I don't know why I bothered to convince Wild Hawk and
his warriors to leave you behind," Judd said, and scowled. "I
should have given you to them with my blessing. I would have,
if your arrival at the reservation wouldn't have invited more
trouble than the Comanche have already!"

His voice boomed like thunder and echoed around the canyon. Kat stopped being angry long enough to actually *listen* to
what he was saying. "*I* made off with the jewels?" she parroted.
"*I* rendezvoused with Westfall and Riggs?"

"Well, at least you have enough gumption to admit it," he
snapped.

"I am not admitting to something I didn't do!" she hissed
in outrage. "I am repeating what you said because I cannot
believe you said it! *You* gathered up everything from the cave,
including the jewels, except for the bedroll I was sleeping on.
You took both horses and rode off. I know that for a fact,
because I looked down from the cave and I saw neither hide
nor hair of you anywhere. I couldn't descend to the trail, so I
climbed to the caprock, because it was the lesser of two unnerving evils for me.

"*You* left me without food, water or a mount. When Chester
and Hugh showed up out of nowhere, they demanded the jewels
in exchange for my life, but they had no intention of letting
me live. I, of course, told them I didn't have the jewels, because

you had taken them, along with everything else. Chester was ready to pull the trigger when the Comanches showed up.''

Judd's gaze narrowed on her. His thoughts roiled with suspicion and doubt.

''Chester and Hugh killed J.P., by the way,'' Kat added. ''I asked them. Hugh blurted out that J.P. threatened to withhold payment because they lost track of me the night I escaped from my prison of a hotel room. They took J.P.'s poker winnings to buy supplies so they could trail after me to abscond with the jewels.''

Judd continued to stare at Kat, marveling at her ability to cleverly twist the truth so that he barely recognized it. Damn, this woman was so cunning it was downright frightening!

''Since you know I encountered Chester and Hugh, then you were obviously following me for the spite of it,'' Kat muttered disdainfully. ''But did you intervene in this so-called rendezvous? No! You watched them die, watched me be taken captive.''

Yes, he had, Judd mused. He had been forced to watch, because he was not in a position to come thundering into the gully to rescue her. Yet he had admired her bravery in the face of catastrophe. So, it seemed, had Wild Hawk.

''You hung around to see if the Comanches would finish me off, so you could go your merry way, toting my jewels,'' she continued bitterly. ''But the raiders must have decided I was more trouble than I was worth after I sang off key and recited for hours. When they rode off, you came sauntering up to cut me loose, because you didn't know what else to do with me.''

She glared at him. ''What happened? Did your guilty conscience truly get to you? And here I was thinking you didn't have a conscience at all.''

Obviously, Kat didn't know that Panther's appearance and subsequent conference with Wild Hawk had altered her fate. He decided not to tell her. She could believe whatever she wanted on that issue, but he was going to straighten out this matter of the jewels and *her* claims of abandonment this very minute!

''In the first place, Diamond, you were the one who had the

jewels in your possession," he informed her curtly. "I tucked
them in the bottom of your sleeping bag as a show of good
faith, then gathered up the rest of my belongings to pack on
the horses."

Kat blinked like an awakened owl. "You expect me to
believe that nonsense? Where are the jewels now?"

Judd shifted uncomfortably. "I retrieved them from your
discarded bedroll after Wild Hawk took you captive."

"Of course you did," she said, then sniffed sarcastically.
"Next I suppose you are going to tell me that you planned to
return to the cave after you vanished into thin air."

"I did return," he insisted. "Haven't I always returned each
time I've gone out to scout the trail? I went in search of your
cohorts who have been following us, but they were no longer
behind us. They obviously changed course because of the storm,
and they were waiting ahead of you at the designated rendezvous point."

Kat stared at him as if he had sprouted antlers. "Designated
rendezvous point? Are you insane, Lassiter? You think I know
where the hell I am? You think those two idiots J.P. hired knew
their way around Texas? You think I made prior arrangements
to meet with those henchmen who turned on my stepfather and
followed me for the jewels? You think I planned to hike off
without you because I trusted *them* more than I trusted *you?*
You are the man I trusted, and you abandoned and betrayed
me!"

Judd was getting confused. Either Kat was one whale of an
actress or double misconceptions had flung them apart. Only
now did it occur to him that Kat actually considered herself
abandoned in the cavern, that she might not have noticed the
pouch of jewels he had tucked inside the bedroll.

It could have happened the way she said, he supposed. He
also supposed—if he were excessively lenient in his presump-
tions—that Chester and Hugh could have come upon Kat by
chance, after being swept off course by the dust storm. But
Judd wasn't absolutely certain that Kat hadn't disposed of her
stepfather or hired Chester and Hugh to ambush Judd for a cut
of the jewels.

Kat could have double-crossed her bodyguards, then lit out of town with Judd, leaving Chester and Hugh to follow the trail of the gems. But Judd would never know for sure, because Hugh and Chester weren't around to tell their side of the story. Wasn't it a little too convenient that everyone who could contest her story was dead?

Judd wasn't sure what part—or how much—of Kat's story could be believed. It didn't matter, he convinced himself. He had rescued Kat, because he had taken the assignment and he was a man who finished a job he started, no matter how difficult or distasteful it became.

Resolutely, he turned in the saddle and rode north, leaving Horse to pick his way through the twisted ravines that led onto the High Plains. He rode through the night, avoiding the soldiers' encampment, setting his sights on the northern rim of Palo Duro Canyon. There he could bed down in the small village of abandoned dugouts the buffalo hunters had occupied before they'd followed the dwindling herds south.

Judd rode in silence, guided by the silvery glow of the Cheyenne moon and his knowledge of this region of Texas. He had crossed this rugged terrain hundreds of times in the last ten years. He understood this wilderness, knew it like the back of his hand.

What he didn't know was if he could trust Kat Diamond to give him the whole truth—and nothing but. More importantly, he didn't know if he could trust her with his life.

Kat wanted desperately to bound off the mare and pace so she could think things through logically. Could she have been operating on incorrect assumptions? Or would she be a gullible fool to accept Judd's boiled-down version of the incident that had played havoc with her day?

It was true that he had scouted the trail on a daily basis to check for trouble, then returned to camp. In the past, however, he had notified her of his intentions before he left.

Since Kat had been asleep, had Judd tried to be considerate by not waking her? Had he truly tried to be thoughtful, courteous and considerate by toting his supplies down the steep hill so she wouldn't have to struggle with the extra weight? Had he really left the jewels in her possession as a gesture of trust, just as she had placed them in *his* care in good faith before they left The Flats?

Kat smiled faintly when she realized she had learned to do her pensive thinking on the back of a horse, as well as pacing in the grass. She reminded herself that every situation she encountered was building her character, making her stronger and more self-reliant. This day had been fraught with disaster, but she had survived. She and Judd had been at the worst of all possible odds, yet he had come to retrieve her and now they were together again.

Of course, she had no intention of flinging herself into his arms, as she had the previous night. She refused to let herself be overcome by newly awakened desire. She was not going to pretend everything was hunky-dory between them, because nothing could have been further from the truth. The fact was that neither one of them had learned to trust blindly—or even conditionally. According to the gospel of Judd Lassiter, presumption spelled impending danger—in any language.

What you think you know, but do not know for absolute certain, will come back to haunt you, he had told her once. *Take nothing for granted and you will never be at the mercy of your own surprise.*

Kat realized she had acted on pure assumption this morning. She had fled from the cave, believing Judd had abandoned her, because he had established a habit of telling her before he rode off to scout or hunt. But because of the emotions she had experienced the previous night in his arms she felt an uncomfortable vulnerability to Judd. She had assumed the worst when he wasn't there to greet her at dawn.

Was it possible that he had experienced that same sort of outraged vulnerability when—*if*—he had returned to the cave and found her gone?

If Judd felt as used and betrayed as Kat did, then he must have spent the day cursing her, just as she had cursed him. It was entirely possible that, given his perception of the situation, he had misread her encounter with Chester and Hugh. That being the case, Judd could have perceived the encounter as a conspiracy.

Now that Kat had set her frustrations aside to consider the turn of events from Judd's point of view, she understood why he had behaved as indignantly as she. There was passion between them, she knew, but trust was slow in coming. They both were quick to think the worst of each other in times of trouble.

Pensively, Kat stared at Judd's silhouette. Would he be willing to reevaluate this situation from her point of view? Did he care enough about her to bother understanding her actions and take her feelings into account? Or was it best to continue their journey with this wall of mistrust between them?

If Kat let herself care too much, if she let herself depend on Judd, it would break her heart when they parted company in Santa Fe. She couldn't let herself fall in love . . .

Kat jerked upright in the saddle, causing the mare to sidestep and prick her ears.

"Something wrong, Diamond?" Judd asked quietly.

It still amazed her that this man had such an acute awareness of his surroundings. His senses were as sharp as his four-legged namesake's. She envied that about him, along with all his other impressive survival skills.

"No, I was just thinking," she said belatedly.

"Really? On horseback? I didn't think that was your style. But of course, I have discovered recently that you are full of unexpected surprises."

Kat ignored his sarcasm. "I am teaching myself to adapt to situations."

"Are you now?"

"Better than you, I believe." She had put herself in his place and viewed the situation through *his* eyes. *He* had not returned the favor, and *he* was the man who said it was best not to assume anything. He was a hypocrite, as it turned out.

"Is that so?" Judd snorted caustically. "I would dearly love to hear how that feminine mind of yours came to that twisted conclusion."

"During our ride I have made use of my time by asking myself if I might have misinterpreted your actions today. If I had known that you tucked the jewels in my sleeping bag—as you *claim* but have no proof of it—I would have viewed your deed as a vote of confidence. Perhaps I would have realized that you did intend to return, as you have each night after you left to hunt and scout. Therefore," Kat went on to say, "I would have waited for you, and I wouldn't have allowed hurt and betrayal to send me plunging headlong into trouble."

Judd frowned as he listened to her explain how she interpreted his absence from the cave. Had Kat actually believed he had left with the jewels?

"I can see now that you might have felt exactly as I did and that you thought I'd gotten exactly what I deserved for traipsing off alone," Kat confirmed. "The truth is, I *didn't* know you left the jewels with me, because I never thought to look for them. I was feeling . . . um . . . awkward and insecure because of . . . what happened between us last night." She looked away after voicing the admission. It hadn't been easy to bare her feelings, not knowing how Judd would react.

When Judd said nothing in response, Kat felt tension rolling over her. His lack of reply led her to believe that he didn't give a damn one way or another about what happened between them last night. And damn it, she was not falling in love with this exasperating man! There was no such thing as love. Her parents never behaved as if the sun rose and set in each other's eyes, never gave in to public displays of affection. Monica Diamond and J.P. Trumball certainly hadn't gushed all over each other, either. Love and marriage did not go hand in hand.

Love was a hallucination suffered by romantics and fools, she reminded herself. She had better not let herself forget that, either! She and Judd had shared passion and sexual desire—that was all. The bond between them was purely physical, Kat tried to tell herself.

"About last night—" Judd said eventually.

"Forget about it," she cut in quickly. "I think it's best if we pretend nothing happened. I certainly have no intention of repeating what was obviously a mistake with a man who refuses to even *consider* that he misjudged my actions. As far as I'm concerned, we have nothing to say to one another until you admit we both reacted rashly and that you broke your own hard and fast rule that living on assumption is dangerous business.''

Judd couldn't contain the smile that quirked his lips. Exasperated as he was with Kat, she was still a unique source of amusement. Furthermore, there was nothing shallow about this female. She possessed keen intelligence and was capable of complex, analytical thought.

Vividly aware of that, Judd was always cautious about being outsmarted by her. In his own defense, the nature of his profession *demanded* that he avoid being outsmarted.

He still wasn't certain he could accept everything Kat said as gospel, because he didn't know what truly had motivated her departure from the cave. He didn't know if she had disposed of J.P. Trumball so she could take sole possession of the jewels, didn't know if Chester and Hugh had acted on her orders or their own decision. He still carried the notice Marshal Winslow had given him—just in case. Judd wasn't going to tear up the notice or ignore it until he knew exactly what had happened to J.P. Trumball the night he had died in that dark alley in The Flats.

The fact that Judd *wanted* to believe Kat worried him to the extreme. The way she stammered through her admission that she didn't know how to deal with the passion that exploded between them had him wondering what their tryst meant to her.

Did he mean something to her? Judd asked himself as he rode beneath the dome of twinkling stars. Did he want their shared passion to mean something special to her, to him? It wasn't as if a promising prospect of a shared future lay ahead of them, he reminded himself. He and Kat came from two entirely different worlds.

Kat Diamond had lived with sophistication and luxury most of her life. She intended to sell the heirloom jewels so that she could resume her pampered way of life, enjoy the sense of freedom she craved.

Judd, on the other hand, avoided civilization as much as

possible. He was a loner who accepted the powers bestowed on him and used the gift to rid the world of men who committed unforgivable crimes.

The fact was that Kat didn't have the slightest idea what he was capable of when he reached deep within himself, when he called to the unseen forces of his guardian spirit. She thought she had seen a vision that night beside Whispering Springs. She didn't know the half of it! She would be horrified to discover what Judd became when he willed it to be so.

Only Three Wolves, the Lone Horseman—and someday Wild Hawk—experienced what the Indian culture referred to as the deep sense of knowing. The concept and the special powers came from living an existence so closely attuned to nature.

White men made the mistake of attempting to conquer nature, not learning from it, living with it. They stole from nature without giving anything back. The mind and spirit and heart held infinite powers that could be harnessed and wielded with time and practice. The legend of the Phantom Panther that called out to the night of a thousand eyes lived and breathed and exerted power. But white men scoffed and labeled what they couldn't explain as superstitious nonsense.

Many an outlaw had encountered the Phantom Panther of the Cheyenne and had died knowing he had lived with the wrong assumptions.

Would Kat Diamond be repulsed if she had seen what Wild Hawk saw tonight? Would she consider Panther a hideous monster? How could she not? She had been raised in white society. The concepts that Judd lived by were totally foreign to her. To put it simply, Kat wouldn't know how to understand.

Judd stared up at the winking stars and glowing Cheyenne moon, telling himself not to become too attached to Kat. They were like two comets blazing through the night, each following its own course. They had burned down the night together, but one night did not destiny make . . . did it?

Judd frowned, remembering that night years ago when he had come to grips with the offered powers of his totem. It was that fateful night when the great cats descended from the hills to claim their prey or name their master—depending on how Judd reacted to their appearance.

That monumental event had altered the course of his life.

The night he met Kat Diamond had also altered his life, his emotions.

You have appeared to me in both spirit and human form, because of the man-woman? What other powers does she possess besides unfaltering courage and bold defiance in the face of possible death? Those powers I have seen for myself and greatly admired.

Wild Hawk's words flowed through Judd's mind like an underground river seething with currents. He knew the answer to that question, but he had refused to offer it up to Wild Hawk, to himself. Yet the damnable truth was that Kat Diamond had the power to hurt, to expose Judd's vulnerability, to make him feel emotions that had been buried inside him for more than a decade.

Kat Diamond had the power to become Judd's greatest strength or his damning weakness.

When a man's heart and soul were at stake, he had to be extremely cautious. Judd had no choice but to reserve judgment on Kat. He needed proof, needed a sign that this forbidden attraction to that green-eyed siren wouldn't lead him down the path of destruction.

CHAPTER FOURTEEN

Bone-weary, exhausted from the emotional roller-coaster ride she had endured throughout the day, Kat battled to remain upright in the saddle. Twice she dozed off and jerked awake the instant before she would topple from the mare. She felt like crying for no good reason, wanted to beg Judd to call a halt to their travels, but she would not give him the satisfaction of letting him hear her bawl like a helpless female. Kat had proved to herself—on a daily basis—that she was made of sturdy stuff. Whining would not accomplish anything.

But ah, if only she could close her eyes and drift off to sleep. If only she could give her aching body and cramping muscles a few minutes' rest . . .

Kerplop.

Judd glanced back to see Kat sprawled in the grass like a misplaced doormat. Weariness had caught up with her, obviously. He was surprised she had stayed awake as long as she had, considering the harrowing events of the day, but he could not stop here to give her the rest she desperately needed. They were too exposed to the towering summits on either side of the canyon. They could be spotted easily in broad daylight.

Effortlessly Judd dismounted, then scooped up Kat. She

mumbled drowsily as she cuddled against his chest. His traitorous body stirred in response, as if she had caressed him. When she slung her arm over his shoulder and nuzzled her face against his neck, her breath whispered against his skin, and warm sensations rippled through his body. Judd tried to resist the tender feelings she drew from him, but it was hopeless. This woman, this wild diamond in the wilderness, touched him in the most elemental way, even while he called himself every kind of fool for succumbing to this attraction.

Balancing Kat in one arm, Judd surged onto Horse's back. The gelding blew out his breath in a snort.

"Sorry, fella," Judd murmured. "You'll earn extra rations for carrying extra weight. Keep your legs under you for another hour and you can eat, drink and rest to your heart's content."

Although Judd hadn't grabbed the mare's reins, the horse followed out of familiar habit. Horse dug in his hooves as they began their ascent along the Indian trail that wound into the very heart of Palo Duro Canyon. The weary gelding stumbled as he moved down the next slope, but Judd shifted to aid in the horse's balance.

In the distance Judd saw the river glistening like a silver streamer. He knew Kat would appreciate the scenery here. She appreciated the rugged beauty of this wilderness, even if she had been raised in proper society. That pleased him immensely. It indicated that Kat could find beauty even where danger prevailed.

Some people gazed across the rolling expanse of the High Plains, broken by rocky ravines and jagged canyons, and saw only difficult terrain to be crossed and conquered. Judd saw it as Earth Mother's handiwork that possessed a striking beauty all its own. Apparently Kat shared his feelings, because she never failed to comment on unique rock formations.

In the morning light Kat would wake to see an 800-foot-deep canyon and towering rock formations that resembled stone lighthouses, ancient castles and animal and human faces etched in colorful layers of brown, purple, green and white sandstone and mudstone. She would appreciate her surroundings even if she wasn't pleased with her companion.

When Kat sighed in her sleep and snuggled up on his lap, Judd tightened his arm around her. Before he realized it, he had brushed his lips over her forehead. He had become entirely too familiar with her, too comfortable with her in his arms.

At least he had made the tender gestures while she slept and he didn't have to answer for them. Judd didn't want to explain himself. He wanted to enjoy the secret pleasures of holding Kat for as long as the moment lasted.

Judd smiled to himself when he heard the quiet whisper of the waterfall that tumbled over the rocks to form a shallow pool. He was anxious for a bath and a few hours of sleep.

After days of hard riding they would rest and recuperate, then begin their journey to Tascosa. It was a town that rivaled The Flats for hellions, vagabonds and renegades, but at least he and Kat could stretch out on a bed again before heading west.

Carefully Judd eased to the ground, then grabbed the bedroll with his free hand. He carried Kat into one of the abandoned dugouts, checked for varmints that might have crawled inside, then kicked out the bedroll. Gently he laid Kat down. She curled up like a kitten and sighed heavily, but she didn't wake up. He hadn't really expected her to. He knew she was physically and emotionally exhausted.

After Judd tended the horses, he stripped off his clothes and climbed the rock stairsteps to the trickling waterfall. He sat there for the longest time, letting the cool water cascade over him.

Later, when he donned clean clothes, he heard a soft whistling call and glanced up to see a trio of midnight-black pumas lounging on the moonlit ledges above him. The creatures were never far away, following like his shadow, clinging to the underbrush, hiding in the ravines, awaiting his summons. Yet tonight the ghost cats had come voluntarily to him.

"I would hate to have to explain you to Diamond," he murmured to the ever-present creatures.

Years ago the cats had left their marks on him. Kat had yet to see the scars on his back—and he planned to keep it that way, planned to withhold the information that wherever he went he was never far from the guardian spirits of the Cheyenne who stood as shadowy sentinels of the night, watching with eyes that glowed like twin flames.

Reentering the dugout, Judd stretched out beside Kat—and found himself wanting her in the worst way. The passion this woman called from him had quickly become an addiction, a weakness that constantly warred with his self-control—which had not turned out to be as unswerving as he used to think!

Judd closed his eyes and begged for sleep to come. It came almost immediately. So quickly in fact that he didn't realize he had gathered Kat's warm, supple body to him—as if she were the other half of his heart.

He slept as soundly as he had when he was a child.

Kat groaned and rolled over to find herself staring up at the mud-and-straw ceiling of a dugout. She didn't remember walking in here, didn't even remember climbing off her horse. She glanced sideways to find a cactus rose on the empty space beside her. Judd's bedroll, saddlebag and weapons were nowhere to be seen—just like yesterday morning. But she knew without question that he hadn't abandoned her.

Smiling, Kat scooped up the yellow rose, wondering if Judd's thoughtful gesture was some sort of peace offering, an assurance that his absence wasn't permanent. Too bad he hadn't been that thoughtful yesterday, she mused. It might have saved her from an overload of anger, frustration and heart-thumping fear.

Rising, Kat walked outside to estimate the time. The sun was bearing down on her, indicating it was nearly noon! Good heavens!

" 'Bout time you got up, Diamond," Judd grunted as he ambled down an eroded slope of rock. "You missed breakfast. Dinner is roasting over the campfire."

Kat glanced in the direction he pointed to see a rabbit cooking on a spit. The small campfire emitted heat, but not smoke that would alert intruders to their presence.

"Thank you for the rose. It was sw—" She swallowed *sweet,*

because she knew Judd would take offense at it, just as he balked at *nice*.

Her gaze lifted to the towering walls of red, gray and green sandstone, marveling at the beauty of this place called Palo Duro. "I would give anything to be an artist so I could capture the panorama of this canyon on canvas and take it with me when I go," she said on a sigh. "Look there!" Kat smiled delightedly when she spotted a stone configuration that reminded her of a lighthouse. "And there!" She whirled to face a towering formation that reminded her of a massive castle.

"This was a favorite Comanche haunt before the soldiers ousted the tribe and killed their horses, and then buffalo hunters descended to stake their claim," Judd reminded her.

"A place for vision quests, I suspect," she said, distracted.

"One or two," he said, smiling enigmatically.

"How is it that you know so much about Comanche customs?"

"Because the Cheyenne customs are basically the same, and because of the alliance formed many years ago between the tribes." He hunkered down to turn the meat above the glowing coals. "I have . . . um . . . a certain understanding of Comanche warriors. Our people suffer the same plague of whites, but we have the same appreciation of nature—"

"Oh, Lord!" Kat interrupted when she spied the shimmering waterfall at the far end of the canyon.

Magnetically drawn, she strode forward, leaving Judd to stare after her in wry amusement. "The waterfall will keep, Diamond. We'll be spending the day here before we travel by night to Tascosa. The next leg of our journey is rife with two-legged predators."

"Worse than the ones milling around The Flats?" she called over her shoulder.

"About the same. You never step onto a street without checking in every direction first. Gunfights are the rule, not the exception there."

At the moment, Kat's least concern was what awaited in Tascosa. "Do I have time to bathe before lunch? I've never walked through a waterfall before."

She looked so delighted by the prospect that Judd couldn't deny her the pleasure he had enjoyed last night, and again this morning. "Go ahead. Just watch your footing. The pool has a few unexpected holes and the depths are at least fifteen feet just below the falls."

Kat couldn't undress quickly enough. She left a trail of clothes behind her as she jogged toward the falls. Laughter bubbled from her lips as she stepped into the tumbling curtain to sip the refreshing spring water.

"Ah, this is glorious!" she called out as she lifted up her face and arms to the sparkling mist.

Her voice carried like a siren's lure. Judd found his footsteps taking him to the cedar trees that concealed her from his view. Okay, so he was a Peeping Tom. A man had to get his thrills when and where he could, didn't he?

His breath clogged in his throat when he saw Kat poised like an Indian maiden paying homage to the Great Spirit. Water streamed over her luscious curves and swells like a lover's flowing caress. Judd's unruly body clenched with unappeased need. Gawking at Kat had its price. How could he have forgotten that?

When Kat eased down the stepping stones to submerge in the pool, Judd chuckled at her rudimentary swimming skills. She was dog paddling, splashing water everywhere. He longed to teach her more refined skills, but there were two very good reasons why he was reluctant to get naked with her right now. First of all, he wouldn't be able to keep his hands off her and his mind on instruction. Secondly, he didn't want her to see the scars . . .

Kat's startled gasp jerked Judd from his reverie. Pistol drawn, he darted toward the waterfall. Kat was too busy staring up at the outcropping of rocks to shield herself when he approached. Difficult though it was to take his eyes off her, Judd raised his gaze and scowled under his breath.

"Do you think they'll attack?" Kat questioned warily. "I thought great cats were usually loners, staking their private domain in canyons and forests and avoiding companionship."

She studied the jet-black pumas that sunbathed on the rocks

and stared intently at her with eyes that held that same eerie glow that she remembered from her experience at Whispering Springs. She glanced speculatively at Judd, who had reholstered his weapon and was muttering at the feline trio.

"Something wrong, Panther?" she asked, appraising him speculatively.

Yes, something was wrong, Judd thought irritably. Those cats were not in the habit of making their presence known, except to him or at his command. So why had they appeared to Kat now? It was as if they were standing guard over her. *Why?* he wondered, baffled.

"Lassiter?" Kat frowned at his sour scowl. "Do you think we have invaded their territory and they have come to object?"

Judd glowered at the lounging cats, willing them away— but to no avail.

"They are magnificent creatures, aren't they?" she said, watching them with open fascination. "They are the epitome of strength, grace and keen alertness."

"Yeah, the epitome," Judd grumbled.

His dour tone drew another of Kat's curious stares. She studied Judd as she paddled toward the shallows. "I would have thought a man called Panther would be more appreciative of these remarkable creatures."

"You'd think," he said neutrally. "We better eat before the meat burns. Maybe the cats will drink from the pool, then wander away. You can continue your swim later."

Kat had been so thoroughly distracted that she forgot she had been paddling around naked while Judd prowled the bank— just as the Phantom Panther had done in her vision at Whispering Springs . . .

A warm blush crept up her neck to color her cheeks, though Kat reminded herself that Judd had done far more than see her stark-bone naked. It was too late for modesty, but nonetheless she shielded herself as best she could and waited for him to turn his back before she emerged from the pool.

Judd smiled when Kat tried unsuccessfully to cover herself. "Got something I didn't find in the cave?" he teased her.

Kat valiantly fought down her blush. "That was different.

It's broad daylight. I'm sure you've seen your share of naked women, but you're the only man—''

When she slammed her mouth shut and turned the color of wild turnips, Judd chuckled. ''Get dressed before you set your face aflame, Diamond.'' He shot a mutinous glare at the lounging cats. ''Maybe seeing you naked is what drew those cats. If you put your clothes on, maybe they'll get bored and leave.''

''I rather like having them standing guard,'' she said, staring at them pensively, then glancing at Judd. ''Their sharp senses might alert us to oncoming trouble.''

''You don't think my instincts are good enough?'' he huffed.

She cocked her head and watched him retreat. ''Why are you so touchy all of a sudden?''

''Maybe because you're naked and I'm not doing a damn thing about it! Ever think of that?''

Kat blinked as he disappeared into the row of cedar trees. Had she aroused him until need made him irritable? Did she have the ability to do such a thing?

Judd was obviously aware of her. The thought brought a deep sense of feminine satisfaction. It made Kat wonder how he would respond if she actually set out to seduce him, to pleasure him as thoroughly as he had pleasured her that night in the cavern.

Forget it, Diamond, pride shouted. *The best you can hope for is a truce with Lassiter. He'll break your foolish heart if you let him.*

''No, he won't,'' Kat argued aloud with herself while she dressed. ''He can't because I don't love him. I refuse to let myself love him, in fact.''

Famous last words—that's what that is, the voice goaded her. *Watch where you step, because you might fall in over your head. You'll never know true freedom if your heartstrings are forever tied to this human tumbleweed.*

''I won't fall in love. There is no such thing,'' Kat chanted on her way to the campfire. She would not let it happen, would not allow the passion she had discovered in his arms to become an all-encompassing bond that was physical as well as spiritual and emotional. She would not let Judd Lassiter turn her soul inside out and that's all there was to it!

Judd muttered at the wayward direction of his thoughts. He had already made up his mind to evacuate the campsite as soon as it was dark, but a silent voice kept whispering that this was his last chance to be alone with Kat. His insatiable need for her had been feeding on itself since he saw her standing in the waterfall that morning. She had reminded him of an enchanting fairy princess amid a cascade of shimmering diamonds. The vision was forever etched on his mind, playing havoc with his male body.

Kat had requested one last swim before they mounted up, and Judd had given her permission. It seemed he was constantly giving in to her wishes. Now he stood in the concealment of the cedars, watching her, aching up to his eyebrows. He told himself to keep his distance, if only to prove to himself that she wasn't an impossible obsession, but he longed to feel her silky body gliding against his in the pool. It was a fantasy he wanted so badly he could almost taste it.

If he went to her now, in the deepening shadows of darkness, she wouldn't notice the unsightly scars that marred his back. He could enjoy one last place out of time and space—the only place a man like him could ever fit into Kat Diamond's sophisticated way of life.

While Kat paddled around the pool, Judd trekked along the uneven stones that led to the elevated waterfall. By the time he reached the ledge beneath the falls, his clothes lay behind him like a trail of good intentions that had gone hiking. He knew that private moments with Kat would be few and far between when they reached Tascosa. Knowing that made it impossible to deny his need for her. He wanted to savor the ineffable sensations she aroused in him, this one last time— despite everything that stood as obstacles between them.

Just this one last time, Judd thought to himself as he stared down at the enticing vision of beauty gliding across a pool of liquid silver.

* * *

Kat gasped when she heard the splash behind her. She paddled around to see nothing but the glittering waterfall above her. When something latched onto her leg, she shrieked in surprise and tried to escape, but she quieted instantly when Judd's grinning face rose from the water's surface.

"I swear you must enjoy scaring years off my life, you rascal," she scolded playfully. "By now I must be back to the age of ten—"

When his hand grazed the pebbled peak of her breast, her breath evaporated and warm tingles danced along her nerve endings.

"Believe me, Kat," he purred softly while his hand did impossible things to her sensitized body. "You don't feel anywhere near ten years old. You feel like a very desirable, alluring woman."

Kat met his intense gaze as his arms folded around her. Delicious heat spread through her as his naked, aroused body glided familiarly against hers.

All her well-meaning lectures faded into oblivion when he said very simply, "I want you."

He didn't speak of the conflict between them, the lack of trust. He spoke only of a need that was his as well as hers. Kat couldn't have ordered him away if her life depended on it, for she had spent her swim wondering what it would be like to have him here with her. Now that he was, one touch left her hopelessly captivated by her own forbidden longings.

When his lips feathered over hers like darkness absorbing the light of day, and his roaming fingertips teased and aroused, Kat knew she was lost. She arched wantonly into his hands, gave herself up to the exquisite flavor that was in his kiss.

Her breath hitched when he curled her legs around his hips, opening her to his intimate caresses. Heat blazed through her, and suddenly there wasn't enough cool water in the pool to douse the fire he ignited deep inside her. The effect he had on her was, as always, spontaneous, uncontrollable, indefinable.

"Panther . . ." she whispered raggedly, her nails digging

into his muscled shoulders to brace herself against the tidal wave of sensations that buffeted her.

"Do you want me?" he asked hoarsely.

Kat stared into those mystical amber-green eyes, helpless to offer anything but the truth. "You know I do. I always have . . ."

A pure male smile curved the corners of his mouth upward. "No matter what, there is this between us, isn't there, Kat?"

She nodded because she didn't trust herself to speak again. His fingertips were gliding over her softest flesh, dipping, retreating, tormenting her with the want of him.

When he bent his head to suckle her nipple, Kat moaned. Shimmering sensations coursed through her body as his hands and lips worked their wild, seductive magic. Panther was indeed a wizard who cast potent spells. He could transform her into a molten mass of desire, and she could do nothing but respond to the pleasure of his touch.

Judd swallowed a groan when he felt Kat pulsing around his fingertip, burning him with honeyed fire. He wanted to be inside her, filling her, driving himself into splendorous infinity. He wanted to lay her down in the plush grass beside the pool, but he knew he would never make it that far. His need for her had already taken him to the limits of self-control. She always left him feeling desperate and impatient. He wondered vaguely, if they had forever together, would he still feel this intense desperation to be one with her? He feared so, and that was what made her such a threat to him. There was simply no cure for his obsession—except satisfying the hunger of it, again and again.

"Panther, please . . ." she whispered as she arched toward him in rhythmic need. "Come here, please . . ."

Judd couldn't deny her or himself. He pressed her hips to his, penetrating her silky heat in one gliding motion, finding that inexplicable sense of satisfaction, that sense of completeness that went far beyond physical need to feed the emptiness in his soul—an emptiness that hadn't existed until the first time he'd made wild, sweet love to Kat.

Even as he moved against her, and she clung desperately to him, matching each hard, driving thrust, he knew he would never experience these unique sensations with another woman. He wished it weren't so, needed it *not* to be so, but that was the one undeniable truth that he knew would haunt him forever.

Why do you risk so much for her, because of her? In essence that was the question Wild Hawk had asked. The answer tormented Judd as he held onto Kat, sharing a need that had grown so ardent and intense that he couldn't tell where her desire for him ended and his passion for her began. They were as one— not two halves of a whole, but one breathing, moving entity that soared, spiraled and skyrocketed through a world of kaleidoscopic sensations.

Judd tensed when he felt pleasure burgeoning out of control. He didn't want the moment to end. *Too soon, always too soon. Never enough, never enough time to experience the magical feelings that converged and exploded . . .*

And then need rippled through him and he shuddered against her, wishing this unprecedented kind of pleasure could go on forever, not sizzle and devour him in one brief moment.

He felt Kat hugging him tightly to her, felt the sweet tremors of passion's aftershocks vibrating through her and into him. He held onto her for a long moment, wishing reality wouldn't return. He didn't want to face the lingering doubts and suspicions surrounding her. He wanted these moments of utter peace that he had discovered only with Kat.

Judd very nearly came undone again when Kat tipped back her head, stared deep into his eyes, then kissed him with astonishing tenderness. He wondered if she, like he, was reluctant to speak and break the mystical spell they created when they were in each other's arms. They both knew it was time to leave their secluded paradise, but they lingered a moment longer, then two, sharing one last kiss.

Ever so gradually Judd eased away, then submerged and swam back to the stone that led up to the waterfall. He waited until Kat waded ashore before he turned his back to her so she couldn't catch a glimpse of his scars in the moonlight. Hurriedly, he gathered his clothes and dressed. When he emerged from the trees, Kat awaited him.

Without a word he linked his fingers with hers and led the

way to the horses. Judd didn't want to spoil the companionable silence, didn't want to put any distance between the memory of their lovemaking in the pool. He wanted to savor those inexpressible sensations throughout the long ride that lay ahead of him. It was as if the mention of their sensuous interlude would tarnish the magic of that moment. To Judd, that memory was more precious than the pouch of priceless jewels.

Several hours later, Judd asked himself if he would allow this fierce, obsessive need for Kat to overshadow his suspicions. For the first time in his life he understood how a man could become a fool for a woman, blinded by his desire for her, wanting to ignore everything except these feelings she aroused in him.

Wanting a woman to absolute obsession could become a man's fatal downfall, he reminded himself. History was teeming with tales of such disaster.

Judd had hours to mull over all those troubled thoughts that chased each other around in his mind. It was a long ride to Tascosa.

CHAPTER FIFTEEN

Kat smiled appreciatively as she and Judd halted on the hillside overlooking a lush grass and cottonwood tree-filled valley. Several bubbling springs and creeks converged into the Canadian River. On its banks stood a thriving community that bustled with activity.

The journey from the shelter of Palo Duro Canyon had been uneventful. Judd had pointed out a group of ragtag riders and stopped in a canopy of cedar trees until the men rode past. According to Judd, they were most likely rustlers who preyed on the ranchers who had recently established homesteads in west Texas.

"Tascosa," Judd announced as he pointed toward the peaceful-looking valley. "It is one of only two towns in the Panhandle. Sweetwater lies more than a hundred miles east." He glanced at her momentarily. "I thought you might appreciate sleeping on a real bed. And," he added casually, "a stage line has recently been set up between Tascosa and Sweetwater and now extends all the way to Las Vegas, New Mexico. You might prefer to buy a ticket on the stage rather than continuing your journey on horseback. The stage will cut your travel time in more than half. Your choice, Diamond."

Disappointment coursed through Kat. She had known that she and Judd would part company eventually. He was giving her a choice as to when and where she would go her own way. From the sound of his voice, it made him no difference to him. That hurt, because he had made such a marked difference in her life. Although she had fought valiantly against her tender feelings for him, the fact was that she *liked* him, enjoyed his company.

Lingering memories of their two nights of splendor stole through Kat. She would never know such pleasure again, she realized. As exasperating as Judd Lassiter could be occasionally, and though he didn't trust her, she knew that no other man could ever measure up to his remarkable standards.

You came west to find your freedom and independence, she reminded herself resolutely. *You have dreamed of this for years. Be content with it and don't ask for more. Judd Lassiter isn't going to become a permanent part of your life. You have always known that, so you better get used to the idea unless you want to leave here with a broken heart that never mends.*

"There's a hotel on the north side of the river," Judd said as he nudged Horse downhill. "I'll rent you a room."

"What about you?" she asked, trying to prevent disappointment from seeping into her voice.

"I'll camp out by one of the springs. I need to scout the area while I'm here."

"Why?"

Judd shrugged impossibly broad shoulders. "Marshal Winslow gave me bench warrants for three men who have robbed stages, rustled cattle and posed as Comanche raiders while committing several murders. I suspect"—actually he knew it for a fact, but he didn't mention that to Kat—"that the Comanches who took you captive mistook you and your companions for the outlaws they were trying to track down. Comanches don't take kindly to vicious white men assuming disguises to bring more trouble to their tribe."

"And you think those three men might be in this area?"

He nodded. "Possibly. Tascosa is a favorite haunt for renegades, because of the lack of law officials and military personnel in the area. Cattle can be rustled and sold to cattle drives headed two hundred miles north to Dodge City.''

Kat was pretty certain this was Judd's way of telling her that he had tired of playing guide and protector, that he preferred for her to catch the stage to New Mexico so he could track down the criminals. Hurt and disappointed though she was, Kat squared her shoulders and elevated her chin. ''I'll check on the stage schedule after I freshen up in my hotel room.''

Judd glanced sideways, noting her determination in the set of her shoulders and the expression on her face. It was just as he'd suspected all along. Kat was ready to divvy up the jewels and hightail it to Santa Fe by stage. He had served his purpose by getting her to a place where she could make stage connections.

Although the notice requesting information about Kat Diamond and her connection with J.P. Trumball's death was still burning a hole in Judd's pocket, he had decided to ignore it. No one in Tascosa would know about J.P. Trumball's death in The Flats, so Kat was safe in showing her face. She could step back into civilized society—or as close to civilized as society could come in the raucous west Texas town—without inviting trouble. There was no city marshal making rounds on the streets, only the sheriff who occasionally stopped by for a few days.

''Where will you be camped . . . in case I need to speak with you?'' Kat asked neutrally.

Judd directed her attention northeast. ''One of the springs that feeds the river is just beyond that hill. The road that winds north to Dodge City is just west of the springs. You'll find my camp without any trouble.''

In silence they forded the shallows of the Canadian River, then rode down Main Street. Kat dismounted when Judd gestured toward the small hotel above a mercantile shop.

''Well, Panther, aren't you a sight for sore eyes!''

Kat followed Judd inside to see a hefty female beaming at him in delight. The middle-aged woman wore a crisp calico dress that billowed around her broad hips. Her graying hair was pinned atop her head.

''Samuel! Come out here and see who has finally showed up!'' Gracie Hampton called out.

A tall, lean merchant appeared from the back storeroom. He hurried over to pump Judd's hand. "Where have you been all these months, my friend? You're the closest thing this town has to law and order, and we could have used you more than once, I tell you for sure." His wide grin displayed buck teeth. "Of course, we have been using the threat of your name and reputation to keep some of the locals from misbehaving," Samuel Hampton said, then winked wryly. "You might want to have a word or two with those rascals, just so they won't think Gracie and I were blowing hot air."

Judd returned the welcoming smile. "My pleasure, Samuel. I'll see to it as soon as I have the little lady settled into your best room."

Gracie and Samuel glanced around Judd's broad shoulders simultaneously. Kat pulled off her hat, letting the tangled curls stream down her back. She gave the two wide-eyed merchants her best smile.

"Land o' Goshen! What a pretty thing she is." Gracie scurried over to give Kat a hug. "It's always nice to have another woman in town. Aren't that many of us yet, but the town is growing by leaps and bounds. We're having a fandango in the street tonight, in fact." She smiled proudly as she glanced at her husband. "It was Samuel's idea for a social get-together. The fiddlers and piano players from the saloons have agreed to provide music."

"What are you celebrating?" Judd asked curiously.

"Our application for a post office has recently been approved," Samuel informed him. "That means more stage line connections to carry more travelers and mail. It will bring more business to our community."

Samuel gestured toward Kat. "You bring your lady to the fandango tonight, Panther. You'll both enjoy it."

"Actually, I'm not his—" Kat tried to explain, but Gracie was shepherding Judd into the storeroom, yammering a mile a minute.

"Gracie hovers over Panther whenever he shows up," Samuel explained, smiling fondly. "We owe Panther our lives."

"There seems to be a lot of that going around," Kat murmured.

She imagined there were dozens of citizens in Texas who were alive and safe because Panther carried out his dangerous profession exceedingly well.

"Panther happened by when two hooligans surprised us while we were locking up the storeroom for the night. They held us at gunpoint and demanded supplies for their quick getaway. They were the two men who had killed a gambler over a poker game in one of the saloons and stole the winnings," he added. "Gracie and I were staring death in the face when Panther just showed up out of nowhere.

"When he snarled at those desperadoes ... well, I guess the name Panther suits him perfectly," Samuel said, nodding pensively. "It was the strangest thing I ever did see, believe you me. One minute he wasn't there and then he was hardly more than a shadow, his eyes reflecting the light like his namesake."

Kat was well aware of Panther's phenomenal feats. She had stared into those mystical eyes on several occasions and had become entranced by them.

"He had a bullwhip in one hand and his dagger in the other and he made short work of the outlaws before they could take me and Gracie hostage against him. Turned out that Panther had been tracking those drunken scoundrels for two weeks and he caught up with them in time to spare me and Gracie a bad end."

Samuel grinned. "Since then, we've told the tale a hundred times, so any desperado who happens into town knows that Panther is a good friend of ours. The tale keeps most folks toeing the line. We haven't had much trouble since, but Tascosa is starting to attract too many of the kind of men we prefer not to have around."

He pointed out the store window toward a nearby hillside. "We buried the ne'er-do-wells that came after me and Gracie up on Boot Hill. We save the best room in the hotel for Panther, in case he wants to make use of it. He's got a special fondness for baths, you know. We sent off for the biggest brass tub we could find. He doesn't know it's here,'' he murmured confidentially.

Kat nearly salivated at the thought of a spacious tub and bubble bath, but she decided she should be the one who camped at the springs so Judd could enjoy the special gift his grateful friends purchased for him.

While Samuel filled in Panther's name in capital letters on the hotel register, Kat glanced around the well-stocked shop. The place bespoke of neatness and meticulous organization. This store made the supply shop in The Flats look like a shack littered with unorganized heaps of goods.

Store-bought dresses, men's jackets and trousers hung on a corner rack. Cedar shelves, neatly arranged with everything from ammunition to flour, sugar, iron kettles and feed sacks lined the building. Kat's gaze lingered on a frilly yellow gown and she smiled whimsically at it.

Judd had never seen her in a dress, only baggy men's clothes and cloddish boots, she reminded herself. Not that it mattered, she supposed. If he wasn't all that intrigued by who she was on the inside, what difference did it make how she looked on the outside? But still . . .

"Something catch your eye, missy?" Samuel asked as he handed her the room key.

"I was admiring a yellow gown that matches a yellow rose someone once gave me," she murmured, distracted. "But I'm afraid I'm short on funds at the moment, so I will have to pass—"

"I will not hear another word about it!" Gracie's voice wafted in from the storeroom. "You take these like I told you to and don't be trying to talk me out of it, you rascal. You can't put a price on Samuel's and my life. We can be generous if we've a mind to, so skedaddle before you make me lose my temper with you!"

Curiously, Kat watched Judd reappear carrying a fashionable pair of trousers, vest, crisp white linen shirt and jacket. Atop the stack was a special blend of grain for Horse.

Samuel grinned at Judd's scowl. "We sent all the way to Chicago for those fancy trappings."

"Don't know where you and Gracie got the idea I needed to look civilized," Judd grumbled, eyeing the garments warily. "You thinking I might need these for my own funeral or something?"

"Certainly not! But a man needs a respectable set of Sunday-go-to-meeting clothes," Gracie said behind him. "And next time we send off for something special for you, I don't want to hear all that grumbling about us spending our hard-earned money on you. If we would have had a son, we would have wanted him to be just like you. But we don't, so we have decided to adopt you and that is that!"

"Thank you," Judd said awkwardly. He wasn't accustomed to being treated like family. Most folks took a wide berth around him and didn't glance in his direction unless they had to. But the Hamptons welcomed him with open arms after he had saved them from disaster.

He glanced at Kat and wondered if she knew what a caring family was like. From what she had told him about her life in Louisiana, he doubted she had experienced the close-knit ties of family, either.

He stared at the clothes in his arms, then at the rack of dresses. Maybe he would get Kat a going-away present. She didn't have proper attire for dining at the restaurant or boarding the stage. He knew she didn't have much money at her disposal—none that he knew about—only a pouch of jewels that no one in Tascosa could afford to buy.

Steal, yes. Buy, definitely not.

"Why don't you go up to your room and get settled?" Judd suggested to Kat. "I need to speak with Samuel and Gracie about the bench warrants I'm carrying."

Kat nodded, then started up the steps, feeling like an outsider. She always had been, even in her own home, she reminded herself. Her mother's ill health had caused her to become self-absorbed. Her father's staid philosophy on raising an unwanted daughter had made him seem more of a stranger than family. Things had gotten worse when Monica married J.P. The man had dreamed up a thousand reasons why Kat should go to her room so she wouldn't be under his feet.

No doubt, Judd was tired of Kat's company and wanted to spend time with his friends. As always, she was inconveniently underfoot.

"I'll send up our assistant with water for a bath," Gracie called to her. "First door on the right."

When Kat disappeared from sight, Judd set aside the stack of clothes and ambled toward the rack of dresses. He didn't have the slightest idea what style or color would appeal to Kat. He could visualize her in each and every gown, with that wild mane of curly hair cascading down her back like a river of fire. She would look bewitching in ribbons, ruffles and lace. She was born to feminine clothes and luxury.

Judd remembered the hubbub Breezy Malone claimed Kat had caused the day she stepped off the stage in The Flats. According to Breezy, everything in breeches was panting after her. Kat Diamond would undoubtedly draw the same attention from the male population in Tascosa.

"Your lady had her eye on that yellow gown," Samuel pointed out. "She said she couldn't afford a dress, but she was sure looking wistfully at that one."

Judd removed the dress from the rack and held it up to gauge the size, then saw the plunging neckline and gulped. Kat would definitely need a bodyguard—or a sawed-off shotgun—to hold men at bay if she appeared in public in this seductive creation.

"It should fit her perfectly," Gracie piped up. "Would you like me to select the proper undergarments to go with it?"

What the hell? thought Judd. Tonight would be the last evening he spent with Kat. She would be on her way to Santa Fe and he would resume his duties as a bounty hunter. With new stage lines frequenting Tascosa, the thieves he had been sent to track down could have set up camp nearby to prey on travelers and ranchers.

"Pick out everything the little lady will need to look proper," Judd requested. "Then wrap them up." Judd dug several bank notes from his pocket. "This should cover the expenses."

Gracie's eyes popped. "You rascal, you know that's more than plenty!"

Judd gave her The Look, and she shifted uneasily.

"This is the price I've decided that all this feminine paraphernalia is worth." He then threw Gracie's words back at her. "I'll not hear another word about it and that is that!"

While Gracie walked off, snickering, Judd turned his attention to Samuel, then drew out the Wanted posters he carried. "Have you seen any of these three men around town recently?"

Samuel took his wire-rimmed spectacles from his shirt pocket and studied the three sketches carefully. "A rough-looking bunch," he murmured, then held up the first sketch to the light. "This one." He pointed to the drawing of Crazy Ben Corothers. "Seems to me that he was in here a couple of days ago. Bought some trail rations and lots of ammunition, as I recall. Paid in big bank notes like you carry."

"I'm not surprised. He and his cohorts have been hitting stage lines from San Antonio to Fort Griffin. They killed a driver and wounded two others. They also murdered a rancher and his wife. According to Marshal Winslow, this wild bunch can smell money when too much of it is stacked in the same place."

"This one." Samuel tapped his finger on the sketch of Arkansas Riley. "I think I might have seen him exiting from the saloon last night when I was on my way home from the town meeting. We're trying to hire a marshal to keep a lid on our town. You want the job?"

"No, thanks," Judd replied.

"I was afraid you'd say that, but I was told to ask the next time I saw you." Samuel turned his attention back to the poster. "Riley's woolly mustache and square face look familiar. If I recall correctly, he is a stout, burly brute with an exceptionally foul mouth."

Samuel carefully appraised the third drawing. "Can't say that Rowdy Jack's face looks familiar at all. If he has been in town, I haven't run across him. You might check with Robert Wilson at the restaurant or Cape Mullin in the saloon. They see their fair share of bad hombres on a daily basis. Don't blame Cape for keeping two loaded shotguns under his bar. Some cowboys who were fired from a trail drive last month came in to drown their frustration and tried to shoot Cape's place all to hell. He ran them out of his saloon and put buckshot in their sorry butts.

"Wouldn't be surprised if that bunch of scoundrels aren't the cause of the cattle rustling that's been going on around here lately," Samuel continued. "For sure, those cowboys know how to cut cattle from a herd. Probably gathering their own stolen livestock to drive to the railhead in Dodge City."

With a nod of thanks, Judd pivoted toward the steps. From the sound of things, he wouldn't have far to look to find thieves preying on the stage and ranchers. The criminal element was entrenching itself in this isolated town in the Texas Panhandle.

Good, thought Judd. He was going to need plenty of time-consuming distractions after Kat boarded the stage and rode out of his life forever. Her new life awaited her in Santa Fe, but he wasn't a part of her future. They had spent too much time in each other's pockets.

Hell, it had gotten to the point that he was too aware of her needs, her moods. He couldn't honestly say he trusted her completely, but he sure had gotten used to having her around.

Too bad he hadn't gotten over wanting her until hell wouldn't have it. Two magical nights hadn't been enough to get her out of his system. He hoped when Kat was out of sight she would be out of mind. Maybe he wouldn't be so distracted as to get himself shot while lollygagging about her.

Damn, he was going to miss those radiant smiles, miss the way she got all sentimental when she viewed panoramic scenery in west Texas. Miss the feel of her luscious body responding instantaneously and making him feel like the greatest lover the world had ever known . . .

Judd's thoughts scattered when Gracie dropped the wrapped packages atop his stack of clothes. When she eyed him perceptively, Judd did something he rarely did. He blushed.

"Go on now," she whispered, smiling wryly at him. "Give the presents to your lovely lady. She is a very lucky woman."

Judd didn't explain that Kat wasn't exactly his lady and that Kat would be taking the first stage west—without him. The forbidden memories of the passion they had shared would be just that—memories in a place out of time, a time when a man and woman who had nothing in common found unexpected pleasure in each other's arms.

He repeated that thought, over and over, on his way upstairs. Kat wanted her freedom to begin a new life in the West. She would adapt to Western culture, which was more tolerant of women of independence. He had nothing to offer her—except endless hours on horseback, wide-open space without comforts and luxuries. She would find a man who could offer her a way of life like the one she had left behind in Baton Rouge . . .

The thought stung like a bumblebee. Judd decided not to think about the man who would eventually replace him, the one who would take Kat to bed and wake up to the sight of her radiant smiles every day of his life.

Scowling, Judd hurled aside the thought and wheeled to the right when he reached the top of the steps. He shouldered his way into the room without knocking, then skidded to a halt.

There, in a corner of the spacious room stood the grandest bathtub he had ever seen. As much as he appreciated the over-size tub, it was the feminine vision of beauty—surrounded with bubbles, smiling in pure pleasure—that stole the breath right out of his lungs.

CHAPTER SIXTEEN

Kat smiled guiltily when Judd barreled through the door, then she sank deep in the fragrant bubbles. "Samuel told me that he and Gracie had ordered the marvelous tub for you. You should have been the first to use it, but it looked so inviting ... What are you doing?"

Kat's eyes rounded when Judd tossed his stack of packages on the bed and peeled off his shirt on his way across the room. He reached down to unfasten his doehide breeches, then tugged off his moccasins. It appeared that he wanted to make use of the oversize tub and he had no intention of waiting to enjoy the surprise gift from the Hamptons.

"If you'll give me a minute, I'll—" Her voice dried up when Judd stood before her in all his masculine splendor and glory, fully aroused. Like a tongue-tied idiot, Kat sat there staring at his bronzed, brawny body.

"I'll admit the sight of this brass tub is inviting, but it wouldn't be half as inviting without you in it," he said huskily.

To Kat's startled amazement, he slid in behind her. His hands glided over her flesh in such a gentle caress that Kat forgot to breathe, forgot how long she had waited to enjoy the privacy of a bath in a real tub. When Judd buried his head in the tangle of curls she had piled atop her head, then brushed his lips over her bare shoulder, she melted like butter in a skillet. Not only did she forget her vow to keep her mind off this sensual wild man, but she couldn't even remember why she had made the pact with herself. It was impossible to think when his hands and lips were skimming over her flesh, eliciting warm, sizzling responses.

When his fingertips plucked at her taut nipples, Kat sighed out his name. She arched helplessly toward his caresses as the room spun in a dizzying whir. When he touched her so gently, she was overcome by so many erotic sensations and needy desires that she could think of not one good reason why she should deny herself this one last memory of him.

She was living only for the moment, savoring every delicious pleasure, absorbing the masculine scent and feel of his sinewy body brushing intimately against hers. His arms were around her, supporting her. His bent legs were pressed against hers, surrounding her with his power and strength.

She moaned softly, raggedly, as his hand glided down her belly to trace the sensitive flesh of her inner thighs. Kat felt herself burning with fervent need when his fingers swept closer to the knot of heat coiling inside her. When he eased her legs farther apart to grant himself access to her womanly softness, Kat held her breath in erotic anticipation, then gasped when he caressed her with one fingertip, then two.

When Kat tipped her head back and whispered his name on a broken cry of pleasure, Judd pressed his lips to the pulsating column of her throat and watched her luscious body tremble in response to his intimate caresses. He rolled her nipple between his thumb and forefinger, at the same moment that he dipped his finger deeper into her soft, moist heat. He felt her shimmering around his hand, calling to him in secret caresses.

Fascinated, he watched her as he caressed her again and again, felt her burning his fingertip like liquid lightning as she all but came apart in his arms. He marveled at the intense pleasure that roiled in him while he pleasured her, as if each sensation she experienced was his own.

"Stop . . ." Kat whimpered, then groaned when he sent her spiraling out of control once again.

"Die for me," he murmured against her ear. "You burn me alive when you respond so wildly in my arms. Did you know that, Kat? Again . . ."

"No—" Kat's protest evaporated when his thumb brushed over the nub of passion and his fingertips filled her, spread her, teased and caressed her. The little death of which he spoke claimed her once again and she convulsed around his fingertips, cried out his name on ragged whispers.

His right hand splayed from one aching nipple to the other, then back again, making her arch from the water, pressing shamelessly against both skillful hands.

"Again," he rasped. Fascinated, he watched her writhe, then melt with the rush of pleasure he had called from her.

"No . . . please . . ." she said brokenly. "I don't want to die again without you, Panther. It's you I need. Please . . ."

He must have gone a little mad, he decided as he lifted and turned Kat around to face him. The tub was oversize, but it wasn't nearly large enough to accommodate what she wanted— what he craved, right here, right now, this very second. But something as insignificant as lack of space didn't concern Judd when Kat was begging him to bury himself inside her, to feel the flame of her desire burning him, fusing them until they were one shimmering essence.

Kat's luminous green eyes locked with his as he drew her down upon him. Her lips parted in the same hot invitation her body offered him as he took possession.

Judd groaned low in his throat, frustrated by the lack of space. He was so hard and aching that he was half blind with desire. He gently turned her so that she was beneath him, then draped her legs over the edge of the tub so he could drive himself home. He heard her gasp as he came to her with more desperation and impatience than he'd intended.

It was always like that with Kat, he realized. Each time with her was like the first time, each sensation bursting into another, leaving him marveling at the intensity of pleasure she drew from him.

Water and bubbles slopped from the tub and dribbled through the cracks in the floorboards. Judd braced his elbows on the side of the shiny brass tub and plunged deeper, harder, faster, driven by needs so profound and intense that nothing in life seemed as important as satisfying her, satisfying himself.

She was his pleasure, he realized suddenly, not the act itself, but Kat.

Again as before, Judd could distinguish no division line between his aching need and her burning desire. They were like some sort of chemical reaction that exploded when mixed together. Like bombs bursting, he felt as if he had been catapulted into the sun, clutching Kat in his arms and waiting to shatter in a million pieces.

Judd felt immeasurable passion racing through him. His arms trembled, his body tensed, awaiting that moment when need spilled from him like a volcanic eruption. Sensation after indescribable sensation pelted him, seared him. He arched helplessly against Kat, shuddered one last time, then collapsed.

His forehead rested against hers and he looked down at their joined bodies that were surrounded by only half as many bubbles and half the original amount of water. He was pretty sure the pools of water disappearing from the floor were trickling from the overhead beams in the storeroom below them. The Hamptons would know exactly how he had christened the tub they had generously purchased for him. There would be no private secrets here at Hampton Hotel.

That being the case, Judd decided to make full use of the room he had rented for Kat. Satisfied, yet still hungry for her, he levered up to his feet, then drew her up beside him. Her gaze never left his as he scooped her up and carried her to the bed.

When he placed her on her back and lifted her legs to straddle his shoulders, Kat stared uncomprehendingly at him.

"I want all of you, in every way I can have you," he whispered.

And then he parted her gently with his fingertips and tasted her with the tenderest, most intimate kiss. Her nails raked over his shoulders like claws, anchoring herself to him as he made love to her with his hands and lips and whisper of breath. She wept for him and he tasted her passion. She clenched around his hand, then quivered in uninhibited abandon. Her nails dug deeper into his shoulders, as if steadying herself against the stormtide of sensations rushing over her.

Judd smiled against her softest flesh as he caressed her with tongue and fingertips. The more pleasure he gave to her, the harder she clung to him. He knew she would leave her mark on his shoulders, but he welcomed the souvenirs of a time when he had brought Kat to the towering height of desire and held her suspended in climactic ecstasy.

He had her down to begging breathlessly, hoarsely. She whispered to him to fill the empty ache he called from her. He trembled with her as she collapsed in shuddering spasms, then he covered her to give her all that she asked, all that he ached for.

With each penetrating thrust and answering response, Judd felt the silken chains encircling him, binding him tighter to her, forging him to her for all eternity. He felt the ineffable need boiling inside him, a need that *she* had created and only *she* could satisfy.

He suddenly realized that it didn't matter if she left her mark on his shoulders, because the passion she summoned from him marked every fiber of his being. She had written her name all over him in places that no one could touch or see. She had branded him to the very core.

Judd gritted his teeth when he felt his control sliding away from him. He could feel the change overcoming him—the kind Kat wouldn't understand if she noticed. He battled like hell to restrain himself from slipping into the deepest reaches where mind and body and practiced discipline combined to create the legend he had become.

"No," Judd whispered hoarsely. But it was too late. He was buried in the throes of ardent passion, helpless to stop what he had learned to do with ease during those moments when desperate situations demanded extreme measures.

And then inexpressible desire overtook him, and he prayed Kat wouldn't open her eyes and peer up at him. Not yet, not when he couldn't control what was happening to him. He had allowed her to see the vulnerability she called from him, but he was afraid for her to witness what he could become.

Passion bubbled like a wellspring, pouring over him, pacifying him, draining his energy and strength. Judd came back into himself by breathing deeply, focusing absolute concentration.

He lifted his head and sighed in relief when he noticed Kat's eyes were still closed and she was smiling dreamily. What Kat Diamond did to him when she gave herself up so generously to the fiery needs they ignited in each other was, quite simply, quite accurately, otherworldly.

Damn, that was close, thought Judd. He hoped like hell that he would have Kat on a stage headed west before some catastrophic event forced him to explain things about himself that she would never understand. She would run away screaming in terror, as others before her had.

His uneasy thoughts scattered when Kat opened those entrancing eyes and smiled at him. She didn't know what had almost happened. She hadn't seen.

Hallelujah!

''I l—'' Kat compressed her lips and swallowed as she stared up at the ruggedly handsome face surrounded with raven-black hair, embedded with amber-green eyes so intense that they appeared gold in the light filtering through the window.

Her boggled brain had nearly slipped up and put dangerous words on her tongue. Worse, she had almost said them aloud.

The damnable truth was that what Kat feared might happen had happened. She had fallen in love with this incredible man. No matter how long and hard she tried to deny it, she couldn't ignore the truth. He had turned her soul inside out and stolen her heart. She would take her secret with her when she left Tascosa. He would never know that she had fallen prey to the tenderest, most consuming emotions that she previously hadn't believed existed—emotions *he* still didn't believe existed.

''I love your new bathtub and the soft feather bed,'' Kat said instead, then reached up to trace the marks she had left on his shoulder. She blushed as she wiped away the trail of blood and remembered how and why the marks had gotten there. "Sorry about that."

"I've had worse and enjoyed it far less," he said, grinning at her.

Judd eased away. Her comment reminded him not to turn his back, for fear she would see what he had taken great care to conceal from her. He came quickly to his feet and grabbed the shirt and breeches that were strewn on the floor.

Unfortunately, he forgot about the mirror that hung over the washstand behind him. He had unintentionally presented the reflection of his back in the mirror.

Kat's eyes widened in alarm as she stared at the deep scars that raked across the rippling muscles of his back. "Panther? My God, what happened to you?"

He muttered several expletives. Before he could yank the buckskin shirt in place, Kat was on her feet, rushing forward to inspect the crisscross scars.

"You were mauled!" she realized and said so. "When did this happen? How did this happen?"

Judd pulled his shirt into place and stepped into his breeches. "Doesn't matter how or when." He glanced discreetly at her, expecting to see her repulsion. Puzzled, he stared harder, wondering if that was compassion he had seen in her eyes.

"It must have mattered at the time," Kat insisted as she scooped up the towel to cover herself. "It must have hurt terribly."

Judd was touched by her concern, even while he was surprised by it. She was perfection, every curvaceous inch of her. He had been marked for life—literally and figuratively. This was yet another difference between them, he reminded himself. Kat deserved a man as perfect and normal as she was.

"Tell me what happened," Kat insisted.

"What difference does it make?" Judd muttered. "I survived an initiation that was more difficult than most. I healed, life went on, and I learned never to let danger sneak up on my blind side."

His refusal to confide in her told the grim truth. To Judd, she was the place he came to to ease physical needs. He didn't trust her or care enough to share his past with her—pleasant or unpleasant.

Judd Lassiter wasn't the kind of man who needed a shoulder to cry on occasionally, because nothing fazed him, nothing got to him. He had taken what he wanted from her when he came upstairs. Now that the passionate interlude was over, he became distant and remote.

The tryst was over. His male body was appeased. Business went on as usual.

Kat frowned when she suddenly recalled what he had said. *Some initiations are more difficult than others.* She stared speculatively at him, wondering . . .

"I brought you something," Judd said, jolting her from her ponderous thoughts.

He could have brought her a pouch of jewels twice the size of the ones she had and she wouldn't have cared. What she cared about was the fact that he had shut her out, wouldn't confide in her.

When Judd extended the first package, Kat stared at it as if it were a poisonous snake. "What is that?"

"Open it and find out," he ordered more gruffly than he'd intended. He wanted to get past her probing questions about his scars, questions he couldn't bring himself to answer. He hoped the gift would soothe her, but she was reluctant to accept what he offered. "Here, Diamond, take it."

When she refused the package, Judd opened it for her, then held the yellow gown to his chest and awaited her reaction.

Her gaze narrowed suspiciously. That was not the reaction he'd anticipated. Samuel had told him that Kat favored this fancy yellow dress with all the bells and whistles and plunging neckline that would draw too damn much attention to her breasts. What more could a woman possibly want?

"Why did you buy that for me?" she wanted to know.

"You're welcome," he replied. "It's exceptionally pretty, if you ask me. But of course you didn't, did you? You didn't even bother to say thank you."

"Why?" she persisted, staring unblinkingly at him.

"Does it matter?" he asked in exasperation.

Obviously it did—for reasons he failed to comprehend—because her face flushed with irritation and she glared flying arrows at him.

"Is this your way of repaying me for that tryst in the cave, in the pool, in the tub and then on the bed?" she snapped furiously. "You think I can be bought like the harlots who entertain you when you itch to scratch your lusty needs?"

Whoa! Judd winced as he watched her temper boil over. He hadn't expected Kat to take the gift the wrong way. But she damned sure had. She stood there in her towel, indignation radiating from her like heat from a potbellied stove.

"Well," she hissed like a disturbed cat. "Was that the reason, Lassiter? Is this your way of saying thanks for the roll in the hay and now that you're on your way to New Mexico—at long last—good riddance to you?"

"No, damn it, that isn't what this dress is saying," Judd muttered at her.

"Then what the hell does this dress say?" she shot back.

Judd took a deep breath, shifted awkwardly and blurted out. "It says I wanted to see you dressed up like the lady you are, not the ragamuffin I dragged through the wilderness and imposed one hardship after another on while I taught you to survive the kind of life I lead. It says you deserve better than I gave you. It says you belong in the lap of luxury, surrounded by the finest things in life, not in a saddle roaming across the unforgiving frontier."

He made a stabbing gesture with his free hand, directing her attention to the other packages that he had dropped in his haste to join her in the tub. "And all those frilly undergarments and the satin slippers repeat what this dress is trying to say. You are a beautiful woman who deserves beautiful things.

"And damn it, Kat, you are not being compensated for . . . er . . . sexual favors, or however the hell you put it," he fumbled ahead awkwardly. "What happened between us happened because you . . . because I . . . Oh hell, when I look at you I want you in the worst way, and the dedicated self-discipline I've practiced since I can't remember when goes up in smoke . . . . Now, what the hell did I say wrong? Why are you crying?"

Kat shook her head, her throat too clogged with emotion to speak. Tears bubbled down her cheeks. She loved this exasperating man so much it hurt. He had impulsively purchased a dress with all its feminine trimmings because he saw it and thought of her, thought of all the necessities and luxuries she had done without while journeying west. She cried because he was going to let her go so she could have her precious freedom that didn't seem so precious anymore. She cried because her heart was breaking and that frilly yellow dress didn't mean half as much to her as the knowledge that he wanted her to have it—just because.

"I'll take it back if you'll just stop crying," Judd promised.

"No. I love it."

"But I thought you said—"

She snatched the gown away from him, reached up on tiptoe and kissed him. "Never mind what I said. I do love the dress. It caught my eye the moment I saw it . . . because it reminded me of the yellow rose you gave me. But you don't have to pay for it. I'll make up the difference when we split up the jewels."

"No, absolutely not," Judd declared firmly. "It was meant as a gift from me to you, not as another expense for this assignment. That's two different balls of wax. You're going to dress in these citified clothes and I'm going to get gussied up in that fancy suit Gracie decided I should have and we're going to dine and dance."

When he realized he was spouting orders at her, he smiled apologetically. "Maybe I better rephrase that before you get all bent out of shape again."

He struck a sophisticated pose, bowed elegantly, then took her hand to kiss her wrist. "I respectfully request the pleasure of your company this evening, Miss Diamond. I shall call for you at seven, if that meets with your approval."

Kat felt her eyes fill with tears again. Judd Lassiter could play the elegant gentleman even while he stood there in rugged buckskin. He was a man of all times, all places, all seasons under the sun, and she loved him with an intensity that put her fragile emotions in turmoil.

"Well, damn, Kat. Don't cry again," he groaned miserably.

''We waded through hell together to get here, and the fact is that I made hell worse for you, just to see what you were made of. You met every challenge with grit and gumption. After all we've been through, you're crying over a few words, as if you have spigots in your eyes.''

The compliment, offered by a man so competent and difficult to impress, really got to Kat. She had longed to earn his respect and admiration since she'd first met him. And now that she had, she was so pleased and relieved that she cried even harder.

''What did I say wrong this time? I'm only trying to act civilized, even though we both know I'm the farthest thing from it. Truth be told, you can't even imagine how upset you would be if you knew what I bec—''

Judd whirled away before he shoved both bare feet in his big mouth. ''I'll be back after I make camp and ask around town about the desperadoes I'm supposed to track down. Check on the stage ticket this afternoon, and please stop crying. Those tears of yours are killing me, damn it!''

When the door banged shut behind him, Kat plunked down on the bed and had herself a proper cry—bawled like a baby was closer to the mark. Why had she fallen in love with Judd, only to lose him, only to remember him in tormentingly sweet memories? Why hadn't she kept her heart out of this bargain? How was she going to live without having him when he was no longer within touching distance?

Resolutely, Kat drew herself up from her slouch on the bed and inhaled a cathartic breath. She was not going to sit here dwelling on tomorrow's misery. She would be sinking into the quagmire of loneliness soon enough as it was. She had stage schedules to check and a telegram to send to Louisiana. Sitting here blubbering would accomplish nothing!

CHAPTER SEVENTEEN

"Goodness gracious!" Gracie Hampton clasped her hands together in delight when Kat appeared at the head of the staircase wearing the yellow gown Judd had given her. "You look wonderful, Katherine!"

Kat descended the steps feeling self-conscious because she had grown accustomed to dressing in men's clothes that allowed freedom of movement, and because so many eyes suddenly homed in on her. Men from every walk of life filled the mercantile store to overflowing. Every one of them turned in synchronized rhythm when Gracie called attention to Kat.

The vivid yellow gown was designed to reveal more bosom than Kat had noticed when she saw it hanging on the rack—but she was certainly aware of it now! Kat felt the urge to cover herself because of the intense male stares, but she knew that would only call more attention to the sharply cut décolletage. There was nothing Kat could do but plunge ahead, with dignity and poise, and fight down her blush.

With head held high, Kat descended in a swish of petticoats—which seemed to gain her even more attention from the cluster of leering men. If stares left fingerprints, Kat swore she would have more smudges than a glass door!

Again, Kat wished for the loose-fitting men's clothes she had grown accustomed to. She had changed so drastically since leaving Baton Rouge that she felt as if she were wearing someone else's skin, someone else's frilly, impractical clothing.

"I wonder if you could direct me to the telegraph office," Kat requested of Gracie.

"I'll hand deliver you there myself, ma'am," Tully Pitt volunteered eagerly.

Kat glanced over her shoulder to see a rugged-looking, bow-legged cowboy approaching. He swept off his straw hat and bobbed his head in silent greeting, clasped his hand around her forearm, then propelled her toward the door. Kat decided she may as well get used to the touch of other men because, starting tomorrow, longing for Judd Lassiter's touch would be unproductive torment.

"I'll go along with you, Tully. I'm headed that way myself."

Kat felt another hand slide around her right arm. To her surprise, two more men fell into step behind her. Amazing how helpless the male population thought she was, just because she had donned a dress. Damnation, this scene she had unintentionally caused was every bit as bad as the day she'd stepped off the stagecoach in The Flats. She did not need to be reminded how it felt to be fawned over and ogled.

She supposed there were some women who basked in effusive attention.

Kat Diamond was not one of them.

She sighed inwardly as the size of the entourage increased as she made her way down the street. She was receiving so much rapt attention that it was laughable. These men were nothing like Judd, she noted. He treated her as an equal, not some royal princess. All this gushing attention offended her, and she wished for the simple pleasure of making her way down the street all by herself.

This had to stop, Kat decided. She was not going to tramp around town like this all afternoon. She felt ridiculous!

"Ah, this must be the place," Kat said, halting beneath the sign that hung above the telegraph office. "Thank you for your time, gentlemen. I will be able to manage on my own from here. Good day.''

Kat shot through the door and closed it quickly behind her. There had been a time, not too long ago, that she could zigzag through the crowded streets of Baton Rouge and not think a thing about the bustling masses. Now she felt suffocated. Amazing how quickly she had adapted to—and now preferred—wide-open spaces.

When the red-haired attendant stared at her with mouth gaping and his gaze lingering on this confounded neckline, Kat strode forward. ''I would like to send a telegram to Baton Rouge, Louisiana,'' she announced briskly.

''Yes, ma'am, whatever you want.'' The attendant fumbled for pen and paper, then waited, all ears—and eyes.

Kat quickly formulated her thoughts. She needed to contact her closest friend. Mattie Barker could spread the word of J.P. Trumball's death and the eventual sale of the plantation . . .

No, Kat decided on second thought. Now that J.P. was gone, she wouldn't be forced to sell her family home. She could return to it whenever she wanted. Once she reached Santa Fe, there would be funds to pay her living expenses. The plantation would continue to pay its employees from the profit now that J.P. wasn't around to drain the cash flow with his gambling debts. In fact, Kat could travel between New Mexico and Louisiana whenever it met her whim, and she might possibly happen on to Judd . . .

Kat stifled that whimsical thought. She could not spend the rest of her life hoping for a chance sighting while she traveled back and forth across Texas. That would be foolish futility.

However, any time loneliness and restlessness overtook her she could board a stage and return to the plantation. The stage lines were expanding rapidly, and railroads were sure to follow. She could make the lengthy journey any time she pleased.

''Er . . . ma'am? The telegram?'' the attendant prompted.

Kat gave Mattie's name, then stated the information about J.P. and ended with: ''I will contact you from Santa Fe.''

Reaching into the small reticule Judd had given her, Kat fished out funds to pay for the telegram. When she wheeled toward the door, she groaned in dismay. The crowd that had escorted her from the hotel had grown into moblike proportions!

Good heavens! Were these men in this frontier town so hungry for the sight of a woman that they gathered like flies to molasses?

Exasperated, Kat stepped outside, trying to glance in one direction, then the other. She couldn't see over the sea of bobbing hats. "Which way is the stage station?"

"Stage station?" Tully Pitt repeated. "Aw, come on, honey, you just got to town. Surely you aren't leaving so soon."

"There is a fandango tonight," someone called from the center of the mob. "I'd be honored if you'd save at least one dance for me."

Kat was bombarded by dozens of similar requests. This was absurd! Annoyed, she tried to push her way through the crowd, but no one would clear a path until she promised a dance. Only when she agreed—and not very graciously, either—did the mob surge forward.

Kat reluctantly accepted the two new sets of hands that latched on to her forearms to whisk her along the uneven boardwalk. The men carried her across the street, so as not to get the hem of her gown dirty, then shepherded her across another warped boardwalk.

Sighing in relief, Kat burst into the stage station. Three scraggly-looking men were standing in line in front of her. Kat sincerely hoped these hooligans were not headed in the same direction she was. The company she might be forced to keep during the trip to Santa Fe would be most unpleasant.

"Well, well, what do we have here?"

Kat kept her expression carefully neutral when the tallest of the three hombres turned to face her. His scraggly, unkempt hair brushed his thin-bladed shoulders. His beard and mustache were as uneven and mangy as his hair. When he insultingly undressed her with his ferretlike eyes, Kat wanted to slap him, but she knotted her fists in the folds of her gown and held her temper.

The other two men pivoted to leer at her in the same insulting manner, but Kat refused to be intimidated or frightened. She looked each galloot squarely in the eye—making certain she could identify them if things got out of hand—and waited her turn at the ticket window.

Eventually the three ruffians glanced past her to survey the crowd waiting outside, then visually devoured her again. After a few moments they turned their attention to the stage attendant. Kat thought it odd that the men requested the scheduled departures of stages traveling north, west and east. She was dismayed when the tallest hombre requested a ticket to Las Vegas. Fortunately, the other men decided not to buy tickets for the following day. They announced they would make arrangements to leave in midweek.

That was a relief, thought Kat. Being closeted in a stagecoach with one foul-smelling scoundrel would be plenty.

Kat stiffened when the men purposely brushed past her close enough to touch her, but she refused to react. She continued to stare straight at the ticket agent.

"Uppity little thing, aren't you?" Tall drawled sarcastically.

"Think you're too good for the likes of us, do you?" Medium chimed in.

Kat flicked a discreet glance at the whisker-faced scoundrel whose short upper lip revealed a large gap between his two front teeth. His teeth, she noted, were a disgusting shade of yellow.

"Might be surprised what you're missing, sugar," Short added with what Kat presumed to be his most provocative wink.

She was not the least bit impressed. The gesture fell pathetically short of its mark. And so did the man. The stout, burly-looking man with his square face, fuzzy mustache and cold, dark eyes was revolting.

When Kat didn't dignify their goading remarks, merely stepped forward to confer with the stage agent, the threesome apparently got tired of being ignored and swaggered through the crowd outside.

Kat breathed a sigh of relief when she was left alone in the office. She had no desire to encounter those three hooligans in a dark alley, not without a bullwhip, pistol and dagger in hand.

In that event, she knew she would be called upon to defend herself. She only hoped that if the time ever came, she could execute the skills Judd had taught her. Otherwise . . .

Kat didn't even want to speculate about what would happen if those three lecherous men did manage to surround her.

Judd frowned irritably when the bartender he was questioning kept getting distracted by something going on in the street. Cape Mullin, proprietor of Wild Mustang Saloon, kept looking past Judd, forcing him to redirect Cape's attention to the papers on the bar. Cape had positively identified Arkansas Riley, but suddenly he couldn't keep his gaze focused for more than a few seconds at a time.

Sighing impatiently, Judd pivoted to see what the hell was demanding Cape's attention. Scowling, Judd watched the woman with flaming red-gold hair, dressed in the eye-catching yellow gown and surrounded by a mob of men, move down the opposite side of the street. Damn, Judd should have suggested that Kat wear her disguise until he returned to escort her to supper. From the look of things, Kat had more than her share of masculine attention. She was probably reveling in it, too.

Judd felt uncomfortable with the unprecedented wave of possessive jealousy that crested on him. He recalled how Gracie and Samuel kept referring to Kat as *his lady*—and how he kinda liked the sound of it.

Judd's first impulse was to burst from the saloon, storm across the street and lay claim to what was his, but he willfully restrained from making a fool of himself. Kat probably enjoyed holding court with that slew of men. After all, most women gobbled that stuff up, didn't they?

Kat could fend for herself if one of her companions stepped out of line, he reminded himself. He ought to know, because he was the one who taught her to defend herself, and he had seen her in action when Wild Hawk and his warriors tried to capture her. They'd had a battle royal on their hands.

Besides, Judd told himself, a beautiful, alluring woman like

Kat was undoubtedly accustomed to drawing crowds. She had drawn one in The Flats. She knew how to handle these kinds of situations.

"Must be a new bit of fluff in town," Cape murmured as he watched the procession troop down the street. "Must be a new prostitute on her way to Lottie's Place. From the look of things, the new arrival will have clients lined up for at least two solid weeks. She must be a real looker."

Judd scowled again, wondering if all those men were visualizing themselves in bed with Kat, touching her familiarly, taking her intimately . . .

The revolting thought left a knot of rage burning in his belly. Too damned bad his conscience wouldn't allow him to gun down a man for thinking lewd thoughts. If so, Boot Hill would have to be expanded by nightfall.

"Take a look at this sketch," Judd demanded gruffly.

"Huh?" Cape Mullin blinked like a man emerging from a trance. "Oh, yeah, the thieves you're after. Right." He stared at the Wanted poster of Crazy Ben Corothers. "Yeah, I've seen that sorry sonuvabitch in here, too. Tried to wreck my place one night last week. I whacked him over the head with the butt of my shotgun and had a few of the men haul his drunken ass into the street to sleep off his binge."

"None of these three men are registered at Hampton Hotel," Judd reported. "Did you happen to notice where the two men you identified headed when they left the saloon?"

Cape shrugged his bulky shoulders, then chawed on the cigar that dangled on one side of his mouth. "Like I told you, the Corothers character was still asleep in the street when I locked up for the night. I didn't pay any attention to where Riley went when he left here. You might check at Tascosa Hotel to see if the clerk recognizes these ugly mugs. You can also check with the cook and owner of the restaurant. Robert Wilson might have seen them around."

"Thanks. I'll do that." Judd pointed to the last drawing. "What about this one? Does he look familiar?"

Cape stared pensively at the beady-eyed hombre known as Rowdy Jack. "Nope, but there's a passel of goons who come through town looking like they're badly in need of a shave and haircut. This one could pass for at least a dozen somebody elses, but I'll keep my eyes peeled, Panther.''

Cape stared at Judd. "Sure you don't want the job of town marshal?"

"Positive," Judd replied. "Remaining in one place for too long gives me a bad case of restlessness."

"We can't pay a salary to match what bounties pay, but you can't blame a man for asking." Cape grinned around his cigar. "You wouldn't mind if I bandied your name about while you're in town, would you? Keeps the riffraff looking over their shoulders, don't you know."

Judd shrugged. "Whatever it takes to keep the lid on, Cape."

"I'll send a message to you if one of these three renegades shows up in my saloon. You staying at Hamptons', as usual?"

"No, I'm camping out by the springs near the Dodge City road."

"No kidding?" Cape said, surprised. "I thought you always—"

"Not this time," Judd cut in quickly.

"Don't forget about the fandango tonight," Cape called as Judd ambled toward the door. "If nothing else, you might spot those renegades in the crowd."

Judd stepped outside to see the mob of men who surrounded Kat surge in the direction of Hampton Hotel. He hoped Kat would return to her room—and stay there until he fetched her for supper.

Well, at least with a shield of men encircling her, she should be protected in case a gunfight broke out on the street, Judd thought. He just hoped like hell that he didn't have to be called upon to break up any fights over *her*, because he was working on a short clock. He had to question the clerk at Tascosa Hotel, pitch camp by the springs, then get himself spruced up for dinner and dancing.

Reminded that he had a job to do, Judd strode down the opposite side of the street, casting an occasional glance at Kat's mob of admirers. A wry smile pursed his lips when an amusing thought occurred to him. Maybe he should suggest that Cape and Samuel hire Kat Diamond as town marshal. Her very presence would discourage rowdy men from brawling. They would be too busy trailing after her like a litter of kittens on the trail of cream.

Judd trotted Horse north of town, dismounted, then built a campfire but left it unlit beside a road at the base of a tree-covered hill. He wanted passersby to know that this shady spot beside the cottonwoods was already taken. It would also allow him to compare the sketches in the Wanted posters to any travelers who rode past.

Unfortunately, Judd didn't see anyone on the road who resembled Arkansas Riley, Crazy Ben Corothers or Rowdy Jack. But as Cape Mullin said: You've seen one woolly-faced, mop-haired renegade, you've seem 'em all—or something to that effect.

Too many men in lawless Texas towns had reason to conceal their facial features with long hair, fuzzy beards and droopy mustaches. Most of them were wanted for something or another. It just took time and effort to figure out who was wanted *where,* for *what.*

The thought prompted Judd to fish out the notice that stated Katherine Diamond was wanted for questioning about the murder in The Flats.

He should light the campfire and burn that notice, Judd told himself. But he didn't want to waste the kindling and fallen tree limbs he had gathered to keep warm when he returned later that night. He was only planning to be in camp long enough to clean up, change into the fancy trappings Gracie had given him, then call for Kat at the hotel.

For a long, pensive moment Judd stared at the notice, asking himself if he would blame Kat for disposing of J.P.—or hiring Chester and Hugh to do it for her. He had seen the bruise on her cheek—a bruise J.P. had put there. Kat claimed J.P. had made her life hell and gambled away the profits from the family plantation. She also claimed Hugh and Chester had double-crossed J.P. and that she had not intentionally met up with the two men before Wild Hawk and his warriors arrived on the scene.

Judd admitted that he had never wanted to believe anyone—believe *in* anyone—as much as he wanted to take Kat at her word. He asked himself a dozen times a day if it truly had been a misconception that had sent her trudging off alone when she accidentally happened onto Chester and Hugh. But how was Judd supposed to know for absolute certain, when Chester and Hugh weren't around to substantiate her claim of innocence—or confirm her guilt?

Well, Judd supposed there was one way to find out if Kat had been totally honest with him. If she hopped the stage without bothering to say farewell, without divvying up the jewels, then he would know she had been playing him for a fool.

Kat didn't seem like the kind of person who would connive and deceive. She seemed decent and honest. Problem was that Judd had become jaded and cynical, because of the criminals he dealt with. He'd learned not to trust anyone, didn't take anybody at their word. That was suicidal.

Judd frowned pensively when he finally realized what the crux of his problem was. Because of the feelings Kat aroused in him, he wasn't as sure of himself, or his judgment, as he usually was. Kat kept him off balance, kept him questioning himself constantly. In all other endeavors Judd never hesitated or wavered, just *acted*. With Kat it seemed he was always *reacting*.

No wonder she left him feeling as if he had lost his solid footing. He had, damn it.

Sighing in frustration, Judd grabbed the citified suit. He wasn't going to spend his last evening with Kat wondering if she planned to betray him one last time before she set her sights on Santa Fe. He was going to enjoy her company, then he was going to let her go her own way while he went his.

For this one night he was going to use the social skills his father taught him and try his best to blend into society—Tascosa-style, at least. He would walk in the world that Kat was accustomed to, behave like a gentleman—or as close to a gentleman as a half-breed loner could come. He would treat Kat like a lady—and hope to hell he hadn't misjudged her, hope he wouldn't have to send a telegram to the marshal in Santa Fe and request that Kat be returned to Marshal Winslow in The Flats for questioning.

Could he do that to Kat? Had she used her feminine wiles on him so that he would be reluctant to turn her in? Would he become that vindictive, if he discovered that she had fed him one crock of malarkey after another since the night he met her?

"Just don't disappoint me, so I don't have to answer those questions," Judd muttered to the bewitching image floating above him. "Just don't give me any reason to doubt you, Kat, because I don't want to be faced with that . . ."

He frowned thoughtfully. Now, what highbrow word had Kat used to describe an intricate dilemma? "Yeah, conundrum," he said aloud.

Squirming uncomfortably in the trim-fitting jacket, brocade vest and itchy trousers, Judd carefully mounted Horse and managed not to split any seams. Since he had left Kat's mare at the livery stable, he wouldn't have to worry about a thief sneaking into camp and swiping the horse. Judd double-checked to ensure he hadn't left anything of value at the site—just an unlit fire and a stake that indicated the space was occupied.

Keeping Horse at a leisurely walk, Judd rode south. Long before he reached town he heard the combined strains of fiddle, harmonica and piano floating on the air. Main Street was lit up with dozens of torches. The future site of the post office had been roped off. Colorful banners flapped in the breeze and a sign had been erected, announcing the opening of the new building.

Clusters of men and women paraded up and down the street, waiting for the fandango to begin. Calico queens and prostitutes noticeably outnumbered proper ladies, and they flirted outrageously with the crowd of men. Judd suspected business at the brothel would be booming when the celebration ended.

Cape Mullin and the Hamptons had joined forces to set out refreshments on the two tables at the end of Main Street. Judd smiled wryly, wondering if the town founders would have dreamed up another excuse for a celebration even if the application for the post office had been rejected. Probably. This was the social event of the spring season. More than likely, Mullin and the Hamptons would dream up something equally as festive for the summer and fall seasons. No doubt, they were trying to give Tascosa some respectability to attract newcomers and outgrow a bad reputation.

Judd dismounted and tied Horse to the hitching post. Tugging at his cravat—noose was more like it, he thought sourly— Judd entered the mercantile shop/hotel. The teenage boy who served as janitor had been promoted to clerk, since Gracie and Samuel were hosting the celebration. Toby Webster was the son of a local sheep farmer who did odd jobs in town to make pocket money. Although the boy reminded Judd of a string bean, and had yet to fill out with muscle, he had a friendly disposition and an engaging smile. Toby didn't shy away from Judd, either, because the Hamptons sang Judd's praises in Tascosa. This, Judd reminded himself, was one of the few towns where folks didn't run for cover when he appeared. He supposed this was as close to a hometown as he would ever get.

"Panther?" Toby croaked, eyes popping. "Is that you?"

Just what Judd needed—to feel more conspicuous and self-conscious in this getup. "Yeah, Gracie's idea. Guess she wanted to try her hand at domesticating me."

Toby grinned. "Well, you look mighty nice all decked out in your finery, if you don't mind me saying so."

Judd grimaced. He hated *nice*. It would ruin his intimidating reputation.

Toby braced his bony elbows on the counter and leaned close to pass along the latest gossip. "Have you heard that we have visiting royalty staying at the hotel?"

Judd elevated a dark brow. "Is that so?"

Toby nodded his bushy blond head. "That's what I heard. Don't know if the Hamptons know yet, because they have been buzzing around setting up for the fandango. But the men who have been in and out of the store this afternoon have been saying we have a real live princess, right here in Tascosa. They say her family markets diamonds."

Judd choked down his laughter and struggled to keep a straight face. "You don't say?"

"I do say," Toby insisted.

Wasn't it amazing how rumors were born—and how quickly they became tangled up in exaggeration?

Unless Kat was the one who had initiated the gossip.

The thought put quick death to Judd's amusement. If Kat started the gossip, then it stood to reason that she was an accomplished liar who spoon-fed Judd to gain his sympathy and cooperation.

Hell and damn, there he went again, getting all cynical and suspicious because he didn't want to end up looking like a gullible, world-class fool.

"Lady Katherine—that's what you're supposed to call her, because she's got such a fine pedigree—went to the telegraph office to send a message to some of her rich relatives in Louisiana," Toby reported. "Then she checked the stage schedule. If you're gonna catch a glimpse of her, you'd better make it snappy, Panther, because she won't be in town very long. All the men claim she's leaving tomorrow, and they are forming a line at the fandango so they can take turns dancing with her."

Judd wasn't surprised to hear that, not after the commotion the "princess" had caused on the streets this afternoon. From the sound of things, Judd would be damn lucky to squeeze in one dance with Her Royal Highness.

When Judd wheeled toward the stairs, Toby frowned. "Where are you going?"

"I'm going to have a look at the princess," Judd announced.

"You can't just march up there and demand a look-see!" Toby howled, aghast.

"Wanna bet?" Judd threw over his shoulder as he headed up the steps.

CHAPTER EIGHTEEN

By the time Judd reached Kat's hotel room door his disposition had turned pitch-black. If he discovered Kat had been traipsing around town, spouting stories about her fabulous wealth and prestigious titles and lining up dances for the fandango, he was going to strangle her. He had gotten all gussied up to impress Kat. Why was that? Why did he feel the need to impress her? He must have suffered a momentary lapse of sanity.

Scowling, Judd rapped his knuckles on the door.

"Who is it?"

"Who the hell do you think it is?" he muttered, glaring at the wooden door.

"Nothing like agreeing to share a meal with a man whose sour mood is destined to ruin my appetite," Kat said as she swung open the door.

When Judd clapped eyes on Kat, he felt as if someone had doubled a fist and buried it in his soft underbelly. "Holy ... hell ..." he wheezed.

Judd was totally unprepared for the startling transformation from cute little ragamuffin to the stunningly beautiful woman poised in front of him. He knew his jaw must be scraping the fancy cravat that was wrapped tightly around his neck, but the impact of seeing Kat in that sunflower-yellow gown stole the breath right out of his lungs. She reminded him of the first glorious rays of dawn burning away the dark of night. He understood instantly why men fell all over themselves to follow her down streets, why Tascosans believed her to be royalty. She looked . . . spellbinding, bewitching.

Kat had pinned that curly mass of fiery gold hair atop her head in a sophisticated coiffeur. Feathery ringlets coiled at her temples and above her eyebrows. Her upswept hair called attention to the slender column of her throat. The plunging neckline showcased the creamy swells of her breasts to their best advantage.

And that gown! Judd's owlish gaze swept up and down, appraising every curvy inch of alluring femininity. The garment looked as if it had been specifically tailored for Kat. It accentuated the small indentation of her waist, her full bosom and the gentle flare of her hips. With that lovely face, and that heavenly body and that dress, well . . . the entire package was enough to knock a man to his knees—and keep him there.

If Judd had had an inkling of how stunning Kat would look in all those frilly, revealing trappings, he wouldn't have sent her to the stage station alone!

Judd shook himself loose of his astonished daze and stepped into the room. "Little lady," he purred as he kicked the door shut with his boot heel. "There ought to be a law against a woman looking as good as you do."

Kat smiled up at him. Commanding attention from the male population in Tascosa wasn't half as gratifying as having Judd stare appreciatively at her. The compliment was icing on the cake, but she was too preoccupied to revel in it. Judd's dashing appearance set her back on her heels. She couldn't take her eyes off him, because he was definitely worth staring at in his well-fitted garments. The black suit and contrasting crisp white linen shirt called attention to his bronzed skin, raven-black hair and powerful physique.

"Lassiter," she said, giving him another sweeping glance, "if you make a habit of dressing like this, you're going to change professions from bounty hunter to lady killer. You look—''

"Do not say nice," he muttered as he tugged at the cravat that constricted his throat.

"Sweet?" she ventured impishly.

He shook his head, then impulsively reached out to trace the delicate curve of her jaw, the lush fullness of her mouth. "I don't think so. I guarantee that I'm not thinking sweet thoughts when I look at you. I swear you would tempt a saint, and I'm nowhere close to being one."

Judd's rakish smile and outright flirtation almost made Kat take offense. Almost. She never put much stock in her looks, because she had nothing whatsoever to do with those God-given attributes. She had been fawned over and bombarded with effusive flattery for years. She hadn't let it go to her head, or her heart, because she knew the male gender used compliments for ulterior purposes when they wanted something from a woman.

In Kat's opinion, men were entirely too visual, too driven by their physical needs. Kat thought Judd was different—at least he had been, until she stepped into this dress. She wanted him to love her for what she was on the inside, not how she looked on the outside. Yet she couldn't deny that the sight of him in his citified clothes made a startling visual impression on her. She would be a hypocrite if she scolded him for carrying on about *her* appearance when she was fiercely affected by *his*.

His fashionable garments were such a drastic contradiction to the man she had come to know that she couldn't stop staring at him. He seemed to have the same problem with her, so she supposed they were even.

Kat was aware that his clothes were a civilized veneer that concealed all that raw power and lithe grace that she had seen in action on numerous occasions. If Judd Lassiter wanted to take civilized society by storm, he could do it, capturing feminine hearts and drawing appreciative gazes with each swaggering step, each roguish grin. But Kat knew that high society wasn't Judd's style. His soul was as wild and untamed as the Texas frontier. He would become bored in civilization, like a predatory cat in captivity. He could play the role for a time, but he would always be drawn to the wilderness.

Judd dropped into an exaggerated bow. "Shall we dine, Your Highness? The common peasants on the streets await another glimpse of you."

Kat glanced at him curiously as she scooped her reticule off the bed. "Your Highness?" she repeated. "What is all this silly nonsense?"

"You don't know?" Though he smiled casually, Judd watched her intently, wondering if she had indeed started the wild rumors.

Kat opened her reticule, plucked up the pouch of jewels he had left with her that afternoon, then stuffed it into her bodice. Sadly, the tight-fitting garment left no room for the gems. In frustration, she stared down at the bulge between her breasts. Where was she going to stash the gems so she didn't have to keep track of her reticule?

"Maybe I should guard the royal jewels this evening, princess. There doesn't seem to be spare room for extra accessories in your bodice."

Kat's breath clogged in her chest when his fingertips brushed the swells of her breasts to retrieve the pouch. Lord, she was so receptive to his touch that her skin burned and desire burst to life instantaneously.

Kat stared at him helplessly. She really did have it bad for this man. Did he know that? Could he detect the longing to have her love returned? Could he see the yearning on her flushed face, read her affection in her eyes?

When Judd's hand lingered unnecessarily, caressing lightly before withdrawing the pouch, Kat's lips parted on a shaky sigh. "Don't do that or we might not see the inside of the restaurant."

"Would you mind that too much, Lady Katherine?" he asked, his voice low and husky, his eyes searching hers.

Kat stepped back apace, pulled herself together before he completely unraveled her, then said, "You already proved your effect on me this afternoon and you damn well know it. And why are you calling me princess and lady? Before I stepped into this gown I was just plain ol' Diamond, your inept sidekick, your sadly lacking protégé.''

Judd studied her closely. Either Kat was an incredibly good actress and accomplished liar or she had no idea what the hell he was referring to. Judd hoped the latter was true, he really did.

"Gossip has it that you are visiting royalty, Lady Katherine. Your prestigious family acquired their wealth from mining and marketing diamonds," he said as he tucked the gems in his vest pocket.

Kat gasped in outrage. "Who started such a preposterous rumor?"

"You?" he asked—but with a deceptively teasing smile.

Her gaze narrowed, and Judd swore he saw flickers of hurt and frustration in those pine-tree-green eyes.

"Is that what you think?" she asked him. "Are you quick to think such things because you still don't trust me to give you the truth? For your information, I am appalled to hear that such rumors are circulating. I can't imagine how they got started, but I want them squelched immediately!"

Judd stared at the beguiling vision of beauty who appeared highly offended and upset by the gossip. Judd hadn't expected Kat to be so irate, but she certainly behaved as if she was. Why was that? he wondered.

Judd wasn't sure, but nonetheless, he stepped out on a shaky limb—hoping Kat wouldn't saw it off behind him—and said, "I don't believe you started the rumors, Kat."

The smile she bestowed on him was dazzling, heart-stopping. She reached up on tiptoe, flung her arms around his neck and kissed him full on the mouth. "Do you have any idea how much I . . ." Her voice dried up.

"How much you what?" he murmured, scrutinizing her closely.

Kat tossed him an evasive smile while she straightened his cravat. That done, she retreated into her own space. "Do you have any idea how much I appreciate your trust?" she said finally.

His gaze never left hers as he wondered what she really intended to say—and hadn't.

There you go, getting suspicious again. Just enjoy the evening and stop pouncing on her every word. The moment the stage rolls out of town, you will know if she intends to keep her part of the bargain. That is the exact same time you will find out if your trust is wasted on her.

This really isn't about a cut of the jewels, is it, Lassiter? It never was, was it? If that is so, then you know what that means, don't you? It means you've got serious trouble here. So what the hell are you going to do about it? Nothing? Just let things play out as originally planned?

What are you going to do, Lassiter? Look the other way, or have Kat locked up for questioning? And how in the hell are you going to cope with either of those difficult choices?

Judd scowled. This was no time to be having an in-depth conversation with himself. He was going to set aside every last suspicion and enjoy these last few hours with Kat. He was *not* going to second-guess her, not going to dig for hidden meanings and leap to cynical conclusions. He was simply going to savor every moment in the company of this strikingly beautiful woman. Tonight he was going to accept Kat at face value and leave it at that.

Pressing his hand possessively against the small of her back, he ushered her to the door. ''Come on, sweetheart, I'm starving.''

Kat felt a warm tingle spread through her body as they descended the steps. She wondered if Judd realized what he'd said, wondered if the endearment meant anything to him. She didn't dare call him on it, for fear it was just a casual comment and she would feel foolish for probing him for a commitment.

But, ah, wouldn't it be nice if she *did* mean something special to him?

Don't go getting all gushy and romantic, Diamond, she chastised herself. *You have one night left to share with Judd. Commit this evening to everlasting memory, but don't look too far into the future, because Judd Lassiter isn't going to be there, doesn't* want *to be there. He isn't going to give up his way of life for you.*

When Toby Webster saw Panther and the princess at the landing, his mouth dropped open wide enough for a prairie chicken to roost. Goggle-eyed, Toby watched their descent. The princess was everything rumor said she was. Why, she was by far the prettiest thing Toby had ever laid eyes on in all his sixteen years!

"Toby Webster, this is Katherine Diamond," Judd introduced, then grinned at the boy's star-struck expression.

"You know Lady Katherine?" Toby tweeted.

Kat flung Judd a quick glance, then turned to Toby, determined to set the boy straight. "I'm very pleased to meet you, Toby, but I prefer that you call me Kat. Although rumor has it that I am titled royalty, that simply is not so, and I would appreciate it if you could help me quell the gossip circulating around Tascosa."

Toby appraised the sophisticated lady poised before him. "Maybe you're not, ma'am, but you sure look like you could be, should be royalty."

Kat graced him with a dazzling smile. "That is very kind of you to say. The next time you hear the gossip, I would like it to end with you. I'm sure that rumor about being a diamond heiress got started because of my last name."

"I'll do my best to set the story straight," Toby said very seriously. "But the tale spread pretty fast and it might take time to correct it. I've heard the same gossip at least ten times since I began my shift at the counter."

Kat stared more at Judd than at Toby. "I only want to be known for who and what I really am. Nothing more and nothing less."

Judd didn't miss the plea in those hypnotic green eyes. Kat was asking him to look beneath the alluring gown and elegant coiffure to see her for what she was—or what she projected herself to be in his presence.

Stop that, damn it! Give your suspicions the night off before you drive yourself nuts!

"What Kat is," Judd said, taking her arm politely, "is famished. If you'll excuse us, Toby, we have an important date with a thick, juicy steak and all the trimmings."

When they emerged onto the street, Judd did indeed feel as if he were Her Royal Highness's bodyguard. Male heads turned in rapid succession to stargaze at Kat Diamond. Every man within shooting distance dragged the hat from his head and doubled at the waist as she passed. It was as if they were paying their respects to a princess on her way to royal court.

"Do you always have such a profound effect on male populations?" Judd asked.

Kat wasn't about to lie to him, though her first reaction was toward modesty and humility. As Judd once said: All he wanted was the truth, and nothing but. "Afraid so, but I consider the attention a nuisance. It is comparable to the unwanted attention you receive when your reputation precedes you from one town to the next."

Judd reckoned she was right. When he appeared in a community, looking more savage than civilized, people stared, pointed and whispered. He had learned not to pay much attention to it. Apparently Kat had, too.

Judd relaxed a bit and became amused when male onlookers parted like draperies as he escorted Kat to the restaurant. Men bowed, scraped and drooled over Kat until Judd shut the door behind them. The ritual began again when Kat walked in to turn every male head in the restaurant. This woman was born in the limelight and collected stares like moths flittering to a flame.

On one hand, Judd felt a sense of pride while he served as Kat's escort. On the other hand, possessive jealously gnawed at him. He would have had to be blind not to interpret the speculative gleam in all those male stares.

Judd also noted that the female patrons were giving *him* a thorough going-over. Whether because of his formidable reputation or the cut of his clothes, he couldn't say for sure. He wondered if Kat felt the slightest twinge of jealousy.

"Speaking of being devoured," Kat murmured as Judd held out a chair for her. "It's obvious the women have made note of your arrival. I told you that you could be a lady killer if you were looking to change professions."

Judd winced when he noticed one particular pair of feminine eyes focused on him. He and the widow who owned the pharmaceutical shop had spent short intervals together a couple of times. Judd knew he had been some sort of novelty to the widow, but his interest in her had waned the moment he left town. So why did he feel uncomfortable having Kat in the same cafe with the woman he had known briefly? Such situations had never bothered him before.

After tomorrow it isn't going to matter, Lassiter. Kat and her pouch of jewels will be long gone. That is for the best and you damn well know it.

"Something wrong?" Kat asked as her gaze glided from the sultry brunette to Judd, who was squirming in his chair.

"Just thinking," he mumbled.

"I thought I smelled wood burning," she teased, eyes twinkling. "A close friend of yours, I presume, judging by her intense stare."

Judd shifted awkwardly, then breathed a sigh of relief when the waiter arrived to interrupt a conversation he didn't want to have.

"The usual, Panther?" the waiter presumed.

Judd nodded.

"And may I say you look very dashing in your dress clothes."

"Thanks," Judd mumbled self-consciously.

"And for Lady Katherine?" the waiter asked. "And may I say you look divine."

"I'm not—"

"She would like the same," Judd broke in.

When the plump waiter waddled off, Kat frowned at Judd. "Why didn't you let me set him straight?"

"Might as well let Tascosans think they have a claim to fame for the evening. The Hamptons drop my name around town when potential troublemakers arrive. Folks might as well tell of the stunning princess who attended their celebration."

Kat stared straight at him. "I do not hold with dishonesty."

She had no idea how much he wanted to believe that!

"I need to speak with the restaurant owner," Judd said as he pushed back in his chair. "I want to find out if the wanted men Marshal Winslow asked me to track down have been here recently."

Judd pulled the folded papers from his pocket, then stood up. When he strode away, Kat noticed the paper that had fallen on the planked floor.

"You forgot—"

It was too late. Judd was out of earshot, and Kat wasn't about to holler at him and draw more attention to herself.

Carefully, trying not to expose herself in the gown with its diving neckline, Kat bent over to retrieve the paper. She expected to see a sketch of one of the murderers and thieves Judd was tracking. She gasped in shock when she saw *her* name and a rough sketch on the notice. Her stunned gaze flew to the kitchen door that Judd had entered, then she stared incredulously at the wrinkled paper.

Judd thought she was responsible for J.P.'s death? Was that why he could never quite bring himself to trust her? Was that why he had accused her of rendezvousing with Chester and Hugh after she left Whispering Springs Canyon?

Kat slumped in her chair, her mind spinning like a windmill. My God, did he think she had killed J.P., then offered Judd a cut of the jewels to guide her away from The Flats before she could be arrested for murder?

On the wings of that haunting question came another. Did Judd think she planned to hightail it out of town without giving him a cut of the jewels?

Kat tried to get herself in hand as the tormented thoughts bombarded her from all directions. Had Judd made love to her, believing she had committed murder and then abandoned him to rejoin Chester and Hugh? Did he believe she had been using him these past few weeks and intended to betray him?

Wounded pride and indignation blistered her. She was such

an idiotic fool, she realized. She had let herself believe Judd cared about her, but obviously he was expecting to be deceived eventually and he had been using her to appease his needs. What did he plan to do? Arrest her the instant before she stepped on the stage? Was this all a setup? Was he planning to have the last laugh on her? Was she going to be locked up in Tascosa, waiting for the sheriff to tote her back to The Flats?

Kat cringed at the thought of being cooped up in the shoddy log cabin that served as a jail. She would probably be forced to camp out with the drunks who celebrated too enthusiastically at tonight's fandango.

While she was rotting away in that shabby calaboose, what would Lassiter be doing? Polishing all the gems he repossessed from her? Laughing himself silly? Was tonight just a charade played for her benefit? Like the last supper before calamity struck?

Kat clenched her fists in the fabric of her gown. She wanted to burst out cursing and screaming in frustration. She had been set up, all right. First came the fancy dress, the night on the town, Judd's gentlemanly attention and compliments to keep her distracted and unaware of his scheme. Just when did he plan to spring this little surprise on her? At the stroke of midnight? At the moment before she raised her foot to board the stage?

How could he trust her so little? she asked herself, then answered bleakly: Because mere physical attraction was all he ever saw in her. He had *used* her, just as he must believe that she was using him. He had taken the Golden Rule and altered it to suit his purpose. *Do unto others before they can do unto you,* Kat thought bitterly.

Had Judd suspected her of killing J.P.—or ordering Chester and Hugh to do it—when he agreed to her bargain?

Kat reflected on the night she had climbed through Judd's hotel window. She had proposed the bargain, then passed out from hunger. He had tied her to the bed, then left to pick up food—or so he wanted her to think. He must have learned about J.P.'s death from Marshal Winslow and decided to take advantage of the situation.

It all made sense to her now. Judd had decided to haul her

through the wilderness, making the trek as difficult as possible, just for spite. Why shouldn't he drag her along for his own amusement? He was trailing the desperadoes and he was heading in this direction anyway. Each time he left her alone—presumably to scout the trail and hunt for food—Judd had kept watch on her, wondering if she planned to rendezvous with Chester and Hugh.

Kat closed her eyes on the tormented realization that Judd had been expecting, *waiting* for her to double-cross him. He may have even convinced himself that she planned to dispose of him when they came close enough to civilization for her to make it on her own, so she wouldn't have to split the jewels with her.

Sweet mercy! He never really trusted her at all—still didn't if he was carrying the notice from Marshal Winslow.

Kat couldn't have felt worse if Judd had drawn his dagger and stabbed her clean through her broken heart. She wasn't going to enjoy the freedom she craved. She was going to be locked up, then transported back to The Flats to stand trial. The two witnesses who could have verified her innocence—if they would have been honest enough, which they probably wouldn't have—were dead and gone.

Oh, God, OH, GOD! What was she going to do? How much time did she have to formulate her plan? She needed to pace. Sitting at the table, while dozens of eyes bore down on her, made it impossible to think clearly. She needed to be alone to contemplate. But she also needed food to sustain her, because there was no telling when she would be able to eat again, if she had to light out of town in the darkness to avoid capture. She had no money to purchase supplies, and she absolutely refused to steal supplies from Gracie and Samuel's store, not even if her life depended on it!

Calm down, Kat! Just bide your time, she ordered herself. *Don't let Lassiter know you are wise to his crafty scheme. Now that you know what he's planning, you can figure out a way to counter him.*

Hands trembling, Kat folded the notice, then stashed it in her bodice. Judd Lassiter thought she had put on an act for his benefit, awaiting the right time and place to betray him? Well, he was the master of deception, and if he thought she had been acting for his benefit, he hadn't seen anything yet!

She was going to put on the performance of her life and pretend she didn't hate him for what he planned to do, what he had already done, for making her fall in love with him! She would never forgive him for that!

CHAPTER NINETEEN

Robert Wilson wiped his hand on his grimy apron, then held at arm's length the paper that Judd Lassiter handed to him. He squinted to read the information on the Wanted poster, then studied the sketch.

"Rowdy Jack, huh?" Robert murmured pensively. "Hard to tell a man's features with that mop of stringy hair, mustache and beard."

"So everyone else in Tascosa says," Judd replied. "But Arkansas Riley and Crazy Ben Corothers have been positively identified. Rowdy has to be nearby. Since he seems to be keeping a low profile, I suspect Rowdy is the brains behind this outfit. I also suspect the trio is planning a robbery, since Riley and Corothers have been seen around town for more than a week. They are very likely casing Tascosa."

Robert's eyes widened in alarm and he swiped his beefy hand over his bald head. "Damn, you think maybe they might hit the bank?"

"Or a stage rumored to be carrying a hefty amount of cash. Or they could be planning to rustle cattle and drive their stolen herd to the railhead in Dodge. This trio has dabbled in a variety of illegal activities," Judd reported. "Tascosa is a prime target area because it is isolated in the Texas Panhandle and the best law enforcement agency is in Dodge City.''

''Yeah,'' Robert grumbled. ''More than two hundred miles north.''

''And from Sweetwater,'' Judd added, ''a hundred miles east, and even farther to Fort Griffin and San Antone. Like I said, a prime target area with several days' head start on marshals and rangers.''

''Are you sure you aren't interested in taking the job of marshal?'' Robert asked hopefully. ''Your reputation would keep ne'er-do-wells like this trio from hanging around.''

''No, thanks,'' Judd murmured, then redirected Robert's attention to the sketch.

Robert studied the drawing very closely, then nodded his bald head. ''I think maybe this character has been in my restaurant a time or two. Must have been last week, because I don't recall seeing him recently. If this is the man I vaguely remember, he ate alone and packed hardware on both hips. Didn't cause any trouble, but looked like he could have if he had a mind to.

''If I were you, I'd check at Lottie's Place,'' Robert suggested. ''Chances are those hooligans passed through the brothel once or twice.''

That was going to be Judd's next stop—once he figured out what to do with Kat while he continued his interrogation. But then, he probably wouldn't have to worry about what to do with her. So many men had requested a dance with Kat that she would be totally distracted during his absence.

Or he could just come right out and tell her that he was going to Lottie's in search of information. It was the truth, after all. He just wasn't sure Kat would believe him.

Would she get upset if he entered the brothel? Judd wasn't sure. He hadn't dealt with enough women in his lifetime to predict how a woman like Kat might react.

Better to keep silent, he decided. No sense causing a problem if he didn't have to. He was going to handle this situation as he had in the past—do what had to be done and keep his plans to himself. Besides, after tomorrow, when Kat caught the stage west, he wouldn't have to consider anyone else's opinions or feelings. He would be back to being a loner.

Then he would do his damnedest to forget that he'd grown accustomed to having Kat around. It was for the best, he kept telling himself. She wasn't aware of the deep secret he harbored, and he planned to keep it that way. She wouldn't understand if he told her, couldn't live with it even if he did tell her.

"Yep, these two scoundrels definitely look familiar," Robert said as he appraised the sketches of Arkansas and Crazy Ben. "They came in together to chow down. They had bottles of hooch stashed in their pockets. Thought they'd never leave. Loud and unruly they were, too."

Judd folded the papers and tucked them in his pocket. "Much obliged for your help."

"My pleasure," Robert said with a nod. "I'd just as soon keep the riffraff out of Tascosa. We damn sure need a marshal around here. Are you *sure* you aren't interested, Panther?"

"I'm sure. You're the third person who's asked, but I'm afraid the answer is still no."

"Figured you'd say that, but I didn't see the harm in asking twice myself." He grinned, displaying the gold caps on his two front teeth. "I don't know who we're going to get to protect this town from bad hombres, but we need to find somebody soon. If word gets out that we're isolated and defenseless, then *wham!* You've got desperadoes swarming around here like bees. No, sir, sure don't want that to happen."

Judd pivoted around to return to his table. He knew one man who might be interested in the job of town marshal, a man whose life would need new direction very soon. He wondered how Wild Hawk would react when Judd sprang the idea on him.

Wild Hawk had been stolen as a young child and had been raised Comanche. Soon, he was going to face a difficult choice. Wild Hawk could remain in confinement in Indian Territory or return to the society that had borne him.

This was the ideal locale for Wild Hawk to start over, because Tascosa was located on Comanche hunting ground. Wild Hawk knew the area, he knew how to handle an assortment of weapons, and he knew how to track. Judd could use his influence with Marshal Winslow and the townspeople in Tascosa. It was time Wild Hawk faced his own heritage and learned to live with it, rather than allowing it to torment him.

After Judd put Kat on the stage, he would track the outlaw trio and locate Wild Hawk. No doubt, the war party was out there somewhere, trying to track down the same trio who had passed themselves off as Comanches on several occasions.

Judd would have to find a way to convince Wild Hawk that it was time to put his frustration with the white invasion to better use. The capable warrior, who considered himself his own worst enemy, needed to understand the white-eyes, to accept his white heritage. Otherwise, Wild Hawk was going to drive himself crazy.

Helluvan idea, Judd complimented himself on the way back to the table. That Comanche warrior would earn a name and reputation very quickly if he donned white men's clothes and reentered the society where he'd been raised.

Judd returned to the table a moment before the heaping platters of food arrived. Hurt and disappointed though Kat was, she put up a cheerful front. Discovering Judd's mistrust had spoiled her appetite, but she was determined to eat heartily, because this would be her last decent meal before she reached Santa Fe. Stage stations were notorious for serving beans and stale bread three times a day.

"You're awfully quiet," Judd observed between bites.

Kat forced a smile. "That's because I'm eating. The food is delicious. I was taught not to talk with food in my mouth. Meals were quiet, dignified affairs in our home, until J.P. Trumball came along," she added deliberately so she could gauge Judd's reaction.

Sure enough, he looked up to watch her closely. Why hadn't she noted how he focused absolute attention on her when she mentioned J.P. before? Her oversight, obviously.

"J.P. yammered through meals, boasting of the grand improvements he had made in the plantation, taking all the credit away from our innovative overseer, and explaining why extra money was needed for expenses. The truth was that J.P. needed money for his gambling debts. In short, he embezzled money to pay for his addiction. My mother never called him on it, but she knew he was draining our finances. She simply wasn't healthy enough to do much about it.''

There, thought Kat; let Judd view the stepfather she had dealt with for ten years for what he was, not the supposedly innocent victim who had been shot down in an alley in The Flats, but rather the man who had schemed to dispose of her so he could take absolute control of the Louisiana plantation.

Judd wanted to take Kat at her word, but he kept thinking that Kat had been taught to scheme and lie by the best. How much influence had J.P. had on Kat's conception of honesty and truth? Judd supposed he would find out tomorrow.

"Well, that will be behind you very soon," Judd murmured as he cut off another slice of juicy steak. "When you reach Santa Fe and sell the jewels, Trumball will be nothing but a fading memory. By the way, did you find out when the stage leaves for Las Vegas?"

Kat nodded. Corkscrew curls bobbled at her temples. "Nine o'clock in the morning. Unfortunately, a very seedy-looking character was in line ahead of me, asking questions about different arrivals and departures to various destinations."

Judd jerked upright. Alarm bells clanged in his mind. "Seedy character?"

"Yes. Not the kind I prefer to spend the day with in the close quarters of a stagecoach. Fortunately, I have learned to protect myself, so I intend to handle whatever situation arises," Kat said determinedly.

Judd's heart hammered. Could the trio of outlaws be planning a robbery with one man inside the coach and two others giving chase? It was a perfect setup. Hurriedly, he dug into his pocket for the papers.

"Can you identify these men, Kat? Was one of them in the stage office?"

Kat appraised the crude sketches, then nodded. "All three of them were there. This one"—she pointed to Rowdy Jack's poster—"bought a ticket to Las Vegas. The other two were in the office with him. They harassed me because I all but ignored them."

That now-familiar feeling of protective possessiveness surged through Judd. He didn't like the thought of Kat brushing shoulders with men who raped, murdered and robbed innocent victims. The thought of letting Kat board the stage with Rowdy Jack made him grimace.

Judd stared at the far wall, his mind racing. He was definitely going to be on hand the following morning when the stage departed. He was going to escort Rowdy Jack to the calaboose.

Then he would accompany Kat on the last leg of her journey. She wasn't going to know it until the stage pulled out, because he intended to give her the chance to hang herself—or exonerate herself. To be on the safe side, he planned to be at the stage station at dawn to check the schedules. He wanted to know if her claim of a nine o'clock departure was accurate.

Outside the restaurant, fast-tempoed music struck up. Violins, harmonicas, banjos and pianos formed a band for the fandango. Judd finished his meal hurriedly. There were more questions to be asked, since he'd discovered that the bandits might be planning to rob the stage. Judd had to find out how much cash was being transported west, and he would need the cooperation of the stage station attendant and driver. He preferred that shredded newspapers be placed in the strong box and the money shipped on a later stage.

Kat was surprised when Judd abruptly hoisted her from her chair and guided her toward the door. "Something wrong?" she asked as he whisked her onto the street.

"Nothing, except that I plan to dance with the visiting royalty," he said as he headed to the roped-off area on Main Street.

Judd had never danced in his life except in rituals in the Cheyenne village, chanting to the powerful guardian spirits his people honored. He doubted it would be the same. He would just have to watch the other dancers and hope he could catch on quickly.

With intense concentration, Judd counted the beats of the music and watched men swirling their partners around the dance area. He could handle this, just as he dealt with everything else in life, he assured himself.

"I better caution you that this is my first time," he felt obliged to tell Kat. "I am apologizing beforehand for trouncing on your feet."

"You mean I get to teach you to do something for a change?" she asked as he clutched her hand and weaved through the dancers. "What an intriguing prospect."

When the band struck up "Little Brown Jug," Kat counted aloud the steps for the double shuffle. She wasn't the least bit surprised that Judd caught on rapidly. The man was exceptionally light and agile on his feet. He had no trouble whatsoever adapting to the waltz when the band played "The Flying Trapeze."

Kat was sorely disappointed when one of the men who had followed her around that afternoon approached to request a dance. Her pride smarted when Judd handed her over to Tully Pitt without the slightest hesitation, then lost himself in the crowd.

An hour elapsed, during which Kat was passed around the male crowd like a tray of hors d'oeuvres. She began to wonder if Judd planned to abandon her now that he had her pouch of jewels in his pocket. Damn it, she wished she could read that man's mind. What was he planning?

If she was going to avoid a stint in jail, and the crushing blow of learning of Judd's plotted betrayal, then she needed to take immediate action. She had to locate Judd and retrieve the jewels, she told herself. She would dream up an excuse to return to her room and she would take the jewels with her. She could pick up the mare from the livery stable and ride west to wait for the stage at one of the stations en route. She had her ticket, so it would be easy to convince the driver to allow her to board the coach. She would give Judd his cut of the jewels— thereby proving that she intended to uphold her end of the bargain. Then she would walk out of his life and pretend she hadn't wasted her heart on a man who didn't have enough faith in her to fill a thimble!

"I'm sorry," Kat said, backing away from her twelfth dance

partner. "The strenuous dance pace is exhausting. I need to fetch a drink."

Despite her partner's protest, Kat shouldered through the crowd of dancers to find Gracie Hampton serving drinks at the refreshment table.

"Have you seen Panther?" Kat asked. "We were separated when another gentleman cut in to dance with me."

Gracie shifted awkwardly, then forced a strained smile. "Um . . . no, I haven't seen Panther lately."

Kat frowned at Gracie's odd behavior. Usually, Gracie was the epitome of cheerful enthusiasm. Now she was subdued. The woman obviously knew something she didn't want Kat to know.

Kat stared levelly at Gracie. "Tell me where he is, Gracie. I know you know."

"I'm sure there is a perfectly good explanation," Gracie said quickly, refusing to meet Kat's probing gaze, wringing her hands nervously. "But I did see him headed toward Lottie's Place . . . with . . . um . . . Lottie."

"Who is Lottie?" Kat wanted to know.

"She's . . . er . . . that is to say, she and her girls entertain—"

Kat caught on quickly. The sense of hurt and betrayal intensified like a throbbing wound. Whirling around, Kat scanned the torch-lit streets. She saw Judd and a woman dressed in red satin passing beneath a flaring torch.

Damn him! Leaving him was becoming easier by the minute. She had a perfect excuse to demand the return of the jewels, to light out of town and never look back. Confound it, she wasn't even gone and already he was turning elsewhere for physical satisfaction! That pretty much said how much he cared about her, didn't it? To him, she was easily replaced and quickly forgotten.

Kat stalked off, her pride and temper rising to full boil. She didn't doubt for a second that the full-figured harlot—which was all Kat had ever been to Judd, curse his fickle hide!—was an intimate friend of his, just like the woman staring at him in the restaurant. Judd didn't even care enough about Kat to spend the last night with her.

But, of course, she reminded herself bitterly, he had stopped by to seduce her this afternoon, so why would he bother coming by tonight when there were other available women within kissing distance?

"Lassiter!" Kat called over the lively music. "I request a word with you."

Judd flinched as if he had taken a tomahawk between the shoulder blades. Damnation, Kat's timing was atrocious. He had expected her to be passed around the dance floor for at least another hour. Reluctantly, he pivoted to see her eyes spitting flames. The expression on her face consigned him to the nethermost regions of hell.

"I'll be along in a minute, Lottie."

Lottie inclined her fiery red head and smiled in amusement. "Good thing you're armed, sugar. Looks like trouble is headed straight toward you," she said before she turned and sauntered into her establishment.

Kat was so outraged that her eyes prickled with tears. She could barely speak past the fierce constriction in her chest. "I want the pouch, now, before the contents are used in payment for services soon to be rendered," she gritted out.

"Kat, it's not what you—"

"Give ... me ... the ... pouch," she said slowly, succinctly—and with venom. "Nothing has been what I thought since we struck off together. You can have your cut of the gems, here and now, Lassiter. The sooner we conclude our bargain, the better."

"We are not divvying up these rocks on a crowded street," Judd muttered. "It would be an invitation for a mugging, but I'm sure you realize that, don't you?"

The goading comment made her teeth clench, her fists knot. She knew he was making reference to J.P. Trumball's death, presuming *she* had stolen the jewels from her stepfather and fed Judd a fabricated tale. God! He had never believed one damned thing she had told him—ever!

"Fine. If you prefer to divvy up after your tryst, we'll do it later."

"When?"

"Later," she all but spat at him. She knew he was pressing her for an exact time because he doubted she had any intention of giving him payment for his assignment.

Assignment . . . the word made a tormented roll through her mind. That was all she had ever been to him—that and the fringe benefits that close proximity provided.

"Since you have other plans for the moment, and far be it for me to interfere, I will look you up at my convenience," she hissed.

"I think we better discuss this situation after you've had time to calm down," Judd said, watching her face flame with anger, her body tremble with barely suppressed fury.

"Oh, we will definitely have a discussion, you can depend on it," Kat snapped. "Now give me the pouch."

Reluctantly, Judd fished the leather poke from his jacket, then stepped closer so that anyone watching would think he intended to steal a kiss from her, not transfer priceless gems to her waiting hand.

"Don't even consider it, Lassiter," she growled as his head dipped toward hers.

"You'll damn well kiss me so onlookers won't suspect you're carrying a fortune in gems. If you won't cooperate, then the jewels remain with me," he muttered tightly.

Kat remained rigid as his arms glided around her. Judd tucked the pouch in her hand and she clamped it in her fist, wishing she could clobber him with it—good and hard. His dark head angled toward hers, and it was all she could do not to bite his lips when they drifted lightly over hers.

She resented the traitorous sensations that streamed through her, hated his ability to stir her even as he was betraying her. She scolded herself when she felt herself melt against him, and then realized abruptly that she should give him a kiss to remember her by, something to curl his toes and make him wonder what they might have had together if he hadn't turned against her.

With that thought in mind, Kat curled her arm over his shoulder and arched into him. She took everything he had taught her about passion and returned it in this one sizzling kiss. She kissed him for all that could have been, for all she would have given him if he could have loved her half as much as she loved him.

To her satisfaction, she felt his male body react, felt his arms tighten around her as she savored and devoured his lips and caressed him with the provocative movements of her body.

When Kat stepped away, Judd stared oddly at her, as if he wanted to say something, but changed his mind. She inhaled a deep breath, hoping he couldn't hear her heart breaking. With the pouch concealed in the folds of her gown, Kat turned away. She cursed herself for caring for this Judas who planned to lead her into a trap and have her locked in jail.

In swift strides Kat headed for the hotel to gather what few belongings she had to her name. She refused to spill the tears that blistered her eyes. She would not allow Judd to know how much he had hurt her.

Kat had turned to only one man in her life, trusted only one man, and he had broken her trust and her heart. She would not make that mistake again. She had been right to seek freedom and independence, to ask for no more than that from life, she told herself as she tramped across the uneven boardwalk. She certainly wasn't going to be foolish enough to fancy herself in love again.

Another lesson learned, Kat mused, battling tears. She was a poor judge of men. She thought Judd was honorable and trustworthy, but she had been wrong. He, like J.P., intended to double-cross her, betray her. Kat's actions and words could never speak loudly, or strongly, enough to earn Judd's trust and loyalty. She had only been his sexual pawn, and he would see her in jail for a murder she didn't commit. She'd lose her inheritance and spend the rest of her days counting all the ways she had played the fool.

Well, you are not going to play the fool for Judd Lassiter, ever again, her pride screamed in anguish. *Never, ever, again!*

CHAPTER TWENTY

Judd cursed colorfully as he entered Lottie's plush parlor. He had hoped to conduct this investigation without involving Kat. Now she was operating on the misconception that he had come to seek pleasure in another woman's arms. The fact that he felt guilty about something he hadn't done, the fact that he had wanted to explain himself, when he wasn't a man compelled to offer explanations to anyone, bothered the hell out of him.

Judd knew damned good and well that it was in Kat's best interest to let her continue her journey without him. Yet he couldn't overlook the possibility of Rowdy Jack planning a stage robbery while Kat was in the coach. Judd remembered what had happened to the last woman Rowdy Jack and company had encountered. The thought had him cursing all over again.

He should let Kat think the worst of him, he told himself. This ill-fated attraction had no future anyway. She didn't know what he was—what he could become—when adversity demanded it. She would not understand. White society couldn't understand, because the powers he wielded could not be measured by any yardstick of civilization.

And damn it all, he'd gotten mixed signals when Kat had glared murderously at him, then kissed the breath out of him.

On second thought, he decided that scorching kiss symbolized the love-hate relationship between them . . .

Oh, hell, he didn't have time to delve into his feelings for Kat, or hers for him. He had an investigation to conduct and he didn't have much time to conduct it. Damn it, he needed something productive to happen—and quickly.

Composing himself, Judd glanced around the abandoned parlor. Most of Lottie's girls and customers were on the street, enjoying the lively festivities. This place would be jumping alive when the celebration shut down.

Judd set aside his inner frustration when the buxom madam, whose ample assets were showcased by a low-cut red satin gown that fit like a second skin, emerged from the hall.

"Now then, sugar," Lottie purred seductively as she sashayed up to walk her fingers down the buttons on his vest. "How many words did you want to have with me before we trot upstairs?"

Judd grabbed her adventurous hand, then reached into his pocket. "I want to know if you have seen any of these three men and can identify them by name."

Lottie pouted prettily when Judd turned her down flat. "And here I thought we were going to enjoy each other this evening." She eyed him perceptively. "You're sweet on that diamond heiress, aren't you?"

Judd almost smiled at the speed with which gossip traveled, but he forced himself to remain somber as he unfolded the Wanted posters. "These men are wanted for robbery and murder," he informed her in a businesslike tone.

Lottie sniffed distastefully when she recognized the man in the first sketch. "He's still going by Rowdy Jack," she said. "The bastard was in here last week. He knocked around one of my girls. Tonight is the first time she has been out of the house since the incident. I told that vicious bully—over the barrel of my shotgun—that he wasn't welcome here. Haven't seen him since, thank goodness."

Judd held up the second poster.

Lottie nodded her red head. "Crazy Ben Corothers has been here a few times. He flashes money at the girls and never asks for the same girl twice.'' She scoffed sarcastically, then added, ''According to my girls, he barely lasts a minute. In fact, they gave him another nickname: the minuteman.''

When Judd pointed at the third outlaw's sketch, Lottie's eyes widened in alarm. ''Damn, that desperado is upstairs with one of my girls right now. It's the first time I've seen him here. Hope the hell he doesn't get his pleasure from beating women, like his friend Rowdy Jack.''

Judd wheeled toward the steps. ''Which room is he in?''

''He's with Trish. Her room is at the end of the west wing.''

Judd took the steps two at a time. At least something had gone right this evening. He was about to make Arkansas Riley's acquaintance and get some accurate answers. Ark Riley was going to be more than happy to tell Judd where Rowdy and Crazy Ben were holed up, what the treacherous trio had planned.

''Trish?'' Judd called as he tapped lightly on the door.

''Go away, you sonuvabitch. She's busy with me right now.''

Judd smiled devilishly as he pulled out his pistol. He kicked at the locked door, splintering the wood. He was in the room before Ark Riley knew what was coming. The prostitute collapsed in relief when she saw the weapon aimed at her abusive client. Judd noticed the welt on the woman's cheek before his gaze homed in on the scraggly ruffian who was groping to retrieve his pistol.

''By the time you find your gun you'll already be dead,'' Judd snarled.

Trish and Ark's gazes flew to Judd, startled by the cold, hollow sound of his voice, the glowing flicker in his eyes.

''Hell,'' Ark Riley muttered as he raised his arms over his head. ''Panther? Oh, hell . . .''

There were times Judd was glad his legendary reputation preceded him. It gave even the most ruthless desperadoes pause.

Like a stalking cat, Judd approached his prey. ''I'll take the pistol and you can have your pants, Riley. But if you're inclined to leave in what little you have on, it doesn't make a damn to me.''

Ark Riley's Adam's apple bobbled noticeably when he swallowed. Judd held the man's uneasy gaze as he spoke to the dark-haired harlot who cowered in the corner. "Go downstairs so Lottie will know you're safe. Ark Riley and I will take the back exit."

Nodding her tousled head, Trish held the sheet to her bare breasts and scurried from the room. Judd kicked the door shut behind her, then smiled devilishly at Ark. "I wonder if you endure torture as well as you dish it out, Ark. We'll see."

"Look, Panther, the girl got what she deserved 'cause she wasn't giving me what I paid for—"

"Put your pants on," Judd interrupted gruffly.

Ark Riley flinched at Judd's intimidating tone and menacing stare, then reached slowly for his breeches.

"Kick the pistol over here," Judd demanded.

Ark did as he was told, then stepped into his breeches. When he thrust out a hand to grab his socks and boots, Judd shook his head.

The outlaw swallowed visibly again. "But I need—"

"You need to do exactly what I tell you." Judd's voice was as cold as a tombstone. "We're going down the back steps, *now.*"

Cautiously, hands held high, Ark Riley approached the door. "I swear on my mother's grave that there's been a mistake. I don't know who you're looking for, but—"

Ark's eyes nearly popped from their sockets when Panther's dagger pricked his neck. Damn, Ark hadn't even seen him pull the knife! The barrel of the pistol dug into Ark's ribs with enough force to separate them. An icy chill ran up and down Ark's spine as Panther's powerful body moved as close as Ark's own shadow.

There was a hazy aura radiating around the bounty hunter known as Panther. It was like a pocket of frigid air giving rise to steam. Panther was so close that Ark swore the man was going to climb inside his skin with him and rob him of breath.

"Move slowly, steadily, or you won't like the consequences."

Panther's voice was so quiet, yet so deadly, that Ark shivered again. He reached out to open the door and was stung by the unholy sensation that this notorious bounty hunter was flowing around him, swallowing him up in that icy presence that caused the temperature to drop a quick ten degrees. Damn! Panther was downright spooky!

What the hell was happening? Ark asked himself shakily. Panther's reputation was just superstitious nonsense, wasn't it? These cold sensations chasing each other down Ark's backbone were caused by fear, weren't they? Panther didn't really possess unnatural powers, did he?

Ark Riley clasped his hand around the wrought-iron railing to steady himself as he descended the back steps. The vacuum of icy air became more defined as it flowed around him, suffocating him. Ark began to panic. He couldn't explain what was happening, didn't recognize the low growl behind him as human, because it sounded like nothing he'd ever heard. Instinct told him to bolt away.

"Nowhere to run . . ."

Ark wasn't sure if he heard or thought those words, but they were penetrating his terrified thoughts and he quivered uncontrollably. In the dark silence of the alley he heard quiet breathing, the deadly rumble of a predatory cat. He felt himself being whipped around and forced down the last four steps backwards. His hands and feet were lashed to the railings so quickly that he didn't realize he'd been tethered until it was too late. Shocked, unable to move, Ark stared this way and that, trying to figure out where Panther was.

Damn, he was there, and then he wasn't!

The iciness gradually faded away, leaving Ark breathing heavily. Ark realized he was alone in the darkness. He asked himself why he thought a confrontation with the devil would be a burning experience. He'd been wrong. Panther was indeed a devil, but the sensations he incited were as numbing as ice.

A short time later, Ark heard the clip-clop of horses' hooves. He glanced over his shoulder to see a buckskin gelding and his own sorrel.

The eerie presence had returned like a chilling wind.

Doomed, Ark found himself thinking. Icy fingers clamped around his wrists to free him from the railing, but his hands and feet remained tied. As if he were light as a feather, Ark was tossed over the back of his sorrel and led down the alley.

Frantic, he tried to bargain with the devil who had taken him captive.

"You want money? I'll split what I have with you, fifty-fifty," Ark groaned as the saddle horn dug into his belly. "I know where there's a lot of money buried. If you let me go, you can have a cut."

He lifted up his head when he heard bone-chilling laughter pouring from the hazy image astride the skittish buckskin.

"I'll have it all, and you will give it willingly, Riley. I've only made one bargain in my life, and it isn't with you."

The lights of Tascosa and the lively beat of music faded into the distance. Ark Riley's thoughts ran wild, trying to conjure up a way to outsmart this man called Panther. How was he going to alert his cohorts? He consoled himself when he realized that Crazy Ben and Rowdy would know something was wrong pretty quick, because Ark was supposed to meet them beside the bank in a few minutes.

Ark told himself to start thinking fast. If he didn't find a way to escape from Panther, he had the unmistakable feeling he wouldn't live through the night. Rowdy and Crazy Ben would come to his rescue, Ark tried to reassure himself. They'd come, and with luck, the threesome would break the curse of this bounty hunter called Panther. If not . . .

Ark decided not to think about that right now, not when he had to figure out how to get loose and run like hell!

Rowdy Jack pushed away from the brick wall of the bank where he was leaning leisurely. He watched the festivities and sipped from the whiskey bottle he had stashed in his pocket. He saw Crazy Ben Corothers shouldering his way through the crowded street, making a beeline for the bank. Rowdy swore under his breath. He had specifically—and repeatedly—ordered Crazy Ben and Ark to keep low profiles around Tascosa. The stupid bastards were always making a public scene, which was the reason Rowdy had pitched camp in the nearby hills rather than booking rooms at one of the hotels. He had chewed both of them out good for entering the stage office while he was asking about schedules, destinations and buying a ticket. Those morons didn't take instructions worth a damn!

When Crazy Ben came charging toward the bank like a runaway locomotive, Rowdy ducked around the corner. The moment Crazy Ben veered around the corner, Rowdy grabbed him by the shirt collar and gave him a good shaking. "Damn it, I told you not to be so conspicuous! You're going to give us away, you idiot! We can't pull off this bank robbery after the town shuts down for the night if folks are suspicious of you darting hither and yon. What the hell's the matter with you?"

Crazy Ben jerked loose, rearranged his twisted shirt, then shot Rowdy a disgusted glower. He didn't like anybody manhandling him. He'd gotten plenty of that when he was a kid growing up in Missouri. His pa used to beat the hell out of him for pure sport—until one night when Crazy Ben fought back with a loaded rifle and ended up with a price on his head. These days nobody put their hands on Crazy Ben, unless he was too drunk to object. That included the boss of this outlaw gang.

"We've got bigger problems than being recognized, boss. In fact, it's too late for that," Crazy Ben muttered sourly. "I just saw Panther. He's here, goddamn it! He's dressed up like a gentleman, but it's him. I know it's him."

The grim news sobered Rowdy instantly. "Damn."

"Damn is right," Crazy Ben grumbled uneasily. "I heard that hotel proprietor named Hampton spouting off about how the legendary Panther had showed up to keep the riffraff in line, so I've been keeping my eyes peeled tonight. And guess what, boss: I saw Panther come swaggering out of the alley, still dressed in his fancy duds. He took Ark's sorrel mare around back of the brothel."

Rowdy jerked upright, glancing every which way at once. "Where's Ark now?"

"That's what I don't know. He was going to get himself a quick poke over at Lottie's Place. He never came out. You know what I think, boss? I think Panther got hold of him—

that's why the half-breed bastard was making off with the sorrel.''

"Hell and damnation!" Rowdy sputtered furiously. "Ark ought to know better than to go spreading some whore's legs while we've got a bank to case and extra horses to round up for a fast exit from town."

Rowdy rammed the whiskey bottle into his coat pocket, then stared thoughtfully into the dark alley. "We've gotta set up an ambush for Panther, blow him out of the saddle before he knows what hit him."

"Well, we better make it quick or it ain't going to do Ark no good. You know what they say about that damn bounty hunter. He gives no quarter. The men he hunts down never live to stand trial. Panther is judge, jury and executioner."

Rowdy snorted. "Not tonight, he ain't. The wild legend that follows him ain't gonna be worth telling after tonight." Rowdy wheeled sideways, staggering slightly. "Get your horse and meet me east of town. We'll follow that headhunter and pick him off when he least expects it."

Crazy Ben zigzagged through the crowd, shoving people out of his way in his haste to cross the street. *We can still pull off this bank heist,* Crazy Ben assured himself. He and Rowdy would make short work of that cocky pistolero, free Ark Riley, then blast the vault open with gunpowder. They would make arrangements to rob the stage, and they would be long gone before Tascosans could figure out who did it and mount a posse to give chase.

Crazy Ben smiled confidently. Maybe Panther had done them a favor by showing up when he did. They could make certain that headhunter wouldn't be tracking them, because he would be six feet under Boot Hill—real soon.

Kat packed her meager belongings and stacked them neatly on the chair beside the commode. She had paced the floorboards for an hour, attempting to get her roiling emotions in hand. But every time she thought of Judd swaggering into the brothel with the well-endowed madam, hurt and disappointment came crashing down like an avalanche.

Kat realized now that her lack of experience in romantic endeavors had caused her to get the wrong impression of her intimate encounters with Judd. He had been so tender and gentle with her that she assumed he cared—just a little. Obviously, gentleness was a technique he relied on to seduce women.

Damn it, how could she have been so naive? How could she have for one moment thought she was woman enough to satisfy a man as experienced as Judd Lassiter? And worse, why had she thought there was more between them than physical attraction?

Kat cursed herself for the umpteenth time. She had brought down these painful feelings on herself. Judd certainly hadn't made any sort of commitment or indicated that he might be falling a little bit in love with her while she was nose-diving into love with him. In all fairness, she supposed she couldn't hold him at fault that she cared more about him than he cared for her.

After the third heart-to-heart talk with herself, Kat ordered her smarting feminine pride to stop laying blame where it didn't belong. No other woman had captured Judd Lassiter's affection permanently. So why had she thought she would be the first and only? Lord, such arrogance!

Kat plunked down on the edge of her bed to sort out the gems. She tucked two glittering diamonds, a ruby and an emerald inside her stocking and replaced the others in the pouch. After tucking the pouch in her clunky boots, Kat headed for the door.

By now Judd should have finished his ... tryst ... with Lottie and was probably headed for his campsite by the springs. Kat decided to approach him in a businesslike manner, give him his share of the gems, then ride west to await tomorrow's stage.

Since the livery stable attendant had abandoned his post to enjoy the festivities, Kat retrieved her mare and struggled to situate herself in the saddle. The cumbersome dress made the task more difficult than ever before, but Kat was nothing if not determined.

Resolutely, she rode out of town, following the dirt road due north. The mare pricked her ears and sidestepped as Kat stared into the distance. A prickle of unease spread across her skin as she glanced sideways.

Maybe riding out alone wasn't such a grand idea, she thought to herself. She had no weapons of defense, nothing but a few hand-to-hand combat skills Judd had taught her.

When Kat noticed the campfire in the distance, she relaxed. She was near Judd's camp—within shouting distance, in fact. Urging the mare into a trot, and telling herself that danger— if there was any—wouldn't have a chance to strike before she reached her destination, Kat rehearsed what she intended to say when she encountered Judd Lassiter for the very last time.

Rowdy Jack crouched in the cottonwood trees that lined the road to Dodge City. A devilish grin pursed his lips when he spotted the woman in bright yellow riding in the moonlight.

"Well, well," Rowdy snickered wickedly. "If it ain't the high and mighty miss we met at the stage office."

Crazy Ben hunkered down beside Rowdy. "Word around town is that Panther is sweet on that lady. I heard that he escorted her to the restaurant, then took her to the dance. The menfolk in town were wondering if they would get their chance to dance with her. Rumor also has it that she has a high-falutin pedigree and lots of money, but she still keeps company with that half-breed savage. Looks like she's headed out for a tumble in the grass with him."

Rowdy chuckled fiendishly. "Well, ain't both of them going to be in for a surprise when we ruin their roll in the hay?"

Crazy Ben frowned, bemused. "What have you got planned, boss?"

"We're going to grab ourselves some bargaining power," he explained. "The prissy lady's life for Ark Riley's. Panther might just have a weakness for that bit of fluff, and we can use it to our advantage."

"You're a smart one, Rowdy, always coming up with a scheme when things get tense."

Rowdy gestured toward the east. "You circle around and we'll attack the snotty lady from two directions at once. Don't make any unnecessary racket, either," Rowdy ordered as he crept through the underbrush to mount his horse. "We don't want to alert Panther that he's about to have company. Know what I mean?"

Crazy Ben grinned nastily. "I got it, boss, and I want first turn with the lady when we're through with Panther."

"Fine, you get her first, but only if you follow my orders," Rowdy said before he took his position in the skirting of trees . . . and waited for the right moment to pounce . . .

"Where are Crazy Ben and Rowdy?"

Ark Riley winced when the menacing shadow fell over him. He had been staked out between two scrubby cedars on the hillside and left alone for several minutes. Then suddenly Panther was back, looming over him, changing forms like an incandescent fog. Ark's nerves tingled as he gaped at "the thing" that had eyes like glowing coals, and a dark shadow within the icy haze. The hair stood up on the back of Ark's neck, and he squirmed futilely against the bands of rope.

"Holy . . . !" Ark's voice dried up when the eerie presence came closer, revealing itself in the moonlight. This was the creature who inspired legends, Ark realized. The Phantom Panther did live and breathe! And worse, the creature raised its shrill, unearthly scream to attract its own kind.

Ark tensed when he heard the answering caterwauls above him on the hill. He twisted sideways to see three midnight-black pumas stalking downhill, their tails whipping like those of scorpions, their eyes burning down on him. Damnation! Those vicious predators were going to make a meal of him!

"Answer me, Riley." The hollow, guttural voice rolled from the dense fog that had taken on the form of a great white puma.

"I-I d-don't know," Ark bleated. "They're still in town, I guess."

"Where are you camped?"

Again the voice drifted toward him like an arctic wind. Ark

shivered nervously. "In the ravine to the east." He sure as hell wasn't going to keep his trap shut and let Rowdy and Crazy Ben get off scot-free. If singing like a stool pigeon would save Ark's hide, then he'd damned sure sing!

Green-gold eyes—like flames burning in ice—bore down ominously on Ark.

"Your plans. Tell me what they are."

"No plans," Ark squeaked, casting anxious glances at the prowling black cats above him. "We're just lying low—that's all—*argh!*"

Ark whimpered when the specter reared on hind legs and spun like a twisting plume of fog. Sharp talons lashed across Ark's outstretched arm so quickly that the path left by the striking paw was reminiscent of a meteor's tail. In horror, he stared at the swirling fog, then glanced at the devil cat poised at his left, another at his right, the third standing guard above his head—ready to pounce.

"We were going to hit the bank, then the stage," Ark blurted out hurriedly.

"When?"

"Tonight after the festivities, then tomorrow. Rowdy is going to be inside the coach so he can take the driver by surprise," Ark panted. "I'll make you a deal, any deal—just keep those killer cats off me! Just don't claw me again, Panther. I've told you what you want to know!"

Ark squealed like a stuck pig when Panther spoke in a foreign tongue and two black cats drew blood with their razor-sharp claws, then toyed with him as if he were a defenseless mouse. "I swear I've told you everything! Get those cats away from me—"

"Where did you bury the stolen money?"

Another slash of sharp claws brought the guarded secret to Ark's tongue. He twittered like a canary to give directions.

Ark's voice trailed off as the evanescent shadow retreated into itself, then faded into nothingness. To Ark's shocked amazement, the black cats vanished as if they had never been there.

"What in the hell?"

His chest rose and fell rapidly as he glanced around, finding himself alone. All he saw was the reflection of predatory eyes watching him from the shadows of the trees. They were out there, waiting, just as the legend said. If Ark hadn't seen the phenomenon with his own eyes, felt the slash of claws, he never would have believed it.

He just wasn't sure he would live to tell about his terrifying encounter with the Phantom Panther and his four-legged executioners.

CHAPTER TWENTY-ONE

Kat jerked in alarm when she heard thundering hooves coming toward her from opposite directions. She'd thought she was close enough to Judd's campsite to escape trouble.

She thought wrong.

Teeth gritted, Kat gouged the mare, then clamped her legs to the horse's flanks, as Judd had taught her to do. She remembered he had told her to ride hell-for-leather and stay low so she didn't present an easy target when she was being chased. She raced off, watching the mare eat up the ground beneath her, hoping the mare had enough speed to outrun the horses galloping toward her.

The riders approached with amazing speed and they were soon upon her. To Kat's dismay, she found herself staring down the spitting end of two pistols.

Kat swore under her breath when she recognized the men she had encountered in the stage office. Rowdy Jack leaned out from his horse to snatch her mare's reins. Kat struck out with her foot, causing Rowdy's mount to bolt sideways and toss him off balance. He hit the ground with a thump and a foul curse. Kat dug her heels into the mare, and the horse leaped over the downed man who still clung to the reins.

When Crazy Ben reached out to snag her arm, Kat took a vicious bite out of his hide and left him howling in pain. Again, Kat tried to urge the horse forward, but Rowdy Jack bounded up to drag her off the mare. His arm slid around her neck, attempting to choke her into submission.

"Lassiter!" Kat screamed at the top of her lungs. "Lass—" She gasped when her assailant cut off her air supply.

"Shut up!" Rowdy Jack sneered as he bent Kat sideways to apply more pressure to her throat. "One more word and you're dead. Hear me? *Dead.* You're gonna get us into that half-breed's camp, free and clear. Now don't give me no more trouble, because I've already lost patience with you."

Kat mouthed an expletive and struggled to draw breath. No way was she going to jeopardize Judd's life. No one was going to use her as a shield of defense!

Kat fought like a cornered wildcat. She struck out with hands and feet in a flurry of bites and kicks that had Rowdy hissing in pain. He reflexively recoiled when Kat took a chunk out of his arm and kneed him in the groin.

Rowdy was still holding onto her when he hit the ground cursing, but Kat was determined to wrest free. She crammed her elbow into Rowdy's underbelly, then kneed him again on her way to her feet.

The horses were prancing nervously around the melee, and Kat backhanded one of the mounts across the muzzle, causing it to rear up. Rowdy rolled sideways before his horse landed on him, and he cursed ripely when Kat hiked up her hindering skirt and sprinted toward the shelter of underbrush beside the road.

"Get her, damn it!" Rowdy hissed as he shook the sting of bites from his arms.

Crazy Ben lowered his head and charged after her. Kat could hear the pounding of hooves and quickly switched direction. She plunged headfirst into the bushes and groped for anything that would serve as a weapon. The first thing she latched onto was a branch. With improvised weapon in hand, she huddled in the underbrush, awaiting her chance to attack, then escape.

What she hadn't expected was for Crazy Ben to ride his

horse over the top of her. The horse reared up, and she heard Crazy Ben swear profusely when his head thumped against an overhanging limb. He somersaulted backward when his mount plunged forward, and he was left spread-eagled in the underbrush.

Kat leaped to her feet to chase down the horse, but Crazy Ben snaked out his hand to swipe at her ankle, sending her cartwheeling across the grass. She managed to land one hard blow to Crazy Ben's head with the tree branch, but Rowdy Jack arrived on the scene to tackle her, leaving her muttering curses into the grass.

"Get hold of her hands," Rowdy ordered Crazy Ben. "And watch out for those claws and teeth. She don't fight like any woman I ever met. Most of 'em just scream and whimper and beg for mercy."

Kat's breath came out in a whoosh when Crazy Ben plunked down on top of her to restrain her arms. "Lassiter!" she shrieked with what little breath she had left. "Run for your life, run—!"

"What does it take to make you shut the hell up, woman!" Crazy Ben snarled as he shoved her face into the grass, then wrenched her arms behind her back.

Kat refused to lie still while her ankles and wrists were bound up. She wiggled and squirmed and bucked, but when Rowdy grabbed a handful of her hair and jerked her head backward, she was forced to her feet.

Rowdy smiled snidely as he hooked his hands under her arms and motioned for Crazy Ben to grab her feet. "Now then, Miss High and Mighty, we're gonna have a nice little chitchat with Panther."

Kat wormed and wiggled while she was carried back to the road. She sent up a couple of shouts and was rewarded with a slap in the face. When the men tossed her over her mare and dropped a noose over her neck—yanking it so tight she could barely breathe—Kat accepted defeat.

Because she had no other choice, Kat lay jackknifed over her saddle. When Rowdy cut her some slack on the noose, Kat took advantage and yelled Judd's name, pleading with him to escape.

"Damn you!" Rowdy snarled as he kicked her in the hip. "You're the stubbornest female I ever came across. Now shut the hell up!"

"Never—"

Pain exploded in Kat's skull when Crazy Ben hammered her with the butt of his pistol. The world turned pitch-black before Kat could yell Judd's name again.

"Damnedest thing I ever saw," Crazy Ben muttered as he reholstered his pistol and stared at the unconscious woman. "Who'd have thought this prissy bit of fluff had so much fight and sass in her?" He grinned nastily. "I can't begin to tell you how much I'm gonna enjoy taking this chit."

"Well, we're gonna get Ark back first," Rowdy said firmly. "After that, I don't care what you do with her."

Judd felt a chill of icy dread sinking into his soul when he heard Kat's desperate screams echoing in the darkness. He had ridden off to locate Rowdy and Crazy Ben's campsite and the buried loot, but thank goodness he hadn't ridden so far away that he hadn't heard Kat. Although she called out for him to run for his life, Judd turned back. He had never walked away from a battle in his life and he wasn't about to start now, especially if Kat needed him.

On the heels of that thought came the wary suspicion that Kat was setting him up for a trap. She had insisted they would divvy up the jewels later this evening, but if she planned to keep the stones for herself, all she had to do was board the stage and leave town.

But then, how to explain the fact that Kat now seemed to be in serious trouble but hadn't asked for his help? Instead she had warned him away.

Despite the unease curling down his spine, Judd felt relief in knowing that Kat was concerned about his safety—more concerned about *his,* apparently, than her own.

Judd jerked Horse to a halt, then glanced toward the eastern slope of the hillside where he had left Ark Riley staked out. There were enough boulders and underbrush on the slope to conceal himself from view. From the sound of things, someone was heading toward his camp, someone Kat viewed as a threat.

Damn, could it be that Rowdy and Crazy Ben had come looking for Ark, and Kat had blundered upon them? That was the only logical explanation Judd could come up with, and he sure as hell didn't like it. Judd knew damned well how this ruthless trio treated women. He wouldn't wish their abuse on his worst enemy.

Judd gritted his teeth against the fierce, protective need that threatened to swamp him. On several occasions, the desperadoes he chased had taken hostages in hopes of saving themselves. Always before, Judd had been concerned about the safety of the hostages, but he had never been emotionally involved with them.

He was definitely involved now.

The simple truth was that rescuing Kat was his foremost concern. Suddenly, this wasn't about apprehending vicious outlaws or putting his life on the line. It was about Kat's life.

Only that.

Judd made a pact with himself, there and then, that he would do whatever was necessary to save her. Whatever it took, even if it meant destroying the image of what Kat *thought* he was and her discovering what he really was, he mused as he dismounted.

Judd stared into the night and drew deep within himself, reaching down to one level of consciousness, then another, and another, finding that mystical source of power, spirit and strength that was his to dispense at will. He breathed in slowly, then closed his eyes, feeling the Cheyenne guardian spirit consume him. When he opened his eyes, he could see two riders approaching, leading Kat who was slung over her mare.

Rage pummeled him, but he channeled the emotion into the great forces that he had been taught to command. He let the powers and emotions feed upon themselves, generating more strength, radiating, expanding, encompassing. He raised his face and his voice to the Cheyenne moon, and the bone-chilling scream of the Phantom Panther brought down the night.

* * *

"What the hell was that?" Crazy Ben chirped, then shifted uneasily when his mount sidestepped.

Kat roused to the sound of the unearthly scream echoing across the valley. Groggy though she was, she recognized that haunting sound, took comfort in it. When a trio of caterwauls answered the high-pitched shriek, Kat knew that Rowdy Jack and Crazy Ben were about to confront the revelation she had witnessed that night in Whispering Springs Canyon. These vicious renegades were going to encounter the living legend, Kat assured herself.

"If I were you, I would turn tail and run while you can," Kat advised her captors.

"Just shut up," Rowdy sneered at her, even as he glanced apprehensively around him, watching the shadows shift and sway on the hillside.

"Only a rare few have confronted the Phantom Panther and lived to tell about it," Kat goaded him. "You are on a fool's errand."

"What do you know about it?" Crazy Ben smirked.

"I was visited by the vision," Kat assured her captors. "But the Phantom Panther's mission is to destroy evil. You won't stand a chance when he calls to the night of a thousand eyes—"

"I said shut up!" Rowdy barked, then immediately lowered his voice. "There's no such thing as the Phantom Panther. It's just superstition—"

A wild, ear-splitting scream interrupted his gruff denial. A dozen caterwauls reverberated down the hill, followed by a dozen more.

"Damn, Rowdy. Sounds like there's a hundred mountain lions prowling on that hill," Crazy Ben said uneasily.

"Doesn't matter if there's a thousand," Rowdy said with brash confidence. "We've got the woman. She's our insurance. Lassiter is sweet on her. You said so yourself."

"Even if that were true, which I am here to tell you that it isn't," Kat inserted, "Lassiter is no longer in the camp. Now he is one of *them*. Unless you light out of here while you still can, you are going to be dreadfully sorry you didn't believe me.''

The loud chorus of caterwauls and shrill shrieks couldn't have been more timely, Kat decided. The eerie sounds left Crazy Ben and Rowdy Jack squirming on their saddles. Unfortunately, though, Rowdy's criminal mentality defied the blatant warnings. He had more rebellious bravado than good sense.

Kat only hoped the conclusions she had drawn—after her vision sighting, the sudden appearance of the three black cats in Palo Duro Canyon, and the "initiation" scars she had seen on Judd's back—meant what she assumed they meant. She sincerely hoped that Panther was everything the legends claimed he was, for Kat couldn't bear to watch him die because of her. That would be the crowning blow. She would not be the Judas goat who caused the destruction of her mentor.

When a man's bloodcurdling scream arose from the hillside, Crazy Ben glanced dubiously at Rowdy. "I don't know if this is such a good idea after all, boss. I vote to cut our losses and let Ark fend for himself as best he can—"

"You can shut up, too," Rowdy snapped hatefully. He jerked his steed to a halt, inhaled a deep breath that made his chest expand noticeably, then hitched his thumb toward Kat. "Get the woman off her horse and hurry up about it."

Muttering, Crazy Ben dismounted. He grabbed Kat roughly by the shoulders and hauled her to the ground. He had a pistol at her throat before he propped her upright. "One false move, princess, and you're looking at a royal funeral," he hissed in her ear. "Don't think for a second that I value your life more than my own. I'll shoot you if I have to and won't lose a wink of sleep over it. You ain't the first woman I dropped in her tracks, I guaran-damn-tee it."

"Lassiter!" Rowdy bellowed at the swaying shadows of the trees. "We've come to make a trade! The princess for Ark Riley. You interested? Or should we take our turns with this highfalutin lady before we kill her?"

Kat stared in amazed fascination as twin pinpoints of light appeared by the hundreds on the hillside. "Night of a thousand eyes," she murmured, remembering the fantastic legend. "Uh-oh, you boys have really done it now. You've made the Phantom Panther killingly mad—''

Kat wasn't allowed to finish her sentence, because Crazy Ben backhanded her, causing her to tumble at his feet.

''I told you to shut the hell up, woman!''

Another unreal scream rose from the hillside, followed by echoing growls and snarls.

''Rowdy, I don't like the sound of things,'' Crazy Ben whispered. ''For all we know, that bounty hunter may have already killed Ark.''

Kat could feel Crazy Ben's tension as he grabbed her arm and jerked her back to her feet. He held her in front of him like a shield, his body rigid and on full alert. He had her neck in a vise grip, and the pistol barrel quivered against her throat.

''Make up your mind, Lassiter. I ain't a patient man,'' Rowdy called out.

''*Let the woman go . . .*''

Kat heard the cold, hollow voice behind her. When Crazy Ben whipped her around to keep her between him and Panther, she found herself staring at the evanescent image she had encountered that night at Whispering Springs. Eyes embedded in a swirl of incandescent fog flared up like dancing flames. The vague image of a white puma rearing upon its hind legs was visible in the shifting wreath of phosphorescent haze.

''Geezus!'' Crazy Ben croaked. ''What is that thing?''

Even Rowdy had enough sense to look uneasy, Kat noticed, but the man couldn't overcome his bullheadedness. He raised his bearded chin to a defiant angle and snarled, ''Let Ark go and you can have this princess.''

When a strange sound broke the silence, Crazy Ben flinched, then glanced left and right. ''What was *that?*''

''Prowling catamounts,'' Kat informed her jittery captor. ''I told you this was a bad idea.''

''Rowdy! Crazy Ben! Help me!'' Ark Riley howled in frantic desperation.

The panicky call set off a chain reaction. Rowdy cursed mightily, Crazy Ben swore, and the hazy apparition lashed out with its great paws.

Out of the corner of her eye, Kat saw Rowdy reach for his pistol. She knew the scoundrel had run out of patience. The specter was getting to him. The outlaw was ready to do what had become second nature to him—draw and fire.

''No!'' Kat bounded from Crazy Ben's grasp in two long leaps. The great creature had no weapon for protection, and he refused to pounce while Kat was in the way. Kat refused to stand there doing nothing, refused to watch Panther be brought down by these worthless outlaws. Panther needed her protection, and she wasn't going to let him die! She couldn't bear to watch it happen!

A haunting scream erupted at the same moment Rowdy fired. Kat felt the searing pain beneath her shoulder blade, felt the tingling sensations in her left arm, but her gaze was fixed on the unearthly vision and those glowing eyes that were riveted on her. Kat's legs folded involuntarily, dumping her on the grass. Her chest ached, but she struggled to draw breath, squirmed sideways so she could keep her eyes on the eerie specter that hovered in front of her.

Agonizing pain and an odd numbness spread through her. Kat felt as if she were suspended in time and space, watching from behind windows that were her eyes. It was the most peculiar feeling she had ever experienced—as if she were there, but she wasn't. While she was floating in this indescribably dizzy state, she realized she had ruined the expensive yellow dress Judd had given her. It felt wet and sticky against her skin, and she looked down to see the garment changing color before her fuzzy vision. *Ruined,* she thought as her breath seesawed in and out and blood pounded in her ears.

She had ruined the only gift Judd had given her . . .

The thought spiraled away when an enraged growl exploded above her, answered by a chorus of vicious snarls. Kat heard Rowdy and Crazy Ben scream as they turned tail and ran from the dark shadows that materialized from the underbrush. Pinpoints of glowing lights converged in the valley. The sounds were deafening, overriding Rowdy and Crazy Ben's horrified screams.

Kat fought to remain conscious, determined to see exactly

what was happening, but a gray haze blanketed her vision and she couldn't muster the strength to keep her eyes open. With each throb of heartbeat she felt her energy ebb like the tide receding from the shore.

There was so much Kat wanted to say to Panther—so many tender emotions that begged to be voiced—but Kat couldn't form the words, because pain paralyzed her. She collapsed on the ground as inhuman growls of outrage mingled with the terrified howls of the damned . . .

An ice-cold mist swept over Crazy Ben as he dashed toward the sound of Ark Riley's horrified voice. Rowdy Jack was hot on his heels, but the powerful swipe of claws that came at him from out of nowhere sent his pistol windmilling from his fist. False bravado fled when Rowdy felt the vaporous specter breathing down his neck.

Maddening, otherworldly screams shouted down the night as the incongruous shadows leaped toward Rowdy and Crazy Ben. It was as if the valley had come alive with glaring eyes that flickered like fireflies telegraphing condemnation and doom.

Frantic, panting for breath, Rowdy scrabbled up the slope to find Ark Riley staked out like a human sacrifice. Rowdy grabbed his knife to cut Ark loose, then staggered back, slamming into Crazy Ben.

"Holy damn!" Rowdy squawked when the ethereal creature—that he thought was right *behind* him—re-formed in a haze that floated on the hillside.

"Oh, God!" Crazy Ben gasped when three jet-black panthers materialized from the darkness to take their places beside the vaporous specter that rose up higher and higher, expanding like a thundercloud.

Crazy Ben turned to run for his life, but there was nowhere to run. The dark cats were multiplying by the second, forming a ring around him. Crazy Ben flinched when something latched onto his ankle. He glanced down to see Ark Riley trying to pull himself to his feet. His shoulders and arms glistened with bloody gashes, and he was whimpering the same way Ark had left his victims whimpering behind his trail of terror.

"You have met your doom and you will die as you have lived. There will be no mercy for your black souls!"

A frigid wind brought the words down upon the three desperadoes. Rowdy, in a last stand of defiance, clawed at Crazy Ben's holster to retrieve a pistol.

"Don't shoot at the thing!" Crazy Ben raved at him. "You'll bring hell down on us all!"

Rowdy didn't heed his cohort's advice; he raised the pistol and fired off four quick shots. His eyes bulged when the phantasmal apparition floated toward him, accompanied by the howling chants of a thousand catamounts. The wind seethed, shadows sprang and devoured. Rowdy felt the slash of unseen claws tearing at his flesh, heard the snarls amplifying around him as he wilted on the ground beneath an oppressive weight he couldn't see, only feel.

He screamed in horror when the flaming eyes of hell descended on him, engulfing him in their icy flames. Behind him he heard Crazy Ben and Ark shrieking, begging for mercy that wouldn't come. The eerie noises, the agonizing pain that consumed him, brought an instant of terrifying revelation. He heard that hollow voice winding toward him, as if through a long tunnel. Rowdy knew, right then, that this was just the beginning of the tortures the damned endured.

It was his last thought before he and his companions were swallowed up by the howls that brought down the night . . .

CHAPTER
TWENTY-TWO

"Damn, double damn, triple damn!" Judd chanted as he knelt beside Kat's lifeless body.

He breathed slowly, deeply, calling himself back from where he had been, wishing the powers bestowed on him included touch healing. He would have given everything he had, everything he was, if he could lay his hand on Kat and bring back her vibrant spirit. But it was not within him to do that.

Hand shaking, Judd touched his forefinger to her neck, praying he would feel her pulse—and alternately cursing her for launching herself into harm's way. What the hell had she been thinking? Why had she put her own life on the line like that? For him? Why?

How much had Kat seen while he dealt with the ruthless desperadoes? He knew she had seen the transformation in him and he grimaced, remembering. Had he alienated her now that she knew the truth about those legends and so-called myths? Had she been so shocked by his appearance that she had cried out, "No!" and leaped toward him in denial? Or had she truly tried to save him from Rowdy Jack's gunshot?

He wanted to believe that when Kat leaped toward him it indicated a desire to protect, despite what she had witnessed.

But in that tense moment she might have leaped toward him out of the need to *be* protected, not to protect.

Judd let his breath out on a ragged sigh and forced himself to concentrate on finding a pulse, but it wasn't easy while dozens of intense emotions were warring inside him. Finally, he felt a faint throb that indicated Kat was alive—barely.

He glanced wildly around him, trying to decide what to do. He wanted to take Kat to the hotel to recuperate in comfort, but he wasn't sure she would survive being transported on horseback, not when she had lost so much blood already.

"Damn it," Judd muttered as he carefully scooped her up in his arms and carried her to the campfire.

Judd ripped strips from her petticoats to use as a makeshift tourniquet, then peeled away the bodice of her gown. He spewed several foul curses when he saw the jagged wound below her collarbone.

Kat had been struck at close range, and the bullet had passed from back to front. The thought of one scar—much less two— marring her body sickened him. The thought that Kat might have risked *her* life to save *his* tormented him to the extreme. Wondering if it had been shocked denial that had sent her toward him, and accidentally got herself shot, tortured him no end. Either way, her life was ebbing from her body *because* of him.

Then suddenly, vividly, unmistakably, Judd realized that all his doubts and suspicions about Kat were ill-founded. She had come to the camp to divvy the jewels. She would never have thrust herself in the line of fire if it had been her intention to double-cross him.

Judd slumped when that realization hit him like a ton of rock. All these weeks he had refused to trust Kat completely. He had kept his heart at a safe distance, for fear of being betrayed. But Kat's courageous feat spoke louder than words, louder than lingering doubt. Somehow he knew that wild leap she had made had been an attempt to protect him, even if she had been stunned by the revelation of seeing him transform into the vaporous creature she had encountered at Whispering Springs.

Kat had cared more about him than about her pouch of precious gems, more than the freedom and independence she had waited for years to enjoy. Judd was awed and humbled by that knowledge—though he still cursed her mightily for throwing herself in front of that damn bullet! It spoke a great deal about Kat's character, though he would have preferred to find it out the easy way, not the hard way. Seeing her unconscious and bleeding was definitely the hard way, because when Kat was seriously injured, Judd did a lot of bleeding himself.

Only twice in his life had he agonized over someone. Bad as it had felt, it had never felt like this.

Casting aside his meandering thoughts, Judd focused on binding Kat's wounds. Then he scooped her limp body onto the bedroll he had spread out for her. When he had the campfire blazing, he hoped the radiating heat would warm the chill in his soul. But nothing could do that, not until he was one hundred percent certain that Kat would survive.

When she was resting comfortably, Judd twisted on his haunches and whistled at Horse. The gelding pricked his ears and looked up from the plush grass where he grazed. The second whistle brought Horse sidestepping downhill. Judd stood up to grab the saddlebag, then quickly unfastened the saddle so Horse could wander off to graze. Judd dug into the medicine pouch he carried with him, anxious to mix a poultice to pack on the wound before infection set in.

In the distance Judd heard the wailing cries of the panthers, voicing the tormented emotions that flooded through his heart. Knowing how wrong he had been about Kat tore him apart. Knowing that Kat had still come to his defense, even while she believed he had betrayed her with Lottie, weighed heavily on his soul. Kat had risked everything to ensure his safety. Judd had never known such steadfast loyalty. The very thought touched him so deeply that emotion clouded his eyes as he stared at Kat's ashen face.

Judd mixed a balm from mesquite tree leaves and the milky juice of cactus that he kept for emergencies. A rueful smile pursed his lips as he spread the poultice on the wound. More than a decade ago he had set aside his emotions, his own pleasures, to pursue the worst elements of society. He supposed his crusade for justice was his way of seeing that the outlaws who had molested and killed his mother all those years ago received retribution.

He supposed he had been on some kind of mission his entire adult life—a mission of revenge against his mother's brutal death, a death that had altered the course of his life. He had been hell-bent on punishing those vicious white bastards and all their kind.

That life-altering disaster had forced Judd into white civilization, forced him to endure the mocking scorn of being a half-breed. Judd had buried his feelings deep inside himself so he wouldn't be hurt again. But Kat Diamond had resurrected his emotions and made him feel too human again, too vulnerable.

When Kat stirred and moaned miserably, tender emotion squeezed at Judd's heart. He knelt beside her to comb those riotous tangles of curly hair away from her peaked face.

"Panther?" Kat licked her bone-dry lips. Her throat felt as if it were filled with sand. "A drink," she requested hoarsely.

Judd reached for the remainder of water in the cup he had scooped from the spring to make the healing poultice. "Here, princess." He levered her head up and pressed the tin cup to her blue-tinged lips, wondering if she would shrink away from his touch now that she had seen him at his very worst, knew the legend to be true. But to his surprise, Kat simply drank the water. He decided she was too dazed with pain to react to him right now. Later, if—*when*—she recovered, she would come to her senses and tell him she wanted no association with the creature she had seen bringing doom down upon those vicious outlaws.

"The outlaws?" she asked hoarsely.

"They will never bother you again," he assured her.

Her dull-eyed gaze lifted to him. "And you are safe and sound?"

"Yes," Judd answered but he couldn't help himself from scolding her. "You should have stayed where you were."

A smile wobbled on her lips. "Couldn't let you die . . ."

When her face turned deathly white, Judd eased her back to

the pallet. "Close your eyes and rest and let me return the favor," he ordered more briskly than he intended. But then, he wasn't sure Kat had heard him, because she slumped unconscious on the pallet before he finished speaking.

Judd worked quickly to apply another layer of medicinal salve to the wounds, then he bandaged her back and shoulder. The notice Kat had tucked in her chemise tumbled free when Judd tried to rearrange her soiled gown. He forgot to breathe as he watched the folded paper plop on the ground. He picked up the notice, then cursed mightily. Kat knew that he hadn't trusted her. Still, she had tried to protect him. Why?

While Kat slept, Judd paced. He halted abruptly when he realized he had borrowed her favorite mannerism. Damn, the woman's influence on him was mind-boggling. She had him feeling every emotion under the sun, had him pacing to do his thinking, and had him wondering how *he* was going to survive if *she* didn't.

Life seemed so damn unfair, Judd thought to himself. To take something as rare, vibrant and beautiful as Kat Diamond and reduce her to pain-ridden sleep made Judd ache to curse all the powers that be. It made him ashamed that he had ever doubted her.

Hell's fire, this was a lousy way for him to learn the truth about her, learn that she had been honest and forthright with him from the very beginning. He was certain now that J.P. Trumball had offered a twisted version of the facts when he'd tried to gain Judd's cooperation. He knew Kat had not conspired with Hugh and Chester, even if they weren't around for him to torture the truth out of them. Kat was right, he decided. She couldn't possibly have arranged a rendezvous with those henchmen, because she wasn't familiar with the area. Judd had simply overreacted, spurred by wariness and mistrust.

Kat Diamond was exactly who and what she said she was. All she had wanted when she left Baton Rouge was to be out from under Trumball's manipulative thumb and his mounting debts. She wanted to find freedom and independence and have the opportunity to make her own choices in life.

Judd vowed, then and there, that he would do all within his

power to make sure that Kat enjoyed her heart's greatest desires. He would tend her wounds, provide her with protection, nourishment and compassion. Like a bird with a broken wing, he would heal her, then let her fly free.

Letting Kat go wouldn't be easy, Judd knew, but he couldn't ask her to stay with him, couldn't ask her to live a gypsy way of life in the wilderness. She was meant for the comforts, luxuries and sophistication of society, and he couldn't bear confinement. He had tried it once and had grown restless in a house that didn't breathe. He had become resentful of walking through crowded streets rather than communing with nature. He was a creature of nature, a half-breed by birth but a Cheyenne warrior at heart.

Judd peered down at the wan face bathed in flickering firelight. He knew what he had to do—he had to let Kat spread her wings and fly. But until that day came for her to board the stage for Santa Fe, he would see that she wanted for absolutely nothing. He would compensate tenfold for every doubt and suspicion he had harbored about her.

Resolved to enjoy Kat for as long as time would allow, Judd eased down beside her, providing his warmth and strength, praying to all the spirits of the Cheyenne nation that Kat would survive the night.

Kat stirred restlessly on the pallet, tossing her head to and fro. Images converged, then receded. The encompassing heat burned like fire and Kat instinctively moved away from it, trying to cool her enflamed body. She rose to a higher level of consciousness, then groaned miserably.

Vaguely, she became aware of the burning pain in her shoulder, the numbness in her arm. She couldn't determine where she was, or how she had gotten here. All she knew was that her body complained about the slightest movement, yet she felt the need to move.

Cold chills replaced the excessive heat, and Kat couldn't control her chattering teeth and quivering body. She felt so weak, helpless, so alone in a hazy world. That was the worst of it, she thought groggily. She was so alone. The man she loved had never learned to trust her, never learned to return her love. So what was the point of fighting for her life? It was an empty and unfulfilled existence. Why not sink into the dark abyss that yawned beneath her and let fate play its trump card?

"No, Katherine Elaine Diamond, you are not *giving up,* came a silent, insistent voice. *You* will *survive. That is what life is about. You must meet every challenge and conquer difficulty. That is what gives you character. You must* make *your own place,* find *your own happiness. Only those who possess unfaltering hearts and unwavering spirit defy difficult odds. You* will *fight for your life with everything that is in you. Fight, Katherine.*

Involuntarily, Kat inched toward the reassuring warmth and strength she felt lingering beside her. She could not allow herself to succumb to that sense of fatalism and despair. She would feed on the strength that seemed to encircle her. She would take comfort in the whispered words she couldn't interpret.

She slept, ignoring the feverish pain that throbbed through her body.

An eternity later Kat felt cool liquid skimming her lips, followed by a pasty substance that made her wrinkle her nose in distaste. Dear Lord, what was that awful taste? The taste of death?

She tried to reject the deadly potion but she felt her mouth being forced open, her throat massaged. As hard as she tried to resist, she swallowed the nauseating potion.

When a cold cloth glided over her pebbled skin, chills rippled through her body. Kat shrank away from the icy touch, yearning for warmth. She was sure she was being tortured, because the throb in her shoulder intensified. And her back! She felt as if someone had buried a dagger to the hilt. She cried out against the burning pain that pummeled her, then felt the prick of something sharp against her flesh. Nausea churned in her stomach, and hazy darkness swirled around her like drifting smoke. She was disoriented and frantic, afraid the sick feelings were going to strip away her will to survive.

As before, a quiet voice beckoned her away from the pit of black silence, refusing to let her give in to the agonizing pain. Yet the pain was so intense that Kat couldn't bear it quietly. She screamed and caught the scent of seared flesh.

Lord have mercy! She must be in hell. She was one of the newly damned who was being tortured by fire. Soon the agonizing ache in her back and shoulder would spread until it consumed her entirely. Why should she keep fighting when it was a hopeless battle? It was too late to survive.

Too late, Kat thought as the unbearable pain buffeted her, sending her tumbling into dark infinity.

Judd sank back on his haunches and wiped beads of sweat from his brow. Cauterizing Kat's wounds had taken its toll on them both, but Judd had done what he needed to do. He refused to let the infection fester and spread, refused to let gangrene set in.

Already, Kat was chilled and feverish. He had bathed her in the cool water from the spring, first thing the next morning, then washed her gown as best he could. He had given her a potion to help her regain strength, but she was so damn pale and listless that it scared the living hell out of him.

Despite the unseen powers bestowed on him by the Cheyenne guardian spirits, he felt helpless in this situation, felt as if he were fighting a losing battle, wasn't sure Kat even wanted to survive the agony that claimed her. He needed her help if he was going to keep her alive. At the moment she didn't appear to be doing her part—and Judd had a pretty good idea why.

The notice Marshal Winslow had given him testified to Judd's lack of trust in Kat. She was living with that while she battled for her life. She had given up on Judd, on herself, because she believed he planned to turn her in.

Damn, he had made such a mess of things with Kat. He had teased and taunted her in the beginning, tested her to the limits. Then he had taken her innocence without offering his heart in the bargain, because he was leery of her hidden motives. And because he hadn't trusted her completely, he hadn't confided in her about the reason for his visit to Lottie's Place. He hadn't expected Kat to come riding into his camp at the same time he confronted those treacherous outlaws who used her for bargaining power. Kat had been caught in the middle of a showdown, and it was all his fault! Worse, he couldn't apologize, because Kat was so delirious with pain that he wasn't sure she knew who or where she was.

Judd climbed to his feet to work the kinks from his back. He had been so tense while cauterizing and stitching the wounds that now he felt as exhausted as Kat looked. He needed to gather more herbs and roots for potions and poultices, and he needed to find shelter from the storm that was brewing on the western horizon. Damn it, could anything else go wrong?

It had been three days since Kat had been shot, and she seemed no closer to recovery than the night she was injured— because of him.

The thought made Judd cringe. Guilt was eating him alive. He wished he could magically wave his arms and turn back the hands of time to replay that ill-fated night. Things sure as hell would have turned out differently if he'd known then what he knew now.

Judd glanced southwest toward Tascosa, wondering if he should transport Kat to the Hampton Hotel. For certain, Gracie and Samuel would help him tend Kat's wounds. But considering all the male admirers she had acquired, she would have so many visitors that she would never get a minute of rest.

Frowning pensively, Judd glanced east. He suspected that Wild Hawk and his Comanche braves were out there, hiding in the gullies and arroyos to avoid the soldiers who unjustly accused them of rustling and murder. Wild Hawk and his men were waiting to catch sight of the outlaw trio who had passed themselves off as Comanches.

Judd made an instant decision, then gathered his gear. Working quickly, he fashioned a gurney from the extra bedroll and tied it between two sturdy tree limbs. He secured it between Horse's and the mare's saddles.

It would be slow going while transporting Kat by stretcher, he knew, but he could reach his destination in three hours.

Then he would have the assistance he needed to care for Kat
and give Wild Hawk the new lease on life that he needed. It
was time for that Comanche warrior to fulfill his own destiny,
Judd decided.

Judd scooped up Kat and laid her gently on the stretcher.
She mumbled something incoherent, then grimaced as she
squirmed to find a comfortable position on the suspended pallet.

"It's okay, princess. I'm here. I won't leave you," Judd
murmured, then wondered if Kat would prefer that he weren't
here. She thought he had no faith in her, thought he had betrayed
her with another woman, knew he wielded powers that altered
his appearance.

So why had she taken a bullet for him?

That question continued to haunt Judd as he rode east, then
descended into the deep canyons that cut through the High
Plains.

When Kat moaned and whimpered, Judd slowed his pace,
trying to cause her as little discomfort as possible, but the path
was rugged. He knew Kat felt every bump as Horse and the
mare picked their way around boulders and skidded in loose
dirt.

It came as a relief to Judd when Kat slumped into motionless
silence again. Every moan and whimper went through him like
sharp needles. He had to find Wild Hawk's campsite soon or
he would have to stop to give Kat an hour of undisturbed rest,
Judd decided. With the sun bearing down on her, and the heat
and wind building as a prelude to the coming storm, he knew
she had to be miserable.

Damn it, where was Wild Hawk? Judd thought, exasperated.
He needed the Comanche's help and he needed it now!

CHAPTER
TWENTY-THREE

Judd's shoulders sagged in relief when he saw Wild Hawk and company on an outcropping of rock above him. Wild Hawk raised his arm in a gesture of welcome, then pointed toward the encampment tucked beneath a sandstone ledge.

Before Judd reached camp, Wild Hawk and his followers weaved down the footpath to await him. Without being given a word of instruction, the Comanches unfastened the ropes between the two horses and carefully lowered the stretcher to the ground.

"What happened?" Wild Hawk asked, staring solemnly at Kat's colorless face.

"She was shot by the three desperadoes who posed as Comanches to rape, rob and murder," Judd explained.

Rage flickered in Wild Hawk's silver-blue eyes. "The white men struck down another victim? When we find them, they will know the full extent of Comanche torture."

Judd knelt down to brush his palm across Kat's fevered brow, then stared grimly at Wild Hawk. "The white outlaws are dead. No longer will they masquerade as Comanches and bring the soldiers' wrath down on your people."

"Panther struck them down," Wild Hawk said. It was not a question, but an acceptance of fact.

Judd nodded as he tucked the quilt around Kat's shoulders. "She took the bullet meant for me, and I struck out with a vengeance in her name, for you and your people, and for all the others—red and white alike—who fell victim to their evil ways."

"Then I owe you a great favor, Panther," Wild Hawk declared. He half turned to speak in the Comanche dialect to the other warriors. Gently they lifted the stretcher and carried Kat beneath the protection of the overhanging ledge.

Judd rose to his feet to stare at Wild Hawk. "I need someone to care for Kat while I gather herbs for healing potions, recover the stolen money the outlaws buried, then ride to Tascosa to fetch her belongings from the hotel."

"It is done," Wild Hawk proclaimed without a moment's hesitation. "Standing Bear, Blue Eagle and the others will keep constant vigil while you and I gather the herbs for the potions." He called instructions to his warriors, then strode off to get his piebald stallion.

Judd set a swift pace north toward the grassy valley beyond the rugged arroyos. "Have you seen the soldiers who were sent to drive you back to the reservation?"

Wild Hawk smirked. "They have been here and gone. We easily outsmarted them, because they are quick to believe what they see, without looking deeper, more thoroughly. We tricked them into thinking we rode north, then we covered our tracks and circled back to the arroyos."

Judd smiled ruefully. "I have been plagued with a few white man's flaws myself lately."

"In what way, Panther?" Wild Hawk asked curiously.

"With the woman," Judd admitted. "I believed the worst about her, because I have trained myself not to trust, taught myself to proceed with extreme caution. A hazard of my profession and upbringing. Sometimes it is not in a man's best interest to trust no one but himself."

"Trusting the devious white man is a rule never meant to be broken," Wild Hawk said cynically. "The whites leave a trail of poisonous lies behind them, a path of broken promises and broken treaties designed to exterminate the Indians and our culture.''

"You were born white,'' Judd had the nerve to point out. He knew that if he hadn't had Wild Hawk's admiration and respect, he would have had a battle on his hands, because to Wild Hawk those were fighting words.

Wild Hawk's chin went airborne and he frowned bitterly. "Do not remind me of the curse that hangs over me, Panther. I know it all too well.''

Judd smiled wryly. "The curse is going to become a blessing in disguise very soon, my friend. You are going to accept your white heritage—''

"Never!'' Wild Hawk spouted off. "I barely survived the massacre of the soldiers. I saw my brothers struck down with army rifles, saw our women violated, our children herded off to Eastern schools where the white man's ways could be pounded *into* them and the Indian ways pounded *out* of them. There is nothing in white civilization that appeals to me. I may have been born white, but I am all Comanche!''

"A proud, defiant Comanche without freedom,'' Judd pointed out. "You will have your freedom and you will become the hand of justice who punishes men like the desperadoes who blackened the name of the Comanche.''

Wild Hawk frowned, puzzled, then watched Judd dismount to dig up several wild herbs. "You speak in riddles, Panther. How is it possible to have freedom that is not mine, to punish the evil whites who turn their kind against us?''

Judd gestured toward a mesquite seedling, indicating that Wild Hawk was to strip the bark and dig roots for medicinal teas. "It is possible to have your revenge, as I have had mine against the three outlaws, and others like them, who violated and killed my mother when I was living in the Cheyenne village. I wanted justice but could not find it living as a Cheyenne. In order to have the justice you want desperately, you must learn to dispense it under the white man's laws.''

Wild Hawk hopped agilely from his horse. He was still

frowning when he took out his knife to peel bark from the tree. "You are still speaking riddles, Panther."

Judd waited strategically, giving Wild Hawk time to gather the needed ingredients and puzzle out where Judd was going with this conversation. He knew Wild Hawk was frustrated with his situation, with the hated confinement of the reservation. But Judd knew something Wild Hawk did not. The government had decided to place even more restrictions on the Comanche and the other tribes herded into Indian Territory. Their activities were going to be regulated and monitored by even more forts inhabited by even more soldiers.

"The government intends to deny the Comanches access to Texas hunting grounds," Judd reported. "The Comanches believed the whites were acting out of spite by killing the buffalo and horse herds. But there was method to the government's cruel deeds of extermination. Indian tribes will be forced to depend on supplies and goods doled out at forts. The bleak fact is that you cannot save the Comanche nation. But you can have your freedom. You can become an example and inspiration to your captive people."

Wild Hawk's shadow fell over Judd while he dug up more roots beside the creek. "All is lost?" he asked grimly.

"Yes," Judd informed him.

"So how is it possible for me to seek justice and serve it when I am Comanche?" he demanded as he thrust the bark, branches and roots at Judd.

"It is simple," Judd said calmly. "You become white again."

Wild Hawk flung back his broad shoulders. His chin shot up again—higher this time than last. "I will die first!" he all but shouted. "I would not be a man at all if I had to sacrifice my pride and turn white!"

"Suit yourself, friend, but Comanche stubbornness will do you no good whatsoever when you're a dead hero. Now, Comanche *cunning*—that is something else again."

Wild Hawk regarded him dubiously. "Explain."

Judd ambled off to cut the stalks from prickly pear cactus and drained the milky substance into a small vial. "Tascosa is badly in need of a town marshal who knows the area well, who can defend himself against outlaws and protect innocent citizens.''

"Why should I care if white citizens are struck down by their own kind? All of them are invaders who have stolen Comanche land," he said bitterly.

Judd got right in Wild Hawk's livid face. "Because victims come in all colors and creeds, from all cultures, Wild Hawk. Times are changing, and you must change with them.

"As a child you considered the Comanche your enemy because they threatened harm when your kin took their land for farming. As a man you consider your previous enemy your family. Like me, you have walked in both worlds. You have been a victim yourself as a man and as a child.

"If you become white, become the extension of white laws, then you will have the power and influence to do what you can to protect your people, to sway the opinions of whites. You will gain honor among whites because of your skills and bravery. As I said, to help the Comanche you must reclaim your white heritage.''

Wild Hawk staggered back as if he had been struck by lightning. He stared openmouthed at Judd, struggling to accept a viewpoint that seemed foreign, taboo.

"I know the concept takes some getting used to," Judd said compassionately. "I admit it took time for me to adjust to the new ways. I have never adjusted completely because at heart I will always be Cheyenne, entrenched in beliefs that are above and beyond the white man's understanding. We know of the knowledge and power born of nature, a strength found in all the creatures that inhabit the wilds.

"I have come to know the whites. They believe that in order to be successful and powerful a man must own land and have many possessions. Whites have yet to comprehend that it is not what a man *owns* that makes him what he is. It is his *honor*, his *courage*.''

Wild Hawk gaped at Judd. "You want me to become the marshal of this town called Tascosa? You want me to walk away from the reservation, from the warriors who follow me? You want me to turn white?"

Judd grinned at Wild Hawk's horrified expression. "I have friends in Tascosa who will hire you on my recommendation. You will be close enough to the reservation to visit occasionally. You will have the freedom to go where you please without soldiers dogging your footsteps. The whites will look to you for protection and guidance, and you can teach them to become sympathetic to the Indian's plight. In a manner of speaking, you will be a chief in both worlds."

Wild Hawk's gaze narrowed as he studied Judd's attire that spoke of both white and Indian culture. "The whites accept you for what you are? A half-breed?"

"They accept what they cannot conquer. They accept a man who defends them when they cannot defend themselves. Whether out of fear or out of respect, they acknowledge my skills with weapons, my ability to eradicate the evil brought down on them by ruthless men."

Wild Hawk stared north toward the hated reservation that lay beyond Red River in Indian Territory. "I will think on what you have said, Panther. I do not know if I can relearn the white man's customs when I have come to despise them for more than two-thirds of my life."

"If you decide to take the job, I will help you make the adjustment," Judd offered. "Kat can also teach you polished ways if—*when*—she recovers," he quickly corrected himself.

"Kat?" Wild Hawk smiled for the first time in days. "She is appropriately named, is she not? When we tried to capture her, she became all sharp claws and bared teeth. She fought more like an Indian than a white."

"Although she was born white, she possesses rare courage, and I have taught her to think like an Indian. She is a victim who needs protection now. And you are a man who has yet to accept the powers of the Comanche guardian spirits. Accept your destiny, Wild Hawk. It is your hatred for your white heritage that stands in the way of your greatness.

"I have heard the voices whispering around you, but you

cannot hear past your own torment to listen and accept the commands.''

Startled, Wild Hawk stared at Judd, who turned away and left him to wrestle with what he had been told.

When Wild Hawk continued to stand there as if rooted to the ground, Judd glanced over his shoulder and arched an eyebrow. ''Are you coming? Kat needs the combined medicine of the Cheyenne and Comanche to get her back on her feet. Together we can heal her, and together we both can learn from her.''

''White,'' Wild Hawk muttered, shaking his head in dismay. ''I tell you, Panther, I do not know if I can eat crow without strangling on it. I swore to the Comanche spirits that I would never go back to the white world.''

''Perhaps that is why the great spirits have yet to empower you, because it was misdirected pride that prompted that vow. The spirits are waiting for you to look through the eyes of your soul and think with your heart.'' Judd grinned devilishly as he added, ''Seems to me that you're thinking like a white man now, Wild Hawk, not a levelheaded Comanche.''

Judd mounted Horse and left Wild Hawk to ponder that last remark. Wild Hawk would have to learn to use his powers where and how they were most effective. It had taken Judd several years to figure that out. By offering advice, Judd hoped he could save Wild Hawk from years of frustration.

After what seemed a century-long nap, Kat roused to consciousness. Her throat was parched and her eyes kept trying to slam shut. She could see two fuzzy faces which seemed vaguely familiar, but she couldn't place them.

''Lassiter?'' she wheezed.

Sweet mercy! Voicing one word required more strength than she ever imagined!

Where am I? Kat asked herself as she glanced in one direction, then the other. The area didn't look familiar to her at all. How had she gotten wherever she was? Kat frowned, trying to remember if she knew what had become of Panther after she had been shot.

Panic clenched in her belly when she couldn't recall seeing or speaking to him after the showdown with the three desperadoes.

Oh, God! Had they killed him? Was this agonizing pain she endured for naught? And how had she ended up with these Comanche braves who looked like the ones she had encountered the previous week? Had she been sold into slavery when the outlaws made their getaway? What was going on?

"Well, 'bout time, princess."

Kat slumped in relief. She definitely knew that voice. Lassiter was alive, though why he was holed up with these Comanches she didn't know. She peered at the unshaven face that hovered over her, feeling gratitude and relief combined with heartache. The man she loved had survived, but he didn't trust her, didn't return her affection. Most likely all she would get from him was sympathy because she was flat on her back, nursing wounds that hurt like hell blazing.

"Take a sip of water," Judd instructed as he propped up her head.

Though her head felt as if it were weighted with lead, Kat raised up to drink her fill. "Where are we?"

Judd sank down beside her pallet. "Comanche camp. I needed to gather herbs to treat your injuries." He hitched his thumb toward the warriors. "I also needed nursemaids to stay with you while I brewed the potions."

"What happened to Rowdy Jack and his cohorts?" Kat rasped.

"Burning in hell," Judd said shortly.

Kat supposed she should pray for their black souls, but she wasn't feeling charitable at the moment. "Good." She studied Judd carefully, looking for wounds, but he appeared to have escaped the showdown unscathed.

Judd reached sideways for a tin cup, then spooned mush into her mouth. Kat pulled a face when the foul concoction offended her taste buds. "What is that awful stuff? Why do I have the feeling you have forced it down my throat before? Did you?"

Judd nodded. He was relieved that Kat didn't remember

every anguishing moment of pain and the torment of primitive surgery. He remembered, and that was agony enough for them both.

"This is a combination of Cheyenne and Comanche medicine," Wild Hawk said as he came to stand behind Judd.

Kat squinted up at the bronzed warrior who spoke English to her for the second time since she had met him. She couldn't voice a greeting because it was all she could do to swallow the offensive slop, then deal with the next spoonful Judd crammed in her mouth.

"You look better," Wild Hawk observed. "Five days is too long to go without food. Eat all you can."

"Five days?" Kat choked out.

"Afraid so," Judd concurred. "I know you're stiff and sore, but if we don't begin rehabilitation on your arm, you might lose the use of it."

Kat stared at her numb arm, knowing she was too weak to struggle with any sort of physical therapy. She just wanted to sleep.

"Sorry, princess, I know you don't want to, but you need to get up."

"I don't know how I possibly can," Kat mumbled wearily. "I can barely hold up my head without wearing myself out."

"Peyote," Wild Hawk said, then strode off to fetch a pouch lying beside the campfire.

"What is peyote?" Kat asked Judd.

"A painkiller of sorts. It is a spineless cactus that grows in the mountains of Mexico. The buttons are eaten for medication and in ceremonial rituals," he explained, then accepted the pouch Wild Hawk extended to him. "Eat these buttons and drink this, princess."

"Stop calling me that," she muttered grouchily. "And what time is it anyway?"

"Time to get on your feet." Judd smiled to himself as he carefully drew Kat into an upright position. She swayed dizzily, so he wrapped a supporting arm around her. The color drained from her face, and he was tempted to change his mind about making her hike around the campsite. But then he reminded himself that she needed to exercise to get her blood flowing and her heart pumping.

Judd urged Kat to take one step, then another. "You will be pleased to know that Tascosa will soon have a town marshal to protect its citizens against outlaws like Rowdy Jack and his ruffians."

"You?" Kat asked as she clung weakly to Judd.

"No. Wild Hawk. He has decided to accept the position."

Kat glanced at the brawny warrior, who gauged her reaction carefully. For some reason her opinion seemed to matter to him, though she couldn't fathom why.

"Tascosans will be grateful," Kat murmured.

"Do you think so?" Wild Hawk questioned earnestly.

"Absolutely."

"There. You see?" Judd put in, grinning. "Once Kat gives you a few tips on how to handle yourself in society, you'll have nothing to worry about."

"Me?" Kat wheezed.

"Of course, you," Judd insisted. "You are the resident expert on social graces. Besides, it's going to take you at least a week to recuperate before you can board the stage. Wild Hawk needs to brush up on his English and his manners, because he hasn't lived in white culture since he was nine years old."

Kat had wondered about this warrior's true heritage. Although Judd didn't elaborate, Kat presumed Wild Hawk had been captured and raised as a Comanche. Now that she thought about it, she began to understand why Judd had convinced Wild Hawk to accept the position of law official in Tascosa. She suspected Judd considered the confinement of reservation life a waste for a man with Wild Hawk's background. This was a golden opportunity for freedom. Kat could certainly identify with that.

Whether Judd would admit it or not, he was a good Samaritan who devoted his life to helping others. He was giving Wild Hawk the chance he needed. He had rescued Gracie and Samuel Hampton from danger. He had saved countless others from vicious desperadoes. Kat admired Judd for that, even if she was disappointed that he couldn't return her affection, couldn't let himself trust her.

As Kat walked in circles around camp—and not under her own power—she forced herself to accept the fact that Judd Lassiter was never going to be a permanent part of her life. She had to keep her emotional distance—beginning now. She had to look upon him as a friend, treat him the same way she treated Wild Hawk, Gracie and Samuel.

She was not leaving Texas with her heart in tatters, mooning over this incredible man who had admitted dozens of times that he had no desire to live in civilization. Panther was, and would always be, a creature of the wild . . .

The thought whirled into oblivion when Kat's meager strength abandoned her. She wilted in Judd's arms like a limp dishrag.

"Kat?" Judd scooped her up before she hit the ground. "Damn it, I pushed her too hard," he chastised himself.

"The peyote may have been too strong for her," Wild Hawk diagnosed. "Let her sleep for a few hours. Next time I won't mix such a strong potion."

Judd eased Kat onto her pallet and stood there staring down at her. Now that she was beginning to recover, he felt confident enough with her condition to leave her in Wild Hawk's care while he recovered the buried money and rode to Tascosa to retrieve her belongings. Judd wanted to have a talk with the town founders. Furthermore, Judd wasn't sure he wanted to be around when Kat recovered her senses and remembered what had happened—what she had seen—that night at his campsite. He wasn't sure he wanted to be on hand when she recalled the vision that appeared before her, realized that he *was* the legend and that the tales she had heard were based on fact.

She would shy away from him, he predicted. Once she got her bearings and her thoughts cleared, she would shrink away from him because he was a freak of sorts.

"Wild Hawk," Judd said, spinning on his heels. "I'm bound for Tascosa to pave the way for you." He halted directly in front of the white warrior. "Take care of her. Keep her occupied by making her teach you white manners and customs."

Wild Hawk nodded. "We will keep constant watch over her," he promised.

"Good. I appreciate that."

Judd walked away, knowing Kat was in competent hands, knowing she would most likely prefer Wild Hawk's company to his. Even though Kat had leaned against him while she walked around camp, he could feel the emotional distance inching between them. It was in the way she refused to look directly at him when she spoke.

He was amazed that he had become so attuned to her needs and moods that he could detect the slightest nuance. It was as if Kat were an integral part of him, a very special part that he had mistreated badly.

Judd knew he had hurt Kat and she was trying to protect herself, but there was too much history between them to part on a bitter note. Judd couldn't bear knowing that he had killed whatever fondness Kat might have developed for him.

One day soon, he and Kat were going to sit down—when she could sit down under her own power and remain awake for more than a quarter of an hour—and have a long talk. He had to apologize for thinking the worst about her, had to assure her that he did trust her, though his trust had come too late for her to respect him for it.

Then there was the incident in his camp and the vision she had seen.

He was going to have to deal with that, too.

Judd squirmed uneasily as he trotted Horse toward the canyon where Ark Riley claimed the stolen money was buried. He wasn't sure how he was going to get through the explanation to Kat, how she would react to it. That was one conversation Judd wished he could avoid, but after what Kat had seen and heard during the showdown, he owed her.

Now all he had to do was figure out how to tell her what he had never before tried to put into words.

CHAPTER
TWENTY-FOUR

"Goodness gracious!" Gracie Hampton hooted when Judd appeared at the door of the mercantile shop. "Where in the world have you been, Panther? Samuel and I have been worried sick."

Judd always marveled at the open-armed receptions he got from the Hamptons. They were only two of a handful of good and decent people who didn't look upon him as a dangerous threat.

Samuel stepped from the storeroom, then slumped in relief. "Well, thank God! I was afraid those vicious desperadoes you were tracking got the better of you. I should have known you were indestructible."

"Not entirely," Judd murmured.

This thing between him and Kat was tearing him apart. Every time he remembered how mistrusting and critical he had been of her, while she had been honest with him, he felt like swearing. He, who had demanded absolute honesty from Kat, had concealed that part of himself that inspired lore and legend. He wasn't ashamed of the transformation that enabled him to wield power and serve justice, but he had withheld answers when Kat asked probing questions. Yet, in his own defense, the

Cheyenne culture frowned on speaking of those mystical powers. They were considered birth-to-death secrets.

Judd knew he should have somehow prepared Kat for that inevitable moment when Panther's guardian spirits appeared. But he had been too much a coward to face Kat's revulsion and shock. Now, each time he touched her he suspected that she remembered the ominous apparition who had sentenced her captors to the pits of hell.

"Panther? You are all right, aren't you?" Gracie questioned, staring at him with intense scrutiny.

"I'm fine," Judd said quickly. "Katherine, however, was injured during the confrontation with the outlaws."

Gracie's eyes widened in alarm. "Oh my, how dreadful! Was she seriously wounded? Will she recover? Sweet mercy, such a vivacious, lovely lady. I hate to think of her suffering. Is there anything Samuel and I can do to help?"

"As a matter of fact, there is," Judd said as he ambled forward. "I need food and supplies. I don't want to risk making the journey to town with Kat until she recovers her strength. I came to collect her belongings. I also need two extra sets of men's clothing."

"Your size?" Gracie asked.

"Yes." Judd figured he and Wild Hawk were close enough to the same size to make a fit. Wild Hawk needed to appear reasonably civilized when he made his debut in Tascosa.

Samuel hurried forward to hand Judd the key to the upstairs room. "Everything is as Katherine left it. The townspeople will be greatly relieved to know she is alive. There has been considerable concern since both of you disappeared without a trace."

Judd still couldn't get used to the idea that so many Tascosans treated him like a native son. It happened so seldom when he passed through frontier towns. "Sorry to have worried you," Judd apologized. "But tending to Kat's injuries was of utmost importance."

"Of course it was," Gracie agreed. "That is as it should be. She is your lady, after all."

Judd didn't correct Gracie's misconception before she bustled off to gather staples, clothes and supplies. With key in hand, Judd climbed the stairs.

A tidal wave of memories swamped him the instant he stepped into the room. He swore he would never be able to walk into this spacious suite without visualizing Kat lounging in that shiny brass tub—and how he had joined her there.

"Damn," Judd muttered as he strode over to collect Kat's neatly stacked belongings. "She's not even gone and I miss her already."

When he scooped up her clunky boots, a smile curved his lips. He remembered those weeks when she'd clomped around in this oversize footwear that made her feet appear too large for her petite body. And these baggy clothes, he mused as he brushed his hand over the plain, homespun garments. From pauper to princess . . .

His smile faded when he compared Kat's transformation to his own. Pauper to princess, Kat could understand—most of the civilized world could. But from bounty hunter to mystical Cheyenne shaman? No wonder Kat had been cool and remote since she regained consciousness.

When Judd tucked Kat's belongings under one arm, the leather poke slid from her boot and plunked on the floor. Judd picked it up, then shook out the jewels on the bedspread. He noted that four gems were missing—the four that he had insisted on as payment for his services as guide and protector.

No doubt, Kat had brought them with her the night she rode to his camp—and ran head-on into calamity. Not that Judd wanted the gems, especially not after he had discovered how wrong he had been about Kat, not after she had practically sacrificed her life to save his.

Why had she done that? That question still tormented Judd, because he couldn't ascertain the answer. Could it be that she preferred death to the prospect of enduring humiliation at the hands of those outlaws, much the same way she had made him promise to end her misery if she were about to be scalped or bound over into slavery by renegade Comanches? That had to be it, Judd decided. Why else? Kat had only chosen her time and place to die—if it came to that.

After Judd tucked the pouch of jewels in his pocket, he pivoted toward the door. Again, the memories of those intimate moments of splendor with Kat threatened to buffet him, but he forged ahead determinedly. He had things to do in Tascosa. Clinging to forbidden memories would accomplish nothing.

Resigned, Judd closed the door and walked away.

"Here, let me wrap up those clothes so they will be easier to carry," Gracie insisted when she saw the loose bundle under Judd's arm. "I gathered everything you'll need for nutritious meals and I packed a few extra blankets."

"Thanks, Gracie." Judd fished into his pocket to pay for the sack of supplies waiting on the counter. He glanced around the shop, then frowned curiously. "Where did Samuel get off to? I have some business to discuss with him."

"He had to attend another town meeting," Gracie informed him, then shook her head and sighed. "We are getting desperate for a law official. The council is trying to decide whether to hire the man who applied for the job." She gave a snort of distaste. "If you ask me, that Thornton character came from the wrong side of the law. He's got a sneaky look about him. If we hire him to keep peace, I don't think we'll be getting our money's worth."

Judd had met his share of shady characters in frontier towns. There were men who took advantage of the position of marshal by demanding that shopkeepers and citizens pay for protection. Those who refused to be bribed were terrorized. Tascosa didn't need a marshal who broke more laws than he upheld.

"Where is the town meeting taking place?" Judd asked.

Gracie placed the package of Kat's clothes on the counter. "Over at the Wild Mustang Saloon. Did you decide to take the job after all?" she asked hopefully.

"No, but I have a friend who is suited for the position and he has agreed to take the job if he is given the council's stamp of approval."

"Who is this man?" she asked curiously.

"Er . . . his name is Hawk."

"Well, I'm sure Mr. Hawk will be perfect if he comes with your recommendation." She shooed Judd on his way. "Better hightail it over to the saloon with the name of your applicant before the council gives the job to that Thornton character."

Judd gathered the sack and packages and strode off. "Kat and I will be back within the week. Thanks again, Gracie."

"You tell Katherine we are praying for her," Gracie called after him.

Judd hurried across the street, hoping he wouldn't arrive too late to put Hawk's name in the hat. The council was about to put Thornton's application to a vote when Judd entered the saloon.

Cape Mullin smiled around the cigar that was clamped in his teeth. "Samuel said you were back in town, Panther." He hitched his thumb toward a bearded hombre leaning negligently against the bar.

Judd took one look at Thornton and pegged him as a seedy gunslinger. Judd had seen the type often enough to recognize Thornton's kind at first glance.

"This here is James Thornton. We're debating about hiring him," Cape reported.

Judd nodded coolly at the tall, scarecrow-thin gunslinger who was helping himself to another glass of Cape's expensive whiskey.

"I have another application for you to consider," Judd announced. "He is a friend of mine. Very qualified. Strong sense of honor and integrity. The kind of man Tascosa needs to discourage riffraff from blowing the lid off this town. His name is Hawk."

"Now hold on, mister," Thornton growled as he spun around to glare at Judd from beneath the low-riding brim of his hat. "I want this job and I damn well intend to have it."

"The choice is up to the council," Judd replied as he sized up Thornton.

Yeah, Thornton definitely had the look of a trigger-happy gunslinger who was itching to build a reputation by sending his competition and personal enemies on a one-way ride to Boot Hill. If there wasn't a Wanted poster out on this hombre, there should be. Judd was willing to bet all the jewels in his pocket that this corrupt pistolero was thirsting for the position of power and motivated by selfish greed. Thornton wasn't going to get his hooks into Tascosa, Judd promised himself.

"This Hawk comes with your recommendation?" Robert Wilson, restaurateur, perked up enthusiastically. "A friend of yours, you say?"

Judd nodded, but he never took his eyes off Thornton.

"He's willing to take this job?" Samuel asked. When Judd nodded again, Samuel turned to Thornton. "We'll be in touch, Mr. Thornton. We plan to interview the other applicant before we make a decision."

Thornton pushed away from the bar and glared at each councilman. "Make sure you make the right decision," he sneered. "Sure would hate to see you pay for your mistake."

"Meaning?" Judd challenged.

Thornton tipped his head back to meet Judd's unblinking stare. "You figure it out, friend."

"A threat then," Judd assumed as he watched Thornton's hands hover above the well-worn Colts that rode low on his lean hips.

"Call it whatever you want, but this job is going to be mine."

"As the councilmen said, don't come around again unless they send for you."

Judd met Thornton's menacing glower with one of equal intensity. When Judd didn't cower to the gunslinger's brand of intimidation, the man spun around and swaggered outside.

"Sure hope we don't have to hire that one," Robert mumbled. "He looks like more trouble than help."

"Exactly what I was thinking," Cape seconded.

"I don't want desperation to cause us to make a costly mistake," Samuel put in. "I'm for giving Mr. Hawk a look-see. If Panther says he's our man, then I'm in favor of giving Mr. Hawk the position."

"Hawk should be in town within the week," Judd reported.

"That's good enough for me," Robert said. "You get Mr. Hawk here as soon as you can. And, by the way, thanks for taking care of those three desperadoes before they cleaned out the bank or robbed the stage, whatever it was they were planning. Samuel told us that you would make short work of them. Guess he was right. Mighty glad you were around, Panther.''

"Tascosa is the closest thing to home I've known," Judd admitted. "I don't want troublemakers to get a foothold here. Thornton probably has a hidden agenda in mind. I've seen *supposed* lawmen terrorize towns until they managed to take over several businesses. I don't want that to happen here."

"You bring Mr. Hawk around as soon as you can," Samuel insisted. "I have no intention of being forced to sell out to someone like Thornton. We want Tascosa to become a respectable town, not a hideout for thieves and murderers."

"If Thornton causes trouble before I return to town, send for me," Judd said as he strode toward the door.

"Well, how are we supposed to know where to find you?" Robert called out.

"Ride northeast toward the gullies and *I*'ll find *you*," Judd promised.

"How will you—?" Cape tried to question.

"You don't ask the legendary Panther how he does what he does," Samuel cut in, grinning. "If he says he'll find us, then that's exactly what he'll do."

Judd walked swiftly toward Horse, anxious to drop off the money he had recovered for safekeeping at the bank, then return to camp. While he was strapping the supplies to the saddle, he felt a presence behind him. Pretending to be preoccupied with arranging his saddlebag, Judd reached over the saddle to grab the bullwhip that hung on the opposite side of Horse.

"Turn around, Panther," Thornton hissed behind him. "We have a matter to settle, here and now. I take offense to folks shoving their noses in my business. I told you this was going to be my town and I damn well meant it."

With his hand draped leisurely over the saddle—the bullwhip clamped in his fist—Judd half turned. Thornton stood with feet apart, primed and ready to instigate a gunfight. A wad of tobacco filled his cheek. He made a spectacular display of spitting at Judd's feet.

"And before you ask, the answer is yes," Thornton added

gruffly. "I've heard of the man called Panther. Don't believe any of those ridiculous legends, though. You're just the nuisance who is standing in the way of what I want. Tascosa is going to belong to me and my friends."

Judd smirked sarcastically when Thornton tried to stare him down. "I don't think folks around here are going to take kindly to having this place renamed Thorntonville, not after the town has been approved for a post office. Too much extra paperwork involved. You and these supposed friends of yours will have to find another town."

"No." Thornton glared menacingly at Judd. "Don't think so. I've already made up my mind to stay. Since you're the only one standing in my way," he growled as he slid a Colt into his right hand, "you'll have to be disposed of—"

The whip popped so quickly, so unexpectedly, that Thornton never had the chance to react. Judd's aim was accurate. The popper of the whip curled around the butt of Thornton's pistol and jerked it from his hand. Thornton stared in disbelief as his pistol slithered through the dirt.

Judd chuckled at the stunned expression on Thornton's leathery face. "I have a hard and fast rule that goes like this: If a man is stupid enough to draw down on me, I take his pistol as a souvenir. Got any objections, Thornton? Draw the other pistol if you want. I don't mind adding both of them to my collection."

Thornton swallowed uneasily as his Colt slithered toward Judd's feet, dancing to the tune of the bullwhip. His hand hovered over his spare Colt, and then he swore foully when Judd jiggled the whip and the pistol on the ground practically leaped into his hand. He twirled it skillfully, then tucked it in his saddlebag.

Even more disconcerting than losing his firearm to Panther was the fact that a crowd of Tascosans had stepped onto the boardwalks to watch Thornton be humiliated by this damn half-breed.

Judd followed Thornton's gaze. "Yeah, friend. I'd say it's time for you to move on. I don't recommend coming back while Hawk is in charge of this town. You're the kind of man he cut his baby teeth on. He might not be as generous with you as I am. He really hates it when bad-ass hombres try to make a big production of a showdown in the street.''

"You haven't seen the last of me," Thornton snarled. "I've got friends hereabout.''

"So do I," Judd assured him, then acquainted the gunslinger with The Look.

Thornton backed up a step and shifted uncomfortably. His pride smarting, he whipped around and stalked toward his horse. "You and I aren't finished," he muttered as he swung into the saddle. "You've made yourself a mortal enemy."

Judd watched Thornton trot west toward the gray clouds that piled high on the horizon, wondering if he had made Hawk a bitter enemy even before he accepted the position as marshal. *Nothing like being tested immediately,* Judd thought as he mounted Horse. He made a mental note to perfect Hawk's skills with a pistol. The Comanche was deadly with a rifle, bow and arrow, but he had a few things to learn about drawing and firing a Colt.

On his way out of town, Judd dropped off the recovered money, then halted in front of the telegraph office to send off a request to Marshal Winslow in The Flats. He wanted to inform Winslow of the buried loot and request information on Thornton. Wild Hawk might as well know what he was up against when he arrived in town.

Thunder rolled above the arroyos, bringing Kat awake. She opened her eyes to see lightning playing leapfrog across the evening sky. The pain that had become her constant companion had waned and Kat experienced an odd sensation of floating, a giddy feeling that left her suspended somewhere between sleep and wakefulness.

It was a pleasant change, Kat thought sluggishly. She could move without sharp stabs of pain making her flinch. She must be recovering quickly, she decided. Five days of drifting in and out of consciousness were five days too many.

Kat rolled sideways on her pallet and smiled when she saw a hazy shadow drifting above her. *It must be Lassiter,* she concluded. She well remembered how his face had condensed in that strange, incandescent fog the night he took on the ruffians in his camp. She also remembered the vivid, colorful dreams that had swirled around her while she slept. Awake or asleep, Lassiter was never far from her thoughts.

"Ah, Lassiter . . ." Kat slurred over her thick tongue. "Come here. I've missed you."

Kat reached out to clutch his shirt when he knelt to brush his hand over her brow. She drew him nearer, longing to feel his surrounding warmth, his sensual lips whispering over hers. She felt no inhibition as she drew him down beside her, because all her silent pep talks had flown off with the approaching storm. She could think of no reason why she should keep an emotional distance between them when this giddy, devil-may-care sensation channeled through her. She was feeling no pain, only a need to hold the man she loved for as long as it would last.

"Kat . . ."

"Sh-sh," she murmured groggily. "Just hold me."

Reluctantly, Wild Hawk slid his arm around Kat, knowing he should explain that he wasn't who she thought he was, couldn't determine who he was because the peyote left her suspended in a dreamlike trance. But when he looked at her he was reminded of a fairy princess. A wild cascade of sunshine fanned around her shoulders, and that dreamy smile on her petal-soft lips was difficult to ignore.

Wild Hawk tensed when her good arm slid around his neck, guiding his head steadily to hers. He knew he had better put a stop to this tantalizing seduction before things got out of hand. Kat was only reacting to the side effects of the peyote buttons he had fed her each time she awoke with a pained moan.

Wild Hawk had experienced the hallucinatory effects himself on a few occasions, and he well remembered the symptoms of slurred speech, blurred vision and vivid colors swirling behind his eyelids. He was certain Kat was imprisoned in a dreamlike trance that allowed her to move about without being tormented by pain. She was squirming sideways, inching closer to him without flinching.

When Kat's lips feathered over his, he tried very hard not to respond to delicious temptation. This was Panther's woman, he reminded himself sternly. Wild Hawk was nothing but a substitute for the man Kat thought she was kissing. But when Kat arched provocatively toward him, her full breasts brushing against his chest, his male body reacted involuntarily.

Instantly, Wild Hawk knew why this alluring woman had so much influence over Panther. She was like a siren calling in the wind . . .

"What the hell is going on here?" Judd growled furiously.

CHAPTER TWENTY-FIVE

Wild Hawk tore his mouth away from Kat's lush lips when he heard that deep, gritty voice boom like thunder. He tried to sit upright, but Kat's hand was hooked around his neck. If he jerked away abruptly, he feared he would cause further injury to her mending wounds.

Apprehensively, Wild Hawk swiveled his head around to see Panther looming over him, his eyes burning with irritation, his lips compressed in a flat line. A backdrop of darkness, exploding with fingers of lightning, made Panther appear even more intimidating—especially when the wind began to whistle through the gullies and swirl around the towering peak of caprock.

To make matters worse, Wild Hawk felt Kat's hand slide down his shoulder to brush familiarly against his chest. He tried to smile good-naturedly, but Panther found no amusement in the scene he had happened upon.

"Glad to have you back, Panther," Wild Hawk said as he stilled Kat's adventurous hand.

"And just in time, too, I see," Judd muttered sourly. "Now, what the hell do you think you're doing?"

"Trying to pacify your woman," Wild Hawk explained, then

grimaced at his choice of words. ''She awoke thinking I was you.''

Judd bit off a curse as he watched Kat smile lazily at Wild Hawk without really seeing him. ''Damnation, you must have given Kat enough peyote buttons to knock two grown men to their knees.'' He regarded him suspiciously. ''Or did you cram more peyote buttons down her throat to keep her partially sedated so you could seduce her while I was gone?''

''We are friends,'' Wild Hawk said, offended by the accusation.

''It wouldn't be the first time *friends* found themselves at odds because of a woman,'' Judd muttered.

''This isn't what it seems,'' Wild Hawk protested. He carefully disentangled himself when Kat slid her leg between his— and heard Panther curse mightily. When Wild Hawk tried to stand up, Kat latched onto his hand and pulled him back to her.

Scowling, Judd stalked forward to still Kat's roaming hand, then tucked the quilt tightly around her. She mumbled incoherently, then slumped back into restless sleep.

Judd glared at Wild Hawk, shocked by the force of possessiveness that speared through him. He wanted to strangle Wild Hawk for sampling Kat's kiss.

''I know you got the wrong impression, but I was only trying to help—'' Wild Hawk explained quickly.

''Help by taking advantage of her oblivious state?'' Judd snorted caustically.

''I didn't initiate it,'' Wild Hawk insisted. Then he switched his attention to Mother Nature's fireworks display as the storm intensified. ''What news do you have from this place called Tascosa?''

Judd squelched his annoyance, reminding himself that he had no right to be jealous because Kat had kissed Wild Hawk. Judd supposed he was going to have to adjust to the fact that there would be other men in Kat's future. Judd just hadn't expected that he would be around to see her in the arms of other men.

''There was another applicant for the job in Tascosa. A man

named Thornton," he explained. "But when I told the town council about you, they were eager to make your acquaintance, before they were forced to hire Thornton."

"Maybe you should not have interfered," Wild Hawk said as he continued to watch the storm gather strength.

"Thornton doesn't have Tascosa's best interest at heart," Judd replied.

Wild Hawk glanced at him. "Neither do I."

"At least are honest enough to admit it," Judd countered. "Thornton isn't. He works both sides of the law to his advantage. He did not come to protect the townspeople, but to prey on them for financial gain. I told the council that I would bring you for an interview when Kat is well enough to travel.

"It's time to start your crash course in returning to white society and learning to handle a pistol," Judd declared.

Wild Hawk muttered to himself. He was still reluctant to give up his Comanche ways, though he had become aware of the benefits and necessity of assuming a new life.

"Tomorrow morning you must send your braves back to the reservation with the news of your employment," Judd insisted.

Wild Hawk jerked his head around, his eyes wide. Judd knew this was a difficult moment for Wild Hawk, but the sooner the warrior separated himself from his past, the sooner he would adapt to his new life.

"Tell them tonight," Judd insisted. "Explain the reasons why, so they will understand this is necessary."

"You are asking me to turn my back on the last twenty-one years of my life," Wild Hawk scowled. "That is not an easy thing to do, Panther."

"I know." Judd glanced back at Kat's sleeping form. "But there are things even more difficult to give up, my brother. This is only the first of many sacrifices you face—"

Thunder exploded above the canyon rim. The earth trembled. Judd heard the voices calling in the wind, calling to Wild Hawk whose personal torment deafened him. Judd felt the charged air swirling around him, knew instinctively that Wild Hawk's moment of reckoning had arrived.

"Go tell your warriors now," Judd ordered as he stared at

the churning clouds. "Your time has come, Wild Hawk. Go alone into the storm." As if of its own accord, his arm lifted, directing the Comanche's attention to the pinnacle of rock silhouetted against the flare of lightning. "The spirits can wait no longer for you to come to *them*. They have come to *you*."

Wild Hawk gaped at the odd glow in Panther's eyes, heard the trancelike resonance in his voice, felt the invisible waves of energy undulating around him.

Wild Hawk had no time to wallow in regret, only time to seek his purpose. He could feel an unfamiliar chill dancing in the air, became attuned to the inarticulate whispers in the wind. When indescribable tingles raced through his body, he knew he was beginning to sense what Panther sensed.

"Tonight you will step through the door to your future to explore the mysteries of life," Panther said in a strange, hollow voice. "When you walk into the storm, you will not return as the warrior you are but rather as the legend you will become. You will be one of the chosen few. Only unfaltering courage and bravery will carry you through this night when you walk alongside the guardian spirits."

Wild Hawk did not ask the swirling mass of evanescent fog that Panther had suddenly become how he knew these things. Wild Hawk stared into those flickering pinpoints of flame and accepted his destiny.

"Despite your white heritage, despite your bitter torment, you will be tested as never before. You will be called upon to safeguard the Comanches through the white side of society. This is your night of reckoning, Wild Hawk."

The great panther reared up, his face lifted to the sky. His scream rivaled the thunder and the wind as he called to the unseen spirits.

"Look into the eye of the storm and tell me what you see and hear."

Wild Hawk gasped in surprise when he saw other pinpoints of glowing eyes materialize from the darkness. On the ridge to the east he saw a plume of smoke condense. The forlorn howl of a wolf swirled in the wind.

"Three Wolves," Wild Hawk whispered in astonishment. "Wolf Prophet of the Comanche."

A chorus of howls exploded on the ridge, then died beneath a deafening thunderclap. As lightning leaped across the threatening sky, Wild Hawk pivoted to stare to the north. To his awed disbelief, condensing from a roiling cloud, he saw the shimmering image of the Ghost Horse rearing up to paw at the air. Upon its back was an incandescent apparition that raised its arm toward the heavens. Dark eyes beamed in the darkness, and the wild scream of the Ghost Horse shattered the night.

"The Lone Horseman," Wild Hawk whispered in astonishment.

Beside him the great panther raised his haunting cry, joining the wolf's unnerving howl and the horseman's eerie call. Wild Hawk felt the Chosen Ones gathering around him, summoning him to the cliff.

"There are three of us watching and waiting for you to become one of us," the wolf called out in the silence that followed the echoing thunder.

"There are four winds, Wild Hawk. They are the symbols of the breath of life, the voices of the guardian spirits," the Lone Horseman called out to him.

"Soon you will complete the circle, Wild Hawk," Panther prophesied. *"We are to become the Mystics of the Four Winds, the inspiration to our people. The storm you see before you is like the conflict between men, of men. You must learn to walk in the eye of the storm. You cannot fight for the right to command the omnipotent spirits if you battle an enemy within.*

"Remember that when the storm gathers around you, threatening to beat you into submission. The weak will not be chosen, only the strong of heart, soul and spirit. Shift your mind to an unused position and absorb the knowledge awaiting you.

"Go quickly, Wild Hawk. Learn to accept the burden and limitations of the mystical powers imposed on you. The great power-giving spirits have summoned you to become one of us. Do not fail us . . ."

Wild Hawk turned away from the Phantom Panther's glowing essence. And then he walked out into the storm, carrying nothing with him but a warrior's courage to follow his path of destiny.

Wild Hawk climbed the footholds on the face of the cliff, feeling the presence of the Chosen Ones behind him, beside him, feeling the storm-generated spirits in the updrafts of winds that pummeled him, threatening to toss him to the canyon floor. Determined of purpose, Wild Hawk struggled upward until he stood on the stone ledge that overlooked the yawning canyon.

Voices carried in the wind like the anguished cries of the Comanches who were now confined to the reservation. Wild Hawk heard the whispers of those who had taken the spirit path to the stars in days gone by, heard the pleas of his people. He felt their pain and sorrow flowing through him.

As the sky opened to rain down the tears of a troubled Comanche nation, Wild Hawk lifted up his arms to bear the weight of his accepted burden. He saw images of hawks riding the wind, rising above the roiling clouds of war and conflict.

Lightning flickered, electrifying the heavy air. Blue sparks danced upon the skin of his upraised arms as Wild Hawk stared up at the omnipotent powers swirling overhead. The spirits of thunder, lightning and wind bombarded him, threatened to weaken his courage to stand against them, but Wild Hawk braced himself to meet the challenge. He felt his hair stand on end as a spear of brilliant light snapped, cracked, then bolted down to the place where he stood.

A wild cry burst from his lips when he was driven to his knees by the impact of silver light. He was blinded and paralyzed by the force of energy the sky spirits hurled at him, chilled to the bone by the tears raining down from the heavens.

In that moment, when he lost the ability to see, to hear, to speak, he battled a sense of helpless panic. Then he remembered Panther's words to look past physical pain and see the triumph of heart, mind and spirit.

Bitterness and hatred became insignificant in the face of the mystical powers churning inside him, seeking to localize and fill the empty spaces where hatred once reigned. And in his sightlessness, deafness and immobility Wild Hawk found himself staring down from a bird's-eye view of the world. He watched the clouds boil and seethe over the land. He experienced the unfamiliar sensation of flying and saw a flock of hawks gathering on his outspread wings. With him as their leader, the great hawks formed a V-shaped pattern as they soared as one through buffeting winds to spiral in the eye of the storm. He heard the hawks' cries echoing beside him, behind him, as he glided above the land the Comanche people once ruled.

He could see the ghost horses thundering across the blackened sky. Long-dead warriors were mounted on their backs, chanting for directions to lead a dying culture. He felt his totem's presence offering the strength to battle the fierce gale as he soared over treetops and canyons, seeing the world from a broad perspective.

For the first time in twenty-one years, Wild Hawk cried out in anguish for the family that bore him, to the memory of a life he had known before his heart had become Comanche.

And suddenly, two contrasting worlds united—like both wings of the hawk providing the power to soar above the earth.

The realization that he was a bird of two wings tore a cry from his lips. He was not white, not Comanche, but a medium of otherworldly spirits that ruled the sun, moon and stars.

As the vision faded away, Wild Hawk collapsed on the ridge and gasped for breath. His energy had been drained like the rain eroding channels in the gullies below. While the storm raged, Wild Hawk stared skyward, without the gift of sight and hearing. He was consumed by a universe of invisible powers moving silently through a visible world. He listened to the whispering voices, felt the spiritual essence expand inside him until it touched every part of his being.

Later, when he could stand, could see, hear and speak, Wild Hawk listened to the three mystical shamans of the Indian nations calling to him.

Then Wild Hawk took his place with the mystics, standing at the fourth corner of the wind . . .

* * *

Judd mentally pulled himself back from the drifting haze. He sent up a shrill scream that mingled with the howl of the wolf and the cry of the Lone Horseman. The hawk called from the storm that rumbled above the canyon, and Judd felt the inexplicable satisfaction of knowing a new legend had been born.

Wearily, he turned back to the glowing campfire tucked beneath the shelf of rock. He focused his attention on Kat's huddled form beneath the quilts. He knew he shouldn't take advantage of Kat's peyote-induced slumber, but he was magnetically drawn to the pallet.

Without disturbing her, Judd stretched out beside Kat, needing to hold her close. He knew she would retreat if she had command of her senses, but she was too drowsy to notice who cuddled up to her in spoon-shape fashion.

Judd smiled ruefully as he ran his hand down her rib cage, over the indentation of her waist, the gentle flare of her hips. He wanted to awaken her with tender caresses and worshiping kisses. He wanted to cast aside all the conflicts between them and recapture that moment out of time where passion reigned supreme.

"I'm sorry," Judd whispered against the swanlike column of her throat. "I sorely misjudged you, princess, and I regret every suspicious thought and cruel comment. You deserved none of my distrust."

When Kat moaned softly and turned toward him in sleep, Judd angled his head to taste the sweet nectar of her lips. Ah, how he was going to miss these stolen moments when he was at absolute peace with himself. When Kat was in his arms, all was right with the world.

"Lassiter . . ." she mumbled drowsily, then sighed against his cheek.

The way she whispered his name stirred him, filled him with incredible longing. He wanted to give her pleasure to counteract her pain. He wanted to absorb her pain as if it were his own and make her well again.

While the Comanche warriors slept in the near distance, Judd tunneled his hand beneath the battered yellow gown to caress Kat's silky flesh. Even in sleep she arched sensuously toward him, purred in pleasure.

Leisurely, he mapped the lush contours of her hips, her thighs, the swells of her breasts. He was ever mindful of her injuries as he aroused her by gentle increments, fed on her quivering sighs.

Her kisses quenched his thirst as he filled his hands with the essence of her, caressed her intimately, languidly. He could feel the heat of her desire, like hot rain pouring over his finger-tips. He ached to sheath his rigid flesh in the honeyed softness of her body and become one with her. He ached for their joining so badly that self-denial didn't even offer token resistance.

He could glide into her body as gently as dawn breaking on the horizon and find his heaven on earth. He could claim her body, though he could never have her heart. It would have to be enough, Judd told himself, because that was all he could ever have from Kat.

When he parted her thighs with a gentle nudge of his knee, she opened to him, welcoming him, even in sleep. Judd freed himself from the confines of his breeches and pressed against her. He cushioned her injured shoulder as he drove deeper, throbbing with the need to give himself up to the maddening urges of his body. But he knew that would be another form of betrayal. He couldn't take pleasure at Kat's expense. She was more than a means to his physical satisfaction—never that. She was the *reason* for it. There was a difference, Judd discovered. But he needed to be one with Kat this one last time . . .

When Kat moved provocatively against him, Judd felt his control slipping from his grasp, making a liar of his intentions. Her good arm curled around his neck, drawing him ever closer as she set an erotic cadence of passion.

He shouldn't, he knew he shouldn't respond so ardently to her, knew she probably wouldn't remember what would be impossible for him to forget. But, the Great Spirit help him, he was moving with her, feeling the crescendo build, feeling the secret fire blazing in his soul, burning him with the indescribable need only she created in him, a need only she satisfied.

Her ragged breath stirred against his neck and he felt her come apart in his arms. And suddenly, unexpectedly, she shattered around him, caressing him with fire. When she trembled against him and whispered his name, she took him with her, sent him cartwheeling over the waterfall into helpless ecstasy.

It was the most incredible sensation Judd had ever experienced, and he tried not to cling too tightly as he shuddered against Kat, for fear he would aggravate her tender wound. For the longest time he lay there, cradling her in his arms, feeling her lips gliding along the tendon of his neck.

These tender emotions he experienced with Kat were going to come back to haunt him, he knew. But for tonight, in the calm that followed the storm of Wild Hawk's reckoning, Judd had come back into himself.

He had come home . . .

The thought lured him into sleep. He knew that in the years to come, wherever Kat was, she would always be home to him. She would be the place his heart longed to visit. But his doubts and suspicions had destroyed her faith in him. The encounter with the outlaws had opened her eyes to what he became when he squared off against the evil forces in this world.

At least he had tonight, Judd consoled himself. It would have to be enough.

CHAPTER
TWENTY-SIX

Kat groaned when pain shot up and down her arm. Although she tried to still the movement, something strong and insistent refused to allow her arm to remain immobile. Head throbbing, mouth dry as dust, she opened her heavy-lidded eyes, then squeezed them shut against the bright light glaring down on her.

Lord, she felt so sluggish, and there was an odd undertaste in her mouth. "Water," she wheezed.

As if by magic, she felt a tin cup at her lips and the refreshing water streamed down her throat. But the pain in her arm continued relentlessly. Again she objected with a loud groan.

"Sorry, princess, this is very necessary."

Kat squinted against the bright light to see Judd sitting cross-legged, lifting her injured arm, then slowly lowering it to the pallet. She looked past the pain to recall a strange, erotic dream that floated on the fringes of memory.

It had been a dream, hadn't it? She had been drifting in a world of brilliant colors and amplified sound, responding to the gentlest of caresses and a whisper of kisses. She vaguely remembered the tingling sensations that had spilled through her while she bobbed just beyond reality's shore. As if hypnotized, she had moved closer to those exotic feelings, likening the wondrous sensations to sparkling rubies, emeralds, diamonds and sapphires from her inheritance. Each one became the symbol of the pleasure streaming through her, around her. Those colorful, exquisite sensations had converged into explosive heat and she had shattered into a million pieces . . .

"Oh, my God!" Kat gasped aloud.

Her wild gaze flew to Judd when realization hit her like a thunderbolt. It must have been those peyote buttons that made her feel so uninhibited and wanton, she thought, humiliated. She must have allowed her subconscious desire for Judd to take command of her body. She had seduced him when she didn't have full command of her senses!

Embarrassment splashed across Kat's cheeks. The heightened color in her face obviously caught Judd's attention because he raised an eyebrow, then grinned at her.

She glared at him, ashamed, humiliated, exasperated. "Do not ever allow Wild Hawk to give me that awful potion of his again," she snapped hoarsely. "And please let go of my arm!"

Judd's smile grew wider. "Ah, not a morning person, I see."

"There would be absolutely nothing wrong with my mood if I wasn't suffering a hangover caused by that dreadful peyote," Kat groused. "Now stop that. My arm is killing me!"

Judd didn't stop. He went right on lowering and raising her arm.

"Damn it, Lassiter!" she all but yelled at him.

"Good morning to you, too, princess."

"There is nothing good about it."

"You're alive—that's a start."

Kat swiveled her head around to see that she and Judd were alone beneath the outcropping of rock. "Where are the Comanche braves?"

"They left for the reservation at dawn. They said to tell you good-bye."

Kat frowned. "Wild Hawk went with them?"

Judd smiled enigmatically. "No, he was called away, so to speak."

"I thought I remembered something about Wild Hawk deciding to take the position as marshal in Tascosa. Did I dream that?"

"No. He is still expecting you to help him polish his social graces when he returns."

Judd gently lowered her arm and then withdrew his hand from her wrist.

"Thank you," she said with exaggerated politeness. "If you care to know, that hurts like hell."

"I realize that, but it cannot be helped. Now turn over so I can check the wound on your back," he requested.

Wincing, Kat eased onto her side, then to her stomach. She flinched as Judd removed the bandage, but she refused to cry out. This was not a man tolerant of whimpering and weakness, she reminded herself.

"Does the wound look better?" she asked through gritted teeth.

"Much. I think you are finally on the mend."

"Good, the sooner I am back on my feet, the sooner I can strike off for Santa Fe. By the way, your cut of the jewels is tucked in my stocking."

Kat reached down to retrieve the stones, but Judd took up the task of rolling down her stocking. The gems tumbled onto the pallet. He scooped them up and set them in the palm of her good hand.

"They belong to you," he said. "They are the price I intend to pay for allowing you to get shot."

"No," Kat contradicted. "That was the price you demanded for guiding me cross-country. I got myself shot for free."

"Kat—"

"That was the bargain," she cut in firmly.

Judd was silent while he applied a fresh poultice to the wound. He felt Kat erecting that invisible wall between them again, saw the proud elevation of her chin, noted the resigned set of her delicate jaw. Judd wanted to apologize to her for everything he had done to make her life miserable since the moment they'd struck off on this journey, but the words tumbled around his mind in disarray. He couldn't figure out a good place to start.

Later, he decided. Later, when Kat wasn't nursing a peyote hangover he would voice his regrets. Now she was waspish and stubborn and she couldn't seem to bear looking at him for more than a few seconds at a time.

"Okay, roll onto your back so I can tend the other wound," he requested.

Stiffly, Kat eased onto her back and stared up at the vault of blue sky—*not,* he noted, at him. Judd scooped out the medicinal ointment and gently dabbed it on the jagged flesh that had faded from angry red to tender pink.

"Just to be on the safe side, we will continue to coat the wounds for the next several days."

"Fine," she said with polite formality. "Whatever you think is best."

"I brought your clothes from the hotel so you can change into breeches and a shirt."

"Good."

He smiled at her crisp, one-word reply. "Something wrong, Diamond?"

"Nothing."

"I realize you prefer that I don't touch you, but—"

"What is that supposed to mean?" She glanced at him briefly, then looked the other way.

"It means *I* know that *you* know, but don't understand. Not that I blame you."

Judd sighed. He was doing a lousy job of broaching the subject that had tormented him since the night Kat had been shot. He knew she was tolerating his touch out of necessity. She was repulsed by the eerie revelation that he could be as inhuman as he was human. Thus far, she had been putting up a bold front for his benefit. Admirable, but unnecessary. He had to get this out in the open, once and for all, he decided.

"Kat, about the night you were shot—"

"Oh, that."

Judd frowned, bemused. "Oh that, *what?*"

Kat rolled her eyes at him. "You really must think me dense, Lassiter. I took every cue you tossed at me about the legends and myths surrounding you while we trekked west. You were subtly trying to inform me that you do indeed possess supernatural powers.

"I knew the moment the image of the Phantom Panther and his guard cats appeared to me at Whispering Springs that I was seeing another part of you, the same part that condensed the night I was shot. I figured it out long before that showdown. You have a second sight, a third sight and a sixth sense that I can't emulate, only marvel at," she assured him. "I was only waiting to see if you trusted me enough to confide in me. Obviously not."

Judd just sat there staring, listening in amazement to her matter-of-fact comments.

"Why do you think I tried to protect you, Panther?" she asked him as she stared at the air over his left shoulder. "Do you think I wanted to see such an incredible legend end? Certainly not. You were meant for greater things. Don't you think I'm aware of that?"

"Well, I—"

"I would have given my life for you and considered it well spent. My life would have been no tragic loss," she said. Her breath hitched and tears glistened in her eyes. "After all, I'm a murderess, aren't I? If you would have left me to die, you wouldn't have to hand me over to Marshal Winslow for questioning. That's what you're planning, isn't it?"

"Kat—"

"I saw the notice that fell from your pocket, Lassiter," she hurried on before emotion caused her voice to crack completely. "You can continue to believe I'm guilty of killing my stepfather. It doesn't matter now. It's *too late* for that to matter."

"What does that mean?" Judd wanted to know.

Kat squeezed back the tears and turned away from him. "I'm exhausted and I want to sleep. And don't you dare try to cram that peyote down my throat again, because I promise I will spit it back at you. I made a fool of myself because of it already. I refuse to repeat my humiliation."

Judd sat there while Kat ignored him. Her comments had him befuddled. She wasn't the one who had cause to be embarrassed and ashamed—*he* was. He had taken advantage of her uninhibited condition. Did she think it was the other way around?

"You're wrong, princess," he said to the back of her head. "That is just one more thing I have to apologize for when you are in a better frame of mind. And I intend to apologize when your disposition evens out."

"This is as good as my disposition is going to get, and you have nothing to apologize for, nothing I want you to apologize for. And that, Lassiter, is all I have to say about that, so go away and let me rest."

Judd did exactly that. He hunted game to cook for lunch, but he never wandered far enough away from camp that Kat was out of his sight. All the while he wondered why she hadn't made much of the revelation that he became law and order's wrathful vengeance when the situation demanded. Hadn't Kat seen him at his very worst? Had she been unconscious when he brought down his fury on Rowdy Jack and his cohorts?

That had to be it, Judd told himself.

He hoped she never had to witness the full impact of his powers. He was sure the encounter would terrify her.

Kat was feeling well enough to sit up on the afternoon that Wild Hawk returned to camp. Almost at once, she realized there was something different about him. It wasn't just the eye-catching streak of silver hair that began at the crown of his head and streamed past his left temple, or the bird's claws that dangled from the leather string that encircled his neck. It was in the expression in his silver-blue eyes, the confident, commanding way he carried himself.

Her gaze bounced to Lassiter, who ambled alongside Wild Hawk, then settled on the Comanche warrior. Although Kat certainly wasn't an authority on the unseen powers at work in this visible world, she was sensitive to the unique auras that vibrated around these two men.

Something very significant had happened to Wild Hawk while he was away . . .

Kat frowned, recalling Judd's cryptic comment when she

had asked about Wild Hawk's disappearance: "He has been called away, so to speak." Kat had the unmistakable feeling the Comanche warrior had been called *upon,* just as Judd had obviously been at some point in the past.

"You look much better," Wild Hawk noted as he halted at the end of her pallet.

She smiled wryly at him. "And you look different. Been on a vision quest? A shame my quest didn't affect me as potently as yours did." She cut Judd a sharp glance. "But then, some of us are called *away* and others of us are called *upon.*"

Judd studied Kat's indecipherable expression, then decided it best not to dwell on her comment. Besides, there was much to do and little time to do it. "After Wild Hawk changes into the garments I brought for him, I was hoping you would feel up to tutoring him."

"Are you planning to pump my arm up and down while I'm tutoring?" she asked, sparing him no more than a hasty, side-long glance.

"I thought I might."

"Then the answer is no. I can't concentrate on improving Wild Hawk's social skills while you are inflicting pain."

"Your rehabilitation is just as important as Wild Hawk's instruction."

"To you?" she said, then sniffed. "I doubt that. You are only feeling guilty because I got myself shot on what you consider *your* time."

"Damn it, Kat—"

"Maybe this is not such a good idea," Wild Hawk cut in before an argument broke out.

"It's a grand idea." Ignoring Judd completely, Kat flashed Wild Hawk a cheery smile. "Helping *you* prepare to reenter white society will help *me* fill these hours of boredom."

"Come on, Hawk, might as well get started," Judd said as he snatched up the package he had brought from town. Motioning to Hawk, Judd led the way to an oversize boulder that would serve as a dressing screen.

"There is trouble between you and your woman," Hawk

noted as he accepted the clothes with a grateful nod, then stepped behind the boulder for privacy.

"You could say that. If you wanted to be more accurate, you could say she hates me," Judd muttered.

"Why?" Hawk pulled off the doeskin shirt and fastened himself into the unfamiliar garment.

"For a dozen good reasons. I should tell you from the onset that dealing with white women will be no easy task, especially if you happen across one as strong-willed and high-strung as Kat Diamond. You probably won't, though, because I doubt any woman can top her," Judd declared. "I've been in and out of white society for several years, but nothing prepared me to deal with the likes of Kat. My advice to you is to steer clear of females until you have been acclimated into your new life and new job. No sense cluttering your mind with more trouble than you can handle."

Hawk stepped into the trim-fitting breeches. "You consider the love of a woman heap big trouble?" he asked, mouth twitching.

Judd did a double take. "Nobody said anything about love."

"I did. Kat Diamond is in love with you," Hawk stated matter-of-factly. "And you are in love with her."

Judd snorted derisively. "That only goes to show how much you have to learn. Whatever respect Kat might have had for me is gone, because I believed the worst about her. Besides, neither of us believe love exists."

Hawk barked a laugh. "You know, Panther, wise and worldly though you are, you can be very blind sometimes."

Judd bristled indignantly. "I have exceptional eyesight, thank you very much!"

"Yes, the keen vision of a panther." He regarded Judd with a sly smile. "But you are the one who told me I had to learn to see with my heart. Now are you telling me that I should do as you say and *not* as you do?"

"Damnation, Hawk, you're becoming as difficult as Kat. You are going to blend into white society much easier than I first thought."

Hawk stepped into full view and looked down his torso. "So how do I look?"

Judd reached out to unfasten the top button of the cream-colored shirt. "Now you don't look so straight-laced. And stop squirming around," he ordered brusquely. "The people in Tascosa will be wondering if you have a rash if you keep worming around like that."

"These clothes are itchy," Hawk complained, and scratched his shoulder.

"You'll get used to it. Once you settle into society you can make your own personal fashion statement by adding buckskin to your wardrobe. The first thing you must do is let the whites get used to having you around, and vice versa."

On the way back to camp, where Kat waited to give lessons on social skills, Judd told Hawk about the good-hearted Hamptons, the restaurateur and the saloonkeeper he would meet soon. Judd also instructed Hawk to be on his best behavior around the councilmen, because Judd considered them allies and friends who would come to Hawk's defense if the need arose.

Judd halted in front of Kat, then bowed gallantly. "May I present your new student Hawk," he introduced formally. "Work your magic, Diamond."

Kat stuck out her hand and smiled cordially. "I am honored to make your acquaintance, Mr. Hawk. My name is Katherine Diamond."

When Hawk stood there, uncertain how to respond, Judd nudged him in the ribs and said aside, "Take her hand and respectfully remove your hat."

"I don't have a hat," Hawk reminded him.

Judd removed his Stetson and plunked it on Hawk's head. "Now you do."

Hawk grabbed the brim and yanked, causing his long hair to stand on end. "I have to remove the hat every time I speak to someone?"

"Only to women," Judd specified. "Men just get the nod."

"Who is giving the lessons? You or me?" Kat questioned tersely.

Judd met her irritated gaze, realizing her irritation was starting to rub off on him. He didn't function well when he and Kat were at odds—and they were definitely at odds. "You are," he said, staring at the air over her head.

"Exactly. So take yourself off to find something to serve as eating utensils," she ordered. "Table manners are important, too."

"See what I mean about women?" Judd said confidentially. "You can set them off unintentionally. Better ask Kat how to get back in a woman's good graces. You'll need to know."

"Then I can convey the information to you, Panther," Hawk said, smiling.

When Judd wheeled around and strode off, Kat relaxed. She knew she was being difficult around Panther, knew it was childish, but she couldn't control herself. She was in love with the man, and it hurt like hell to know he didn't feel the same way. He didn't have the slightest faith in her, didn't consider her worthy of his respect.

She tried to treat Judd indifferently, but it was impossible, because he stirred so many emotions. How was a woman supposed to treat a man as if he didn't exist when she was totally and hopelessly aware of everything he said and did?

"Now then, Hawk," she said, discarding the unproductive thoughts. "Let's try the formal greeting from the top."

"The top of what?" he asked, confused. "From the top of the hat?"

Kat chuckled in amusement. "Sorry, that is a theatrical expression. Society has hundreds of clichés and catch phrases you will need to learn."

Hawk groaned aloud. "I only have a few days. How am I going to figure out all these clicks?"

"Clichés," Kat corrected patiently. "They are trite phrases such as: water under the bridge, which means the past is past and there is nothing you can do about it."

Hawk nodded pensively. "That makes good sense."

"To go against the grain is a saying that applies to you," Kat explained. "Returning to white society is the opposite of your true inclination. When you run your hand against the grain of a rough cut of wood, you are bound to be pricked by splinters. That is where the saying originated.''

Hawk nodded in understanding, then smiled. ''You are very perceptive, Kat Diamond. These breeches I'm wearing definitely go against the Comanche grain.''

''Try wearing a skirt,'' Kat said, laughing. ''Masculine clothes are far more practical. You don't have it as bad as you think you do.''

Within a few minutes, Kat and Hawk were at ease with each other and the tutoring session was under way. Kat tossed out a few more catch phrases, gave their definitions, then instructed Hawk to use them in sentences. Hawk was an easy teach, because he was quick-minded and determined to learn all he could in the limited time he had. Since Hawk had begun life in white society, several of her instructions jogged half-forgotten memories of childhood and made the lessons easier.

Hawk's quest in the wilderness had armed him with the self-confidence needed to begin his new life. Kat's instructions provided him with the social tools to make his reentry into civilization easier. She spoke of customs and behaviors, declaring that basic human emotions and flaws were similar in most cultures. The trick was to become a student of human nature and learn to gauge reactions to anger, to joy, greed and cravings for power so Hawk would quickly recognize signs of impending trouble.

Three hours later, Kat was certain Hawk would have little trouble meeting the upcoming challenges. He stopped squirming in his new clothes, learned to shrug nonchalantly and tossed out a few clichés every now and then. His manner of speech was still a bit stiff, but Kat knew he would learn to pick up the rhythm patterns of the English language when he was surrounded by people who spoke fluently. In short, Hawk was well on his way to becoming a star pupil.

''Now then,'' Hawk said as he sat down cross-legged beside Kat. ''Panther insisted that I learn how to deal properly with women. He says your kind can be difficult.''

Kat bristled. ''He did, did he? Well, that only goes to show how little he knows. Women are not so difficult to understand

and relate to. We want exactly the same things men want. Courtesy, respect and consideration are important to everyone. No one wants to be taken for granted, overlooked, or treated as if their feelings and opinions count for nothing.

"Your friend Panther could do with a few lessons in social graces himself. He can be impolite, less than gracious, stubborn as a pack of mules and mistrusting for no logical reason!"

Kat slammed her mouth shut when she realized her voice had risen several decibels.

"And women become emotional about those flaws in the men they love," Hawk presumed, biting back a grin. "That is no different than the Comanche culture."

"Nobody said anything about love," Kat muttered, busying herself by tucking the quilt around her hips. "Now who is supposed to be giving lessons to whom here?"

Hawk shrugged. He had perfected the shrug with amazing ease. In fact, it was becoming his trademark, Kat noted.

"An old Comanche proverb states that there is much to learn from every living thing in the world around you. A wise man never forgets that."

"You are absolutely right, Hawk. Now let's move on to proper table manners before the last of my energy deserts me."

Kat handed Hawk the improvised fork, spoon and knife Judd had fashioned from twigs and presented to her a few minutes earlier. Then she showed Hawk how to hold his wooden fork so he could eat in a socially acceptable manner, how to handle the knife when cutting different foods.

Kat glanced up in surprise when a hawk swooped beneath the shelf of stone and, amazingly, landed on Hawk's shoulder. Kat estimated the buzzard hawk had a four-foot wing span. The bird fluffed its feathers, then turned its head to stare down its hooked beak at her. Its light-colored eyes gave it a fierce appearance, and Kat was amazed that Wild Hawk's eyes were nearly a perfect match for those of the bird of prey.

"I see that you picked up a pet during your wilderness vigil." She nodded in understanding. "Not unlike the black pumas that appear from time to time in Panther's presence."

"I have named him Buzz, for obvious reasons." Hawk

grinned, but his expression sobered an instant later. "You understand the way of things in the Indian culture, but you are not wary?"

"Let's just say I have an easier time accepting the fact that you and Panther are rare men who have been granted exceptional gifts. I am more awed than frightened, though Panther somehow got the impression that I am disturbed by it."

Hawk appraised her pensively. "I do not think all whites are as open-minded. Spirit powers can be unnerving when called upon in full force. Have you seen Panther at his most dangerous?"

"Well, no," she admitted. "I passed out shortly after I was shot. When I asked Panther what became of the three outlaws, he said they were in hell. He didn't explain how they came to be there."

"He put them there, wielding the powers of his guardian spirit," Hawk said simply.

"Which means *precisely* . . . ?" Kat prodded.

Hawk's expression sobered as he stared directly at Kat. "The same way a vicious panther attacks its prey. The same way Three Wolves disposes of wicked men who follow wicked ways. The same way the Lone Horseman calls the wild mustangs of the plains to trample evil."

Kat grimaced as she visualized how powerful predators attacked unmercifully. Maybe she didn't want the grisly details, after all. Maybe Panther, and men like him, were hesitant about having eyewitnesses view them at their deadliest.

Kat had been close enough that fateful night to witness the shocking transformation Judd had undergone. She had felt the energy swirling around him, heard the changes in his voice. She had seen the look in his eyes, the silvery haze that indicated the man she knew had become something more than human.

Bemusedly, Kat stared at the sharp-eyed hawk perched on Hawk's shoulder. She noted the razorlike claws, the pointed beak, the alertness that stated the creature was aware of everything transpiring around it. She wondered how Hawk changed when he wielded the mystical powers bestowed on him.

"I tell you, Kat Diamond, I'm not sure how I will react if

someone other than my mortal enemies sees me call down the powers of my totem. It is personal and private."

Kat began to understand that Panther was uncomfortable, uncertain of how he would be viewed—judged—by witnesses. Did he see his supernatural gift as an insurmountable obstacle between himself and Kat? Was he holding back deeper feelings because he didn't want to make her uncomfortable?

Suddenly Kat realized that it was not Panther who must make a gesture of acceptance, but she. But how? And what if Panther had no deep feelings for her? Then she would make a fool of herself with him all over again.

No, maybe it was best to catch the stage west and not look back. Even if Judd Lassiter wanted a future with her, what kind could it be? Judd had accepted who and what he was, so why did she think her brief appearance in his life would become some pivotal point?

"Lessons are over for the day," Judd announced as he strode into view. "Diamond needs to exercise, then rest."

"I can exercise my arm by myself," Kat insisted.

"No," Judd contradicted. "You won't be as relentless a taskmaster as I will."

"You're certainly right about that," Kat mumbled. "It's hard to keep doing things that hurt, whether they are physical or emotional."

Biting back a grin, Hawk rose to his feet and touched the brim of his hat respectfully. "Good afternoon, Miss Diamond. I will be looking forward to visiting with you later."

Judd's brows shot up when Hawk delivered such a polished farewell. "Damn, you learn fast, Hawk."

Hawk inclined his head. "Mr. Lassiter, nice to see you again," he said, then strode away, with the ever-present Buzz riding on his left shoulder.

Judd nodded approvingly at Kat. "Nice work."

"He's a receptive student."

Judd knelt down to peel off Kat's tattered gown. She took immediate offense. "What do you think you're doing!"

"Helping you change clothes."

"I can do it myself."

"No, you can't, not without splitting a stitch. I don't want to have to sew you back together again. Once was unnerving enough."

Kat frowned darkly. "Don't expect me to believe it was harder on you than it was on me."

"Fine, don't believe it, even if it's the truth. You think I didn't beat myself black and blue the whole time I performed primitive surgery, knowing it was my fault you will bear these two scars for the rest of your life? Two scars that mar absolute perfection? Believe me, I've thought about it a lot."

Kat blinked. Her mouth opened and shut like a door, but no words came out.

"Well, it's true," he said as he shook out the clean shirt and breeches. "You were perfect until I nearly got you killed."

He thought she was physical perfection? Kat was flattered, but she reminded herself once again that she wanted much more than Judd's physical attraction.

Her thoughts flitted off when Judd drew the stained gown to her waist, baring her breasts to his heated gaze. Kat felt a flush creep up her neck to stain her cheeks while he looked his fill.

"Still perfection in my eyes," he murmured as he picked up the oversize shirt. "You may not want to hear my apology, refuse to accept it, but I am truly sorry this lovely body of yours got in the way of a flying bullet. If you did it to protect me, then I am humbled by your bravery. No one ever took a bullet for me before, Kat. *No one.*"

Kat had difficulty keeping her resolve when he bent to graze her lips in a wispy kiss. Oh, God, how was she going to live without this man? She couldn't even remember what it felt like not to love him, not to have him in her life. He had become as necessary to her as breathing, and she would die inside when he walked away.

When he lifted his dark head and smiled at her, Kat wanted to throw her arms around him—her good one, at least—and hold on tightly for as long as he would let her.

"Now the breeches," he prompted as he carefully eased the gown down her hips. "I also want to apologize for doubting your claim of innocence. I'm not turning you over to Hawk so he can telegraph Marshal Winslow. Anyone who would throw herself in front of a bullet is not the kind of person who would aim and fire at her stepfather, no matter how much he probably deserved a good shooting.

"I was wrong, Kat, and I'm dreadfully sorry for ever doubting you. You are exactly what you seem. Honest, trustworthy and reliable. My problem is that I haven't spent much time with people who possess those virtues. I couldn't recognize a good thing when it was staring me in the face."

She searched his eyes, wanting to let the words in her heart fly free. "Judd, I—"

"There's something else you need to know," he rushed on. "I know you think I betrayed you when I went to Lottie's Place, but you are mistaken. I showed the sketches to Lottie and discovered Ark Riley was upstairs. I was able to apprehend him and take him to my camp. I should have explained, but I didn't. I hurt you and I'm sorry for that, too.

"And now I'm going to hurt you again," he continued, smiling apologetically. "Not because I want to. I've done enough of that already. But I am not going to allow you to lose the use of your left arm."

Kat braced herself for the discomfort when Judd helped her into her breeches, then lowered and raised her arm to limber up the stiff muscles. Carefully she formulated her words, trying to think past the screaming pain caused by his repetitive exercises.

She asked herself if merely telling Panther that his mystical powers didn't disturb her would convince him. She doubted it. She had told him she was innocent of crime and he hadn't believed her. She had to find a way to show him that she not only accepted the dangerous side of his persona but approved of his calling, had no fear of him.

How to make the point? she asked herself while he worked her arm like a water pump.

Twenty minutes later, when Kat's brow was beaded with perspiration and her face was ashen with pain, Judd halted his ministrations. "Rest," he ordered gently. "You've earned it for being a courageous patient. And, Kat?"

"Yes?" she said tiredly.

"I—" Judd closed his mouth, then reached out to brush his forefinger over her cheek. "I'll have supper ready when you wake up," he promised before he rose and walked away.

CHAPTER
TWENTY-SEVEN

"Not bad, Hawk, not bad at all." Judd nodded approvingly as Hawk slid the well-used Colt into Judd's spare holster. The pistol that had belonged to James Thornton now hung on Hawk's hip.

The hawk, which had flitted off when lead started flying, returned to Hawk's shoulder.

"I had a good instructor," Hawk said as he stared at what was left of the cactus he used for target practice.

Judd cocked a brow to survey Hawk. The man was an absolute marvel. Hawk had learned quickly and he had learned well. He was damn fast clearing leather, and his aim with a pistol was accurate. As for his command of English, Hawk's hours of tutoring with Kat had certainly paid off. Hawk was well on his way to adapting to his new life.

"Only one more thing left to do before we ride into Tascosa," Judd announced.

"What's that?"

"That long hair has to go."

Hawk jerked up his head and threw back his shoulders. "Why? Yours is long."

"It wasn't when I started in this business," Judd informed

him, then pivoted toward camp. "Right now, Comanches are still a touchy subject in Texas, same as white-eyes are touchy subjects in Indian Territory. The first thing you have to do is get a foothold there; then you can adapt your clothing and hairstyle to suit your tastes."

Hawk grunted sourly as he fell into step beside Panther. "Anything else I have to sacrifice to become white?"

"No, but I advise you to steer clear of whiskey," Judd said. "It affects your reflexes and your senses. That can get you killed."

"Cut my hair, avoid women and whiskey. Dress like a white man, speak like a white man, think and eat like a white man—"

"Only white on the outside," Judd cut in, then tapped his chest and smiled wryly. "On the inside you're still one hundred percent Indian. One day, when the white-eyes kill off each other because of their greed and hunger for power, we can have our hunting ground back. Patience is the name of the game, Hawk."

Hawk chuckled. "Outwait the enemy. As a warrior I grew up with that philosophy."

"It always applies ..." Judd's voice trailed off when he saw Kat silhouetted against the glorious colors of sunset. She was hurling his dagger at the dead cedar tree that protruded from cracks in the face of the cliff.

"Quite a woman," Hawk murmured as he followed Judd's distracted gaze. "She is not as difficult as you made her out to be."

"Around *you,*" Judd clarified.

Judd had to admit that he was envious of the easygoing friendship that had developed between Kat and Hawk during their long hours of tutoring. Judd had heard their laughter drifting from beneath the outcropping of stone, heard them talking companionably.

While Kat and Hawk had grown close, Judd and Kat had grown distant. He could feel her slipping away from him, hour by hour, day by day. Even though he knew it was for the best, it didn't hurt any less to know he was losing her.

Damn it, she was going to leave a hole the size of Texas in his heart when she boarded that stage.

Don't think about it, fool. You know this is for the best. Like you told Hawk: There are burdens and limitations to these imposed powers. Kat deserves more of a life than you can give her. You are, and will always be, one of the Mystics of the Four Winds. You vowed to come when the voices call.

Judd waited until Kat launched the dagger with practiced ease, watched the blade quiver in its target, before he announced his arrival. "Company coming, Diamond," he called out to her.

She turned to grace Hawk with a smile, then stared past Judd's shoulder. It was becoming a habit of hers that annoyed him.

"How is our star pupil doing?" Kat inquired.

"Passing with flying colors," Judd replied.

Hawk nodded, then grinned. "Another cliché."

"Exactly right." Kat flashed Hawk a smile that made Judd's heart twist in his chest.

"How are you at cutting hair, Diamond?" Judd questioned.

"Passable, I suppose, but not with flying colors." She bit back a smile when Hawk grumbled and toyed with his flowing mane. "Sit down on that chair-size boulder and let me try my hand before we lose the light."

Judd strode over to fetch his saddlebag and withdrew the small kit that held his razor, scissors, needles and thread. He handed the scissors to Kat, noting she was careful not to let her fingers graze his hand.

You've lost her. She avoids even the slightest touch.

Glumly, Judd plunked down on the ground to watch Kat clip Hawk's long, dark mane. They chatted casually while she moved around him, making a conscious attempt to give Hawk a respectable-looking cut. Judd felt more like an outsider than ever. He had been alone most of his adult life, but he couldn't remember feeling this lonely.

This is what you deserve for letting yourself get emotionally attached, idiot . . .

When a wailing sob that was his name echoed around the

canyon walls, Judd's thoughts scattered and he vaulted to his feet. His heart slammed against his ribs when he recognized the distressed voice.

"Pan-ther . . !" The haunting sound ricocheted off the stone cliffs again.

Judd whistled to Horse. The gelding jerked up his head and came trotting from the grassy knoll when Judd gave a second whistle.

"Stay here," he instructed Hawk and Kat.

Judd picked his way up the gully, bareback, following the distress call. When he reached the caprock, he flattened himself against Horse—in case he was being lured into a trap.

He swore ripely when he saw Gracie Hampton swaying atop a sorrel mare. Her gray hair was in wild disarray. Tears bled down her smudged cheeks, and her gown was torn and soiled. Her lips were cracked from long hours of riding in the sun and wind.

Rage burst through Judd when he noticed the purplish bruise on her jaw. "Thornton," he muttered furiously.

"Panther!" Gracie wailed in torment and relief. "Thank goodness I've found you at last!"

He swore foully when he realized Gracie's hands and feet were tied to the saddle. Judd motioned her toward him, refusing to sit upright and move from behind the jutting rocks. This was not a good time to become an easy target.

"Oh, Panther," she whimpered brokenly. "That awful man came back to town with a vengeance."

"Easy, Gracie," Judd murmured as he leaned away from Horse to untie her wrists and ankles. "You can tell me all about it when we reach camp and you've quenched your thirst. Use the travel time to get yourself in hand. Whatever is wrong I will fix it," he promised the weeping woman.

Gracie used the time it took to weave around the obstacle course of rocks and boulders to have herself a good, loud cry. By the time they reached the campsite, she was fresh out of tears and down to shuddering sobs.

"Gracie!" Kat came running the moment she saw the once-cheerful hotel owner who had been reduced to teary anguish. "What on earth has happened?"

Judd gently drew Gracie from the saddle. She flung her arms around his neck and squeezed the breath out of him before turning her blurry gaze on Kat. "I'm afraid the town council has made a formidable enemy in that scoundrel Thornton," she said hoarsely. "He means to take over the town, lock, stock and barrel. He and his ruthless friends descended like a plague of demons."

"Hawk, fetch Gracie a canteen. Hawk, Gracie Hampton," he added in hasty introduction.

After Kat guided Gracie to the pallet, she blotted the woman's flushed face with the hem of her shirt. "Everything is going to be fine," Kat said consolingly. "Hawk and Panther will take care of this situation—"

"But they can't!" Gracie howled in torment. "They will be walking into a trap with our town council as bait."

Kat glanced worriedly at Judd, who sank down on the pallet to hand Gracie a drink.

The older woman gulped hurriedly, drew a shaky breath, then plowed on. "Thornton came riding into town last night with a troop of ragtag cutthroats at his heels. They ransacked our hotel and stole merchandise from the shop. Then they swarmed Robert Wilson's restaurant and dragged out the tables and chairs and lit a bonfire.

"And that was only the beginning," Gracie said bitterly. "The raiders took the whiskey from Cape Mullin's saloon and got themselves rip-roaring drunk. Then they lassoed Samuel, Robert and Cape and dragged them up and down the streets, demanding that Thornton be hired as marshal."

Gracie burst into tears and buried her face in her hands. After a moment, she swiped at the tears and forced herself to continue. "Samuel was the only one still conscious after the torture session that produced no results. Samuel told Thornton that Panther and Mr. Hawk would send them all to hell for their abuse and destruction."

Kat grimaced. She could well imagine what poor Samuel had suffered for his defiance. "Is Samuel all right?"

"Not very all right," Gracie blubbered. "Thornton kicked him in the chin and declared that the only way Panther and Mr. Hawk could reclaim Tascosa was over his dead body."

"If that's the way he wants it, I'll accommodate him," Judd growled vindictively.

"It gets worse," Gracie whimpered. "The raiders decided to exchange your lives for Samuel's, Robert's and Cape's. They hauled them to a box canyon west of here and staked them to a mesquite tree."

"Are you speaking of the place the Comanches call Devil's Canyon?" Hawk asked.

Gracie shrugged. "I don't know it by name, but the rock formations are reminiscent of dragon spines. I saw it for myself, because the raiders threw me over a horse and took me with them after I tried to object to their cruelty."

Judd glanced grimly at Hawk. His protégé was about to be tested to the full extent of his newfound powers. He would be asked to save people who meant nothing to him. Judd waited, giving Hawk the chance to decide if he was prepared to reach deep inside himself to save strangers—*white* strangers at that.

"Go on, Gracie," Hawk prompted as he sent Judd a speaking glance.

"If you ride into that box canyon, it will be like riding into the jaws of death," Gracie said brokenly. "Thornton has twenty gunmen with him, all of whom are exceptional marksmen. According to Thornton's drunken boasts, he and his men didn't care much for the fact that the Confederacy lost the war and Union soldiers destroyed their homes. The raiders have been on a rampage since the war, gathering a larger force of bitter renegades who plunder helpless communities.

"Thornton and his men recently came down from Montana, after the last town they bled of profit dried up. They preyed on miners until there was nothing left. Now they have cast their greedy eyes on Tascosa and the cattle herds that are driven up the trail on their way to Dodge.

"Dear Lord! What are we to do?" Gracie blurted hysterically. "They sent me to lure you out, but two men cannot go up against an army. It's suicide! I cannot ask you to save the lives of three men who will most surely be lost, whether you succeed or fail. We are doomed to live under the reign of that tyrant and his vicious army. God help us all!''

When Gracie flung herself down on the pallet to have another good cry, Kat patted her quaking shoulder and stared at Judd. She knew he and Hawk intended to take on the lopsided odds, knew—for once and for all—that her whimsical dream of sharing a life with the man called Panther would mean the sacrifice of too many innocent lives. Gracie, and people like her, needed the help of men like Panther and Hawk. They dared to go where others feared to tread. They accepted their destinies and fought force with force.

When Judd rose to his feet, Kat could sense that strange aura gathering around him. ''Kat, do you feel up to taking Gracie back to town after she has a chance to rest?''

Kat wanted to shout to high heaven that she needed to go with him and Hawk, not huddle on the sidelines and await the outcome. Panther touched so many lives that she couldn't bear to think of his defeat. She wanted to assist him any way she could . . .

Suddenly Kat knew how she could help, how to provide a necessary distraction—though Panther would undoubtedly refuse her offer. That being the case, she wouldn't ask permission—she would simply act. She had the inescapable feeling that Robert, Samuel and Cape would become the first targets when all hell broke loose. After all, Kat reminded herself, the councilmen were the ones who had denied Thornton's application. Thornton was probably planning to place his own men on the council after the smoke cleared.

''I will see that Gracie is resting comfortably,'' Kat said. And she would, but Kat wouldn't be around to watch Gracie rest.

''The time has come,'' Judd murmured, then turned away to saddle the horses.

Kat waited until Hawk and Panther skidded down the slope, then she reached for the pouch Hawk had left in camp. ''Gracie, I want you to chew these buttons. They work like a sedative,'' Kat said hurriedly.

"What are they?"

"Just take them," Kat ordered. "We won't leave here until you have a chance to rest. I will be back for you later."

"But—"

Kat didn't have time for explanation. She grabbed the bull-whip and dagger, then pulled herself onto Gracie's mount to make a quiet departure. She knew the success of her deceptive ploy could be the difference between the life and death of the councilmen. She had to give them a sporting chance.

Devil's Canyon, she mused as she kicked the horse into full gallop. *Hell of a place to have to ride into without an impenetrable coat of armor.*

Judd led the saddled horses up the rocky slope, then stared, bemused, at the campsite. A sense of icy dread filled his veins when he noticed only one silhouette sprawled on the pallet, and the telltale absence of the sorrel mare.

"Damn it to hell, Kat," Judd growled ferociously.

"What's wrong?" Hawk questioned as he came up behind Judd.

Judd didn't bother to reply. He handed Horse's reins to Hawk, then raced toward the pallet. He sputtered a curse when he saw Hawk's open pouch. "Kat fed Gracie peyote buttons to sedate her."

Hawk glanced around. "Where is the extra horse?"

"Under Kat," Judd muttered angrily. "Headed directly toward Devil's Canyon, is my guess."

"What?" Hawk crowed in disbelief.

"I told you headstrong white women could be difficult, if not absolutely impossible."

"She will get herself killed. What is she thinking!"

"Smoke screen," Judd replied pensively.

Suddenly Hawk understood. "She is planning to provide us with a distraction."

Judd nodded as he placed the canteen at Gracie's fingertips, then mounted Horse. He thundered off like a house afire. Hawk was at his heels. Judd wanted to strangle Kat for her reckless daring—and wondered if she would live long enough for him to satisfy his frustration with her.

Hell and damnation, he had endured untold torment when Kat threw herself in front of a flying bullet. Now the odds of survival were worse. Why was she doing this?

The answer came with startling clarity while Judd rode with fiendish urgency. Kat knew what it was like to be a helpless victim. She had unwillingly played that role most of her life. Now she had become a martyr, determined to do all within her power to save the men held hostage by merciless raiders.

Judd knew as well as Kat that the councilmen were not going to be allowed to walk away from Devil's Canyon. They were to become examples for Tascosans who defied the takeover. Resistance would mean death for anyone who didn't march obediently to Thornton's drum.

Difficult though it was to concentrate on the task ahead of him, Judd focused his attention, refusing to let himself become preoccupied with concern for Kat. His ability to strike swiftly, unerringly, was all that would save her from her own selfless courage.

If anything could save her at all . . .

Judd shoved away that dismal thought and breathed deeply, steadily. He closed his eyes and descended into the depths of absolute concentration, leaving Horse to guard his own steps in the darkness. Judd didn't care if he never emerged from the farthest recesses where he sank to find strength. If remaining within the omnipotent spirits for all eternity was the price paid to save Kat, then so be it.

Through an icy fog, Judd heard the piercing whistles of the circling hawk, and Panther responded in kind. He reached out with mind and spirit to accept the power source at his command. His voice rose in another bone-chilling scream, summoning the Mystics of the Four Winds into a united force, for it was going to require the combined magic of powerful shamans to destroy the evil that gathered in Devil's Canyon.

* * *

Kat stared down the moonlit path that led into Devil's Canyon. A campfire blazed near the lone tree that Gracie had described. Kat could make out three silhouettes tied upright to the scraggly tree. Flames from the campfire flickered across the men's downcast heads.

Anger and outrage roiled inside Kat as she pulled off her cap and shook out the golden strands, letting them tumble over her shoulders. She wanted it known that only a woman was riding into the canyon.

Kat glanced around the looming rock walls and mazelike ravines that formed spined barriers in the canyon. There were too many places for sharpshooters to hide, she mused. The raiders had undoubtedly entrenched themselves in the narrow gullies so the impenetrable ridges of rock would protect them from flying bullets.

This Thornton character knew how to select the perfect sight for his trap, Kat mused bitterly, and not just because of the canyon's name, either.

Although frissons of uneasiness channeled through Kat, she focused on her plan of action. Judd had taught her to be prepared for anything. She had forgotten that rule the night she blundered toward his encampment outside Tascosa, and she had earned a bullet for her carelessness.

Kat decided to head directly toward the three captives so she could ascertain the seriousness of their condition. All she had was one weary horse to transport the men, and herself, from the jaws of hell. She wouldn't have much time before the raiders realized her intention and opened fire.

There was also one more hurdle to overcome, she reminded herself. Although she wanted the raiders to realize she was a woman, and hoped they wouldn't view her as a threat, there was a possibility of being hauled from the horse and—

Kat cut off the repulsive thought. She would have to talk swiftly and continuously to provide a distraction.

Marshaling her composure, Kat urged the sorrel down the

twisted path. She prayed for the ability to think clearly and move quickly when disaster struck—which it inevitably would.

Kat's only regret, as she descended into the raiders' den, was that she hadn't worked up the nerve to tell Judd that she loved him—just in case things didn't go according to her optimistic plan. She would have liked for Judd to know that no matter where he was while serving his calling for justice, that he was loved and admired and needed. She wished she could tell him that wherever she was—in this world or another—he would be remembered until long past forever.

"Here's to justice," Kat said aloud. "And to every innocent victim who prayed for deliverance that came too late . . ."

CHAPTER TWENTY-EIGHT

Thornton spit tobacco juice as he watched the lone rider follow the winding path to the canyon floor. His eyes widened in surprise when moonbeams glinted off the long golden tresses.

"Well, hell, Thor," Dex Fuller, Thornton's second in command, whispered as he watched the rider descend. "That's a woman!"

"Sure as hell looks like one to me," Thornton said before taking another swig of Cape Mullin's fine liquor.

"So where's this Panther and Hawk the councilmen think so much of? Did those lily-livered cowards send a bit of fluff to do their fighting for them?"

"Hey, Thor," one of the raiders called from his concealment in the V-shaped arroyo. "What the hell's going on? Do you have to make an appointment to fight that legendary spook?"

Thornton took another gulp of liquor, then wiped his mouth on his shirtsleeve. "Don't know. Can't figure why Panther and Hawk would send a woman. Guess we won't know until we hear what the gal has to say."

He turned to wave his arm in an expansive gesture. "Hold your fire until I find out what's going on. Pass along the word, boys."

Kat heard the command and breathed a sigh of relief. She would have provided a lousy distraction if she had been shot out of the saddle immediately.

Strategically, she reined the sorrel toward the cadaver-thin renegade who wobbled toward her, his shiny new Sharps rifle—undoubtedly stolen from the gunsmith shop in Tascosa—aimed at her chest. Kat made certain the renegade couldn't see the right side of the saddle where the bullwhip was coiled within easy reach. The dagger was tucked in her right boot. Her left arm was of little use in a fight, and Kat hoped she wouldn't have to defend herself with it.

"Where are those two cowards?" Thornton scowled in question. "Can't be hiding behind your skirts because you aren't wearing any."

Muffled chuckles echoed in the darkness. The sounds assured Kat that most of the raiders were fanned out in front of her. Only a few men were positioned near the escape route—in case their enemies made it through the barrage of bullets on the canyon floor.

"I came to inform you that Panther and Mr. Hawk are indisposed," she said very formally. "Your summons came at an inconvenient time. They have other fish to fry at the moment."

As anticipated, Thornton immediately disregarded Kat as a threat. The fact that she was a woman, and spoke in a cultured manner, worked to her advantage. She could tell Thornton had let down his guard. His thin-bladed shoulders slumped, and so did the rifle barrel.

"Well, la-di-da," Thornton smirked. "Indisposed, you say? Now ain't that a crying shame." He glanced briefly at the councilmen who were bound to the tree with a lariat. "You hear that, fellas? Your salvation just ain't got time to save your hides tonight."

Thornton wobbled forward to scoff up at Kat. "You go back and tell that legendary Panther and his sidekick that if they don't show up here tonight there won't be anything left here to do, except see to the burying. These councilmen die at dawn. Then me and my men are going to ride back to town and take over. If anybody in Tascosa has an objection, he'll hang high."

"I'm sorry, sir, but I cannot do that," Kat said with exaggerated formality.

"Why not? Oh, yeah," Thornton smirked. "I forgot. *Indisposed.* Well, you tell them to get *disposed* real fast. Tell Panther—"

"Tell him yourself, James Thornton."

The hollow voice rolled down the eroded walls on the south rim of the canyon, causing Thornton and his men to wheel in search of the eerie sound. Kat heard rifles and pistols being cocked, saw those unnerving pinpoints of light flickering against the inky walls of the cliffs. With each heartbeat, more phosphorescent eyes reflected in the moonlight.

"Tell me, *James Thornton."*

Another unearthly voice drifted into the canyon from the eastern ridge. Heads turned in synchronized rhythm. Kat stared up to see the silhouettes of buzzard hawks circling in symbolic flight over the dead—or about to be dead. With each spiraling rotation, more birds of prey joined the formation. Taunting whistles and chattering calls filled the air, then faded into silence.

Kat flinched when a wolf's unnerving howl rose toward the moon. Incongruous plumes of smoke drifted along the caprock.

"Damnation. What is that?" someone called out.

Kat swiveled in the saddle when thundering hooves resounded behind her. To her amazement the image of the fabled ghost horses raced along the ridge above her. Then the dark shadow of a rider, his cape billowing out behind him, appeared on the back of a stallion that was the color of the devil's heart.

Kat blinked as she glanced in one direction, then another. She could feel the density of tension in the air and swore she could slice it with the bullwhip. On the wings of that thought came the realization that this was her time to act. Haunting howls, shrill screams, piercing whistles and thundering hooves overlapped each other, as if the demons of the night had congregated. Vengeful devils from the four corners of the earth had come to collect the souls of the eternal damned.

Kat grabbed her dagger and whip, then slid from the horse.

She was cutting the rope that bound Samuel's chest before Thornton and his raiders knew what she was about. All attention was focused on the western rim where a floating fog took the form of a great white puma with glowing eyes. An unholy scream slid down the face of the cliff as the Phantom Panther slashed out with razor-sharp claws. Caterwauls resounded in eerie accompaniment as pinpoints of shimmering light moved from higher elevations to lower, descending like a deadly plague.

"Thornton! What the blazes is going on?" one of the raiders called anxiously. "I thought you said the legend was a hoax. This doesn't look like a hoax to me!"

Wolf howls overrode the raider's voice. Shadowy images of buzzard hawks formed a tornado-like funnel above the canyon rim. Kat felt a frigid chill seep down her backbone and into her soul. Her hand shook as she cut Robert Wilson loose, then offered him support when his knees buckled beneath him. Clearly, the restaurateur had been injured and had difficulty standing alone.

Although the hair on the back of Kat's neck was standing on end, she reached out to saw at the rope that held Cape Mullin. The moment he was free he wobbled slightly, but he braced himself against the tree.

"Get Robert on the horse," Kat instructed Samuel. "Do it now. We don't have much time."

Without a word Samuel slid his arm around Robert's waist and moved toward the horse that pranced uneasily, ears pricked, eyes wide with fear.

Another round of caterwauls, screams, howls and whistles rose up in the night. The specters of runaway horses pounded against the caprock like rolling thunder heralding the arrival of doom.

Kat shivered as the ground shook beneath her feet. She could feel the omnipotent forces coiling upon themselves, then fanning out like a glacier of ice sliding into the canyon, devouring all within its path.

"Oh my—" Kat's throat closed when four evanescent apparitions rose at the four corners of the caprock. Distorted, menacing faces appeared in the swirls of fog, smoke, cloud and shadow that expanded toward the sky.

Run for your life!

The silent command came out of nowhere. Kat wheeled to follow the horse and riders that trotted down the escape route. She had taken only three running strides when she felt a man's arms clamp around her knees, sending her plunging headfirst into the prickly grass.

"You ain't going nowhere, witch!" Thornton snarled as he plopped on top of her and grabbed her by the throat. His bony fingers dug into her windpipe, making her choke for breath. "Call off those demons!"

Kat could barely breathe, but she could smell the whiskey and tobacco on Thornton's panted breath. He loosened the stranglehold just enough for Kat to catch a quick gulp of air, then he jabbed her in the ribs.

"Do what I tell you, witch," he snarled.

Kat raised her hand and slammed the stock of the whip in his face. When he reflexively shrank back, she rolled to her knees to strike him with the coiled whip.

"Move away. It is not safe."

The hollow, gravelly voice came from behind her. It was like sound echoing in stone. Kat didn't turn around—she was too mesmerized by the look of horror that claimed Thornton's homely features. The man's face had turned deathly white as he wobbled back against the mesquite tree, groping out with a shaking hand to support himself.

In the near distance, gunshots whined and ricocheted off the rocks. Terrified screams of agony quickly followed. Inhuman howls, growls and shrieks billowed from the spiny rims of rock that formed the gullies and arroyos. The sounds became deafening, unnerving. Kat stood her ground—more accurately, she was transfixed to the spot by the deep, penetrating pocket of cold air that coalesced in the fog that swirled around her.

The eerie force of living power flowed past her—through her. Kat wobbled off balance and collapsed to her knees, her mouth gaping, eyes popping. She sat motionless, watching Thornton be consumed by the incandescent specter of the Panther. It was as if the man's wicked spirit was being drained from him to feed the churning apparition.

When Thornton's horrified scream died in silence, Kat felt the strangest sensation overcome her. She stared toward the rock formations where gray-black shadows swooped, dived and pounced, launching their attack on the raiders from every direction at once. She heard the repetitive thunder of hooves as the ghost horses plunged off the cliffs to feed with the great cats, wolves and buzzard hawks.

The air was so charged with energy that Kat felt as if an oppressive weight was bearing down on her shoulders, forcing her to lie prone on the ground. The howls and screams multiplied tenfold, a thousandfold, as the chill froze Kat's bones, her soul. She tried to cry out in alarm, but no sound came—it was frozen in her chest. Darkness swirled like vultures, then converged on her.

For a frantic moment Kat feared she was about to die as Thornton and his raiders had—consumed by sharp fangs and claws, pecking beaks and trampling hooves, before the very life was drained from them.

The destructive storm of violence raged and consciousness bled away. Kat sought a safe haven—away from the night of a thousand eyes, a thousand tormenting howls, shrieks and hoof beats.

"Kat Diamond, you are a dozen kinds of daring fool."

Kat stirred beneath the icy, oppressive weight that held her prone on the ground. As if in a dream she saw the shifting apparition at arm's length. There was a sparkling haze within the frigid wreath of fog, around which three black pumas circled continuously. Unafraid, Kat stared at the mystical form, then looked beyond to see three incongruous shadows with glowing eyes that watched her from a distance.

It was as if four omnipotent forces of nature hovered in attendance, insuring she survived this nightmare. Kat knew who they were, because Panther had mentioned them when he spoke of lore and legends. The Lone Horseman who trampled demons. The Comanche shaman who called in the wolves to devour evil. The Hawk who swooped down to deliver the wicked to their doom. And the Panther who struck with knife-like claws to tear the worst devils to shreds.

"You see me now for all that I am, Kat Diamond," came a voice that dripped icicles with every syllable. *"You see us all. Mystics of the Four Winds. You see our gifts and our curses, the total, absolute destruction of violence clashing with violence. Only by our will have you survived, when nothing, no one else, was spared.*

"Breathe, Kat Diamond. Live . . ."

Only then did Kat realize she was suspended somewhere between the darkness and the light. She felt air expanding in her lungs, unaware that they had been burning like fire until they filled to give her life. Kat took what breath she had been granted to speak the words in her heart, even if this was to be her last breath, and, by expending it, she would fall into the dark abyss.

"I . . . love . . . you . . . Always . . ."

Like the high tide rushing ashore, dark silence flooded over her, then towed her away with its forceful current.

"I'm getting worried, Mr. Hawk," Gracie murmured while she sat beside the bed in the hotel, holding Kat's limp hand. "It's been two days and Katherine hasn't responded when I try to feed her or offer a drink. Exactly what did you say happened to her in Devil's Canyon?"

Samuel hobbled up to pat Gracie's shoulder. "It's not easily explained," he said, glancing at Hawk. "Katherine managed to cut Robert, Cape and me loose and put us on the horse, but she—"

"Took a fall," Hawk supplied. "I'm told these things take time."

Gracie peered up at Hawk in concern. "How much time?"

Hawk shrugged nonchalantly. "Another day or two perhaps. Depends on whether or not Panther can find the right potion to treat her. Why don't you help Samuel put the mercantile shop back in order," he suggested. "I'll keep Katherine company."

Gracie stared at Kat, then shook her head dubiously. "Are you certain she didn't eat those foul-tasting buttons she gave me? It certainly took a couple of days to recover from that stout sedative."

"If Hawk says Katherine will recover soon, then she will," Samuel declared as he hoisted his wife from the chair. "Come along, dear, we have left Panther to make all the necessary repairs downstairs too long already."

Gracie glanced back as Samuel shoved her out the door. "If Katherine wakes up, send for me at once."

"As you wish," Hawk murmured.

When the door clicked shut, Hawk ambled over to the window, watching the townspeople join forces to clean up the path of destruction left by Thornton's Raiders.

It amazed Hawk that news of the showdown in Devil's Canyon had met him and Panther on the outskirts of town. They had been treated to a hero's welcome, and Samuel had pinned a badge on Hawk's shirt the instant he dismounted. People had lined the streets and sent up a round of cheers and applause when Robert and Cape stepped forward to officially introduce Hawk as the new marshal.

Hawk's transition from Comanche culture into white society had been incredibly easy, especially with Kat's tutoring. He had the townspeople's instant respect and gratitude for fighting their battle for them. No one asked any questions about the buzzard hawk that swooped down to perch on his shoulder while he made his rounds. In fact, the hawk, and the legend circulated by the councilmen, had become Hawk's trademark. Folks on the street had chanted: "When the hawk flies, a ruthless outlaw dies." It was the most amazing thing Hawk had ever seen or heard.

Hawk missed his association with his people, but Panther was right about one thing. The freedom to move about unrestricted was a wondrous feeling . . .

When the door swung open unexpectedly, Hawk pivoted, his hand reflexively moving toward his pistol, but he knew by the silence of the arrival who was there. Panther's brawny frame filled the open doorway, and his attention immediately shifted to Kat.

"How is she?" Judd asked.

"The same." Hawk fixed him with a meaningful stare. "I've been making excuses for you to the Hamptons. Now, when are you going to do something about Kat's stupor?"

The question had Judd pacing in a manner reminiscent of Kat. When he realized what he was doing, he stopped in his tracks. The last two days had been hell—and then some—for Judd. His heart and good sense were in total disagreement when it came to Kat. The words she had whispered that night in Devil's Canyon were tearing him apart.

Hawk ambled over to the bed to brush his fingertip over Kat's pale cheek. He smiled fondly at her. "Eyelashes like butterfly's wings, lips like a budding rose, skin like creamy satin. She is too full of life to be lying here, seeking the warmth to overcome the chill that reaches into her soul. When are you going to give her back the light so she will no longer wander in the cold darkness?"

Judd shifted uncomfortably. "Maybe you should be the one to do it," he mumbled.

Hawk's gaze flew to Judd. "Me? But she is your woman. You should be the one to bring her back from where we left her when the Mystics of the Four Winds brought down their fury in the night. Why have you refused to touch her since the moment she whispered the words that the rest of us heard so clearly?"

"Because . . ."

"Because why?" Hawk leaned on him—hard. "Because you are afraid she didn't really mean what she said in her dazed stupor? Or because you think she *did* mean it?"

Judd turned his tormented stare on Hawk, beseeching him to understand. "You are one of us now. You completed the shamans' circle. I answered the call of my totem years ago. Will she understand and approve when I am summoned, as Three Wolves and the Lone Horseman were summoned that night in Devil's Canyon? Kat saw the Mystics of the Four

Winds hurl down destruction. She felt the oppressive strength crushing her, heard the rumbling spirits, tasted death.''

"And after all that she still spoke of love," Hawk pointed out.

"Or was it misdirected awe and stupefied fascination?" Panther offered in explanation.

"How do I know? I'm new at this, aren't I? But—"

"And what of the freedom Kat craves?" Judd cut in, posing the question that had been haunting him. "Your freedom has been returned after six years of confinement. Are you glad to have it?"

Hawk studied Kat's still form for a long moment. "Before you walked in here, I was thinking how good it felt to move freely, without armed soldiers looking over my shoulder. Thanks to you, I have become the master of my own destiny, a medium of my totem's power."

"Exactly. The same things you were denied and now enjoy are the same things Kat has waited twenty-three years to reach out and grasp. Her destiny awaits in Santa Fe, in civilized society where her aunt lives. Kat's medium of power is in the wealth she will gain from the priceless jewels she carries with her."

Judd walked over to pull the poke from Kat's oversize boot. He poured the glittering gems into his hand, then offered them to Hawk. "This is her heirloom inheritance. These sparkling stones will afford Kat the freedom and independence she has spent a lifetime craving. I was only the guide who was hired to lead her to her waiting dream."

Hawk stared directly at Judd. "So you are going to let her go." It wasn't a question, but rather a statement of what Hawk saw in Panther's eyes.

"I would not deny her freedom any more than I would deny yours, Hawk. You both mean a great deal to me."

"Still, Kat cannot go forward while she is suspended in this trance of our making," Hawk argued. He frowned when a flash of understanding struck like a thunderbolt. He jerked up his head to gape at Panther. "You love her! You *truly* love her!"

Judd staggered back as if Hawk had struck a physical blow.

"It's true." Hawk burst out in snickers. "That is why you haven't come to provide the warmth and will to live. A power only one of the Mystics of the Four Winds can offer her. As long as she is here, you can still see her, keep her in your life, hold her in limbo."

"That's not why," Judd loudly protested.

"No? Then why, Panther?" Hawk questioned, then frowned ponderously. "Seems to me that I recall a fairy tale about a prince who offered a sleeping beauty a kiss to give her life, or something to that effect. What is it that you're afraid of? The kiss itself, or the loss of this woman in your life?"

"Damn, if I'd known you were going to be such a pain in the ass I would have left you floundering with your hatred of your own white heritage," Judd groused.

"Disappointed that the veil of blindness caused by my hatred has lifted so I can see your greatest weakness, Panther?" he taunted unmercifully.

"Damn, I used to appreciate the Comanche's wry sense of humor until you came along," Judd grunted irritably. "Isn't there somewhere you need to be?"

Hawk grinned broadly. "As a matter of fact, no. There is no turmoil for me to resolve in Tascosa at the moment. The only problem I have to resolve is how to arrange the furniture in the new office and living quarters the townspeople are building for me."

"You could help with the construction," Judd muttered. "Wouldn't hurt you to learn to use a hammer and saw. Maybe I'll be lucky and you'll saw off your tongue and hammer your mouth shut."

Hawk's light-colored eyes twinkled. "If you want to get rid of me so you can give Kat the kiss to bring her back to reality, why don't you just come right out and say so?"

Judd's finger shot toward the door, as if Hawk was too stupid to know where to find it. "Out!"

"Fine. I'm gone."

"Good!"

The door eased shut. Judd spun toward the bed, asking himself if Hawk was right. Had he delayed in giving Kat her life

back because he couldn't bear the thought of watching her
board the stage and rumble west? Was he leaving Kat in limbo
because he was afraid to find out if she really meant what she'd
said that nightmarish night? Or if she was too deeply entranced
to know what she had said?

This cannot go on indefinitely, Judd told himself as he stared
down at Kat's still form. *You know what you must do, Panther,
so do it!*

CHAPTER
TWENTY-NINE

Kat felt a strange, satisfying warmth pouring over her as she wandered aimlessly through the darkness. By gradual increments the icy glaze that surrounded her heart and soul melted away. She stirred slightly, inching toward the heat radiating beside her. She became faintly aware of gentle heat gliding over her arms, her belly, her legs.

Along with the infused heat came a hunger that had been locked in motionless time. Instinctively, she knew who provided the needed warmth. She reached out in eager response, seeking those sensuous lips that tasted of gentleness and strength, pleasure and sweet torment. Panther, whose inexhaustible power had passed through her during the living nightmare, had returned to breathe life back into her.

The instant his lips slanted over hers the world came into sharp focus. It didn't matter where she and Panther were, it only mattered that he was with her, caressing her, holding her. Kat felt an overwhelming need to shower him with the love that burst from the cold like the sun blazing over the frozen arctic. It was vitally important that she express her deep feelings—now, here. No words were needed, because she had already spoken them. For now and always, Panther would know that her kisses and caresses were overflowing with love for him.

Judd blinked in disbelief when Kat emerged instantaneously from her trancelike state to become an alluring seductress. He had expected her to rouse gradually when he kissed her, held her. But that wasn't the case at all. Like sorcery, she wove a provocative spell around him, setting off a chain reaction of fiery sensations that left him hard and aching.

In broad daylight, he watched Kat curl up beside him. Her tangled hair fanned around her bare shoulders to shift temptingly over the swells of her breasts. Sunlight beamed through the window, spotlighting her silky flesh. She was like a glowing halo of beauty hovering beside him, holding him spellbound.

Even though Kat stared straight at him with those shiny, luminous eyes, he wasn't sure she actually saw him. But when she smiled, he knew she had returned from the suspended plateau where he had left her so long.

Her hands splayed over his chest in tantalizing caresses. Judd flinched, stunned to realize he had become sensitive in places he never expected. The touch of her fingertips swirling around his male nipples left him burning. When her wandering hand drifted over the washboard muscles of his belly, his entire body clenched with desire.

"Sweet mercy," he wheezed when every nerve and muscle suddenly unclenched and he felt an uncontrollable melting sensation coursing through him. "What are you doing to me?"

His voice dried up when she lowered her head to press whispering kisses over his chest, his navel. The power and strength Judd had learned to command seemed to be leaking out of him with each arousing kiss and caress. He felt boneless, weightless, wildly receptive.

His breath hitched when her hand slid over his thigh, then trailed down to his knee and up again. Her moist kisses followed the erotic path of her hands. Her silken hair flowed over him in another kind of alluring caress.

Judd groaned aloud when she measured the hard, throbbing length of him with her forefinger—once, twice, three times. Then he whimpered—whimpered!

When her petal-soft lips grazed his erect flesh, Judd clawed at the sheet to get a steadying grip with his fists. The world was sliding out from under him, taking his self-control with it. "Kat . . . stop . . ." he said hoarsely.

But she didn't stop, and the ardent sensations she incited with her hands and lips had him begging for mercy. "Please . . . I can't—"

"You can do anything and everything, Panther," she assured him softly. "I know, for I have seen and felt your powers. Now you will see and feel mine . . ."

Her mouth closed over his most sensitive flesh. Her hand stroked, then cupped him gently. His mind spun like a top, putting him in a delirious tailspin. He couldn't breathe, couldn't even remember why he should have to. His heart pounded like a captive bird trapped in his rib cage. Desire, like a Phoenix rising from the depths of the earth, soared and exploded through him.

Judd moaned in unholy torment when Kat nipped at him delicately with her teeth, teased him with her flicking tongue. The playfully intimate caress was almost too much to bear, especially when her hand folded around his pulsating flesh, drifting up and down in a rhythmic motion that made him arch helplessly toward her.

"No—" Judd hissed through his teeth when he felt the silvery drop of need betray his control. She tasted his need for her, then skimmed her lips over his chest to claim his lips. Judd shared the taste of his own blazing passion in a kiss so tender yet potent that his body became utterly boneless. Muscles turned to liquid, flesh vaporized as Kat left a burning trail of kisses over the place where he was most a man.

Over and over again, she kissed and caressed him intimately. Judd's willpower fled the holocaust of passion that burned hotter than a heaven full of stars. He couldn't endure much more of this wild, sweet torment without going up in flames.

"Come here," he demanded urgently. "Now, Kat—"

"I have always been here," she whispered against his sensitive flesh. "Just a touch away, since the beginning of time and until the end of it."

The meaning of her softly uttered words was beyond him, because his mind pinwheeled and his body sizzled. He was a helpless slave to her captive mouth and chaining hands. He, who commanded the greatest forces of power, was being defeated by a gentleness beyond description. Kat touched him so deeply, so completely, that she dragged him into his own depths, down to places he reached to wield mystical forces.

"Oh . . . damn . . ." Judd's voice turned hollow and he felt the transformation overtake him—as if Kat, not he, controlled the will of his guardian spirit.

With each heated lash of her tongue, the stroke of her hands and whisper of lips on his rigid flesh, she was summoning more than just his male body to full alert. She was calling the Panther from his hidden depths and making him respond.

Controlled by her seductive magic, he became a flowing essence of unshackled power, billowing like an incandescent thundercloud. The great cat roused to life, growling in hungry need.

To his stunned amazement, he noticed that Kat didn't look shocked when he transformed before her. She lifted her head and stared straight into his glowing eyes and smiled at him—the kind of triumphant, playfully seductive smile that sent him right over the edge to oblivion.

"Kat Diamond." His rumbling purr echoed around the room. *"Your magic is stronger than mine. You have taken control of what I am . . ."*

Her luscious body slid over his to join him in the swirling fog. She took him as her possession, and the Panther's shrill scream greeted the twilight in helpless abandon.

She was a part of the effervescent haze that churned around him. She was the flame within a vault of ice, burning through him, until all that he was was what they became while they swirled through passion's rumbling storm.

In mindless desperation Judd clutched her to him, unaware that Panther had left his mark on her shoulder. Need had such a fierce and unruly hold on him that he could only respond with wild urgency. He arched against her, feeling her match each deep, penetrating thrust, feeling her caress him as he caressed her.

Then the most startling event happened. The world crumbled, passion flowed forth like a bubbling geyser, and the strength and power he wielded multiplied, intensified, as they shuddered in each other's arms. What he previously considered a dangerous weakness became inexhaustible strength. Where icy-cold caverns once echoed, fire leaped and filled the dark hollows with searing heat.

Then, just as suddenly as the omnipotent forces fed upon the flames, sensations exploded in shattering climax. Judd collapsed beneath the onslaught of intense pleasure that coursed through him. Every ounce of energy drained away. He lay there, spent, unable to move—wasn't sure he wanted to, not when these deliciously erotic sensations were thrumming through him.

He tried to breathe deeply, bring himself up from the nethermost depths, but he barely had enough air to nourish his starved lungs.

Absolute, devastating defeat—the kind a man welcomes as much as he fears—had a fierce and mighty hold on him. When he made love to Kat, no part of him remained unmoved, untouched. Even the mystical Panther bowed down to the immense power Kat wielded.

His eyes drifted shut of their own accord. With arms flung above his head, legs sprawled, Judd sank into the soft mattress beneath him and fell into a deep, restful sleep.

Kat moved away from the relaxed masculine form. She was filled with a sense of completeness and belonging that no words could describe. For once she had lain with *Panther,* and she knew all there was to know of him, felt the extent of his powers—both fierce and gentle. Now her love for him was complete. She had proved to him that neither who he was nor what he became changed her view of him. He was still, would forever be, the man she loved unconditionally. She had given him her heart, soul and all the power of mind and spirit to fortify his strength. She wondered if he would recognize the significance of her gift.

In time, perhaps, Kat thought hopefully. Perhaps one day he would realize that not only had she been prepared to sacrifice her life to save him, to assist him, but she had willingly offered everything *she* was to make him even stronger.

"I love you, Panther, and you, Judd Lassiter," she whispered as she trailed her index finger over his lips. "And because I do love you with all my heart and soul, I will let you go."

Kat rose silently from the bed. When she saw the new gowns Judd had purchased, neatly folded and waiting on the nightstand, she smiled appreciatively. Judd had exchanged the tattered yellow gown for three elegant replacements, plus all the unmentionables and slippers to match.

Although she was still a bit clumsy with her mending arm, Kat managed to fasten herself into the lilac-colored dress, then retrieved the pouch of jewels. She placed two diamonds in Judd's left hand and an emerald and ruby in his right. She bent to place one last kiss to his lips, then stared down at him until tears clouded her vision.

"I will always love you," she whispered brokenly.

Kat scooped up her belongings, rolled them up and tucked them in the carpetbag that sat at the end of the bed. Another gift from Judd, no doubt, she mused as she moved quietly across the room.

Blinking back tears over what could never be, Kat stepped into the hall and drew a steadying breath. It was best for her to leave town immediately, before her whimsical dreams whispered for her to stay and make their parting more difficult than it was already. She knew there was a stage departing shortly, because she had checked the schedule the day she arrived in Tascosa. If she hurried, she could be on that stage, headed for Santa Fe and the freedom that awaited her there.

When she ventured downstairs, Gracie and Samuel weren't to be seen. Young Toby Webster was manning the counter.

"Lady Katherine!" he called enthusiastically. "I'm so glad to see that you're feeling better. We were all worried about you."

"Thank you, Toby." She glanced toward the storeroom. "Are the Hamptons in the back?"

"No, most everybody went over to Wilson's Restaurant to enjoy the first meal served since Thornton's Raiders burned the tables and chairs in the bonfire. Everybody pitched in to build picnic-style tables and benches for the customers."

"And Hawk? Is he with them?"

Toby beamed. "Mr. Hawk is the guest of honor. He doesn't know it yet, but the townsfolk chipped in to give him a bonus for accepting the position of marshal and dealing with Thornton. I think everybody around here wants to make sure Mr. Hawk is well paid so he won't follow in Panther's footsteps and turn bounty hunter too soon."

"I'm sure Hawk will appreciate the gesture of welcome and good faith," Kat replied. "Do you happen to have a pen and some paper? I would like to leave Hawk and the Hamptons a note."

"Sure thing, Lady Katherine."

Kat put her farewells on paper, then handed them to Toby. "Please see that these are delivered after the banquet. Good-bye, Toby."

He blinked, dumbfounded. "Good-bye? You sound as if you are leaving."

"I am, but I'll be back someday, on my way to Baton Rouge. I will be sure to look you up to see what a fine young man you've grown into."

"Godspeed," he called as she exited the shop.

Kat heard the laughter streaming from Wilson's Restaurant and smiled ruefully. She would have enjoyed being on hand for the celebration, but it would be a difficult good-bye. It would be best if she headed directly to the stage office.

When Kat heard the last call for departure, she took off running, cursing the hampering skirts every step of the way. When she reached Santa Fe she was going to set a new trend— or be labeled as an outlandish eccentric. But these confounded dresses had to go. They were much too confining for the sight-seeing trips she planned to take while she was in New Mexico and Colorado.

She hoped being on the move constantly would prevent Judd's memories from overtaking her. With any luck, the day would come—say in ten years or so—that she could remain in one place without his image, the haunting sound of his voice, his masculine scent and his gentle touch, swamping and depressing her.

Kat skidded to a breathless halt in front of the stage agent, then dug through her reticule to find her ticket. Smiling, the stage officer took her hand to assist her into the coach.

"Sure good to see you up and around again, Lady Katherine," the agent said. "Hope you're feeling better."

"Much."

Kat plunked down on the seat closest to the driver and guard. She had been told that riding with one's back to the horses allowed more rest, and with half the bounces and bumps that passengers endured on the opposite seat. Although riding backward oftentimes caused motion sickness, it wore off during long journeys. Kat decided that battling a form of seasickness would take her mind off the man she left behind.

She nodded politely to the woman and her young son who sat in the opposite seat, then leaned back to endure the ride. The coach lurched forward, swinging on its suspension belts. Kat closed her eyes and sent up a prayer of thanks that she hadn't eaten before she left Tascosa. She doubted the driver would stop for a bout of nausea and heartache that would throw him off schedule.

Hawk read the note Kat left for him, then muttered under his breath. Taking the steps two at a time, he reached the second-story hallway and barged through the door to see a sleeping form on the bed.

"Panther?"

Nothing, not so much as a peep.

Hawk lit the lantern, then blinked in surprise when he saw that Panther was stark-bone naked. Hawk yanked the sheet up to Panther's waist to preserve his modesty when he awoke.

Although Hawk gave him a firm shake, he received nothing for his efforts but a groggy moan.

"Panther! Time to wake up!" Hawk all but yelled.

Judd opened his eyes to see shadows cast on the ceiling by flickering lamplight. He turned his head to find Hawk looming over the bed. "You again," he mumbled. "Go 'way."

"Can't. Your devoted friends, and now mine, gave me a key to the city, whatever that means. I just took it and smiled gratefully. Then the good citizens handed me a pouch of money as a reward for a job well done in Devil's Canyon. Everybody here loves me, so I can't leave."

For a man whose English had been until recently slow and stilted, Hawk was speaking too rapidly for Judd's sluggish mind to keep up. He stirred, then became aware of the gems resting in his closed fists.

Gone, with nothing but fists full of jewels to remember her by. No, more than jewels, he corrected himself. *Her memory is as much a part of you as breathing.*

The thoughts came to him in a tormented rush, and Judd cursed under his breath.

Hawk's mouth quirked as he watched Judd stare at the gems he was holding. "It is not difficult to tell who brought whom back to life, and who nearly killed himself doing it. I was under the impression that a long-drawn-out kiss or compassionate embrace would suffice in these situations."

Judd's gaze narrowed as he watched Hawk's broad shoulders shake with amusement. "Suffice?" he repeated mockingly. "New word?"

"Yes, Kat taught it to me. Made me learn five new words a day and use them at least five times. So why did you let her go?" he asked abruptly.

Judd shut his eyes and drew a deep breath, trying to summon his wits and his strength. "I didn't let her go."

"I see. She left you sprawled out like a human sacrifice before she boarded the stage. Now there is nothing you can do about it, even if you wanted to . . . Do you?"

Judd made a sound that could have meant anything.

"Did you ever figure out if you were happy or disappointed that she fell in love with you?"

Judd emitted another neutral sound.

"Well, as Kat would say: It is all water under the bridge. She's gone and you're here. Are you staying?"

"Just long enough to help Tascosans put their town back together," Judd mumbled. "When I received the telegram from Marshal Winslow, offering information on Thornton's Raiders, he also sent word about a couple of desperadoes who were terrorizing ranchers near The Norrows."

"Wolf country," Hawk mused aloud. "Three Wolves should have that covered. What other excuses do you have for not going after Kat?"

Judd nailed Hawk with The Look, but it didn't faze the new marshal. Hawk just grinned wickedly. "Don't push it, Hawk," Judd growled. "I'm not in the best of moods right now."

"Because she is gone," Hawk said matter-of-factly. "Understandable."

Judd flashed him a glare hot enough to scorch hell. "Why don't you go tuck yourself in the room Gracie and Samuel rented to you and I'll make your evening rounds for you?"

"You think wandering the streets will help?"

"Help what?" Judd snapped grouchily.

"Help you forget. It won't," Hawk predicted. "I knew the day you appeared and commanded me to leave Kat behind in the canyon that she had a powerful influence over you. How is it possible that you can't see that, too?"

Judd snatched up a pillow and hurled it into Hawk's taunting smile. "Don't you understand, damn it? She loves her freedom more than whatever she might feel for me. She left. That is statement enough!"

"Maybe she left because she believed that was what *you* wanted." Hawk threw the pillow back at Judd. "Did you ever tell her different?"

"Hell's fire, Hawk, you of all people know what I am. Would you wish your way of life on a woman like Kat? I've nearly gotten her killed twice. I won't make her live with that, wandering around like a damn tumbleweed!"

Hawk was silent for a moment. "To tell the truth, Panther, I cannot say how I would react if I wanted a woman as much as you want Kat, while I was bound to follow the calling. But there has to be a workable solution. You are a man of solutions, after all. Think of one."

Hawk swooped down to retrieve Panther's discarded breeches and shirt, then tossed them to him. "Come make the rounds with me, Panther. Pacing seems to clear Kat's mind. Perhaps it will do the same for yours."

Judd got up and dressed. He followed Hawk downstairs and onto the street. A half hour later he was no closer to a solution than he was while lying abed.

A half day later misery set in.

A half week later loneliness was following closer than his own shadow. Even after hours of wandering through the rugged canyons east of Tascosa, with the three black pumas and Horse as companions, he couldn't find a cure for what ailed him.

The Panther prowled in his habitat, and his wild, shrill screams echoed through the ravines. He called to the omnipotent spirits for direction. Although his powers were greater than before, his keen sight sharper, his hearing more acute, his strength doubled, the ache in his soul burgeoned with each passing night that Kat's forbidden memory descended on him.

At last, the answer came to him in the whisper of the winds, as dawn broke over the jagged spires of caprock. Panther knew what he must do with the precious gift the Great Spirit had bestowed on him.

Panther saddled Horse and rode toward sunrise.

CHAPTER THIRTY

Kat knew she was drawing all sorts of attention when she ventured from the elegant hotel in Santa Fe. She, however, paid no mind to the gape-mouthed stares and disconcerted snorts from pompous ladies and gentlemen. She had instructed the seamstress at the fashionable boutique to stitch together a half dozen pair of breeches and matching blouses that enabled her to move about unencumbered and ride comfortably on horseback.

Although Kat had been in town for a only month, she had developed a reputation as the Southern "Original." She ate like a field hand when she was hungry, instead of picking delicately at her food as fine ladies were taught to do in public. She strolled the streets alone, with a derringer tucked in her purse and a sharp-pointed parasol to discourage aggressive men from crowding her space. She discarded frilly bonnets for a practical Stetson. Slippers were replaced with tailor-made leather boots that she could tuck the hem of her breeches into.

In a word, *eccentric*. The name Kat Diamond had become the signalment of feminine freedom and independence in Santa Fe.

Ignoring the usual amount of attention she drew, Kat hiked

down the street to the livery stable. Thus far, she had viewed all the interesting sights in and around Santa Fe. Now she was prepared to head north to the spectacular canyon rumored to lie in the Colorado mountains.

Kat had never climbed a mountain, but she intended to—soon. She had never stared up at the panoramic waterfalls that travelers she interviewed claimed cascaded hundreds of feet into a crystal-clear pool which was said to be sacred ground to the Cheyenne. She had never seen the monolithic stones in the Garden of the Gods or ventured into the Cave of the Winds—yet.

Kat Diamond would see it all now. She would fill up her senses with the majestic beauty of Mother Nature's handiwork.

And somewhere—Kat sincerely hoped—the ever-constant memory of Judd Lassiter would wander off and lose track of her.

It could happen. Nothing was impossible, because she had seen the impossible and lived through it, Kat reminded herself.

Bystanders parted like the Red Sea to let Kat pass on the boardwalk. Eccentrics, she had learned, were as much of a curiosity as legendary bounty hunters. "Kat Diamond is a mite odd," she heard it said when gossipers were unaware she was within earshot. "Harmless but strange, she is. Any woman who allows herself to be seen tramping down the streets in men's breeches, designed specifically for her, obviously thumbs her nose at conventionality and propriety. Kat Diamond is an outrageous nonconformist who can afford to do exactly as she pleases, wherever she pleases, anytime she pleases."

Those comments followed Kat wherever she went. However, she had never been influenced by others' opinion of her anyway, and she had no intention of starting now. Wrapped in a cloak of freedom and independence, her free-spirited attitude had become decidedly stronger.

"Good afternoon, Miss Diamond," the livery stable owner greeted. "Everything is packed and ready, just as you requested."

"Thank you, Homer." Kat pulled coins from her pocket and

presented them to the rotund proprietor who was known to have a gift for handling horses and mules.

"Off on another adventure, I presume," Homer said, handing her the reins to a sturdy mountain pony and a durable pack mule that was laden down with supplies. "Which direction are you headed this time?"

Away from the memories, she thought to herself. "North to Colorado," she said instead.

"Fine country up that way, I've been told," Homer said conversationally. "But a bit dangerous, too, you know." He gestured his head toward the new bullwhip tied on the saddle and the shiny rifle resting in its leather scabbard. "I cleaned and loaded your weapons, as you requested. The dagger is sheathed just beneath the pommel for easy access."

"Thank you, Homer. As always, you have paid strict attention to every detail."

"When shall we expect you back, Miss Diamond?"

"About the time you see me coming," she answered with a smile. "You know how I am, Homer. When the spirit moves, so do I."

"And the spirit moves with her, Homer."

Kat froze to the spot when that deep, resonant voice that was a part of living memory rolled toward her from the entrance of the livery stable.

Homer staggered back when he spied the sun-drenched form of a man in buckskin and the three large black pumas that circled around his legs. Homer yelped when he tripped over the stool he used while he trimmed horse hooves. Arms flapping like a goose, he landed on his back with a thud.

"Dear God! It's the man called Panther!" he wheezed as he scrabbled onto all fours, then bolted to his feet to dash out the back door.

Kat spun around to see Panther's muscular physique silhouetted against the bright sunlight. She opened her mouth, but no words came out—her tongue had suddenly become stuck to the roof of her mouth.

"Hello, Diamond." Judd stepped deeper into the interior of the livery stable. Out of habit, his keen gaze swept his surroundings; then he surveyed the expensive cut of fabric that comprised Kat's colorful breeches and blouse. He grinned in amusement. "I was anxious to meet the Eccentric everyone in town is yammering about."

"W-what are you d-doing here?" Kat stammered as she filled her eyes with the precious sight of him.

"I rode toward sunrise and here I am," he said cryptically.

Kat frowned. "Toward sunrise? Then however did you get here from Tascosa?"

He didn't reply, just sauntered toward her, his all-encompassing gaze sweeping up and down to note every detail. "You're thinner than I remembered."

YOUR TORMENTING MEMORY HAUNTS THE NIGHTS. "Sleep deprivation. Too busy seeing the world to take time for rest." She studied him astutely. "You look a bit leaner yourself, Lassiter."

I CAN'T SLEEP WHEN YOUR IMAGE TORMENTS MY MIND. "Insomnia," he replied. "Great cats caterwauling all through the night. Keeps me awake."

Kat flicked a glance at the catamounts that curled around his legs like oversize kittens. "What's wrong with your pets?"

"Incurable case of lonely. At least that's what Hawk diagnosed. Damn Comanche thinks he's turned doctor. Folks in Tascosa treat him like a king and it's gone straight to his swelled head. He said to say hello."

Kat smiled morosely. "I would have liked to watch my star pupil come into his own in Tascosa."

"The Hamptons send their best." He stared over her shoulder at the horse and pack mule. "Going somewhere, Diamond?"

"Yes, as a matter of fact. To Colorado."

"Beautiful country. I was raised there, you know."

"I remember," she murmured, then wondered if her trek to the mountains was her subconscious attempt to find a part of him, to walk where he had walked, to see the world through the eyes of the young warrior who had been summoned by his totem spirit to battle the worst men in order to save the best.

He stared at her for a long moment. "You're happy then?"

NO! I'VE BEEN MISSING YOU LIKE CRAZY! "Very happy. And you?"

I'VE BEEN MISERABLE AS HELL WITHOUT YOU! "Can't complain. Did you find your aunt well when you arrived in Santa Fe?"

Judd frowned bemusedly when Kat shifted from one well-shod foot to the other and refused to meet his gaze. "What's wrong, Diamond? Your aunt is still alive, isn't she?"

"No, not exactly."

Judd's brows flattened over his narrowed eyes. "How is that possible? A person is either exactly *dead* or exactly *alive* . . . for the most part, at least."

She finally met his gaze head-on and blurted out, "My aunt doesn't exist. She was a figment of my imagination. I *lied* to you, and I know how much you despise lies."

Judd felt a presence—more than one, actually—lurking behind him. He pivoted to see curious onlookers peeking around the doorway. Obviously, Homer had raced down the street to alert everyone that the legendary bounty hunter had approached the Eccentric of Santa Fe. Were they expecting a showdown? he wondered. Did they think he had arrived to apprehend Kat for a crime they were unaware she'd committed?

"Is there somewhere we can go for privacy? I don't think we'll have much of it here," he said.

Kat nodded, grabbed the dangling reins, and bounded into the saddle with practiced ease. "We can ride north, away from pricked ears and wagging tongues."

When Kat ducked beneath the doorway, while sitting astride her pony, onlookers scrambled a safe distance away. Judd followed in her wake, causing the crowd to back off a few more paces to avoid the snarling cats that bared their fangs for effect.

Judd mounted Horse and reined north, falling into an easy pace beside Kat.

One mile later, Judd asked. "Why did you lie about your fictitious aunt?"

"It was the prefabricated tale I gave J.P. Trumball when I decided to escape the intolerable situation in Louisiana. I told J.P. that my father's older sister lived in Santa Fe and that I intended to move west to be with what was left of my blood family.

"That was a mistake, because I unintentionally provided J.P. with the opportunity to hire henchmen to make sure I never made it to New Mexico alive. Then the plantation would be his to control, or squander away because of his incurable gambling."

Kat decided she may as well clear her conscience completely while she had the chance. "I didn't sell off the jewels in order to rent the luxurious room at the hotel or to pay for my sightseeing trips."

"No?" Judd's brows shot up like exclamation marks. "Then what did you do? Rob a bank?"

"I used my inheritance."

Judd frowned, puzzled. "I don't follow you, Diamond. I thought the jewels were your inheritance."

Kat reined the pony to a halt and stared Judd squarely in the eye. "Do you recall that rumor I squelched in Tascosa?"

Judd nodded his shaggy head. "The one about being a diamond heiress and entrepreneur?"

"That's the one. I don't know how it got started, but oddly enough, there was much truth to the rumor."

Judd's mouth scraped his chest. He stared at Kat, goggle-eyed.

"I told you that I was a bitter disappointment to my father, because he wanted a son to carry on the family name. That was true. But when war broke out between the States, Papa feared his legacy would be stolen while he was away fighting for the Southern cause. He refused to let that happen, so he had his vast fortune sent west and established a trust in my name. He planned to retrieve the fortune my great-great-grandfather amassed during his years as a colonial sea captain. With a name like Diamond, he thought it only fitting to deal with the acquisition and sale of fine jewels. Each generation built upon the staggering fortune. It was passed down to my great-grandfather, my grandfather—"

"I get the picture," Judd cut in, smiling wryly. "The Diamonds dealt in the finest jewels and kept getting richer."

"Yes," Kat affirmed. "When my father was killed, my mother continued living on the fortune *she* brought into their marriage. The jewels I brought west were the ones my father mounted in a necklace and presented to my mother after their wedding, more for show than a symbol of his affection. My mother received no jewels to commemorate my birth because she failed to deliver the much-awaited son.

"To make a long story short, I came to Santa Fe to live off the investments of the trust that has multiplied the last sixteen years. The truth is . . ." Kat paused, then blurted out, "I am disgustingly rich and I have decided to amuse myself by seeing all the sights the West has to offer. I simply cannot remain in one place for too long before restlessness torments me."

"I know the feeling."

"I knew you would." She stared at him. "That is the whole truth and nothing but. Now, tell me what you meant when you said you rode west to find the sunrise. That is astrologically impossible. And what was the comment about the spirit moving *with* me supposed to mean?"

Judd shifted uncomfortably in the saddle. He stared down at the three black panthers that had plunked down in the middle of the road to peer steadily at him.

Tell her the truth, Panther. That's what you rode all the way out here to do, after all.

"Lassiter?" she prompted when he simply sat there, as if he were visually communicating with the big cats.

"It means"—Judd turned slowly toward her, his eyes glowing with an inner light Kat had witnessed on several occasions—"that, for me, the sun rises in your face, Kat Diamond. It means that since you left Tascosa I've lost my sense of direction. It means that every important, memorable event in my life—save one—happened with you. Without you, I have been on a very personal and intimate downslide to loneliness. I went through life never knowing what I was missing until you came along, and I couldn't endure missing you for another day."

Kat's gaze never wavered. She was too intent on what he

said. Hope filled her empty heart and her shriveled soul. Was he implying what she *thought* he was implying?

"And the other part?" she asked, her voice crackling. "The part about the spirit moving with me?"

"All that I am gravitates toward you." He reached across the small distance separating them to limn the elegant line of her jaw, the creamy curve of her cheek. "When you left Tascosa I came to realize that the power vested in me, the power I felt when we were one, is the greatest power known to men and their gods. I didn't know that until there was you, Kat."

"Oh, Panther! Do you mean it?"

Kat flung herself toward him. He hooked his arm around her waist and drew her onto his lap. She rained kisses on his bronzed cheeks, his eyelids, his smiling lips. Tears ran like rivers down her face as she hugged the stuffing out of him. "I love you so much," she whispered, her heart in her throat.

"As much as I love you, Kat?" The words he had never spoken in his entire adult life sounded foreign when they tripped off his tongue. He tried again as he held her close to his heart. "I love you."

Judd glanced around, wanting the privacy to show Kat exactly how much she meant to him. A well-traveled road in broad daylight would not suffice—as Hawk would say. A bed of roses fit for an heiress, yes. A dusty road, definitely not.

He grabbed the reins to her horse and pack mule and veered toward a grove of pines near the hillside. When he reined Horse to a halt, Kat slid to the ground. Her luminous green eyes were shining up at him. He had never seen that much love and devotion staring back at him. It took his breath away.

Already he was hard as granite, wanting her in the most private, intimate ways a man could want a woman. A month without Kat felt like a lifetime. He was starving to death for her.

The moment his feet hit the ground, he scooped her up in his arms and carried her to the lush carpet of grass in the shade of the trees.

He came down on one knee, and while he was there, he said, "Marry me."

"Yes. Anytime, anywhere." Kat smiled radiantly at him, then pressed a heartfelt kiss to his parted lips. "But don't ask me to settle down in one place, Lassiter."

"Why not, Diamond?" he asked as he eased her down in the grass, his body half covering hers.

She grinned playfully. "Because I spent entirely too much time with my mentor, learning to appreciate the beauty of the whole outdoors. I've developed a streak of restlessness. I want to see the place where you were born, where you grew up, the mountains you roamed before you were unwillingly confined to civilized society. Then I want you to see my home in Baton Rouge and stay in a few disgustingly luxurious hotels along the way."

"The kind that boast spacious living suites and roomy bed-rooms and oversize brass tubs?" he asked as he brushed the pad of his thumb over her soft lips.

"The bigger the better," she insisted.

"There's a problem."

Kat's face fell, but she plowed boldly onward. "There is no problem we can't solve together."

"The father I told you I lived with in St. Louis . . ." he began awkwardly.

"Yes? What about him?" Kat questioned anxiously.

"Well, I wasn't exactly honest with you, either. Not that I outright lied. I just omitted a few details."

Her delicately arched brow lifted. "What details?"

Judd stared solemnly at her. "Fur entrepreneur. Disgustingly rich. Remarried a disgustingly rich widow. The trust has been drawing interest for ten years."

Kat burst out laughing. "Diamonds and furs? Dear Lord, Panther, what are two disgustingly rich people going to do with so much money lying around?"

He cupped her chin in his hand, then bent to graze her lips. "Pass it along to their privileged children, along with a legendary kind of love," he suggested.

"Our children will not be restricted from learning all that life has to teach them, whether they be male or female," she insisted.

"Agreed. No one will be locked in the attic for the unpardonable sin of learning to ride horseback," he promised. "All in good time, Kat. But there is something else we need to discuss."

Kat smiled, knowing what he was going to say before he said it. "There will be times when you are called away, just as you called to the other mystics. I expected no less, and I wouldn't have it any other way."

"But even while I'm gone, a part of me will always be with you," he murmured as his hand glided over the pearl buttons on her blouse, watching them come magically undone. "You will always have my heart, because you *are* my heart, Kat Diamond."

Judd parted her shirt to brush his fingertips over her beaded nipples that lay beneath her silk chemise. He caught sight of the three black panthers staring at him with glowing eyes. "Find something else to do. I can take it from here."

Kat blinked in surprise when the cats rose gracefully and walked into the shadows, vanishing as if they had never been there at all. When her attention shifted to Judd, he was staring at her with eyes that glowed brighter than those of the black pumas. A misty haze began to radiate around him, around her. She could feel the power of combined affection growing in intensity, and she pulled him down to offer him all that she was, all that she had.

Panther took her into his soul, and hand in hand, heart in heart, they climbed love's mystical stairway to bask in the glow from the Cheyenne moon. "This is the legend I want to be remembered," he whispered softly. "The legend of my love for you."

And so it was . . .

Dear Readers,

I hope you enjoyed Panther and Kat's story. The Mystics of the Four Winds began with the legendary Three Wolves and his lively English duchess in *Comanche Promise*, my July 1998 release from Zebra. By popular demand, the legend continues with Wild Hawk's story, followed by the tale of the Lone Horseman.

Thank you so much for all your cards and letters expressing your enthusiasm for the mythical heroes of the Four Winds.

Enjoy the magic,

Carol Finch

Put a Little Romance in Your Life With
Fern Michaels

__**Dear Emily**	0-8217-5676-1	$6.99US/$8.50CAN
__**Sara's Song**	0-8217-5856-X	$6.99US/$8.50CAN
__**Wish List**	0-8217-5228-6	$6.99US/$7.99CAN
__**Vegas Rich**	0-8217-5594-3	$6.99US/$8.50CAN
__**Vegas Heat**	0-8217-5758-X	$6.99US/$8.50CAN
__**Vegas Sunrise**	1-55817-5983-3	$6.99US/$8.50CAN
__**Whitefire**	0-8217-5638-9	$6.99US/$8.50CAN